W9-BMU-971

SAINT X

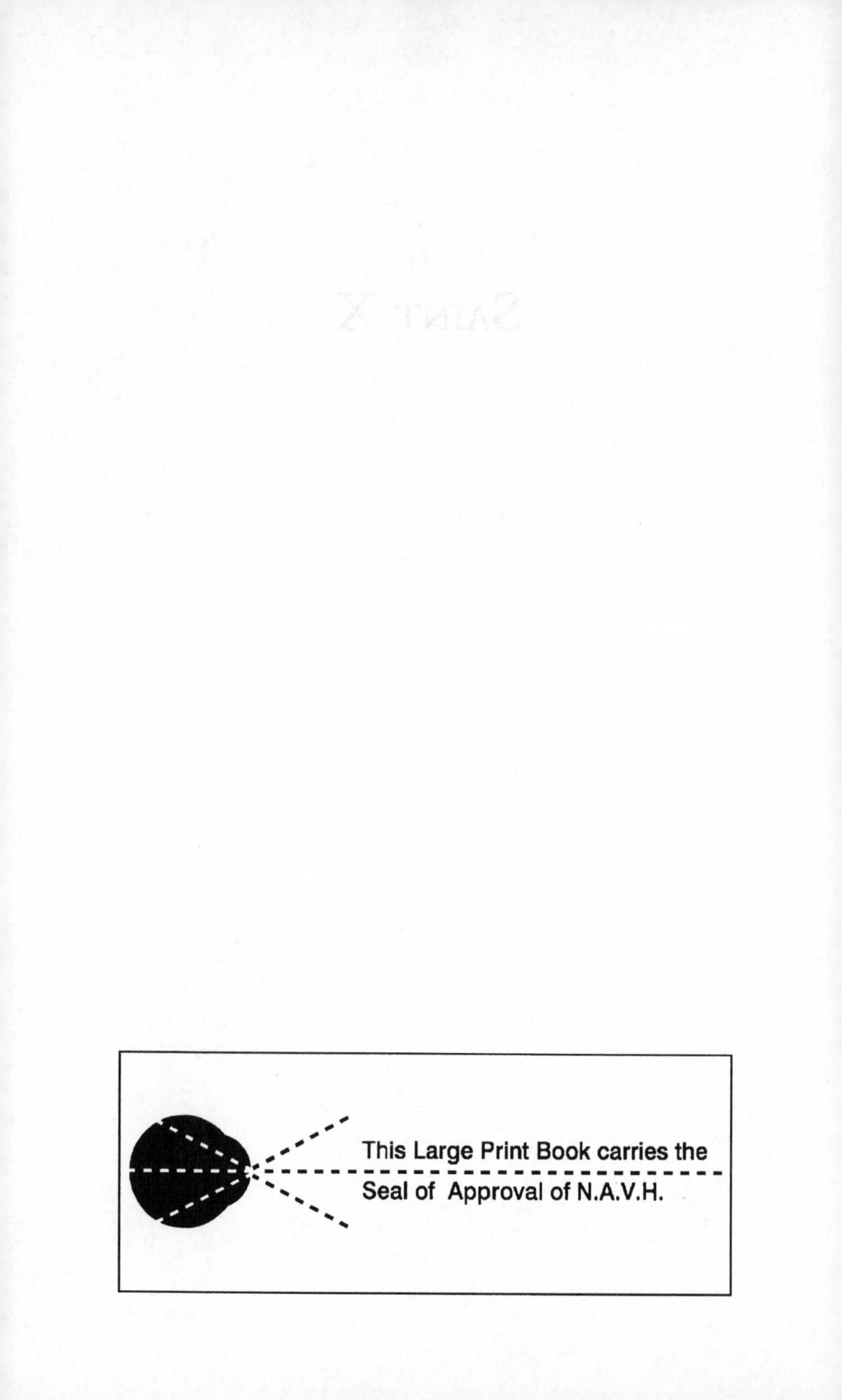
This Large Print Book carries the
Seal of Approval of N.A.V.H.

Saint X

Alexis Schaitkin

THORNDIKE PRESS
A part of Gale, a Cengage Company

Thorndike Press® Large Print Basic
The text of this Large Print edition is unabridged.
Other aspects of the book may vary from the original edition.
Set in 16 pt. Plantin.

LIBRARY OF CONGRESS CIP DATA ON FILE.
CATALOGUING IN PUBLICATION FOR THIS BOOK
IS AVAILABLE FROM THE LIBRARY OF CONGRESS

ISBN-13: 978-1-4328-7247-2 (hardcover alk. paper)

Published in 2020 by arrangement with Macmillan Publishing Group, LLC/Celadon Books

Printed in Mexico
Print Number: 01 Print Year: 2020

For M & E

CONTENTS

INDIGO BAY 9

EMILY OF PASADENA 77

ISLANDS 141

THE LITTLE SWEET 153

OUR BEAUTIFUL DAUGHTER 183

GOGO 211

EVIDENCE 243

GHOSTS 275

VOICES 303

THE REAL WHEREVER 355

SARA 411

THE SECRET CITY 437

SNOW 463

STARLIGHT 505

THE GIRL 523

FARAWAY 561

REMEMBER THIS 593

SAINT X 603

AUTHOR'S NOTE AND ACKNOWLEDGMENTS 613

Indigo Bay

Begin with an aerial view. Slip beneath the clouds and there it is, that first glimpse of the archipelago — a moment, a vista, a spectacle of color so sudden and intense it delivers a feeling like plunging a cube of ice in warm water and watching it shatter: the azure sea, the emerald islands ringed with snow-white sand; perhaps, on this day, a crimson tanker at the edge of the tableau.

Come down a bit lower and the islands reveal their topographies, valleys and flatlands and the conic peaks of volcanoes, some of them still active. There is Mount Scenery on Saba, Mount Liamugia on Saint Kitts, Mount Pelée on Martinique, the Quill on Saint Eustatius, La Soufrière on Saint Lucia and also on Saint Vincent, La Grande Soufrière on Guadeloupe's Basse-Terre, Soufrière Hills on Montserrat, and Grande Soufrière Hills on tiny Dominica, which is beset by no fewer than nine volcanoes. The volcanoes yield an uneasy sense of juxtaposition — the dailiness of island life abutting the looming threat of eruption. (On some islands, on some days, flakes of ash fall softly through the air, pale and fine, before settling on grassy hillsides and the eaves of rooftops.)

Roughly in the middle of the archipelago lies an island some forty kilometers long by twelve wide. It is a flat, buff, dusty place, its soil thin and arid, the terrain dotted with shallow salt ponds and the native vegetation consisting primarily of tropical scrub: sea grape, cacti, wild frangipani. (There is a volcano here, too, Devil Hill, though it is so small, and the magma rises to its surface so infrequently, that it is useless as both a threat and an attraction.) The island is home to eighteen thousand residents and receives some ninety thousand tourists annually. From above, it resembles a fist with a single long finger pointing west.

The north side of the island faces the Atlantic. Here, the coast is narrow and rocky, the water seasonally variable and sometimes rough. Nearly all of the residents live on this side, most of them in the tiny capital town, the Basin, where cinder-block schools, food marts, and churches mingle with faded colonial buildings in pastel hues:

the governor-general's petal-pink Georgian mansion; the mint-green national bank; Her Majesty's Prison, eggshell-blue. (A prison next to a bank — a favorite local joke.) On this coast, the beaches' names bespeak their shortcomings: Salty Cove. Rocky Shoal. Manchineel Bay. Little Beach.

On the south side of the island, the gentle waves of the Caribbean Sea lap against sand fine as powder. Here, resorts punctuate the coast. The Oasis, Salvation Point, the Grand Caribbee, and the island's crown jewel, Indigo Bay, all of them festooned with bougainvillea, hibiscus, and flamboyant, beautiful deceptions meant to suggest that this island is a lush, fertile place.

Scattered in the sea around the island are a dozen or so uninhabited cays, the most notable of which are Carnival Cay, Tamarind Island, and Fitzjohn (famous, at least locally, as the home of the Fitzjohn lizard). The cays are popular spots for excursions — snorkeling, romantic picnics, guided expeditions through their limestone caverns. The closest of the cays to the main island is the ironically named Faraway Cay, which sits not five hundred meters off the coast at Indigo Bay and which, owing to its nacreous beach, its wild landscapes, and the pristine waterfall at its center, would be a popular destination like the other cays, were it not overrun by feral goats, which survive on sea purslane and prickly pear.

The island's visitors have little sense of its geography. If asked, most would be unable to sketch its basic shape. They cannot locate it on a map, cannot distinguish it from the other small landmasses that dot the sea between Florida and Venezuela. When a taxi brings them from the airport to their hotel, or from their hotel to a Caribbean fusion restaurant on Mayfair Road, or when they take a sunset cruise aboard the catamaran *Faustina,* or disembark their cruise ship at Hibiscus Harbour, or when a speedboat whisks them to Britannia Bay to tour the old sugar estate, they do not know if they are traveling north or south, east or west. The island is a lovely nowhere suspended in gin-clear water.

When they return home, they quickly forget the names of things. They do not remember the name of the beach on which their resort was situated, or of the cay where they went for their snorkeling excursion. (The beach there was littered with sand dollars, as if they were entirely unprecious.) They forget the name of the restaurant they liked best, remembering only that it was some exotic flower. They even forget the name of the island itself.

Zoom in closer on Indigo Bay and the resort's features come into view. There is the long drive lined with perfectly vertical palm trees, the marble lobby with its soaring domed roof, the open-air pavilion where breakfast is served until ten each morning, the spa, the swimming pool in the shape of a lima bean, the fitness and business centers ("CENTRE," on the engraved placard outside of each; the American guests are charmed by this Briticism, which strikes them as quaint and earnest on this island so distant from England). There is the beach where lounge chairs are arranged in a parabola that follows the curve of the bay, the local woman set up on a milk crate beneath a sun-bleached blue umbrella at the beach's edge, braiding young girls' hair. The fragrance is tropic classic, frangipani and coconut sunscreen and the mild saline of equatorial ocean.

On the beach are families, the sand around their chairs littered with plastic shovels, swimmies, impossibly small aqua socks; honeymooners pressed closely together beneath cabanas; retirees reading fat thrillers in the shade. They have no notion of the events about to unfold here, on Saint X, in 1995.

The time is late morning. Look. A girl is walking down the sand. Her gait is idle, as if it is of no consequence to her when she arrives where she is going. As she walks, heads turn — young men, openly; older men, more subtly; older women, longingly. (They were eighteen once.) She wears a long, billowy tunic over her bikini, but she has a teenage knack for carrying it with a whiff of provocation. A raffia beach bag is slung casually over her shoulder. Apricot freckles crowd the milky skin of her face and arms. She wears a silver anklet with a charm in the shape of a star, and rubber thongs on her long, archless feet. Her russet hair, thick and sleek as a horse's, is tossed into a bun of precise messiness with a yellow elastic band. This is Alison, never Ali.

"Good morning, sleepyhead," her father says when she reaches her family's lounge chairs.

"Morning," she yawns.

"You missed a cruise ship go by right out there. You wouldn't believe how big that thing was," her mother says.

(Though the guests at Indigo Bay are apt to complain when these hulking ships lumber into the vista, they also derive a certain satisfaction from these moments, when the bad taste of others reaffirms their own quality — *they* have not chosen to spend their vacations in the vulgar opulence of a ship with all the beauty of an office park.)

"Sounds riveting." Alison drags a chair out of the shade of an umbrella and into the sun. From her beach bag she removes a yellow Walkman. She lies down, puts on her headphones, and pulls her sunglasses over her eyes.

"How about a family swim?" her father says.

Alison does not respond. Not pretending she doesn't hear him over whatever she's listening to, her father decides, just ignoring him.

"Maybe in a little while everyone will be more in the mood," her mother says with prodding cheerfulness.

"Hey, Clairey," Alison says. "I'm going on a treasure hunt and I'm bringing a starfish."

She is speaking to the little girl sitting in the sand between her mother's and father's chairs, who until this moment had been piling sand into small mounds with intense focus.

"I'm going on a treasure hunt and I'm

bringing a starfish and a dog," the little girl says.

She is as peculiar in appearance as her older sister is appealing. Her hair is nearly white, her skin extremely pale. Eyes gray, lips blanched. These features combine to create an impression that manages to be at once arresting and plain. This is Claire, age seven. Clairey, to her family.

"I'm going on a treasure hunt and I'm bringing a starfish, a dog, and a piccolo."

"A piccolo," Claire whispers. Her eyes widen with wonder.

The father flags down one of the men who work on the beach. There are two of them, both dark-skinned, in white slacks and white polos with the resort insignia embroidered on the breast pocket in gold thread. The skinny one and the fat one, in most of the guests' mental shorthand. The man who approaches the family now is the skinny one, Edwin.

When he reaches them, Alison sits up and smooths her hair.

"How are you all doing this morning?" he asks.

"Excellent," the mother says with a bright display of enthusiasm.

"First time to our island?"

"Yes," the father confirms. "Just flew in

last night."

The family vacations at a different resort on a different island every winter, weeklong respites from their snowbound suburb that steel them for the remaining months of darkness and cold. They have seen palm trees bent to kiss the sand. They have seen water as pale as glaciers and walked on sand as soft as cream. They have watched the sun transform, at the end of the day, into a giant orange yolk that breaks and spills itself across the sea. They have seen the night sky overcome with fine blue stars.

"Look at our island pulling out she most beautiful day for you." He gestures generally with his skinny arm at the sky, the sea. "What can I be getting you this morning?"

"Two rum punches and two fruit punches," the father says.

Alison emits a small sigh.

The skinny one returns some time later. (Too long, the father thinks, as fathers all along this stretch of sand think; the skinny one is a chatterbox, and a dawdler.) He bears a tray of drinks garnished with maraschino cherries and hibiscus blossoms.

"We have a volleyball match this afternoon," he says. "We hope you will join us."

"Oh, honey, you would love that!" the mother says to Alison.

The girl turns to face her. Though she wears sunglasses, the mother has no doubt that behind them her daughter's gaze is withering.

The skinny one claps his hands together. "Excellent! May we count you in, miss?"

The girl adjusts her sunglasses. "Maybe." (She has developed a talent lately for delivering even the most innocuous words as thinly veiled innuendo. The mother has noticed this.)

"More of a sunbather, are we?" the man says.

Alison's face turns crimson.

The father reaches into his wallet and pulls a few singles from the thick stack he took out yesterday at the bank. (Was that really just yesterday? Already he can feel the island beginning to work its rejuvenating magic on him.)

"Thank you, sir." The skinny one tucks the money in his pocket and continues down the beach.

"Nice guy," the father says.

"Friendly," the mother agrees.

"Well?" the father says, and raises his glass.

The mother smiles. Clairey stares intently at her cherry. Alison swirls her fruit punch with practiced boredom.

"To paradise," the father says.

■ ■ ■ ■

In the hot afternoon sun, the fat one makes his way down the beach, pausing at each cluster of chairs. "The volleyball match will begin in five minutes," he says softly. He nods uncomfortably, tugs at the collar of his shirt, and walks on. The guests watch as he passes. He is big, the kind of big that draws attention. This is Clive. Gogo, to those who know him.

"You best sell my game hard, man! We still four players short!" the skinny one shouts from the volleyball court, hands cupped around his mouth. "Volleyball of champions! Last call!"

People who were sleeping or reading shake their heads at his shouting and smile indulgently. They understand that the skinny one is an essential element of this place, granting the beach its energy, its sense of fun, its luscious, gummy vowels.

Alison takes off her headphones and stands. "Want to come watch me play, Clairey?" She reaches her hand out to her sister.

As the sisters cross the sand to the volleyball court, young men rise from their chairs and stroll casually in their wake. They are in the mood for some volleyball after all.

The skinny one counts off the players, one, two, one, two. Claire takes a seat on the sideline.

"You're my extra pair of eyes, little miss," he says to her with a grin. He tousles her hair and she stiffens at his touch.

Just before the game begins, Alison slips her tunic up over her head and drops it in the sand beside her sister. The eyes of the other players land on her, noticing while trying to appear as if they have not noticed the large conch-pink scar on her stomach. For a moment she stands perfectly still as they take in her secret spectacle. Then she snatches the ball from the sand and tosses it into the air.

It is not much of a game. A few high schoolers and college kids, a couple of young dads with some lingering fitness, a woman who ducks whenever the ball comes near her, a husband and wife in their mid-thirties — a slight paunch spilling over the waistband of the husband's pink dolphin-print swim trunks, the wife's immaculate body casting off the aura of frantic hours at the gym — and one genuinely skilled guy whose overinvestment in the game (unnecessarily aggressive spikes, the frequent utterance of the phrase "a little advice" as he attempts to whip his team into shape) quickly begins to grate on everyone.

As the game progresses, the players converse about the usual things. It is established that two couples are from New York, one is from Boston, and another from Miami. The woman who ducks is from Minneapolis. A Chicagoan on his honeymoon has left his brand-new wife, whose langoustine last night must have been off, holed up in their room.

"She made me leave," he adds quickly. "She said there was no point in both of us missing the day if I couldn't be useful anyway." Having repeated his wife's words, he furrows his brow; it occurs to him that he may have misunderstood her and failed one of the first tests of his marriage.

"Welcome to the next forty years of your life," says the overinvested man. He and his wife have been at Indigo Bay for two days. Don't get him wrong, it's fine, but they prefer Mallиouhana on Antigua, or was it Anguilla?, where they stayed last year. The couple from Miami has friends who swear by Malliouhana.

"Are we the only ones who find the food

here pretty subpar?" the overinvested man asks.

The woman from Minneapolis finds the food delicious but outrageously overpriced.

"It's because they have to bring everything in on boats," says the man in the dolphin swim trunks.

"That's just what they say. It's because we're a captive audience," corrects his wife.

"And the service charge is killer."

"When the bill comes, I don't look. I just sign."

"Smart man."

"Almost, honey!" the wife of the man in the dolphin swim trunks says when he serves the ball into the net. The trunks embarrass him, but they were a gift from his wife, and she was so excited about them he didn't want to offend her by returning them, though he suspects she was excited not because she thought these trunks would make him happy, but because they made her happy, because on some level she wants a husband she doesn't have to take seriously. He noted this but said nothing, figuring it would be cruel and pointless to call her attention to the ugliness in intentions she believed to be pure. When they separate three years from now, he will become aware of how many things he noted silently, of how much time he spent smiling at her while rebuking her in his mind.

A discussion is had about the pros and cons of the various excursions offered by the resort. Somebody wonders whether the snorkeling trip to Carnival Cay is decent.

"We went yesterday. You'll see so many fish you'll be sick of them," says a husband from New York.

Someone has heard that the scuba excursion, to the site where a ship called the *Lady Ann* was wrecked in a hurricane fifty years ago, is not to be missed. Somebody else spent the morning golfing and can report that the course is top-notch. The wife of the man in the dolphin swim trunks has decided against the tour of the old sugar estate and rum distillery. Another husband from New York highly recommends the romantic picnic on Tamarind Island. The beach is exquisite. He and his wife had it all to themselves. He does not mention the fake rose petals he kept finding on the beach, half buried in the sand, remnants of other people's romantic picnic excursions on Tamarind Island, and how they have burrowed into his mind, souring his memory of an experience he knows was very nice.

The boys who followed Alison down the beach include a short, muscle-bound kid with a frayed braid of hemp around his neck; a boy who wears a T-shirt emblazoned with the Greek letters of his fraternity; and a tall blond boy who, when pressed, admits to attending Yale. There's a girl, too, a communications major. For a few minutes they run through the people they know at each other's schools, looking for connections. The ex-girlfriend of the boy with the hemp necklace is in Developmental Psych with the fraternity brother. The sleepaway camp bunkmate of the communications major is in orchestra with the blond boy from Yale. The blond boy plays the cello. He is going to Saint Petersburg on tour in March.

"Small world," the blond boy says when he puts together that a teammate from his high school soccer team is in Alison's dorm at Princeton.

"In the sense that our worlds are small," she retorts.

He laughs. "Good point, Ali."

"Alison."

"Good point, *Alison.*"

The players serve and spike against a dichromatic backdrop of sand and sky. They clutch their knees and say, "Whew," after a particularly aerobic play. They watch Alison. She leaps and dives, flinging herself after the ball with abandon. Her body is lithe and athletic. Even when she's still, an energy simmers about her. When the wife of the man in the dolphin swim trunks catches him staring, he pretends to be extremely absorbed in the view of the ocean.

From her spot in the sand, Claire watches and wonders whether the sluicing beauty of her sister's movements will be hers, too, someday, when she grows up. She doubts it, but this doesn't really make her sad. It is enough to bask in the warmth of her sister's light.

When the game ends (defeat for the team of the overinvested man, who now declares the game to have been "all in good fun"), the blond boy approaches Alison. They talk a bit. The other boys eye him with annoyance and self-recrimination, then turn their attention to the communications major, reassessing. The blond boy touches Alison's shoulder, then trots off down the sand. When he's gone, she brings her hand to the spot he touched and brushes her fingertips against her own soft skin.

As afternoon slips into evening, the guests drift away from the beach. They spend the hours before dinner recovering from the day — the sun, the heat, the booze, beauty so vivid their eyes crave a rest from it. They shower. They check in with the office. (Their expertise is needed to resolve some particularly thorny issue, and they provide the solution with relief; or they are told to enjoy their vacation, things are chugging along just fine without them, and for the rest of the evening they are cranky and short-tempered.) They have sex in the fluffy white hotel beds. Afterward, they eat the mangoes from the welcome baskets, letting the creamy juice run down their hands. They investigate the small bottles in the minibars. They flip on televisions by force of habit, watch a few minutes of a news program from Saint Kitts, a *Miami Vice* rerun, a documentary about a reggae singer who is neither Bob Marley nor Jimmy Cliff. They sit on the balconies, smoke loose joints rolled with the mediocre grass they've managed to procure on the island, and watch the night begin: the sun go down, moths bloom from the darkness, the palms turn to shadowy windmills, the first faint stars pierce the sky.

The sisters lay side by side on Claire's bed and let the air conditioner blitz their bodies. One day on the beach and already Alison has turned nut-brown. Her freckles, faint apricot this morning, are auburn sparks. Claire's skin, meanwhile, is angry pink.

"You poor thing," Alison says.

She fetches the bottle of aloe vera from the kit in the bathroom and squeezes some into her palm. She soothes her sister inch by inch. Claire closes her eyes and slips into the blind dream of her sister's touch.

Alison has been away at college for four months. Sometimes at home Claire goes into her sister's room and sits on her bed. The room looks as if Alison went out just a minute ago. On the desk there are messy piles of snapshots and, mixed in with the pens and pencils in a blue ceramic mug, a tube of sparkly strawberry lip gloss. (Once, she opened the tube, slicked some on, and inhaled her sister's smell on her own lips. She has not dared to do this again.) There are band posters on the walls. The clothes her sister didn't take to college are sloppily folded in the dresser. But the room no longer feels inhabited. Sometimes, when she closes her eyes, she cannot picture her sister's face. She cannot hear her voice, and when this happens a wave of panic washes over her.

Now the hotel room they share is humid with Alison's presence, and everything Claire has missed comes rushing back. Her sister's savage nail biting. Her habit of stroking her scar through her clothes when she's thinking. The way she dances a little, small private movements, when she moves around a room. Her sister is a secret whispered in her ear.

What does a father think about when he wakes at dawn on the second morning of vacation? The damned birds. The roosters crowing away, from somewhere behind the resort. Some incessant yellow-breasted bird making a high-pitched racket on the balcony. (This is the bananaquit, an infamous island nuisance.) He throws on a robe, goes out to the balcony, shoos the bird away, and returns to bed. But it is back a minute later. He does this three times, thinking with increasing agitation of some prior guest in this suite who must have offered the bird scraps from his room service *pain au chocolat.* He tells himself to relax. He's awake anyway now, might as well get his day started. He kisses his wife, who is still sleeping soundly, and steps onto the balcony to appraise the morning. It is a clear day. A few squat clouds move slow as cruise ships across a pure blue sky. Faraway Cay appears so near he half believes he could reach out and touch it. He can make out individual palm trees on the shore. He can see the cay's black rock faces, mossed with growth, and the shadows of its ravines. The cay's intense greens simply do not exist at home. A father reflects momentarily that most people will live their whole lives without getting to see a place this beautiful. He reiterates to himself, as he tries to do often, that he is fortunate. He paused to allow a similar reflection on the shuttle ride from the airport to the resort, a journey whose features — children playing in dusty yards; women sitting somnolently behind dented tin pots at roadside stands; concrete houses that must once have been turquoise, yellow, pink, but whose paint had nearly all peeled away; strays — summoned the equivalent features of his own life: his beautiful daughters, wife, house (the eaves tufted now with shimmering snow), Fluffernutter the dog.

His thoughts are interrupted by a mechanical noise. A tractor is making its way along the beach. He notices now that the sand, which was immaculate yesterday, is strewn with mats of brown seaweed. Two men in overalls are raking the seaweed into piles. The tractor follows after them, scooping up the piles. Behind the tractor, a fourth man uses a push broom to smooth away the tread marks.

A father stands on the balcony and watches this procedure for some time. He understands now that the beach is not naturally pristine, which, he admits, should have been obvious, and this knowledge taints his enjoyment of it. His reaction bothers him. Why should these men's labor make him appreciate the beach less instead of more?

As his second day at Indigo Bay unfolds and he grows accustomed to the resort's beauty, to the bushes everywhere weeping pink blooms and the brazen teal water, he begins to perceive a new set of information. He notices, for instance, that the milk at the breakfast buffet in the open-air pavilion is ever so slightly sour, leaving an unpleasant aftertaste on his tongue. He does not say anything about this. He does not ask the woman who greeted his family so warmly at the pavilion's entrance to rectify the situation. He simply registers it. He also registers that in a few places at the resort he routinely catches the whiff of certain unmistakable odors. At the far side of the swimming pool, warm garbage. At the turn in the gravel path that leads from their room to the beach, sewage. He would never dream of complaining about such things, as other guests might. He likes to think he wears his affluence tastefully. He does not move through the world expecting things to be perfect. He tries to like everything and everybody as much as he can. Even this orientation toward the world he recognizes as a benefit of the position he occupies. It is easy to make allowances when you live a fortunate life.

Only now it is all a bit spoiled, isn't it? This same disappointment every year; childish, he concedes, but there it is: he still hasn't found paradise, not quite. Because, like everywhere else, when you get down to it, it is all just bodies and their manifold wastes and where to put it all, it is all just disorder two days from taking over. The week before he flew down here, a blizzard had prevented trash pickup in Manhattan for a few days. On his walk from Grand Central to the office, the sidewalks were piled five feet high with black trash bags. At street corners, the garbage pails were overflowing, the pavement around them littered with chicken bones, half-eaten hot dogs, diapers, frozen rivers of old coffee. He saw a little terrier in a red sweater urinate at the base of a pile of trash bags; he saw a thick beige puddle beside another pile, and stared at it curiously for a moment before the smell hit him and he realized it was vomit. As he walked past all of this he had fixed an image of a tropical beach in his mind and thought, *Thank god I'm getting out of here.* But now that he is out, now that he is here, he cannot help but wonder whether the only damned difference is the bougainvillea, whether this place is nothing but the same old ugliness, spackled with an unconvincing veneer of beauty.

A yellow rubber ball rises high in the air. A dozen children dash across the sand to catch it. It is ten in the morning, the start of the resort's daily hour of children's games and relays. While the children play, their parents use the free time. At the moment the yellow ball reaches its apex, a mother shudders with the force of her first orgasm in a month. Another mother is getting close and hoping ferociously that her husband lasts. A husband and wife who fully intended on sex snore in bed. Couples drink tequila sunrises in the hot tub, read on the beach, pound away side by side on treadmills in the fitness center. A wife poses for her husband in front of the ocean, trying her best to hide her soft thighs. For a moment their children slip from view. Briefly, they seem not to exist at all.

Claire is no good at games. She falls during the crab walk. "Come *onnn,*" her partner urges during the three-legged race. Two strides into the egg-and-spoon relay the egg rolls off her spoon and cracks on her foot. But most of all she is no good at the mysterious process by which children sift out into pairs and clusters, securing their buddies for the week. Even Axel from Belgium, who doesn't speak English, slips right in with another rowdy boy. They kindle friendship so quickly it leaves her dizzy, as if she's been spinning; when she stops, the world tilts back into place and the business of making friends is done, settled, without her.

The fat one brings the family's lunch. They watch him come up the beach, the heavy tray balanced on his shoulder. He stumbles. French fries rain onto the sand.

"I apologize," he says when he reaches them. "I'll bring you more chips."

"Oh, don't bother. There's still plenty," the mother says encouragingly. "Clairey, sweetheart, no writing."

The little girl freezes, caught with her index finger in midair. The word she had been writing was *chips.* She was up to *p.* She shoves her hand down at her side. She can feel her finger itching with the half-finished *p* and the *s.* She will have to finish later.

"Leave her alone," Alison snaps at her mother. She takes Claire's hand, raises it to her lips, and gives it a peck.

The mother sighs. This habit of her younger daughter's emerged a few months ago, her index finger wiggling and looping through the air. "I'm writing," Claire had mumbled when the mother asked what was going on. They'd met with the school psychologist, a mistake — after that Claire got furtive about it, sneaky, only doing it when she thought no one was paying attention. It is a constant struggle for the mothers: How do you know what is merely odd and what is worrisome? How much damage can you inflict upon your child if you treat something like it is one when it is really the other?

After Clive sets out their food on the low tables between their chairs, he takes a small towel from his pocket and wipes the sweat from his brow.

"Must be hot out here in long pants," the father says.

Alison shoots him a disapproving look, which he ignores. If fathers only said things their teenage daughters approved of, they would never speak at all. The mother and father exchange glances. A change has come over their daughter. Lately, her teenage moodiness carries a whiff of moral judgment. Newer still is this sighing dismissiveness, as if they are hardly even worth the effort of her judgment. Make no mistake, she's a college girl now.

"It's not so bad," the fat one mumbles. "Are you having a cold winter at home?"

"Brutal," the father says. "It's been snowing nonstop. I envy you, waking up to this every day."

"We do have our hurricanes," the fat one says.

"You had a bad one this season, right? José?"

"Luis."

The father claps his hands together. "Luis! That's the one."

"We had six hundred homes and many of our schools destroyed."

"How awful," the mother says.

The father cannot comprehend how people can be willing to live in a place where something like this can happen. He decides that a sense of the perpetual potential for destruction, for incurring a total loss, must be baked into people's temperaments here from birth, so that living like this is easier for them than it would be for him. Which is not a deficit in his character, for presumably if he had been born here he, too, would be such a person, able to bear unpredictability with stoic equanimity. He pauses to imagine himself as such a person — a pleasurable leaving-behind of himself as he enters a self more connected to and at peace with the planetary vicissitudes.

"Tell me something," the father says. "Where do you recommend for some local food? You know, something authentic."

The fat one gives him the name of a restaurant in town. His friend works there; his friend gives tours of the island and the cays, too, "At a good price." The mother and father smile and thank him, but something silent is exchanged between them: they enjoy receiving local knowledge, but they are also on guard for local slipperiness.

Up and down the beach, fathers sign bills for lunches and drinks. They try not to think about the numbers. Five bucks for their kid's Orangina, eighteen for their wife's goat cheese salad. They do not want to linger on the ways they are being nickel-and-dimed in paradise. Besides, what price can one put on such moments? Here is the sea, the blue water and the milky froth. Here is the soft, sun-warmed sand. The grains of sand on earth, a father read somewhere, are fewer than the stars in the universe. How unlikely, then, what an unbelievable stroke of luck, his family on this beach.

Some time later, the skinny one comes to clear the family's plates.

"What are the sisters planning the rest of the day?" he asks.

"We're going to build a castle, right, Clairey?" Alison says.

"Did you know I was this year's Carnival Sandcastle Competition champion?"

"Is that so?" Alison sweeps her hair off her neck and gathers it into a ponytail.

"For true. Well, honorable mention." He grins. "If you girls need any consultation on your design, just let me know."

"We like to build our sandcastles solo, thank you very much," Alison says with a fetching smirk.

Edwin squats in front of Claire. "And you, little miss? Do you, too, prefer to build your sandcastle *solo*?" He smiles at her.

Claire nods rigidly.

He laughs. "Okay, little miss." He tousles her hair. "See you later, sisters."

As he heads off down the beach, the mother notices that her daughter has her eyes on him, watching him go.

The skinny one is the prince of the sand.

The social hierarchy of the guests flows through him. Those he anoints with his gregarious approval seem to possess an invisible status. It is true he takes a lot of breaks and his tendency to stop and chat slows down service on the beach, but this is forgiven, even embraced. What's the rush? They're on island time. He is adored, too, by the young children, who follow him around like a fan club.

Then there is the fat one, Gogo, clumsy in the sand, clumsy with a tray of cocktails on his shoulder, clumsy adjusting the umbrellas to keep up with the movement of the sun, his voice rarely rising above a mumble. But he is Edwin's friend. The closeness between the skinny one and the fat one is clear. When they pass each other on the sand they exchange high fives and chummy insults. Often, Edwin returns from his break with a grease-spotted paper bag in hand — lunch for Gogo.

When a guest asks Clive about their friendship, he says simply, "We're best mates."

"Me and the Goges?" Edwin says, asked the same question. "We come up together from small. Me and he go back to primary. Who you think it was named he Gogo? I'd tell you why but he'd kill me."

One sundown, the man with the dolphin swim trunks is jogging down the beach when he sees Edwin struggling to drag a stack of chairs across the sand. Clive hurries over and, without a word, lifts the load from him. The man feels something crack in him. He loves his wife, don't get him wrong, but somehow he had forgotten until this moment — maybe he has forced himself to forget — the sweetness of friendship.

The sisters do many things together. They collect seashells. They trade underwater messages in the pool: "Mayonnaise is gross." "Fluffernutter is the world's best dog." In the ocean, Alison scoops Claire into her arms and Claire wraps her arms around her sister's neck.

"Our ship sank and Mom and Dad and everybody else is dead," Claire says. "We're in the middle of the ocean."

"See that island out there?" Alison says, pointing to Faraway Cay. "We're going to have to swim for it. It's our only chance. Can you make it?"

Claire nods, sober and brave.

They build castles, Claire happily submitting to her sister's vision and management. She fetches buckets of water and collects twigs and pebbles, while Alison carves bridges and archways and spiral staircases to the sky.

Edwin comes by and appraises their progress. "Look at your bridge there caved in. Guess you girls aren't having much luck building *solo* after all." He grins.

"It's a ruin," Alison replies. "We're building something ancient."

A ruin, Claire whispers to herself as she fetches more water. *A ruin. A ruin.*

A celebrity has arrived at Indigo Bay. He is an actor, a man in late middle age known for playing offbeat characters, mostly sidekicks, with a signature misanthropy. He has brought with him a supple young girlfriend, black-haired and splayfooted.

News of his arrival spreads quickly among the guests, who go intensively about the business of pretending not to recognize him. The chairs to either side of the actor and his girlfriend at the pool remain unoccupied. When the newlyweds (the wife by now recovered from her bad langoustine) find themselves in the hot tub with the actor, the husband goes so far as to ask him what he does for a living.

In the actor's vicinity, the guests laugh more loudly. The men stand straighter and touch their wives more. The women sway their hips. (They tell themselves, though, a bit smugly, that they would not go to bed with him. He was handsome once, but he has let himself go and turned flabby and dissipated. They've heard rumors for years that he is in and out of various rehab facilities in the California desert.)

Though he has been a public figure for more than three decades, the actor has never grown accustomed to the way people adjust themselves in his presence. He can feel it, a shrill solicitousness like a current in the air. While his girlfriend gets a massage, he takes a seat at the poolside bar and orders a vodka with a twist. The couple at the barstools next to him hush. Then the man says loudly to the woman that he wishes there were bigger waves here; he would love to go surfing. He begins to recount a story from long ago. Hawaii, a big wave seized at the perfect moment and how he rode the white curl of it to shore. The actor understands that this is one of the man's moments of personal greatness. One of the unusual features of his life is how often such stories are offered up for him to overhear.

This man could not know that the actor himself possesses a paralyzing fear of the ocean. This trip is his girlfriend's idea.

(Whose idea his girlfriend is, is anyone's guess. He has a way of finding problems and holding tight to them. Always has.) If it were up to him, he would vacation in the comfort of his own house, just take a week away from people. After all, it is people, not work, from which he craves respite.

When they arrived here, his girlfriend flung open the curtains in their room and urged him out onto the balcony. Beyond the sand, the ocean arranged itself in bands of deepening blue. The sun blinked on the water like infinite strobe lights.

"See? Not so scary, right?" She patted his arm as if comforting a twitchy dog.

Then it happened as it always did. The sea rose into a wall, higher and higher, until there was no end to it. He opened his mouth and the water flooded him.

Every family has its documentarian. Say it is the father. He squats in the sand, a position his sorry knees can barely handle these days, and captures his girls at work on their castle. At dinner, he nabs an action shot of Alison cracking a lobster claw with her hands. He snaps Clairey marveling at the whorls of a seashell. This task falls to him because his wife never takes pictures; she says she will but she forgets, or doesn't bother, he's not sure which. Anyway, it has worked out. He has found an avocation and become, if he says so himself, a pretty decent amateur photographer. What a relief to find, in middle age, that there are still interests waiting inside you to be discovered, that you just might have more artistic heft than you long ago made your peace with having.

At home a family's walls are decorated with photographs from their travels. The father and mother went on an African safari last year to celebrate their twentieth anniversary. A black chain of elephants against an orange sunset. A flock of birds like a vast swath of silk in the sky. A gathering of local children craning their faces up at the camera. Their guide, Buyu, kicking at the embers of their campfire with his black rubber boots.

And what a disappointment it is to see, on the walls of their friends' homes, *their* fauna silhouetted against the sunset, *their* gathering of enthralled local children, *their* diminutive guide in black rubber boots. (All over the world, it seems, in Tanzania and Vietnam and Peru, short, wiry men lead tourists across savannas and through jungles and up mountains in these same black rubber boots.) For fleeting moments, he bore witness to something beautiful; to see these moments of personal sanctity duplicated — a father knows it shouldn't matter so much.

It's a relief to be on a straightforward beach vacation. No endangered species or ancient city walls to capture. Clairey at play. His wife, modest and lovely in the whisper of early evening. After many days of disinterest and outright refusal, he prevails upon Alison to let him take some pictures of her. She takes her hair out of its ponytail and lets it fall around her shoulders; she leans against a palm and looks at the camera with a pensive expression, her lips slightly parted. He is so touched by her effort to style herself that for a moment he pulls the camera away from his face and simply looks at her.

In the distance he sees the fat one and the skinny one coming up the beach. He catches the skinny one's eyes on his daughter. If the father is honest, if all the fathers of teenage daughters here are honest, they do not like the way this man looks at their daughters. He is so informal. There is an unconcerned quality in his gaze, as if the father's daughter, while appealing, is not special.

They can acknowledge that their concern has at least partly to do with the color of this man's skin. But they aren't even *con-*

cerned, really; they are merely entertaining the possibility of concern. It is nothing. The people here are simply very friendly. It is their culture, the warm and open way of people on a small island. You know you've gone too long without a vacation when you start seeing friendliness as some kind of problem.

One afternoon, the blond boy from the volleyball game stops by the family's chairs on the beach. The mother watches Alison wave at him as he approaches, a gesture she executes with delicious casualness.

"What happened to your leg?" he asks when he is standing beside Alison's chair.

The mother looks over and sees that her daughter's calf is scraped and bloody.

"Tripped," Alison says, and shrugs.

The mother wants to tell her daughter to get bacitracin and a Band-Aid at the front desk and clean out the cut; she wants to get the bacitracin herself and patch up her daughter's scrape, but she holds her tongue.

"I'm going to hit some golf balls into the lagoon. Thought you might want to come," the boy says.

The mother watches him. His hair falls shaggily around his face — he wears it long and a bit disheveled. His skin is golden, like the outside of a perfectly baked vanilla cake. He wears his swim trunks slung low on his waist. On his chest, she sees a few strawberry blond hairs.

"Sure," Alison says. "Why not?"

The mother watches her stand. She walks beside the boy down the beach with an aloof strut, just right. This age, this moment. A woman flares in ultraviolet bursts on the hot surface of her child.

By their fourth day at Indigo Bay, the mother and father doze on the beach with ease. Sometimes they nod off with their books still in their hands. The longer they are on the island, the more easily and frequently they slip into sleep. All around them, other guests experience this same psychic loosening. In their regular lives, they make choices with high stakes every day: forty million dollars, the life of a patient, a thousand manufacturing jobs in the Midwest. If you catch her in a vulnerable moment at the bar, the wife of the man in the dolphin swim trunks will confess that by the time she leaves the office at night, sometimes the choice of where to order takeout is enough to crumple her. At Indigo Bay, they unwind into a world of choice without consequence. Beach or pool? Beer or margarita? They submit to the tonic regiment of such days gratefully. They begin to fantasize about saying goodbye to their lives back home. They could quit their jobs, buy a little villa down here, and never look back. They could spend every day on the beach and never tire of it. They could remain here forever.

"Don't let them get into any trouble while I'm gone," Alison tells Claire, nodding at their dozing parents. Claire watches her sister until she disappears down the beach, then she turns her attention to the bucket of seashells she and Alison collected earlier in the day. She spreads them out in the sand and sorts them into rows according to size, then piles them together and sorts them according to shape, color, favorite to least favorite. She goes down to the shore and spells her sister's name in the sand. She watches a wave wash the letters away. She returns to her seashells. She holds her favorite tightly in her fist and closes her eyes.

The mother opens her eyes and yawns. "Where's your sister?"

"Bathroom?" Claire says, though her sister has by now been gone a long time. When she finally returns, their mother asks her where she has been.

"Just went for a walk. It's really beautiful down at that end." She points to where Indigo Bay ends at a barrier of black rocks. "Hey, Clairey, I'm going on a treasure hunt and I'm bringing a lime."

Her sister has told a lie. On her breath, as she says *lime,* Claire smells smoke. It's her turn, but she can't think of a word.

"I'll be back," Alison says the next day. It's the in-between time after the beach and before dinner, and Claire is coloring at the coffee table in their room. After her sister leaves, Claire counts to ten, then follows.

She keeps her distance. Her sister walks back to the beach. She moves along the water's edge, skimming her toes in the froth. Claire takes big steps, planting her feet in her sister's melted footprints. Alison does not go to the pool, or to the bar. She walks past the water-sports cabana, the kayaks and Sunfish lined up tidily on the sand. She walks to the end of the beach and continues onto a narrow path, then disappears into the sea grape.

When Claire reaches the path, she hesitates. It is getting dark. What if their parents open the door that connects their rooms and find that they are gone? She takes a deep breath and steps onto the path. After a minute or so, it ends abruptly at an asphalt parking lot full of small shabby cars, their windshields covered with accordions of silver foil.

She hears laughter, a man's, and follows the sound. The asphalt burns her feet, but she stays quiet. There, next to an eggplant-colored car, her sister stands between the fat one and the skinny one. The skinny one digs into his pocket. He pulls out a small box and, from it, a cigarette. Her sister leans toward him and he slides it between her lips.

Husbands and wives have lost track of time. It is Tuesday or Wednesday, but perhaps it is only Monday. They have been on the island four days, no — five, possibly six. Within these lost days are lost moments, hours, mornings. Minutes diffuse like perfume into the air. The passage of time is of consequence only for the spectacles it reveals: The sea transforms to liquid silver as the day draws to a close. Sunset yields to the lavender fleece of twilight. Stars blink awake.

Night. At the hotel bar, couples drink elaborate cocktails as the lilting cadences of reggae float through the speakers. An elderly widow steps into the pool for her nightly swim. (She doesn't swim during the day. The pool is too busy then with the splashes and laughter of people together with their people.) A security guard with a corona of white hair plucks an empty chip bag from a bed of portulaca and deposits it in the trash.

In their room, the sisters lie together on Claire's bed. Alison weaves her sister's hair into a loose braid, unspools it with her fingertips, then braids it again.

"I'm going on a treasure hunt and I'm bringing a pearl," Alison says.

"I'm going on a treasure hunt and I'm bringing a pearl and a pizza."

"I'm going on a treasure hunt and I'm bringing a pearl, a pizza, and the stars."

"You can't bring the stars."

"Why not?"

"You can't carry them."

"I'll bring whatever I want."

A rainy day. Guests flip fruitlessly through the television channels. They sit on balconies and watch the rain. They order room service. They doze and make love, make love and doze. Some perceive the rain as a personal slight from the universe, a tax on their happiness. Others are secretly grateful. The rain absolves them from the burden of spending the day well; they hole up in their rooms with peculiar relief.

In the afternoon, Alison finds a cartoon for Clairey on TV.

"I'm going to the gift shop to poke around. Back soon," she says, not asking if her sister would like to come along.

Though she does not like cartoons, Claire watches dutifully. When the show ends, Alison is still not back. Claire walks out to the balcony. The rain falls in silver curtains. Palms toss in the wind. She looks out at the ocean. There is a person out there, swimming — she can see the head bobbing in the waves; it glints in and out of visibility in the surf, there and not there, back then gone again. Far out, the swimmer stops. The head bobs in place, facing away from shore, in the direction of the little island that is shrouded in mist, like a place in a fairy tale. As Claire looks at it, her heart flutters, and she remembers again the disappointment of mist — how you can never be *in* it; how as soon as you walk into it, it vanishes through your fingers, so that the little island as it appears from here is a place you can never, ever reach, no matter how you try.

The swimmer begins to stroke again. Claire watches as the figure moves around the black rocks that jut out from shore at the edge of Indigo Bay and disappears.

"Got you something," Alison says when she returns to the room later.

From a shopping bag she removes a puka shell necklace. Claire bends her head and her sister slips it over, twisting it into a double strand.

"Look at you, pretty," Alison says.

Her hair is wet.

That night, Claire is awakened by the sound of a key rattling in the lock. As she surfaces from dreams, she watches the door to the hotel room open. Her sister tiptoes across the room and slides into bed. In the morning Claire wakes at dawn to find her sister's bed empty. She is on the balcony, her eyes fixed on something in the distance. It seems her sister is hardly sleeping at all.

The actor cannot set himself at ease. The ocean is too near. His girlfriend tests him. She frolics in the waves, dives into the crests. Each time she disappears, fear grips him. She knows this and enjoys it, and the pleasure she derives from his fear makes him want to wring her.

She keeps pestering him about chartering a boat to Faraway Cay. The concierge has advised against this, on account of the goats, and recommended Tamarind Island instead, but she has decided this makes Faraway Cay off the beaten path and, therefore, more desirable. She says the beach is supposed to be even more beautiful than at Indigo Bay. (Is Indigo Bay not beautiful enough? Is there no such thing as enough beauty, as all of it you could possibly need?) In Faraway Cay's interior there is a waterfall. They must see it. He must overcome this silly fear once and for all. She will help him. (How nice for her.)

At night he dreams of death by water. A whirlpool sucks him into its maw. The deep seas swell and swallow him. Dead, underwater, he feels his body bloat and stiffen. He hears the roving cries of gulls.

On New Year's Eve, Indigo Bay holds a dinner barbecue on the beach. There is a live calypso band — three men in matching tan fedoras and short-sleeved floral button-downs, the cheerful reverberations of a steel-pan. Tiki torches. A buffet of local specialties — roasted sea crayfish, conch creole, mashed dasheen; chicken nuggets and spaghetti for the children. The guests drink piña coladas. They pick and suck the crayfish clean and lick the sweet ocean juice from their fingers. Small children toddle, woozy with happiness, before the torch-lit faces of the band.

When the band begins to play "Day-O," Alison sings along.

"Come on, Clairey. You know the words," she prods.

Claire is tentative at first, her voice barely a whisper, but as the song continues, it grows louder.

Six foot, seven foot, eight foot bunch.

The mother and father smile. Their shy little Clairey letting her voice be heard. Alison seeming finally to have unclenched. The mother and father join in. For a moment they are a family, singing.

Daylight come and me wan' go home.

A father knows it already: this is a memory.

As the night deepens, people kick off their sandals. Husbands reach for wives. They dance and drink and feast beneath the star-crammed sky. All the while, though they don't feel it, sand flies devour their flesh. The next morning at breakfast the guests scratch furiously at their limbs.

"I didn't feel a thing."

"Sneaky little suckers."

Claire is bitten terribly. Her legs and feet are covered. A bite on her eyelid causes it to swell so that she can hardly open her eye. The mother purchases Benadryl at the resort shop and Claire spends the day in a groggy haze, scratching.

Alison takes her sister's hand and pulls it away. "Don't." She presses her palm to her sister's skin. For a brief moment Claire is soothed. "Poor Clairey. You're just too sweet."

During the last days of vacation, adults begin to speak of their return.

"When we get home, remind me to take the car in."

"Let's be sure to call the Vitales about dinner."

"Don't let me forget to sign the boys up for Little League."

The sisters' parents are no different. Two days before their departure, as they lie on the beach, the mother remembers that she has unread library books, by now overdue, on her bedside table. When they get home she will return them and take out new ones, and this time she will actually read them. This vacation has reminded her how much she loves to read. The father announces that when they get back he will start going to the gym in the morning before work like he used to, no excuses. They are energized. Excited, even, to be off this island and back home, where their plans can be implemented, this energy put to use. The vacation has served its purpose — it has made them eager to be home.

A few days ago, they imagined leaving their jobs, their houses, their lives behind and moving down here. Some of them even spent an afternoon viewing properties with a Realtor. Now they see that they were simply indulging a fantasy that, like most fantasies, is not something they actually want. They would grow bored here. The bright colors would grate on their eyes. The sound of the ocean would torment them.

Guests depart daily. The resort shuttle takes them in reverse, up the palm-lined drive, onto the rutted public road, past concrete houses, roosters and goats, clothes on clotheslines fluttering over sandy yards. At Sir Randall Corwin International Airport, they walk back across the tarmac, up the stairs onto a plane, speed back down the runway, and lift into the sky. They touch down in Boston or New York or Chicago amid a papery snowfall and drive the dark roads home.

Inevitably, they leave things behind — in their rooms, by the pool, buried in the sand. The staff gathers these objects at the lost and found, but they are rarely claimed.

Once a month, Gwendolyn from the spa drives the items to Bendy Harbour Baptist Church. A gold necklace with an amethyst pendant. A denim jacket. A red shawl. Infinite sunglasses. A camera (the roll of film inside never to be developed). A legal thriller. A wristwatch with a green face.

On the day before they return home, Alison, Clairey, and their father walk down the beach to where the local woman who braids hair sits beneath a faded blue umbrella. Their father hands the woman sixty dollars, takes a picture of the girls (the woman looking up briefly — humorlessly, the father thinks — from combing Claire's fine white hair), and returns to his lounge chair.

As the woman braids Claire's hair, the sisters sift through the basket of beads, picking out purple and white.

"I'll come back to check on you," Alison says. She pecks her sister on the forehead and is off.

The braiding takes nearly two hours. The woman does not try to get her to talk, which is a relief to Claire. She likes sitting here, the silence and the feeling of the woman's hands working quickly yet gently through her hair. The sun is hot, the bites on her legs beg to be scratched, but she stays still, fortified by an image of herself returning to school with these braids, the beads tinkling as she walks, and how, for a rare, brief time, the other girls will envy her.

When the woman is finished, she hands Claire a clouded plastic mirror. It is better than she dared hope.

The woman looks at her. "My, you a patient child."

That night, Claire claws through her sleep. No matter how she scratches at the bites, she can't make the itching stop. All night she tosses in and out of dreams. When she wakes up it is dawn, barely light. The bites on her legs are crusted with dried, rust-colored blood. The blood has stained the crisp white sheets, too, blots so perfectly red it makes her dizzy. She looks around the room. Alison is gone.

What do a mother and father do when they are awakened by one child to the news that the other is missing? First, they tell themselves not to panic. Their daughter must have simply gone off somewhere on the resort grounds. It is a large property and there are any number of places she could be. Perhaps she has gone for a jog, or to smack tennis balls against the backboard at the courts. The small red blip of a kayak far out on the water might be her — maybe she decided to squeeze in one last water sport before their departure. Perhaps she got too drunk at the hotel bar last night and is sleeping off a hangover in the room of one of the other girls her age. (The parents are not naïve; they know that a teenager is apt to have one daiquiri too many after her parents have gone to bed on the last night of a Caribbean vacation.) Surely she will come groggily across the sand anytime now, and how furious they will be! And how pleasurable it will be to be furious with a daughter who is perfectly fine, and who will be snotty and dismissive when they tell her how worried they have been.

But she is in none of these places doing none of these things. By late morning, a mother and father's faith that their child will turn up any moment has given way to terror. Everything but Alison is forgotten. Breakfast, lunch . . . Claire is starving but says nothing.

Word spreads quickly among the guests.

"Did you hear? That pretty girl with the auburn hair is missing."

"The one with the scar?"

"They're saying she never came home last night."

The police are summoned. The chief of police asks the mother and father a series of questions, and they tell him about their vacation in precise, dutiful detail. As guests sun themselves by the pool and climb the StairMaster to oblivion in the fitness center, the Royal Police Force of Saint X combs the property. The time for the family's flight home comes and goes.

On the first night after Alison's disappearance the sunset is the most beautiful yet, a flashy display of scarlet and violet that deepens, as the sun slips below the horizon, until it is the shade of a bruise. On the balcony, a mother watches the sun go down, then sinks to the floor. She crouches on hands and knees and dry-heaves over the cool terra-cotta tiles. A father goes to her, holds her. He tells her that everything could still be okay. She repeats this. Everything could still be okay. Hearing these words echoed back to him from his wife, a father breaks down. They remain on the balcony, intertwined, for some time. A sense of distance from the day's events comes over the mother and she wonders, with detached curiosity, whether she is becoming — whether she is already — the one thing none of the mothers ever want to be. A father is seized by the most unaccountable memory: Alison, one year old and bald as could be, blowing raspberries against his cheek.

From inside, where she has been set up in front of the television, Claire watches her parents. Later that night, they put her between them in their bed. In the middle of the night she wakes to the feeling of a hand on her back; for a moment, she thinks it is Alison. Then she remembers. It is her father's hand, checking for the rise and fall of her breath. Claire lies awake, eyes wide open in the dark.

On the second day, the chief of police asks the mother and father to take him through their time on the island once more. The father tells him again about their arrival, ten days ago, on a TWA flight out of Kennedy. Alison slept late the next morning. She drank a fruit punch.

"He was after her all week," the mother interrupts. Her body trembles. "That blond boy. He couldn't leave her alone." As she speaks, a film reel of horrible possibilities flickers through her mind. She'd liked this boy, found it sweet the way he lingered, at once cocky and unsure, around her daughter. What if she'd misjudged him? What a fool she'd been, thinking herself a good mom, a fun mom, for letting her daughter go off with him. How had she allowed herself to forget that in the end a mother has only one job? Suddenly she cannot breathe. The warm tropical air clogs in her throat. When she begins to hyperventilate, the chief of police calls for the hotel doctor, who arrives promptly, examines the mother swiftly, and writes a prescription for a sedative. A porter is sent to the local chemist's to collect it. The doctor pulls the father aside. "I might suggest that you have a babysitter called for the little one," he tells him quietly, gesturing at Claire, who is sitting in a wicker chair, eyes on her mother. "Give yourselves some time and space."

"If you think we're going to let our daughter out of our sight, if you think we're going to leave her with some person who could be anyone, you're out of your mind."

"Of course. I apologize."

"Everyone here could be anyone. *You* could be anyone."

"I'll go now, sir."

The couple in the room next to the family's asks Indigo Bay's manager, very tactfully, if they can be relocated.

"It's so awful, what's happened. The thing is, we can hear them," the husband says.

"Going through . . . what they're going through," the wife adds. She places a hand protectively over her stomach; she is four months pregnant, this trip a last hurrah before their lives change. She laces her other hand through her husband's and squeezes, a gesture that means, *Something like this could happen to us.* Her husband squeezes her hand back, an assurance that it won't and, more generally, that this thing that has occurred is not a bad omen, not some harbinger of terrible things on the horizon. (He will turn out to be right. Often, in the decades to come, as their son grows up and their family's own small troubles reveal themselves, the wife will think that this ruined vacation was the darkest of blessings, because however her child struggles, however he tests her, hurts her, what does it matter when she carries within her the indelible sounds of another mother's undoing?)

The manager upgrades them to a private villa.

The rest of the guests do their best to balance concern with the pleasure of their days. They do not know the girl, after all. Their worry is tinged with excitement. There are rumors.

"They say the police are questioning that

blond boy."

"Did you hear they're talking to the skinny one and the fat one?"

"I heard the police picked them up for something the night she went missing. People are saying they spent the night in jail."

"It's always the pretty ones, isn't it?"

The island is turned upside down with searching. Members of the civil service are given days off to join the search. Prop planes loaned from a larger island nearby scan the shallow seas. The lagoon into which, mere days ago, Alison watched the blond boy hit golf balls is trawled to no avail.

The search turns up answers to other, older mysteries. The body of a beloved family dog, who disappeared during a storm last season, surfaces in the thickets beside a salt pond. A wedding band is found in the dusty lot behind Paradise Karaoke. In a limestone cavern on Carnival Cay, a customs worker uncovers a small black notebook in which are recorded the debts of a local man who left the island in an unexplained hurry last year. But no sign is found of Alison.

When the chief of police arrives at the family's hotel room on the third day after her disappearance and delivers this update, the father looks around — at the marble floor, the scarlet orchid in the white vase, the canopy bed — his gaze darting and unfocused, as if the coherence of these things is beginning to come apart before his eyes. "I don't understand. What's taking so long? Where is she?"

"I assure you we are deploying every available resource. Our officers are working in fifteen-hour shifts. We are coordinating with the Federal Bureau of Investigation. We have search-and-rescue units from three islands and a patrol ship from the British navy devoted to finding your daughter."

"But this island is tiny." The father squints at the chief of police. "Why the hell can't you find her?"

The actor's girlfriend finally persuades him, grudgingly, to charter a boat to Faraway Cay. As they slice through the water, he keeps his eyes shut tight and listens as his girlfriend chats up the two men who comprise the boat's crew. ("I *love* reggae. That whole rasta spirituality, you know? I've always found that so interesting." "I'm an L.A. girl. But he" — gesturing, he knows, at him — "grew up in a really small town in Kentucky." He knew she'd tell these men this; she mentions Kentucky to anyone who will listen. It hurts him. His childhood was not a happy one. If he asked her to stop mentioning it he knows she would, but she wouldn't understand why, so he doesn't ask.) Each time the boat lofts over a swell, time becomes a glass cube he's trapped in.

The cay is only a few hundred yards off the coast, so the ride must take only five minutes, though to him it feels much longer. They anchor offshore, so he has to climb the metal ladder down from the boat and wade through the shallows; he keeps his back to the open water, his eyes fixed on the land. She's right — it is beautiful. The cliffs are covered in green growth, a color so vivid it seems to cast out vibrations. The beach is a crescent of sand so brilliant he has to shield his eyes. Palms curve outward in invitation.

While the men prepare a picnic for them on the beach, the actor and his girlfriend hike a path inland to the waterfall. When the ocean slips from view he feels like himself again. At first, they climb steeply uphill through humid green growth, the birdsong so thick you couldn't sort through it if you tried. The understory is a sprawl of ferns and vines and the buttressed roots of trees that rise to form a nearly solid canopy high overhead. (The trees are silk-cotton, and have stood for centuries.) After half a mile or so, they summit abruptly onto an arid plateau, silver scrub and cacti and dust, a transition like leaving one dream and entering another. A few stark, knotty trees jut from the cracked earth, leafless and stunted. Lizards that seem made of nothing but dry air scuttle in and out of the scrub. A small white butterfly floats over the hot earth.

Not far from the path, a cluster of goats snort and chomp at the scrub.

"Gross," the actor says.

"I think they're cute."

"I think *you're* cute."

Whether he says it because he means it or because he doesn't but wishes he did or simply because it's the sort of thing he knows she wants him to say, he couldn't tell you.

The path descends back into dense and steamy thickets. He smells growth, soil, sweet wet rock. He hears falling water. They are close.

Around a bend, and there it is. The water sluicing down the rocks is glitter and mist. The pool into which it tumbles is utterly circular and glassy. At the pool's edge, mosses fur the stones in newborn green, and white flowers bloom, their perfume carried lightly on the vapor cast off by the waterfall. He has the feeling then that he is seeing something he shouldn't be seeing, that maybe there really is such a thing as too much beauty, as so much you can never move on from it.

"You like it?" his girlfriend says. He notes the curl of triumph in her voice and a familiar urge rises in him to fuck her till she hurts for days. But then he looks at her and sees that there are tears in her eyes. She laughs at herself, wipes them away. "I know, I'm a sap."

He has been unkind. All she wants is his happiness. Is that so terrible? He takes her in his arms, feeling the blunt realness of her. What the hell is wrong with him? Where is the problem here? He leads her to the water's edge, holding her hand in case she should slip on the slick rocks, and they wade in. He surrenders to it. They swim together to the very center of the pool. The water is so crisp and clean you could understand how a baptism could change everything. He squeezes his hands together and squirts her.

"Hey," she splashes back.

He wraps his arms around her. "You're mine."

She shrieks and kicks and protests with

delight. "Let me go! Let me go!"

"Never." He makes a silent vow. From now on when she asks for things he will do them, give them, say them.

They swim to the waterfall. They dunk their heads beneath the rushing water and let it pummel them. They slip behind the curtain of water. They kiss. She reaches for him but he shakes his head.

"Lie back," he says. He cradles her head as she lies against the wet rocks. When she comes, her cries are lost in the roar of water.

After, they float, spent and open on the surface of the pool.

"They'll be waiting for us," he says finally.

"Do we have to?" she pouts.

Together, they stroke toward the edge.

Years from this moment, the girlfriend, who by then will have been the girlfriend of quite a few Hollywood men, will publish a memoir (the back cover promising to reveal "the juicy private details of the lives of some of America's favorite leading men"). In the chapter about the actor, these details will include his thalassophobia and his various chemical dependencies, which the girlfriend will theorize stem from a loveless childhood. It goes without saying that the memoir will recount this day: the boat ride across the topaz shallows to the cay, the birdsong and the goats, the waterfall and how, just before leaving it, the girlfriend looked down and saw an arm, puffed and white, reaching up from the bottom, as if frozen in the act of beckoning.

"Why did the chicken cross the road?"

"To give Officer Roy the busiest day of his life."

This is a popular joke here and I don't mind it. The things the police handle on this island are mostly small. Mr. So-and-So cut down Miss So-and-So's sugar-apple tree. A scuffle at Papa Mango's. Floyd Vanterpool operating an unlicensed taxi again. We do see a few cases of domestic trouble each year.

Much of my job involves helping our children here grow up safely and become upstanding citizens, and I like this work. Every year I visit the island primaries and teach a lesson on bicycle safety. For my demonstration I ride a small pink bike with streamers on the handlebars, and this always receives a good laugh. When children see me around they shout, "Officer Roy!" "Officer Roy!" just to say hello.

When the young folk have a late-night bacchanal on Little Beach I have no choice but to bust it up, but I try not to be too cross with them when I do so. I try to remember that I limed on Little Beach myself in my time. While they clean up their rubbish I make jokes. If I see a boy and girl coming out of the bushes together I say, "She out of your league, man!" If I see a boy who's small for his age I say, "Who invited this nursery child to the party?"

If I see some youths clustering outside Perry's in the Basin I pull up beside them and say, "This is loitering. I'm going to have to write you up." You should see how some of the toughest ones look like they might soil themselves until I start laughing.

"Aw, man, don't do that shit to we!" they say, but they're not really mad. "Do it up, Officer Roy!" they beg when I prepare to drive away. "*Please,* Officer Roy?" I turn on my lights and my siren and drive off to their cheers. I have a rapport with them, you could say. I watch these kids grow and I play my part.

Edwin and Gogo — I used to shoo them

away from the radio tower when they were snot-nosed little boys. I came up with Gogo's daddy, God rest his sweet soul. I pulled those two and their hooligan mates over for drunk driving all the time and took them in to sleep it off. I never saw it as punishment. I never wrote them up. I was protecting them from their young stupid selves, like pulling a baby back from the water's edge. My wife and I couldn't have children. The island children are my children.

I must have picked Edwin and Gogo up a hundred times before that night. That's how I know something happened and they were part of it. Because the ninety-nine other times I pulled them over, on the drive to the station they joked with me and made chitchat. But that time, the night Alison Thomas died, neither one of them said a word.

Emily of Pasadena

On my first day of kindergarten, after my father took a picture of me on our front steps in my purple overalls and before I climbed onto the yellow bus, my mother prepared me for Cody Lundgren. She squatted so her eyes were level with mine and told me that there would be a boy in my class who was different from other children, and that I must not be afraid of him, but, on the contrary, must treat him with special kindness. With a child's logic, I assumed this was simply one more part of going to school. In kindergarten, one rode the bus and learned to read (though I already knew how, and was rather smug about it), one had recess and homework, and one was especially kind to the boy who was different. I was a shy child, at once excited and tentative about taking these steps.

As soon as I stepped into the classroom

that morning and saw him, I knew I could not do what my mother had asked. Cody Lundgren terrified me. His limbs jerked. His mouth hung open. Saliva pooled on his lower lip and dripped in glistening cobwebs, darkening his shirt. Worst of all were the sounds he made, viscous gurgles punctuated by high-pitched keening. Every day, while the rest of us learned our numbers or studied butterflies — larva, pupa, fly away — Cody sat with his personal aide, making his sounds and collapsing on occasion into horrible tantrums.

Then, one Monday in February, Cody Lundgren was not in school. Our teacher, Ms. D'Elia, gathered us in a circle and told us that Cody had died over the weekend. We were each made to say one thing we would remember about Cody. This struck me even then as a poorly conceived exercise, dependent as it was upon five-year-olds possessing the subtlety to craft a pleasant fiction about who Cody had been to us. (Ms. D'Elia was new that year, and more than once I'd overheard my mother on the phone with other mothers describing her as "out of her depth," which led me to imagine Ms. D'Elia in a yellow bathing cap, performing a synchronized swimming routine, her legs treading furiously beneath the water's surface.) All of the other children shared the same memory, of the cupcakes Cody's mother had brought on his birthday. They were not the homemade ones the rest of our mothers packed in Tupperware for our birthdays, but fancy ones from a bakery, with sugar flowers and perfect whorls of buttercream. It was a memory that had nothing to do with Cody, really, and everything to do with his mother's love for him. When my turn came, I said I would remember how much Cody liked to sing. Every morning during music time, Cody would squawk and moan along to "Funga Alafia" or the Erie Canal song, terrifying sounds of unmistakable pleasure. I would not actually remember this fondly, but I understood that it was the sort of thing Ms. D'Elia had in mind. Next, she read us a picture book, a parable in which a family of mice grieve and heal after one of them is eaten by a cat, and that was that.

The truth is I was relieved Cody Lundgren was dead. Death meant never seeing someone again, and I was glad I would never again see Cody or hear the yelps and gurgles that so disturbed me.

A few months later, my mother and I ran into Cody's mother at the supermarket. Mrs. Lundgren was tall, with silky black hair, far prettier than any other mother I knew, prettier than I'd previously understood a mother could be.

"Look how big you've gotten!" she exclaimed to me. Her smile was so hard and desperate that I reached for my mother's hand like a younger child than I was. I left the grocery store with a pit in my stomach, rocked by an emotion so new to me I could not identify it, though looking back I know it was shame.

This was the extent of my experience with death when my sister's body was found on an uninhabited cay in the Caribbean, many years ago now. Looking back, the things I remember most clearly from the days after Alison went missing and before she was found are strangely inconsequential. For example, I remember the hunger I experienced on that first day when my parents forgot about breakfast and lunch, and how I felt sorry for myself about it in the banal way any child feels sorry for herself when she finds herself overlooked in a flurry of attention devoted to her sibling. I remember hiding out in the bathroom to devour a Toblerone bar and a tin of mixed nuts I'd scavenged from the minibar. I was hiding because I wanted to see how long it would take my parents to realize they'd forgotten to feed me, so that I could take the full measure of their neglect. Once they *did* realize, I have vivid memories of the room service food with which I was plied, or soothed, or distracted (I'm not sure what to call it) in the days that followed — cheeseburgers and fries and sundaes and a personal pan pizza with delightful miniature pepperonis. I cleaned my plate at every meal; if my parents noticed this, I'm sure they thought my appetite was unaffected by what was happening because I was too young to grasp the seriousness of the situation, but that wasn't exactly right. I was terrified during those days, but not because of what might have happened to Alison. Even as the people around me grew increasingly frantic, I was not worried for her. I literally did not understand that what had happened to Cody Lundgren could happen to my big sister. I thought — I *knew* — that she was playing an elaborate game with us. She was watching it all, the dapper policemen with their braided gold epaulets, the resort staff in a tizzy, the entire spectacle she'd created, from some hidden perch with a smile. No, it was not Alison's disappearance but my parents' terror that terrified me. Their distraction and anguish shook the foundations of a world that had, until then, seemed to me absolutely stable.

Other memories from those days are less distinct. They have the quality of a fever dream — hazy and inconsistent, the swirling world resolving for brief instants into crystalline clarity. I remember lying between my parents at night, my father's hand on my back measuring every inhale and exhale. His words to the doctor. *If you think we're going to let our daughter out of our sight.* I remember the chief of police questioning my parents, and my mother telling him about the blond boy who'd taken such an interest in my sister. As she speaks, my mother's eyes have a wild, darting quality. The tone of her voice shifts from word to word, turning raw, then affectless, then raw again. I don't really understand what she is saying, what she is accusing the boy from the volleyball game of having done. I know only that before my eyes my mother is becoming someone I never understood she could be.

In short, a terrifying knowledge came over me in those days. It was the knowledge that I would never be safe again, because I never had been, not once in my whole life, only until then I hadn't known it, because I had believed so absolutely in the power of my parents.

The chief of police questioned me, too. My father sat me on his lap and my mother explained to me that one of the nice men who was helping to find Alison wanted to talk to me. This was the first moment I remember feeling truly afraid for my sister. I think I understood that if the police were looking to a child for help, something must be very wrong. I felt a familiar prickling in my fingertips, and as I sat in my father's lap I began to trace letters in the air. A-L-I-S —.

My mother reached out her hand and placed it over mine, stilling it. "No writing, Clairey. Please. This is important."

At the time of our family's vacation, this compulsion had been with me for several months. I'm not sure how or why it started. I would hear a word, and it would feel absolutely necessary to write it in the air. When my mother lifted her hand away, I tensed my fingers against the need — my sister's name vibrating in my bones, desperate to get out. Alison. Alison. Alison.

The chief of police smiled at me. I drew away from him. I did not like being smiled at by strangers. He asked me if I knew anything about what my sister had been doing, if I had seen anything out of the ordinary.

What did I know? I knew my sister came and went, was there and not there. I knew that eyes followed her wherever she went. I said nothing and hid my face in my father's chest. He smiled weakly at me and told me what a good job I had done, how brave I had been, which even at that age I didn't believe. A dish of vanilla ice cream with a maraschino cherry was brought for me. I hated how the bright red bled onto the ice cream, but I ate.

On the third morning after Alison's disappearance, my father announced with unconvincing cheerfulness that he was taking me swimming. I'd been holed up in my parents' hotel room all that time, and I understood that he'd decided this would be good for me. I changed into my swimsuit, buckled my jellies, and out we went. When we stepped onto the marble pool deck, a hush fell over the other guests. I looked at them looking at us and gagged. I had the distinct sense that they knew something about us we didn't, and that if they looked at us long enough we would have to know it, too.

"It's okay," my father said, nudging me

forward.

We were not in the water long, twenty minutes at most. My father gathered me in his arms and tossed me into the air. We raced the length of the pool. We did underwater flips and handstands — my father pushed himself into an elegant plank, toes pointed. I see now that we were trying to respool time. If only we could forget what we were beginning to know, maybe we could play ourselves back to when this vacation was just a vacation. When we got out of the water, my mother would wrap me in a fluffy white towel. *Look at you, sea monkey,* Alison might say.

A few hours later, there was a knock on the door of my parents' hotel room. When my father opened it, I saw the chief of police standing very still in his uniform with the braided epaulets. A cartoon was put on the television for me, and my parents went out into the hall with him. Sometime after that, they must have told me what he told them: that Alison had been found, that she was gone. But I don't remember that part. I remember those epaulets, how they seemed like something from a beautiful story.

What is known about the night Alison disappeared: At approximately 8 P.M. she was seen walking from the swimming pool to the hotel bar by an elderly security guard named Harold Moses. At the bar, she met the blond boy, a fact confirmed by the boy and three other witnesses. Alison and the boy went to the staff parking lot and smoked a joint together. At 8:45 P.M., he returned to the bar without Alison. At approximately 10:15 P.M., Alison returned to the parking lot, where Edwin Hastie and Clive Richardson picked her up in Edwin's car, a 1980 Vauxhall Astra, eggplant in color, and the three of them drove across the island to the Basin. They spent two hours at a local watering hole called Paulette's Place, where my sister was seen with the two men, smoking pot and drinking rum and dancing. Several patrons at Paulette's Place confirm that she departed with the men at approximately 12:45 A.M.

At 1:30 A.M., a police officer named Roy Cannadine pulled the Vauxhall Astra over on Mayfair Road for erratic driving. Only Clive and Edwin were inside. Officer Cannadine did what he always did with the young men who could frequently be found weaving down the island's roads late at night. He drove them to the eggshell-blue prison to sober up for the night. In the morning they were released, the car keys returned, and they set off on the two-mile walk to fetch the car from the side of Mayfair Road. They arrived at work on time.

Can you see it? A bar, PAULETTE'S PLACE painted in white on a driftwood sign out front. Dancing and drinking and a haze of cigarette and pot smoke and, in the middle of it all, a russet-haired girl. She dances with the men. She drinks the drinks they hand her.

When she leaves with them, they tell her they are taking her someplace special.

"It's a surprise," they say.

"You'll love it."

Drunk and high but most of all naïve, she lets the twisting in her stomach push her forward when it should hold her back. They drive to the beach beyond the black rocks at the edge of Indigo Bay, where a boat is waiting. They bring the boat into Faraway Cay slowly, and she hops out into the knee-deep water and smiles, for the sea is warm and lovely and she knows that she — her thighs exposed to the starlight, the hem of her skirt soaked by the gentle waves — is lovely in it. They tell her there is a waterfall at the island's center, and they set off for it on foot. She still thinks they are having a good time.

"Not far now."

"Keep walking."

Their voices, though still friendly on the surface, have a coldness to them. No, she tells herself. She is just imagining it. Everything shifts so quickly that by the time she understands what is happening, it is too late to think about what to do. (Anyway, what could she do, way out there?)

They pull her into the scrub. She struggles at first, but one of them slaps her across the mouth. After that she is too afraid to fight. More than this, she knows there is no point. They have wanted what they wanted since the first time they saw her on the beach at Indigo Bay in the white tunic she thought made her look so very fetching. They untie her halter top, shove her denim skirt up, yank her panties down. Maybe this was their plan all along. Or maybe the night has gotten away from them. Maybe as they thrust against her, pressing her body against the hard roots of a manchineel tree, the ground littered with its sour, rotting fruit, they experience no pleasure, only terror, because it dawns on them that, having done this, they cannot allow her to live. When it is over, they dump her naked body in the waterfall. On the boat ride back to the mainland, they toss her clothes into the water, never to be seen again.

Or perhaps it was a terrible accident. They are carousing at Rocky Shoal when she trips and hits her head against one of the sharp volcanic rocks for which the beach is named. Or she stumbles into the sea and they realize too late that she is in no condition to swim. They panic. They do the first thing they can think of; they heft her lifeless body from beach to car to boat to cay.

One might imagine it differently. One might imagine it any number of ways, really, the details shifting, the outcome the same. Clive Richardson and Edwin Hastie were taken into custody.

The night after Alison's body was found, I took off my clothes to change into my nightgown and saw that my shoulders had begun to peel. Mere days ago, my sister had rubbed aloe on my sunburned skin. If I concentrated on the memory, I could still feel her fingertips. Now I was shedding that skin. Soon there would be nothing left of me that she had touched.

For the first time since she disappeared, I cried. I was an only child now, hopelessly insufficient. I picked at the skin, wanting the new sadness I would feel when all of it had flaked away. I wanted all the sorrow I could gather.

A few days later, as my parents went busily about arranging the funeral and the transportation of my sister's body back to New York, the chief of police arrived with the shocking news that Edwin Hastie had been released and that Clive Richardson, while still in custody, was being held not as a suspect in my sister's death, but on charges related to drugs and paraphernalia that had been uncovered during the investigation. Despite the circumstances surrounding Alison's death, the chief of police explained, they did not have sufficient evidence to charge the two men, and they could not hold them if they could not charge them. Apparently it had been determined that the window of time between when witnesses saw Clive and Edwin leave Paulette's Place with Alison and when Officer Cannadine pulled them over on the side of Mayfair Road was not adequate for them to have traveled to Faraway Cay and back.

As you would expect, my parents were incredulous. I remember sitting with my mother on their bed, her patting my back with increasing vigor and turning up the volume on the television as, out on the balcony, my father argued more and more loudly with the chief of police.

"Explain to me, if you can, how you can be so sure the window of time was inadequate," my father said. He paced back and forth, hands jammed in his pockets.

"In the course of our investigation we have conducted numerous simulations, with boats leaving from every feasible location. The window of time during which the men in question were unaccounted for simply is not sufficient."

My father snorted. "How can you be so sure about that window? How can you be so confident it wasn't half an hour longer, or even more?"

"We have three witnesses corroborating the time of their departure from Paulette's Place. The witness who next saw them is one of our own officers."

"How convenient for you."

"I can assure you his testimony is his own."

"Well, your assurance certainly makes me feel a whole lot better. Now I have complete faith in the — what was it you called it? The course of your investigation?"

"That's correct."

My father stopped pacing. He took a step closer to the chief of police and held him in his gaze. "Those men are part of this. Maybe they weren't working alone. Maybe someone else took her out to that island, I don't know. It's not my job to know — it's your job. But I know one way or another they're involved, and you know it, too."

"I understand you are very upset."

"Oh, yes, *upset.* That's just what I am."

"I have some questions for you, sir, but perhaps we should continue this conversation at a later time."

"By all means, let's proceed." My father spread his hand in withering invitation.

The chief of police hesitated a moment, then continued. "Had you noticed any changes in your daughter recently?"

"What kind of changes?"

"For example, had she been agitated? Had she engaged in any reckless behavior? Had she been not herself or had she perhaps exhibited any signs of depression?"

My father laughed then, cold, hollow laughter. "So that's the story you want! Can't have a murder, can we? Bad for business, I'm sure."

"The only story we want is the truth."

"The truth is Alison is the very definition of a kid you don't have to worry about." He paused. "Was."

"I understand."

"Really? Because I'm not sure you do, so you listen very carefully. My daughter was killed here, on your island, and if I get the impression that you aren't really looking for the truth, I promise you I will get on every news network in America and call for a total boycott of your pretty little island, and I will not rest until every last dive shop and rum bar shuts down."

"I understand, sir. Thank you for your time."

A week after Alison was found, we flew home. My father pulled two suitcases through the airport on Saint X, his and Alison's. How small we were, the three of us, barely a family at all.

"Time to go back to reality," the man seated beside my mother on the plane said sociably as we pulled away from the gate.

My mother smiled and nodded politely. She closed her eyes and did not open them again until we touched down in New York.

I had a window seat. As the plane lofted into the sky, I pressed my nose to the pane. At first the island filled the window. But quickly it reduced to a thin slash in the pale sea. Within seconds it was gone and we were moving through a vast heath of cloud.

■ ■ ■ ■

My braids turned limp and scraggly. Frizz haloed my scalp. There would be no grand moment of showing the braids off at school, and this disappointment still stung even in light of what had happened. Most of the time, my parents seemed not to notice how wild my hair had become. But at odd moments, one or the other of them seemed to see me vividly; they would look at the braids, then reach out to touch them as if they were some sort of curious relic.

Finally, the night before Alison's funeral, my father had me stand in front of the bathroom mirror. He unwound the rubber bands, dropped the beads into a plastic bowl, and uncoiled the braids one by one. He worked with exquisite gentleness. I think this was a necessary ritual for him, one he'd put off until he was ready for it. My hair tangled around his fingers. Loose strands floated to the floor.

"All done," he said hoarsely when the braids were out. Then he wandered off down the hall.

Hundreds of people came to the funeral. High school and college classmates of Alison's, women who'd served on PTA committees with my mother, colleagues and clients of my father's. Even, in an uncomfortable gesture, the ambassador from Saint X to the United States.

The funeral is mostly a blur. Too many people. Too much perfume in the air. An itchy gray dress, purchased hurriedly for me by one of my mother's friends. What I remember most is the beautiful teenagers crying. After the service, they gathered in tight clusters on the sidewalk outside the church. The girls wore black dresses that exposed their legs and cleavage. They must not have owned clothing appropriate for a funeral, or maybe they did but chose these skimpy outfits instead because they relished this rare opportunity to explore a sad, tragic sensuality. They cried in the arms of solemn boys who, cast into this moment, appeared spontaneously to have been made into men. Among them, most beautiful of all, was Drew McNamara. Drew was my sister's high school sweetheart. They began dating in the spring of their freshman year and remained inseparable until my sister broke up with Drew the week before leaving for college. I had been heartbroken when she did it — I had believed I would scatter rose petals down the aisle at their wedding. Now here he stood, one among them. I looked around at them, these alive girls and boys, so attractive in their grief while I felt so wrong, a freak, in my own.

In those early months after Alison's death, the investigation consumed both of my parents, though it consumed them differently. My father took a leave from work; Alison became his full-time occupation. He was in frequent communication with the FBI, and he called the police on Saint X constantly to monitor the progress of their investigation, which he became increasingly convinced was not inept, but rather a dexterous charade intended to preserve the island's reputation as a place you could take your family, your kiddos and wives and pretty daughters. His desk in the basement was covered with papers and files. At one point, he even hired a private investigator to dig into Clive Richardson and Edwin Hastie, though I don't believe anything ever came of this.

My mother retreated into herself. Though she did not speak of it, it was clear to me that her thoughts never wavered from what had happened. I could see questions and theories spinning behind her distant gaze. Sometimes I overheard her speaking to herself: "I know it. I know it." In books and movies, the bedrooms of dead children become temples — untouched, everything preserved just as they left it. But my mother lived in Alison's room. I would return from school to a silent house and know she was in there, curled up in Alison's sheets. One day I opened the bedroom door to find her sitting at Alison's desk, cupping something in her hands. It was a nest of Alison's hair, pulled from her yellow brush.

For my part, if before Alison's death I had been prone to some mildly compulsive behavior, in the aftermath this spiraled into a genuine affliction. I felt the prickling in my fingertips, the need to write in the air, constantly. Alison. Alison. Alison. I also developed a second, intertwined compulsion of thinking up scenarios in which those I loved might die. It was a ritual of protection: If I imagined a specific death, it seemed nearly impossible that it would actually happen in exactly that way, so the more scenarios I imagined, the safer the people I loved became. After my mother tucked me in at night I lay awake for hours, tracing Alison's name while conjuring visions of my parents lying in parallel hospital beds succumbing to a rare infection, of our dog Fluffernutter crushed by a falling tree limb, and crying because I was exhausted and desperate for sleep and my powerlessness in the face of these rituals terrified me. I wanted to wake my parents but knew I mustn't add to their worries. I faced the long night hours alone, until the sky began to lighten and, my watch completed, my mind finally released me to sleep.

Depending on where you lived then, maybe you remember how brutal the winters were in the mid-nineties, how the Eastern Seaboard bore nor'easter after nor'easter from December straight through April. During those winters, a good number of Americans found themselves stuck inside for months on end, huddled around televisions and desperate to be entertained. If you were one of them, you will remember how Alison was all over the news the winter she was killed, as Nancy and Tonya and JonBenét were during other winters around that time. It seemed the national appetite craved — demanded, even — a dramatic story about an American beauty. (Nancy in all those crystals, glittering across the Lillehammer ice. JonBenét the way I loved her best, *sans makeup,* as my mother would say, her natural brown hair waving out of a cowboy hat, a red bandana around her slender neck.) News vans loitered on our suburban cul-de-sac for weeks. I was forbidden from playing in the front yard. But one day I disobeyed this rule. It had snowed the night before. While my parents were still asleep, I put on my snow pants and my puffy purple jacket and slipped out the front door. I clomped through the knee-deep snow, lay down on my back, and fanned my arms and legs back and forth. I looked up at the sky. It was white, but the color didn't seem to reside anywhere. It was like the turquoise in the water at Indigo Bay, colors that were everywhere and nowhere. Had my sister slid into the infinity between color and object? Was she out there, in some incomprehensible elsewhere, watching me? Inside my mittens, my hands worked furiously. Alison. Alison. Alison.

A few minutes later my father opened the door and shooed me inside. That night, my mother was draining pasta for dinner with the small white television in the kitchen tuned to the local station, when there I was, swishing my arms and legs through the snow. "The search for answers in the death of local teen Alison Thomas continues," a woman in a magenta blazer said. "Meanwhile, on this snowy day, her sister could be seen making angels."

■ ■ ■ ■

In April, the chief of police on Saint X called our house. We had just sat down to dinner. My father answered the call on the phone that hung on the wall beside the stove, and I watched as he listened, twisting and untwisting the cord. The chief of police had called to inform him in advance that he would be holding a press conference the next day, at which he would announce that all suspects in my sister's case had been cleared, and the department had concluded there was not sufficient evidence that Alison had died as the result of a violent crime to continue the investigation.

My father flew into a rage. I don't remember what he said, but I do remember his shouting, and how I looked down at the drumstick and green beans on my plate like maybe if only I stared hard enough it would all go away — this moment and all the others since I had awoken to find my sister gone. When my father's shouts became choked with sobs I thought I would be sick. I began to trace Alison's name furiously on the kitchen table.

"Stop that, Clairey," my mother said.

I wanted so badly to stop for her, but I

couldn't. My eyes filled with tears. She put her hand over mine, but I shook it off. I cried harder, pressed my fingertip against the tabletop so hard it hurt.

"Clairey, please," she begged.

My body began to tremble.

Then my mother knelt next to my chair and looked straight at me. For the first time in months her eyes seemed animated not by some scene playing out in her mind, but by the present we shared. Though I was much too old to be carried, she lifted my tensed body out of the chair. I let myself go slack in her arms, and she carried me upstairs and tucked me into bed. She stayed there with me, stroking my hair, until I was asleep.

A few weeks later, my parents surprised me with the news that my Aunt Caroline would be taking me to Paris. A present for my eighth birthday, they said. Aunt Caroline was my mother's older sister. She had never married and had no children. She lived in the East Village and was the only adult I knew who smoked. For a week she and I shared a little *chambre* in the Marais. Every morning we had bread with butter and raspberry jam and espresso at a café in the Place des Vosges. ("See how butter *tastes* like butter here," Aunt Caroline said.) I forced the espresso down, trying to convince myself I liked its sophisticated intensity. We did not go to the Eiffel Tower or Versailles, nor to any of the kid-friendly attractions my parents would have sought out: wax museums, puppet shows. We did what Aunt Caroline called "being *flâneuses.*" We wandered. If we passed a *fromagerie* with logs of goat cheese pressed with lavender in the window, we bought some. We ate long leisurely dinners during which Aunt Caroline drained carafes of plum-dark wine. We lazed in parks all afternoon.

Alison had never been to Paris. I had nibbled a *brioche aux pralines* in the Luxembourg Gardens and she never would. I would have this on her forever. I would have every day on her for the rest of my life. In Paris with Aunt Caroline, I finally began to understand that my sister was not gone the way she'd been gone when she was off at college — vanished from my days but still out there, living her life. She was gone not just from me and my parents and Drew McNamara, but also and above all from herself. My parents' grief might lessen, I might heal, Drew might move on, but Alison's loss — of a future, a life — would never change.

On the plane back over the Atlantic, Aunt

Caroline slept with her mouth snapped open like a crocodile's for seven straight hours. I remained awake. I was anxious about returning home. I was wary of my father and even more so of my mother — how when I got home she would squeeze me in her arms so tightly I would be able to feel her thinly veiled terror that I, too, might vanish.

But when my parents met us at the airport, my mother's smile was light and clean. She'd gotten a haircut. My whole life her hair had come down past her shoulders; now it barely skimmed her chin. She was wearing a blue chambray dress and sandals.

"Did you have the very best time?" she asked.

Things were different after that. My father went back to work. If he continued to be in contact with the police on Saint X, he kept it to himself. When I got home from school in the afternoons, my mother was no longer in Alison's room; she was waiting for me in the kitchen with a glass of milk and a plate of Oreos. Always a voracious reader, she began to check out books from the library again. My father rejoined his Sunday squash game. At night from my bedroom I sometimes caught the faint sound of a laugh track — they were watching *Murphy Brown* in bed.

Every so often in the years that followed, my parents received a briefing from the police. A former maid at Indigo Bay had remembered something that might turn out to be consequential. A man from Chicago had called with a tip that seemed bogus, but which the police would of course pursue with diligence and expediency. My parents did not fixate on these developments, and in the end none of them ever amounted to anything.

When someone asked my mother how many children she had, her response was always the same. "We had two daughters but our eldest was killed."

This, in our house, was the final word on Alison. She *was killed.* Passive voice. As if Alison were the recipient of a fate inflicted by nobody.

That summer, my parents sold our house and we moved across the country to Pasadena. I was angry at my parents about our move. I thought they wanted to forget Alison. I see now that we didn't have much of a choice. The victims of tragedies almost always depart, sooner or later. Everybody in our small suburb knew what had happened to us. Cody Lundgren's mother had made me sad and uncomfortable when I saw her at the grocery store, and now we did this to other people wherever we went. To stay would have been, frankly, *inconsiderate.* (The Lundgrens had decamped for Philadelphia not long after Cody's death.)

In New York, we had lived in a large white center-hall Colonial. There had been five bedrooms, a swimming pool out back; Alison and I each had our own bathroom. Everyone I knew lived this way, and I was young enough not to understand that most people didn't. But we lived differently in Pasadena. We moved into a small sage-colored bungalow in the hills. My mother hung wind chimes along the eaves. In New York we'd had a sprawling acre of lawn; here there was a tiny jewel-box garden. Our home in Pasadena was not inexpensive by any means, and we still lived in the sort of neighborhood that would be described as "prestigious" in a real estate listing. But the little bungalow was decidedly, *intentionally,* modest. If I found myself in the car with my mother, driving past some newfangled McMansion or an ersatz Spanish revival estate in Oak Knoll, she would scoff and say, "So tacky," and I understood she meant much more — that the people who lived there were drawing the universe's eye, leaving their good fortune out in the open, when they ought to be secreting it away.

The night before the first day of third grade, I told my parents that at my new school I wanted to go by my middle name. I could feel them exchanging meaningful looks over my head.

"Try it out," my father said. "You can always go back to Claire if you change your mind."

I never did. From that day on, I was Emily.

Everything changed for me in Pasadena. I'd always been a reticent, prickly child, more comfortable in the company of my family than with my peers. I had struggled to make friends and accustomed myself to spending time alone. But in Pasadena I was new and therefore presumed interesting. Soon I was playing school and orphans in the purple enclaves of other girls' bedrooms. To my surprise, I found myself sharing with these girls the intimacy of friendship. We confessed our secrets; stuck out our tongues and touched the tips together, giggling at the contact of wriggling, tasteless muscle; carved sacred spaces in the putty of our suburban world — forts and clubhouses, hideaways in the rhododendrons. The compulsions that had plagued me for so long faded away, evaporating in the dry air of my new life. For a very long time, until the winter of my twenty-fifth year, which would find me in New York City, where events would transpire that would change everything for me again, and irrevocably, I didn't think of them at all.

At some point, my father must have taken the rolls of film from our vacation to be developed, because a few months after our move to Pasadena I found the photographs in his home office, in the back of his desk drawer. Every so often I would sneak into his office and take the photos out. My father had them printed in triplicate. I did not skip through the copies. I looked at each one with the same disbelief. How could it have been real? In one picture, Alison and I were building our sandcastle. In another, the two of us smiled for my father as the woman under the faded blue umbrella braided my hair. There was a series of pictures of Alison posing beside a palm tree. On the back of one of these pictures, in my father's tidy all-caps penmanship: *MY ALI.* There were pictures of Alison and my mother walking on the beach, and of me examining a seashell with a look of wonder . . . swims and games and boat rides and half a dozen incomparably gorgeous sunsets. At first, I went to the photographs when I missed my sister. As time passed, I went to them when I had not missed her in a while and wanted to.

The eleven-year gap between Alison and me is notable, and requires some explanation. I was not an accident, nor had my parents been trying for years to conceive again. I know because when I was in fifth grade I asked my mother why my sister and I had been so far apart in age, unlike my friends and their siblings. She told me that at first she and my father thought they only wanted one child. But then they realized how much they loved being parents and decided to have me. Those were her exact words: "We decided to have you." As if they had known, when they chose to have another child, that the child would be me.

When she told me this I felt sick to my stomach. I remembered something my father had said to the chief of police, when he was asked if my sister had appeared troubled in the days leading up to her death: "Alison is the very definition of a kid you don't have to worry about." His words had stayed with me, surfacing from time to time like a nagging ache. Because to say such a thing, you had to know what it was like to have a kid you *did* have to worry about. In my mother's words, I sensed her betraying insistence that it was exactly me they'd wanted. I don't mean they didn't love me; they did, everyone loves their children. But they loved me differently than they loved Alison. I don't think my parents understood their own desires when they decided to have another child. They thought they wanted to raise another kid. Really, they wanted to raise Alison again.

As the years passed, my mother and father continued to fulfill their parental duties. They signed me up for AYSO and pottery and displayed my endless output of pinch pots on the living room shelves. We went on trips to Yellowstone, London, Washington, D.C. They helped me with long division and took away my television privileges when I sassed. In summary, they behaved. Always fair, always reasonable. Wonderful parents, in a way. We lived on the surface, skated figure eights over a frozen sea.

When I was ten, a women's television network of the feuding pageant queens and psychopathic stepmothers variety premiered *Dying for Fun,* an eight-part true crime series about young women whose hedonistic pursuits — wild parties, gap years, vacations — had gone horribly awry. Each episode was a dramatic reenactment of one woman's story. At the time, I knew only that something was being made about my sister and that my parents were upset about it, though their lawyer had told them there was nothing they could do.

The night *Dying for Fun: Alison Thomas* premiered, my parents took me to a Dodgers game. We ate hot dogs slathered in ketchup and mustard. We stood and cheered when Mike Piazza hit a home run. We sang "Take Me Out to the Ball Game" too loudly, laughed for too long, and generally tried not to think about the fact that in millions of homes across America, people were sitting on couches and tossing cheese puffs into their mouths as they watched a person who was not my sister die some version of my sister's death.

It's hard for me to remember exactly what I was told about the details of Alison's death when it happened, and what facts I acquired later on. I'm fairly certain I didn't know it was the actor who'd found my sister, or who he was to begin with. But at some point I must have learned this, because there were two periods during my adolescence when I became oddly fixated on the actor. The first such period was in fifth grade. I often had sleepovers on the weekends then, which typically involved renting a movie. If the sleepover was happening at my house and it was my parents taking us to Blockbuster, I would do everything as usual, and we would come home with *Free Willy* or *Homeward Bound* or something like that. But if I was sleeping out and it was someone else's parents taking us, I'd try to make it happen that we would rent one of the actor's movies. The actor was not in children's movies, so this involved convincing my friends that a film about a bank heist or prohibition-era Chicago was something we would like. "This is supposed to be hilarious," I'd say, or, "I heard this is Sean Sawyer's favorite movie," Sean Sawyer being the boy we were all in love with. "Are you sure?" the mom or dad would ask when we handed them our selection, and if I'd done a good job, my friend would nod just as enthusiastically as me. Because the movies were actually not at all the kind of thing that interested us, often my friends would doze off after not too long, and then it would just be me, on a beanbag cushion in their playroom in the dark, watching the actor and looking for something I couldn't explain.

The second period came a few years later, when I was thirteen or fourteen and my friends and I were obsessed with *YM* and *Bop* and at night I dreamed steamy soft-core dreams about the shy, sensitive members of various boy bands. For a while during this time, I played out these extended scenarios in my mind where the actor reached out to my family seeking resolution, which he found in talking with me. Our unlikely friendship led to invitations to be his guest at awards shows, where I wore gowns and was photographed on the red carpet, stoic beauty radiating from me like an aura, and I won the attention and sympathy of all the stars I adored. I was ashamed of these fantasies, but I was helpless to stop them, unable to resist the maudlin potential of my own story. I thought I was awful, but now I think I was no more awful than any teenage girl — I simply had more potent material to spin.

I lost my virginity in tenth grade. My boyfriend was a bassist in a band called Skar Tissue and a budding cartoonist who drew pictures of me with big anime eyes and hair made of flowers. His own hair was black streaked with violet. I helped him dye it every other week in his bathroom. My hands were perpetually stained purple, as if I'd gorged myself on berries. For as long as we were together, I was a skater girl, which didn't mean I skated, but rather that I stood around with a few other girls while the boys skated. I wore thick black eyeliner and dog cuffs on my wrists and slouched proprietarily against the gym wall when Skar Tissue played at school dances. At homecoming, they debuted a song called "Emily." I was a girl whose boyfriend wrote songs for her and played them in front of the whole school. I marveled at this, held it proudly in hand.

Four months after we started dating, on a night when my parents were at a dinner party in Toluca Lake, I told him I was ready. He treated me like I was made of glass, and I liked this. He treated sex with the seriousness of death, and I liked that, too. Afterward, it occurred to me that if Alison were alive, I would have told her every detail. Then something else occurred to me: If Alison were alive, it would not have happened at all. There was another life I might have been living, a life in which I was not Emily of Pasadena, but Claire. This other life ran alongside mine like the scenery falling away at the side of a speeding train. While Emily had sex in Southern California, Claire wrote up the mealworm lab in New York. Emily was pink-skinned from the California sun, her white-blond hair cut in a stylish crop. Claire was pale as flour, her haircut the same since she was five. What was I supposed to do with the fact that I was thrilled, I was so very relieved, to be Emily and not Claire?

I knew the exact day I outlived Alison. Eighteen years, three months, twelve days. I had calculated the date when I was fifteen, working it out in the back of my notebook as Magistra Kouchner chirped Latin conjugations. *Io credo, tu credi, lui crede.* For years, I dreaded the day. When it finally arrived, I marked it in secret. I considered telling my friends, who were at that time packing up one by one and saying tearful farewells as we scattered to the well-regarded colleges we would attend. (I would be the last to leave, bound for a highly ranked liberal arts college in the Midwest.) In the end I told no one. I was suspicious of my own impulse to calculate and mark the date. It seemed a theatrical and self-absorbed thing to do. Maybe part of what it means to be eighteen is to feel perpetually caught between the intensity of one's desires and the dawning self that judges them.

On the morning of the day I outlived Alison, I awoke to find my world suffused by a peculiar falsity. The sunlight streaming through my bedroom window seemed *incorrect* somehow, a shade too lemony. When I walked into the kitchen, where my mother was eating a bowl of cereal, and she said good morning, her voice, too, seemed to have shifted, like a piano gone almost imperceptibly out of tune. All day I couldn't shake the feeling that I had been transferred in my sleep to a vast simulacrum. I drifted from room to room, picking up and setting down books, beginning and abandoning the tidying of my bedroom, sitting in the garden, and then, shaken by a sense that I'd remained there too long, moving to the living room. Even my own face seemed to me a not-quite-right facsimile — I studied myself in the mirror and saw Alison's features skewed just enough to look distorted and unharmonious, my pale skin and hair like some ghostly afterimage. I'd been awaiting this day for years, but I don't think I ever really expected it to arrive. Now that the critical juncture was behind me, the tension went out of everything. My world hung slack as a sail on a windless day.

When I arrived at college, for the first time since I moved to Pasadena as a girl, I found myself regularly around people who didn't know me or my story. The usual challenges and possibilities of freshman year — making new friends, conveying one's identity to others (with some fresh tweaks and adjustments from one's high school iteration) — were complicated for me by the knowledge that at some point I would have to tell these people who I was, which is to say, who my sister was. I can't express how much I disliked doing this. Though I'd come out of my shell in Pasadena, I was still relatively shy, and there was simply no way to tell people that I was Alison Thomas's little sister without drawing attention to myself.

The worst part was seeing people's surprised reactions. I don't mean the inevitable surprise of realizing that someone you know is connected to such an infamous incident. I mean the surprise, plainly visible on their faces, that this had happened to *me,* that this story was *my* story. How confused they seemed, how disappointed: something had happened to me, something huge, and yet, somehow, I had managed not to be made interesting by it.

I dated a few boys in college. There was Nick, a pre-med soccer player who loved nothing so much as the sight of me topless in his uniform shorts. Avi was a stoner from Toronto. Scattered between these longer relationships were brief interludes with Dave and Jordan and Zeb (whose first name was really Richard), all of them so different from one another it was like trying on funny hats in a store. With each of them I changed, shape-shifting until I fit into their world. I prided myself on my chameleonic transformations, and on not having a "type," which I thought indicated that I was open to the world, and that my essential self was so solid it could inhabit any number of forms.

They had different approaches to getting me to talk about her. But one way or another, they all tried.

"I just want you to know you can be completely open with me. Like, if there's ever anything you want to talk about."

"My uncle died when I was seven. He was basically my second dad. It really fucked up my world, you know?"

"You don't have to talk about it if you don't want to."

I could never shake the humiliating sense that, whether they realized it or not, these boys were in love with some idea of me as a tragic, wounded girl, that when they looked at me they saw a sort of double exposure — me and the sister I had lost, a second self whose presence they could sense whenever they were with me, and that it was she, not me, they were really after, that as they kissed and licked and squeezed me they were trying to draw themselves closer to her, to touch the infinite, exquisite void of a beautiful, lost girl.

(But when I refused to open up to these boys about Alison, was it really because I couldn't bring myself to, because it hurt too much, or did I withhold to gain their admiration at my stoicism? Did I, actually, enjoy being their tragic, wounded girlfriend? Deep down, did I revel in the way Alison's death made me more than myself to these boys? To what extent was my pain a thing I cultivated, a thing I *used*? Is it possible that these relationships, these boys, were ultimately little more to me than a platform for displaying my suffering and, in doing so, for shoring up my claim to this tragedy, to the death of a sister I was barely old enough to know?)

■ ■ ■ ■

Despite these difficulties, I would describe my "college experience" as pretty normal, which is to say that everything I did, whether a winter day spent dug in at the library or a night of dancing capped off by three A.M. pizza, felt equally, salubriously formative. I majored in English and minored in environmental studies. I made plenty of friends. The one worth mentioning, because of how she figures into my time in New York, is Jackie. Jackie was a friend I acquired at the beginning of college more due to proximity than anything — she lived across the hall. Despite our having little in common, our friendship turned out to have staying power. Jackie was an actor ("*not* musicals"). She saw nothing pretentious about referring to herself as a "thespian," and though I found this ridiculous, I was also impressed by her sheer gumption. Our relationship consisted mostly of her baring her soul and me listening and proffering advice.

Sometimes I wondered whether, when she wasn't with me, Jackie brought up her connection to the Alison Thomas murder to people as a kind of currency. I could imagine her, back home in Bethesda for Christmas break, sitting around in someone's basement with her girlfriends, drinking Yellow Tail:

"You know my good friend Emily I've told you about? Her older sister was Alison Thomas. Remember that story from when we were, like, seven?" (I would be referred to as a "good" friend not because Jackie and I were, in fact, especially close, but to emphasize Jackie's own proximity to Alison.)

"Whoa, seriously?"

Jackie would nod solemnly as if, while her friends might simply consider this to be some novel information, to her it was personal, heavy.

Oh, I didn't *wonder* if this happened. Surely it did. There was no doubt in my mind that Jackie trotted out my story for her own benefit. I didn't even feel mad about it, really, because it was so obvious she couldn't help herself, and how could you be mad at someone for being the person they were? At least at the time I thought that was why I didn't feel mad. Thinking about it now, though, the reason seems different. I never let myself get mad about anything back then.

After college, I found a job as an assistant

to an editor at a publishing house in Manhattan. When I told my parents I would be moving to New York, they were supportive in the polite, aloof way I had come to expect. With Jackie and two Craigslist strangers, also recent college grads, I found an apartment in Prospect Heights. The kitchen was the size of a closet and my bedroom had no closet at all. The apartment was on the ground floor, and out back a cracked concrete patio was littered with things tenants on higher floors tossed out their windows — beer cans, cigarette butts, losing scratch tickets. We figured with some twinkle lights strung up it would be heaven.

Before I moved in and began work, I flew west to spend one last summer with my parents. Two months at home with mom and dad while my friends worked fun, sunburned jobs in resort towns in New England or retraced Che Guevara's motorcycle journey as far as Valparaíso. My parents had not asked me to do this, nor did I want to do it. It wasn't just that without Alison I felt I had to fulfill the role of two children. I did things that, were Alison alive, neither one of us would have done. I pitied my parents in a way I did not pity myself. It is easy to discern the contours of other people's pain, much harder to recognize one's own.

My parents were in their mid-fifties. My father's hair had thinned and grayed. My mother had recently had her first knee replacement. Over and over they told me how happy they were that I was there, how wonderful it was to spend "quality time" together. My mother cooked my favorite foods. My father bought tickets for the things we used to do when I was a kid — Dodgers games, sci-fi movies. Their insistence gave them away. I don't mean they weren't happy I was there. I could see it in their eyes — a love so strong it hurt. That's what I mean. They would be relieved when I left. The house would turn quiet again, and they would feel better.

One day when I came back from the gym, I entered the house quietly, and before I let them know I was back, I watched them. Through the kitchen window, I could see my father out in the yard, tending his jewel box garden. My mother sat in the sunny window seat in the living room, a chenille blanket over her feet, reading. I was seeing them without me: two people living out their separate lonelinesses side by side.

A few days before I flew to New York, I went into my father's home office. There, in his desk drawer, I found the photographs of our vacation at Indigo Bay. They were faded and splotched with fingerprints, and I wondered if looking at them had turned into a kind of compulsion for my father. Perhaps he had looked at the photographs so many times he no longer really saw Alison, had drained the power out of the images years ago. Maybe, subconsciously, that had been the point of the triplicate images to begin with: to stare at my sister until she lost coherence, like reading a word over and over until it starts to crack up. I removed one copy of each picture and brought them with me to Brooklyn. I put them in a shoe box under my bed along with a few other mementos — graduation tassel, prom corsage. The box gathered dust while, above it, I watched Netflix on my laptop while eating salt-and-vinegar chips; cuddled with Jackie after her boyfriend dumped her; had sex, often inebriated, with friends of friends. I rarely took out the photographs. It was enough just to know they were there.

Looking back, what strikes me is how ordinarily my life developed for years after Alison's death. I had friends and boyfriends. I excelled academically. Experimented in typical quantities with the kinds of drugs a fundamentally risk-averse girl could feel more or less comfortable with: I smoked pot on weekends, nibbled once on shrooms in Prospect Park, imbibed a few sips of absinthe at a party. I fretted about my weight, hamster-wheeled on an elliptical machine after work, caved and ate two egg rolls for dinner. At work, I decorated my cubicle with a framed photograph of myself on the rim of the Grand Canyon and a mediocre sketch I'd done of a cathedral during a semester abroad in Grenoble. My job paid a pittance and was glamour-adjacent, and therefore fit perfectly with a certain vision of what a girl's early years in New York ought to look like: fetching coffee for a MacArthur genius; ferrying a portfolio of illustrations through the sleet to the West Village brownstone of a writer I adored; referring to best-selling authors in the informal parlance of the office, according to which Astrid Teague was just "Astrid," and Ian Mann's forthcoming book was simply "the new Mann." On first dates, there was a nifty trick I liked to perform, where I would pull the boy into a bookstore, pick up a novel off the display table, flip to the back, and show him, in the acknowledgments, my name. Every Sunday afternoon I posted up at a café, pen in hand and the pages of a manuscript stacked before me, and when I caught the glances of people at nearby tables I quickly looked back down in a way that conveyed that I was busy making an important contribution to the creative economy.

As it happened, the editor I worked for mostly acquired mysteries. Ian Mann published a book a year about a psychologically damaged private investigator. Astrid Teague wrote atmospheric whodunits set in Cornwall, where she'd grown up (and where she was now rehabbing a dilapidated manor house, which had recently been captured in all its shabby-chic glory in a *Martha Stewart Living* profile, "Astrid Teague Comes Home"). Many of the books I worked on turned on the mystery of a girl's death. A beautiful young body turns up in small-town Maine or in an eightieth-floor hotel room in Shanghai. Sometimes the girls didn't turn up at all — they vanished without a trace, evaporated into their surroundings. In my favorite of Astrid's novels, *The Girl in the Picture,* a woman's body was discovered by a boy and his English setter in a cave on the Cornish coast. The woman had no wallet on her, no identification of any kind. Nobody came forward to claim her, nor did she match any missing person reports. But she did have a camera, and the photographs she had taken before her death became the clues a local detective used to uncover the identity of a hauntingly beautiful woman nobody seemed to miss.

It was pure coincidence, me working on these books. I had applied for over a dozen jobs, after all. I hadn't sought this genre out intentionally, any more than the girl in the next cubicle who worked on popular science, or the girl down the hall whose domain was military history and the occasional sports memoir. My boss didn't know my personal history, and I was proud of the professionalism I brought to this work. For instance, one of my responsibilities was to write discussion questions about these novels for book clubs.

What do you think would have happened if Leah had survived the fire? Would she and Colin have reconciled? Why or why not?

While Rose Van Kleef believes that Emmaline might still be alive, Orrin knows that she is dead. Which do you think is the more difficult circumstance, knowing that a loved one is dead, or not knowing?

How did you react to the comic moments

in this otherwise dark novel?

I would write these questions, and my boss would tell me I had done a good job, and her praise would make me happy. If for fleeting moments the whole arrangement began to rankle, I would remind myself that people had every right to enjoy these stories, just as I enjoyed books about all kinds of terrible things that had happened to other people but not to me. What else, in the end, were stories *for*? This sentiment instantly made me feel better — not, it seems to me now, because I believed it, exactly, but because it seemed a very adult stance to take.

In any event, my living situations, too, affirmed a certain vision of what twenty-something urban life ought to be. For two years I stayed in the shitty Prospect Heights apartment. (On cool summer evenings, when the sky was the brushed-velvet way it gets after a nine P.M. sunset, the twinkle lights really did grant a celestial loveliness to that cracked patio.) From there, I moved to a brownstone in Bed-Stuy where a dozen creative types had set up a communal living system — a rotation of cooking and cleaning duties, weekly "family meetings." When the novelty of this arrangement gave way to weariness at its perpetual high drama, I left for an illegal sublet in the basement of a formerly grand, now-dilapidated old mansion on the far eastern edge of what might, with some fudging, be considered Ditmas Park, just a few blocks from the heart of Caribbean Flatbush. My studio had two half windows at the top of one wall, with a ground-level view of the sidewalk, so that from my desk I could watch the disembodied feet of passersby: black stiletto boots, duct-tape-patched Adidas sneakers, green galoshes. The room was lit by the harsh yellow light of two bare bulbs hung from the ceiling.

I didn't have to live like this. A tidy allowance from my parents flowed directly into my checking account every month. I suppose I chose this arrangement because I was a privileged kid eager to prove to myself that I didn't need the comforts I'd never been without (and eager, too, I might add, to do this before I got too old to enjoy it). It was the sort of thing, in other words, that you do not because you want to do it, but because you want to *have done* it, to have a story you'll share, you imagine, years later at a cocktail party or on the sideline at a soccer game (your child pure magic clomping through the grass in tiny cleats).

I admit I was rather impressed with myself for living in a building where I was one of the only white tenants. What a sharp little pride I felt, riding the 2 home from work and watching the other white passengers empty out, and what a sweet triumph it was on those nights when I outlasted them all. When, six months after I moved in, construction began on a luxury condo three blocks from my studio, I felt genuinely aggrieved. I suppose I must also have thought myself pretty high-minded to live where I did, among the people I lived among, despite what had happened to my sister. This must have been part of why I chose to live there, on the fringe of the largest Caribbean neighborhood in the city, right? To get to think these things about myself.

I took it as my working assumption that for my neighbors my presence was not entirely welcome, and so I smiled very warmly at everyone but spoke to no one, what I thought of as "not bothering people." All in all, I thought I was doing a pretty good job of charting a course through my life in New York that was as palatable as possible. I had not chosen to live in the lily-white postgrad brovana of Murray Hill. I was a gentrifier but, I imagined, an unobtrusive one. I see now that it was not so simple, that in keeping myself apart from my neighbors I was trying to collect a moral credit for living there without really *living* there, and that this was bound up with a set of more general misapprehensions: that unobtrusiveness was some sort of high virtue; that it was even possible at all; that I could inhabit this building, borough, world, life, without casting out ripples. But I was twenty-five — not so young I couldn't have known better, but young enough that I didn't.

Because of this stance, I came to know my neighbors only by their quirks. A stooped woman who must have been at least eighty fetched her mail each evening in a nightgown and a pair of bright white Reeboks. An old man who spoke Spanish wore a NASCAR cap and was never without his terrier, Jefe, a yappy, trembling creature with cloudy cataracted eyes. I assumed my neighbors identified me in a similar way. I was the white girl who came home from work every night toting a premade chopped salad. The only other white tenant was a man with a scruffy beard and an affinity for scarves who lived on the first floor and played guitar from two to three-thirty A.M. nightly, a habit which would have been merely aggravating someplace else, but which I found genuinely distressing here, convinced that it reflected poorly not only on him but also on me, on *us*.

During those first few years in New York I was, in short, living in that period of playacting, of whimsical elective poverty — improvisational dinner parties with mismatched plates, Saturdays scavenging secondhand shops for the perfect two-dollar blouse — that is so common among the children of affluence. The word I would use to describe myself then would not be *happy* — not that I wasn't; I was, or at least, I thought I was — but *unencumbered.* I believed I was enjoying my present life while anticipating, with a minimum of anxiety, the arrival of the next life stage, and the one after that. My illegal underground sublet in "Ditmas Park" would become a one-bedroom rental in Boerum Hill would become purchasing a brownstone in Park Slope, or a condo on the Upper West Side. Pithy remarks at editorial meetings would become acquiring my own books would become launching a best seller. That's what really strikes me, I guess, about that time. It's not that my life was ordinary, but that I fell for it so completely, that I failed so utterly to detect within myself the darker currents that must have been there all along.

■ ■ ■ ■

Sometimes I thought I saw Alison. She picked up a box of cereal in the Flatbush Co-op and scanned the nutrition information. She jogged past me in Prospect Park, a beagle on a red leash tugging her forward. She slipped into a taxi in the rain. The Alisons darted. They slipped around corners. They were there and not there. They were always teenagers.

One day, I ducked out of the office at eleven A.M. for my annual dermatology checkup. It was early October, one of those blue-skied, ludicrously crisp days when the bustling midtown sidewalks seem to hum. At the dermatologist's I sat for over an hour in the waiting room, occupying myself with whatever inexplicable magazines the office subscribed to. In the examining room, I changed into a paper gown. "Sorry for the wait. I was held up by a gangrenous toe," Dr. Schwartz said when he finally came into the room. He made small talk as he inspected my skin with a small magnifying glass. *Did you have a good summer? How are things at work?* He had a strategy of pretending he remembered who you were. "You wear sunscreen," he said in that doctorly way — not a question, but an entreaty for me to reply in the affirmative, whatever the truth, so that we might move this thing along.

"See you in a year," he told me when he'd completed his examination. I crunched out of the paper gown and changed back into my work clothes. I had been away from the office for nearly two hours, much longer than I'd intended, and I was in a hurry to get back. I walked quickly to Lexington, weaving around a girl with her nose in her phone, a towheaded family pointing up at the Chrysler Building. At Fifty-fourth Street, I held out my arm just as a taxi turned the corner into view — a small, delicious victory.

I spent the short ride to the office checking work e-mail on my phone — a nervous missive from Kris in publicity about an author's botched radio interview, a note from the marketing director inviting the assistants to help ourselves to the tray of leftover wraps in the kitchen. When the taxi pulled up to the curb in front of my office building a few minutes later, I entered a tip on the touch screen and swiped my credit card.

"Thank you," the driver said softly from

the other side of the Plexiglas partition.

My eyes landed on the taxi license affixed to the glass: a photograph, poor in quality, of a dark-skinned man against a white background. Beneath the photo, the driver's name. Clive Richardson.

Could it be? I wanted to do something, say something, but my mind was blank. The taxi idled at the curb. My door was already open, propped ajar by my foot.

What I did next was more instinct than intention. As I climbed out of the taxi, I found myself slipping my phone beneath the driver's seat and out of view. Then I slammed the door behind me. Within seconds, the taxi rejoined the yellow sea speeding uptown.

We know what to do with death when it's close to us. Your mom dies, or an old friend, and you grieve. Maybe you're not good at it, maybe the death fucks you up, but it's supposed to be hard, it's supposed to fuck you up. We know what to do with death when it's far-removed from us, too. A sports star or a celebrity chef dies and you read the obit. You start off your lunch meeting by saying, "Did you hear about . . . ?" You read the hot-take remembrances on social media for a day or two. You move on. But we don't know what to do with the deaths of people we knew just a little.

I didn't even know Alison Thomas's name *was* Alison Thomas until she went missing. Before then, can I say this? She was the girl my wife kept catching me checking out all week. She was the reason I wanted to dish out a killer serve in the volleyball game, to impress her and to make up for the embarrassment of the stupid fucking pink swim trunks I was wearing with the dolphins on them. She was the reason my wife said this supremely condescending "Almost, honey!" when the ball landed in the net instead. In the mornings, while my wife chipped away at herself in the fitness center, I took these long, ridiculously hot showers and undressed that blithe teenage body in my mind.

I am not some pervert. We see nice bodies, young bodies, we enjoy them. We all do this, okay? It is *allowed.* But what the hell do you do when the girl you've been jacking off to every morning for a week turns up dead?

The night my wife told me she was filing for divorce, she said, "You know when I knew you were a block of ice right down to your soul? When that girl was killed and you never said a word about it. Every time I tried to get you to talk about it, every time I brought her up, because I was *reeling,* I was just *devastated,* you shut me down."

I wonder sometimes if we'd still be married if Alison Thomas hadn't been murdered.

Don't get me wrong, our love was hardening into a battle of wills long before then. But that trip drove a wedge between us that never went away. I couldn't give my wife the satisfaction of knowing the number that girl's death did on me. I couldn't stand to hear her crying her self-serving dramatic tears over a girl who, let's be real, she'd viewed as nothing but competition. I would listen to my wife crying, and know that she was waiting for me to wrap my arms around her from behind and deliver some sort of Emotionally Appropriate Response, and when I tried to recall what I'd loved about her and why, in our early years together, I'd felt like the luckiest fucker on earth, I couldn't come up with anything at all.

Islands

People are always leaving things behind. Umbrellas. Wallets. Coats. Shopping bags filled with souvenirs: I LOVE NEW YORK T-shirts, snow globes in which replicas of the Statue of Liberty or the Freedom Tower stand suspended in perpetual winter. Sometimes the objects are more uncommon, hinting at the lives of the strangers who have forgotten them. A bouquet of sunflowers, a note attached with twine: *Evelyn, forgive me.* A Senegalese driver at the garage once had a customer jump out at a red light, abandoning a tank that held a lime-green snake. Years ago, when he was new to this job and the job itself was so much more dangerous than it is now, he found a switchblade wedged between the seats at the end of his shift. He still has it, in the plastic bureau where he keeps his belongings, along with a jumble of other objects acquired over the years. A child's pink plastic watch. A ring with a translucent white gemstone, which flickers with rainbow flecks when held up to the light. A camera with a finished roll of film inside.

You were supposed to turn these things in at the garage, but it was no secret that Larry and his numbskull son with the gold chains around his pimply neck just kept the items for themselves or sold them. What he's doing is stealing, too, he supposes, but it doesn't feel wrong. Just the opposite — he is rescuing these things from the careless people who have forgotten them. Though on some nights, after a few beers or a blunt ashed into a Coke can, he wonders if this notion of the righteousness of his thefts is just a bullshit justification. Lately, it seems to him that he keeps these objects as compensation, pitifully insufficient, for his own lost things.

Today he returns home from his shift with an iPhone, the latest model, in a light-gray case, not something he can keep. Anytime now the phone will ring and he will speak to the person to whom it belongs. Maybe it will be the banker he picked up in midtown, who shouted into his phone the whole drive to La Guardia. Or perhaps it will be the Park Avenue mother in those tight black leggings with SOUL in big letters down the thigh, with the little boy in the blazer and the little girl in the blue jumper; he'd dropped the girl at Brearley, the boy at St. Bernard's, the mother in front of a cycling studio on Eighty-third. Or it will be a Russian tourist he drove to Chanel, or a sixteen-year-old girl he picked up in Dumbo who probably has no clue how much her phone costs, or a chef bound for Williamsburg, a tattoo of a pig's butchery cuts on his own fleshy hock. And when he confirms that, yes, they left their phone in the taxi and he has it, has held on to it for safekeeping, they will tell him how grateful they are, and that old feeling will come over him, a feeling that is not so much annoyance or anger as dispassion: You are invisible to them, you are the back of a head, and then suddenly you are indispensable. Suddenly they are, *like, super-appreciative.* Suddenly you are *a lifesaver, boss.* When he meets whoever it is this time to return the phone, and they try to hand him five bucks, or fifty (how variable, their sense of the value of what he has done for them), he will shake his head and politely refuse, as if it is pleasure enough just to be of service to them. His refusal will trigger a shift in the way they look at him, and he will know that they are thinking that he is a deeply good person. Probably they will tell this story: the taxi driver who returned their phone and wouldn't even accept a reward, though surely he could use the money. When they look at him in this approving way, he will simultaneously feel so good and so disgusted with himself for feeling good, for wanting that look, for chasing it, for giving one shit what they think, that he'll regret not taking the money in the first place. Because they're not wrong — he could use it.

It is early autumn, the days still mild, the trees just beginning to turn. But already he can detect faint signs of what is to come. Soon dead leaves will cover the sidewalks, revived for brief moments by swells of wind. At night the sky will turn blue-black as the open ocean, with that same tumbling depth and pitiless beauty. Then the cold will come, and with it the snow, and he will spend his shifts grinding through ice and slush, getting slammed by wakes of snow cast off by passing plows, maneuvering through the city in search of some sorry bastard in ruined wing tips trying to make it to Grand Central before the tracks ice over and the trains north shut down.

From the kitchen comes the click, click, click of a burner failing to ignite — his roommate Les reheating takeout on the stove. Through the thin wall that separates his bedroom from the next one, he hears Leon making his nightly call to his wife. Cecil has taken up residence in their small common area, the television blaring one of the reality shows the rest of them can't stand but Cecil loves, or at least seems to require, for he never exactly appears to be enjoying himself as he watches; rather, the shows seem to be a way of making time pass without feeling the granularity of each moment.

He has lived here for two years, replacing a man from Trinidad who returned home to live out his retirement in the house he'd built for his family. Les and Cecil were already living here when he moved in. Leon arrived four months ago, from Carriacou by way of Canarsie. Of these men he knows only what can be gleaned through proximity: who has a family to phone and who does not, who works the day shift and who the night. Their eating habits. The sounds of their sleep.

It is his ninth apartment in nearly two decades, all of them more or less alike — nondescript buildings in Flatbush, grease-encrusted kitchenettes, radiators that clang and keen and hiss. In his early years in New York, he had bothered to befriend his roommates. When he moved in here, Les and Cecil had tried to make conversation with him. Where was he from? How long had he been in New York? Did he have a wife? Children? To these questions he gave gruff answers or dodges, and they quickly learned to leave him alone. Now he comes and goes like a ghost. His roommates step aside when he wants to use the stove, the bathroom. They are a bit afraid of him, a big man with a look of warning in his eyes. Let them be.

At work it is the same. When he first started driving, there were many others at the garage from the West Indies, but the population has turned over several times since then, and now it's almost all Gujaratis, Sikhs from Punjab and Chandigarh, Bangladeshis, and West Africans. Their foreign tongues draw a curtain around them, leaving him to himself.

At night in bed he feels waves, mild and gentle, against his skin.

Sometimes he misses the water so much his bones ache with longing. Yet it is, ironically, all around him. In New York, he has never lived more than five miles from Manhattan Beach, hardly farther from the water than his grandmother's house had been. During his shifts, he shuttles passengers over the East River on the coral steelwork of the Williamsburg Bridge, under the Hudson through the Lincoln Tunnel, crosses the Harlem River on any number of quaint bridges. New York is a city of islands. When he was freshly arrived, he'd purchased an old guidebook from a dollar cart outside of a used bookshop. In the back of the book, along with sections on tipping and local slang ("flying rat," "bridge-and-tunnel," "yooz"), there was a map. Manhattan and Long Island and the glassy-sounding Staten Island — these he knew. But there were other islands he'd never heard of: Randall's, Roosevelt, Ellis, Wards, Hart, Governors. Over his years here he has learned many more: North and South Brother, South and East Nonations. Goose and Hog and Rat. Hunter and Shooters and Swinburne. Mill Rock and Heel Tap Rock. The Blauzes, the Chimney Sweep Islands, Canarsie Pol. Ruffle Bar and Rulers Bar Hassock and Hoffman. U Thant and Mau Mau and Isle of Meadows.

But though in New York he lives on an island surrounded by islands, sometimes — as he walks from the fleet garage to the N after his shift, or wrestles a bunch of grapes into a plastic bag at the Korean grocery on Beverley, or scrubs the toilet on a Tuesday — it will occur to him that he is, at this moment, on an island, and he will find this impossible to believe. He cannot feel the *islandness* of New York.

One day when he had been in the city two months, he took the subway out to Coney Island. He'd never seen a roller coaster before and he watched as load after load of people careened shrieking over the wooden tracks. He strolled the boardwalk, got fried clam strips and a hot dog with onions at Nathan's. It was September, and warm. After lunch, he walked down the boardwalk steps to the sand and slipped off his loafers. He walked to the water's edge, cuffed his pants, and waded in a few steps. But even then, with the water lapping against his ankles and the seabirds circling overhead and the vegetal scent of shallow water in his nostrils, he did not quite believe it was the ocean he was feeling and seeing and smelling.

Back home, whether you could see the sea or not, you sensed it. He'd sensed it in the schoolyard, tasted it in the blood from his split lip after a boxing match with his friends. When he bicycled down the road to work at dawn, the ocean was a magnet, pulling his feet through their slow revolutions until he crested the rise by the radio tower and there it was, the sea, tossed before him like a net. He'd felt it in the island's interior spaces, too, in his grandmother's kitchen with the white curtains and the refrigerator rusted by the salted wind, at Paulette's Place where he and his friends drained bottles of Cruzan and Bounty, and especially within the walls of the eggshell-blue prison on Commerce Street, where he sometimes put his cheek to the moist concrete floor and thought of wet sand warping silkily beneath the weight of his steps.

He found it impossible to separate his life there from the sensation of being surrounded by water, a sensation he hadn't realized he'd felt all day, every day, until he touched down in New York and felt its absence for the first time. It wasn't just that at home he could smell salt everywhere, or feel the humid breezes tossed off by the sea, or gauge his nearness to the water by the way the light shifted, while in New York, so remarkably, arrogantly immune to its environs, he could not. At home, the sea was consciousness itself. Always, you knew it was there, and that within it was everything else: answers and mysteries, that which could be seen and that which could not, those things that were remembered and those that had been forgotten. In New York the ocean was an irrelevancy, a vestigial thing beyond and apart from the thing itself, the city: the buildings packed in tight as tissue stanching a nosebleed, a glass-and-steel rising that pierced the sky.

There is another life he lives. It flows beneath this one. He feels it like being far out in the water and sensing all that depth beneath you. In this other life, he has never driven a taxi through the snow-hushed streets of New York. He has never spent a birthday eating stale samosas in the holding lot at JFK. He has never lain awake at night listening to his roommate's snores. He has never been to New York at all. He never took a plane away from his home, never watched the island disappear into the sea as the plane lifted into the sky. Never the eggshell-blue prison. Never the shocked faces of everyone he'd ever known. Never that night and never that girl. Never and never and never.

On the table, the iPhone in the gray case rings. The ringtone is that maddening banana song. *Six foot, seven foot, eight foot bunch.* Go fucking figure. He picks it up and says hello.

■ ■ ■ ■

The Little Sweet

■ ■ ■ ■

Could it be? Surely it wasn't him, I told myself as I sat in my cubicle that afternoon. There could easily be five men named Clive Richardson — ten, two dozen — in the five boroughs, never mind that I had no reason to believe that the man who had been a suspect in my sister's death was in New York in the first place. I stared at the manuscript for "the new Mann" on my computer, unable to think, let alone work, for the rest of the day. At five-thirty on the dot, I fled.

Back in my studio I sat on my bed beneath the harsh light of the bare bulbs. It wouldn't be accurate to say I was thinking about what to do. I had not been thinking when I left my phone in the taxi and I was not thinking now. It was more like I was waiting for my body to writhe into instinctive action and carry me along with it. I ate a few bites of my salad. I sat and felt the time drip. Then I dug a handful of quarters from the change jar on my desk, ran out of my studio and up the stairs, and went out into the evening in search of a working pay phone.

I hadn't used a pay phone since I was a middle schooler calling my parents for a ride home in Pasadena. I couldn't recall the last time I'd noticed a pay phone in New York, but it turned out there was one not a five-minute walk from my apartment. Apparently I had been walking past it for over a year without noticing it, and though rationally I knew it had been there all along, that in the city one's mind renders much of the detail in the landscape invisible out of necessity, still, in that moment, I had the uncanny impression that this sorry-looking kiosk spackled with bird droppings and gum and Sharpie graffiti tags faded as the names on an ancient gravestone, had been planted here just now, for me, to make possible whatever was going to happen. I picked up the phone and heard, to my disbelief, a dial tone. I deposited my quarters and dialed my own number.

The phone rang and rang. I was about to lose my nerve and hang up when a soft voice said hello.

"Hello?" I replied.

"Yes?" the voice said.

"Yes," I echoed. "Are you the taxi driver?

I'm the one who accidentally left this phone in your cab."

I regretted the word *accidentally* as soon as I said it. Nobody who had actually left something by accident would bother to say so. It was a tell, a slip. But I was being paranoid. He would take no notice of the word. Why would he?

"My shift begins at five A.M. I could meet you in midtown tomorrow morning to return it."

"Can I come to you? I'd like to get it tonight if possible. I need it for work."

I did not need it for work. But the lie flowed seamlessly. I had to see him tonight. I had to — what? I had no plan. I felt only a need to lock eyes with this man, to speak to him, to make something happen and see what it would be.

"That would be possible. But I live in Flatbush."

"No way!" I said cheerily. "I'm practically your neighbor."

"Small world," he said with a (genuine? perturbed?) chuckle. "In that case, there's a place called the Little Sweet on Church. I can meet you out front if that would be convenient."

I knew the place; it was one of several popular Caribbean restaurants clustered near the Church Avenue subway stop on Nostrand. I had passed them many times with interest, but I had never gone inside, figuring the people there probably didn't want people like me encroaching. (Or was this a justification for staying away from places that made me nervous?)

I told him I could be there in fifteen minutes. "I seriously can't thank you enough," I said before hanging up. "I'm wearing a blue blouse. I'm Emily."

As I made my way to the Little Sweet, I told myself it wasn't him. Though I could not deny that the voice on the phone had a familiar softness, it simply could not belong to the same Clive Richardson who'd spilled my french fries in the sand all those years ago (chips, he'd called them, and how I'd loved that), the one everybody had called Gogo, the man with whom, along with Edwin Hastie, my sister was last seen alive. I would meet him on the sidewalk and see immediately that his face was all wrong, or that he was too short, or too light- or dark-skinned. I would give him twenty bucks, thank him, and be on my way, and though I might be shaken for a couple of days, my life would quickly snap back to its usual dimensions. Whether I hoped for or dreaded this outcome, I'm no longer sure.

The landscape changed as I walked north and east. Though the building I lived in was run-down and situated on an unlovely block of vacant lots and midrise apartment buildings, it was also not far from the Edison-bulb eateries along Cortelyou Road, from cafés whose menus featured an entire section of "alternative milk" options (soy, almond, cashew) and boutiques where one could purchase a vintage Berber rug or an olive-wood cheese platter for exorbitant sums. I was just a few minutes' walk from an especially picturesque stretch of Argyle Road, where in the summertime the Victorian mansions with their wide front porches and twilight-hued hydrangeas seemed to have been lifted from some seaside idyll and set down gently on this street in central Brooklyn. Though I prided myself on living beyond such places, it was also true that I found comfort in my proximity to them. As I neared the Little Sweet, I left all of this behind. The signs on the commercial thoroughfares became more urgent: CHECKS CASHED! PLAY NOW! WIRE CASH LOW FEE!

By the time I reached my destination, the sky was dingy pink, darkness touched by neon storefronts. The Little Sweet was a take-out spot with half a dozen tables, a long steam table behind the counter, and an illuminated menu with stock photos of combination platters hanging above it. It was located between a MoneyGram and a Chinese takeout called Hunan Star, across the street from a West Indian grocery and a discount shop with a hodgepodge of merchandise on the sidewalk: coolers and pushcarts and mop heads, reflective vests and nursing scrubs. Farther down the block, a Creole and English bookstore transmitted ESL recordings into the night: *I run to the house. She bakes a cake. He goes to sleep.*

I stood in front of the narrow storefront and tried to appear occupied. I put a twenty-dollar bill in my pocket to give to the man as a reward. I cleaned out my handbag, disposing of fistfuls of receipts and a cough drop that had been floating loose in my bag, stuck with grit and lint. It had not been necessary to specify what I was wearing. I was the only white person here, with the exception of a man about my age, bearded and man-bunned, who sat at a table in the center of the Little Sweet and alternated between eating and drawing in a sketch pad.

When I saw Clive Richardson coming up the sidewalk I knew at once it was him. It was his walk. The hunched shoulders, the bowed head. He moved like he thought he took up too much space and was sorry. I clenched my jaw to quell the chattering of my teeth and willed myself to be still.

In a flash I saw my parents. They would be sitting down now to one of their abstemious locavore dinners in their kitchen in Pasadena. I imagined them seeing me seeing Clive Richardson on this sidewalk in Brooklyn. I felt them reaching out, pulling me back into the safe, blind world our family had inhabited all these years, our aftermath of SoCal sunshine and ceramics and racket sports. Forget my phone. Turn around. Run straight home and don't look back. That's what they would want me to do.

"Emily?"

I nodded. I couldn't raise my eyes to look at him.

"I hope you didn't wait long."

"Not long at all."

He pulled my phone from his pocket.

"Thank you so, so much. You just have no idea how much I appreciate this." I held out the twenty-dollar bill to him.

"I can't accept this." He spoke softly, as if worried his refusal would offend me.

"Please take it," I implored.

"I would prefer not to."

"You're sure?"

"Yes, miss."

Miss.

I looked up and for the first time our eyes met. Clive Richardson must have been at least forty now, and he looked it — his hair had already started to go white and his forehead was deeply lined. My body trembled. My jaw was clenched so tightly it would ache later. At the same time, my mind spasmed as it tried uselessly to understand that this ordinary man standing before me in a windbreaker and black loafers was *him.*

I tucked the money back in my pocket. "Well."

We stared at one another awkwardly. The moment was lifting away from me. Could it be that I would do nothing? That I would simply let him leave? But what else could I do? Even as I wondered this I was saying, "Thanks again. I really appreciate it," and Clive Richardson was telling me it was nothing, and I was wishing him a good night. The bells on the door of the Little Sweet jingled as he opened it and stepped inside. I turned and hurried down the sidewalk. My eyes filled with hot, stinging tears. It had happened too fast. I hadn't been ready, had missed my chance. My chance for what, exactly, I wasn't sure, but

I was filled with the sense that I'd failed to capitalize on this extraordinary convergence and, more than this, with a sense that this failure was at the center of who I was — a person who let things slip through her hands.

That night I dreamed I walked out of my apartment to find that a stone staircase had opened up in the middle of the sidewalk, leading down. Only the first few steps were visible. After that, the staircase disappeared into the darkness below the city. The stairs went on and on, and I walked for what felt like an eternity in the pitch-black, *step, step, step,* down and down and down, until I found myself standing on a beach. White sand, curving palms, mint waters. It had been here all along — this place, this past, waiting only for me to return. (In the dream I knew without having to know that I was Clairey again, a child.) Some distance from me, standing at the water's edge, her ankles lapped by the gentle waves, was Alison. She was turned away from me, staring out. When I reached her, she looked down at me and smiled, and I smiled back. She raised a finger to her lips. *Shh. Don't tell.* She tossed back her head and laughed.

I awoke drenched in sweat and full of self-recrimination — I hardly ever dreamed of Alison and I'd ruined it, expulsed myself from the dream prematurely. For the first time in months, I took out the photographs from the shoe box under my bed. I needed to tell her what had happened to me and how helpless I'd felt as I thanked Clive Richardson and walked away. All this time, he had been right here. How was it possible that I hadn't known it, sensed it?

There she was, nut-brown from the sun and grinning at dinner with a giant red lobster on her plate. Singing at the beach barbecue. Smiling beside me beneath that faded blue umbrella. *My, you a patient child.* The photos felt volatile, as if they might burst into flame in my hands. There she was on a paddleboard, clinking glasses with my mother, listening to her Walkman in the shade. There she was leaning against a palm tree in her bikini, hands on hips, salt in her hair, looking off down the beach. My father had taken this picture. I remembered watching Alison pose for him. Now, looking at the photograph for the thousandth time, I saw something I'd never noticed before. Down the beach, so far in the background their bodies were nothing but tiny, blurred silhouettes, were Edwin Hastie and Clive Richardson.

I perceived something else, too. A distance in Alison's eyes. It was as if she saw Faraway Cay in her mind's eye and knew that, in the subtext of each moment, as we swam and giggled and tried to tie knots in the stems of maraschino cherries with our tongues, she was moving through the becalmed cerulean water toward it. It occurred to me that maybe I hadn't known my sister very well at all.

At work the next day I was distracted and unsettled. I reread the same sentence over and over without grasping its meaning. The photograph my father took of Alison gnawed at the edges of my mind. For whom had she really been posing?

Eventually I gave up on work. Instead, I opened Facebook and searched for Clive Richardson. There were dozens of profiles, but eventually I found the one I was looking for. His profile picture was a selfie blurred by a burst of light from a lamp behind him. He was not active on the site — he had posted no other photos and had only two friends. The first was a man named Ousseini. This man did have an active social media presence; his timeline was filled with family photos and inspirational quotations set against backdrops of sunsets and mountains. Clive's only post was a birthday message to his one other friend, a man named Bryan Richardson. The post was several years old and was written the way people who do not understand Facebook write messages: *Dear Bryan, Wishing you a very happy birthday. Sincerely, Clive.* Presumably, Bryan Richardson was a relative, though he looked nothing like Clive — he was tall and slender; in his profile picture he wore a trim-cut suit and sat at a keyboard, his hands touched down lightly over the keys.

Edwin Hastie had no profile. A Google search for his name turned up nothing but old articles about Alison's case.

Next, I typed "Alison Thomas" into Google and the autocomplete options popped up:

Alison Thomas murder
Alison Thomas Dying for Fun
Alison Thomas obituary

I had never read my sister's obituary. I was too young to have read it when it came out, and in more recent years, when I might easily have found it online, I hadn't looked for it. Not that it hadn't occurred to me. But I had absorbed a lesson from my parents not to permit myself to plunge into the depths. I clicked on the link and found the brief notice that had been published by our local suburban paper.

> **Alison Brianne Thomas,** 18, died January 3rd, on a family vacation to the island of Saint X. She was born September 8, 1977, to Richard (Rick) and Ellen (Wolfe) Thomas.
>
> Alison was a talented performer and athlete who loved modern dance, swimming, tennis, and the great outdoors. A budding scientist, she had aspirations toward a career in medicine and had just completed her first semester at Princeton. While her life was cut far too short, she lived every moment to its very fullest and gave so much joy to her family and friends.
>
> She is survived by her parents and younger sister, Claire, as well as grandparents Sylvia, Edward, Jean, and Fred, and great-grandmother Helen.

A life, pared down to what were at once its most essential and meaningless facts. I was surprised to read that Alison had "aspirations toward a career in medicine." I had no memory of my sister expressing any desire to become a doctor. Come to think of it, I didn't remember her expressing an inclination toward any particular professional path at all. Maybe I'd simply been too young to attend to those aspects of her life, but I didn't think so. Something about this line rang false. Who had written the obituary? My father, presumably. Maybe he wished to suggest to the world that my sister was more directed, more fully formed, than she really was. *Here was a girl with plans!* But I think something deeper was at play: with this brief mention of Alison's "aspirations," she became not just an eighteen-year-old girl but also a medical student, a resident, a fellow, chair of Pediatric Cardiology at Brigham and Women's. *Aspirations toward a career in medicine.* A false claim, and a necessary one. To mourn a budding physician was a terrible task, but it was a thing you could do. To mourn a girl with infinite futures was to mourn infinitely.

What is the neurological experience of a person? When you think of someone, what sound, image, scent is summoned? For instance, in my mind, my father is forever bent over his African violets in our garden in Pasadena, inspecting them for aphids. My childhood friend Kelsey Johnston is the hyper-particular hammy odor of her farts. Aunt Caroline is gray roots at the nape of a long, graceful neck.

Alison is flowers and white teeth. I know where this image comes from. The high school dance recital, Alison's senior year. She wore a dove-gray leotard and a flowing chiffon skirt and leapt across the stage. I don't know the name of the song she danced to, but I remember its melancholy sound. Watching her was like watching the music itself spin and bend through the air. How deeply I felt her feeling it, infusing the auditorium with a snowy perfume of longing. I remember sitting there, watching the other people in the audience watching her. My sister. Mine.

Afterward, in the auditorium lobby, my parents and Drew McNamara and her friends piled bouquets into her arms. She wore glitter on her cheeks. She grinned. Flowers and white teeth.

This was a child's version of a person. My parents' version of Alison was different but, it occurred to me now, no more accurate. When they spoke of her, it was not to reminisce about the past, but to imagine her into the present.

Of the mandarin tree that grew in our tiny yard in Pasadena:

"Alison would have loved this."

"She would have eaten the fruit right here

under the tree."

At times, their invocations struck me as almost willfully inaccurate.

At Yellowstone, beholding Old Faithful:

"Alison would have thought this was so neat."

Would she really? Alison had never been one to be especially *impressed.*

In my parents' version, Alison was buffed like a piece of sea glass, her edges and points worn away over time and yielding to a pleasing smoothness.

That evening I once again traveled to the Little Sweet, drawn there as if by a spell. As I neared my destination, the racing of my heart became almost unbearable, but I did not turn back. I had to find him. I could not let him disappear. Still, I didn't expect to actually come upon him, and when I arrived and looked through the plate-glass and saw him, seated at a table in the corner beside a potted palm, a plate of crimson stew and a blue can of beer on his tray, I had the sense that this image was not, could not be, real. He sat with his shoulders hunched, his legs squeezed awkwardly beneath the small table, casting off an aura of both physical and metaphysical discomfort.

I lingered only a moment outside, terrified that he would lift his head and see me. Then I crossed the street. Hidden by the shadow beneath the awning of the West Indian grocery, I watched him. From the speakers of the bookstore down the street, a lesson on daily tasks reverberated. *They drive to work. I go to the store. He comes home.* Clive ate his meal in slow, distracted bites while he watched what I assumed must be a television on the wall, out of my view. He finished his beer and purchased another. He nodded a wordless hello to a fellow customer. With a paper napkin he kept crumpled in his fist, he wiped the crimson stew from his lips. Ordinary actions, objectively of no interest. I couldn't look away.

Back at my apartment later that night, I found *Dying for Fun: Alison Thomas* on YouTube. In it, my sister is played by Selena Richter, an actress who, a decade later, would rise to superstardom when she played the heroine in a trilogy of dystopian films based on a popular book series. Someone had posted each episode in the series: Kristin Broekner, Maggie Donohue, Flora Salter, Alicia Madigan. I changed into my pajamas and got in bed with my laptop to submit myself to *Dying for Fun: Alison*

Thomas (Selena Richter in Early Role!!!).

The episode had been viewed some 47,000 times and received approximately 2,400 thumbs-up and 650 thumbs-down. (Whether these "dislikes" were meant to indicate disapproval of the quality of the film, or of Selena Richter, or of the dated anti-feminism and clunky moral suasion of the entire *Dying for Fun* enterprise, I don't know.) The comments section was no more illuminating:

OMG I loved this when it aired and watching it now is a blast from the freaking past.

This is '90s AF.

Selena Richter = overrated.

I can't even with those platform shoes.

Selena Richter looked nothing like my sister. She was voluptuous and busty, while Alison's body was straight and athletic. Her portrayal of Alison featured an entire register of all-wrong sounds: squeals of delight, giggling fits, the occasional deployment of a pouty-lipped baby voice. She had none of Alison's bristle, no flash of intelligence in her swimming-pool-blue eyes. I appeared in a few scenes, though for some reason I was called Katie. I was played by an angelic child with golden ringlets and rosebud lips. When Alison's body was found, Katie cried harrowing, captivating tears, and I felt like some failed version of what Alison's sister should have been.

According to *Dying for Fun,* my sister was a sheltered girl lured to her death by tactics only a total naïf would fall for. For simplicity's sake, I assume, Clive Richardson and Edwin Hastie had been streamlined into a single character named Apollo, with dreadlocks and a gold hoop earring.

"I've never done a body shot before. Won't you show me how?" Alison implores Apollo in an early scene.

"First ya must be lickin' da salt wit ya tongue," Apollo says.

Alison gets down on her knees and licks a line of salt from his muscled abdomen. She looks up at him with guileless eyes and giggles.

In this version, my sister lies bathed in moonlight on a beach that appears made of stardust and allows Apollo to unzip her dress.

"Relax," he says with blatantly evil eyes. (The acting is uniformly one-note and overblown.)

"I want you to be my first," she whispers into his ear. She flushes and pants as if shocked by her own arousal; she is a pale pink peony, poised on the edge of blooming. "Don't you dare be gentle with me."

He presses his hands over my sister's nose and mouth. She struggles. He thrusts. The whole thing slouches to its terrible conclusion as a thousand housewives squeeze their pillows.

"I gon' be ya last."

I couldn't sleep that night. I kept replaying the final moments from the movie in my head. Only instead of Apollo, I imagined Clive Richardson, as I had seen him earlier that evening, transposed into each scene — laying her in the sand, unzipping her dress, smothering her with the same hands he'd used to wipe the stew from his lips. Could he have done it? Could he have played a part? Apollo was an obvious cliché, not a person but simply a murderer. But the man I had observed earlier that night evinced no coldness or cruelty at all, and this chilled me to the bone. Yes, of course he could have done it. You see a mug shot on TV and think, *Him? But he has such a kind face. But his eyes are so gentle.* Nannies drown children they cared for lovingly for years. Perfect couples become a husband who shot a wife. We see so little of people. We forget how much submerged darkness there is around us at every moment. We forget until we are forced to remember.

■ ■ ■ ■

Over the week that followed, I watched the remaining episodes of the *Dying for Fun* series. I had felt guilty for ignoring the other girls. But I admit I also watched at least partly for the same reason anybody else would, for the trashy, low-fi, comically dated pleasure of it. I'd been aware of their stories to varying degrees when they happened. Perhaps you remember them, too. Maggie Donohue (Thailand, Ecstasy, a dalliance with an Aussie on his gap year). Kristin Broekner (Mykonos, an entanglement with the scion of a Russian oil baron). Flora Salter's story captured the American imagination for a few weeks' time, owing to its tragic outcomes — the apartment set ablaze in Montmartre, the suicide of that handsome young tennis phenom. Maggie. Kristin. Flora. Alicia (whose name was pronounced like satin ribbon — *A-lee-see-a*). What is the appeal of such stories? You know the kind I'm talking about. All the pretty dead white girls. The one backpacking in Eastern Europe and the one at the full moon festival in Bali and the blossom-cheeked blonde in Aruba. You see their photographs on the evening news. They wear graduation caps or prom dresses or a peasant blouse and a wreath of white flowers — it's Halloween and they're the darnedest little hippie you ever did see. You hear the eyewitness interviews. "I saw her get on the back of his motorbike." "I think she was on something." "She always had to be the life of the party." You think how stupid it was of them, whatever they did to end up as they did. You feel a bit indignant, actually. You see their honey-blond hair, their red ringlets, their auburn ponytail frozen mid-swish in the photographs, their blue, green, caramel eyes, and always, a smile so blunt it's like they don't have even the faintest notion that anything bad could ever happen to them. You find them naïve and smug. Maybe they are. Maybe Alison was.

During this same period, I walked to the Little Sweet every evening. Now that I had found Clive, it was simply not possible to stay away. He was always there, and he always sat at the same table, in the corner beside the potted palm. I would watch him from the shadow beneath the awning of the grocery across the street for as long as I felt I could without becoming conspicuous. Then I would loop the block a few times, slowing my pace as I passed the Little Sweet. I would duck into one of the nearby stores. Browse the GED prep guides at the bookstore as if they held genuine relevance for me. Peruse the unfamiliar produce in the grocery store — cassava, turmeric root, dasheen — and smile periodically at the elderly Korean couple behind the counter, purchasing a pack of gum on my way out to justify my presence.

Over these nights of observation, my inchoate need to keep tabs on Clive Richardson, to bear witness to his presence, coalesced and sharpened into a sort of plan. I would uncover everything I could about Alison, searching for clues with which to build a portrait of my sister — her emotions and relationships, the dramas and preoccupations of her life, anything that might help me to understand the kinds of dangers to which she might have been vulnerable at the time of our vacation. And I would continue to surveil Clive, watching and waiting for even the smallest detail, the tiniest slip of evidence that might point me toward the truth about the kind of man he was and the role he might have played in my sister's death. What this evidence might look like I didn't know, but I had to believe that a person couldn't take a life and simply melt back into the human crowd — such an act must leave traces, scars, and if I was vigilant, if I could attune myself to this man, I would find them.

I shared none of this with my parents. I told myself I was protecting them. But looking back, I think the real reason I didn't tell them is because I knew that if I did, they would make me promise not to seek Clive out anymore, for my own safety, and I would do as they asked because I always did as they asked, and because it still would have been possible for me to loosen my grip on him then, in the fall, in a way it no longer would be by the time winter came. I would be relieved, their concern just the permission I needed to leave it alone, to go back and continue living my life as if Clive Richardson were not living his just a few blocks east. I could no longer abide such cowardice in myself. I saw clearly now that cowardice is what it was, what it always had been — our nice family life, so remarkably functional, so totally cut off from the depths of our own pain. It fell to me. If my parents could not, would not, then I must inhabit the depths alone to uncover the truth, no matter what.

What a mindfuck. In high school I get treated like shit because I'm Shelly the theater kid, Shelly the freak. Then I show up in Hollywood, change my name to Selena, and I get treated like shit all over again, but now it's because I'm just a pretty face. I'm a weird girl, then I'm an "it" girl, and five seconds later I'm "overexposed."

I leave the house in some shit my stylist put together for me, I'm fake. I leave the house in sweatpants with greasy hair, I'm trying too hard to look like I'm not trying.

I just love how Selena Richter doesn't conform to what Hollywood wants her to be.

Ugh, Selena Richter, I just hate how self-righteously nonconformist she is.

I'm obsessed with how minimalist her acting is.

Why do people keep casting that fucking block of wood and expecting her to carry a film?

I slouch and bite my nails during an interview, where's my poise? I focus on my posture, where's my personality? I point fucking any of this out and, *Boo hoo poor Selena Richter, it must be so hard being rich and famous.* I am not saying it is harder than being a bricklayer, fucking straw-man idiots. I am saying our society is sick with a poison of its own making.

If you need proof, here is a list of just some of the shit that happened to me with my first actual role bigger than a Gushers commercial:

1. When I'm offered the part of Alison Thomas, I tell my agent I'm not sure I want to take it because it creeps me out to play a real-life dead girl. He says to me, "This is not your last dead girl, Selena."
2. The crew is the same for all the *Dying for Fun* episodes. Sometimes in costume or hair and makeup, they do me up a certain way and then consult with each other like, "Is the braid too Alicia?" "Is this skirt too

Kristin?" "Whoa, you're giving me Maggie Donohue flashbacks with that nail polish."

3. In the last scene I'm supposed to say, "Don't you dare be gentle with me," and I very politely ask if we can maybe consider cutting that line, because who says that? Like, why does she need to be such a bimbo? The director gets pissy and goes, "Say your lines, sweetheart." To put me in my place, he has us do dozens of takes. He makes me say it over and over again. The first few takes, I'm standing next to Mike, who plays Apollo. Then the director has me press myself against Mike. Then he has Mike pin my wrists against a tree. Then he has me take off my shirt so I'm just in a string bikini top.

   "Please," I say. "Can we be done?"

   "Are you tired, Selena? Are you parched? Somebody get this bitch a Perrier." Fucking asshat.

   Poor Mike is so uncomfortable.

   I lose count of how many times I've said it. Finally, Mike says, "Come on, man, she gets it."

   The director puts down his stupid

> clipboard and walks over to me. He pulls the string on the bikini top and then I'm standing there with my breasts out in front of the whole crew. He whispers in my ear, "Do you *get it,* Selena?"

But I'm not Selena. I'm not Shelly, either. They think they've got me. They think they've pinned me down. They're not even fucking close.

Our Beautiful Daughter

From "Remembering Alison Thomas" by Jessica Nazarian, January 10, 1996, *The Daily Princetonian:*

On Sunday, students trickling back from Christmas break returned to a campus that had been transformed into a winter wonderland of glittering quads and frosted trees. But one member of the freshman class was not among them. Alison Thomas died over break during a family vacation to the Caribbean. As the investigation into her death continues, students here paused to remember a beloved friend and classmate.

"She was really smart," said Mike Chernin, her lab partner in Molecular Biology 100. "I definitely had to step up my game with her."

Larissa Venable, captain of MoDE (Modern

Dance Ensemble), shared that Alison was one of only three freshmen admitted to the selective squad this fall. "Usually the frosh hang back in rehearsals, but she was throwing out choreography ideas right off the bat. Her ideas were totally integral to our 'Like a Prayer' routine."

Alison's roommate, Nika Ivanova, reflected, "I still can't believe she won't be here when I wake up in our room tomorrow. I just want to say we will always remember her." . . .

From "For Vacationers, Grief and Questions After a Daughter's Mysterious Death" by Vince Cerusi, January 17, 1996, *The New York Times*:
. . . "Alison was an absolute sweetheart," her aunt, Colleen Thomas, said. "Just the sweetest, gentlest soul you could hope to meet. My dog is a rescue and he really struggles with trust, and she was just wonderful with him." When asked about reports that her niece was seen drinking and smoking marijuana at a popular local bar on the night of her disappearance, Colleen Thomas replied, "I don't care what the police down there say. It's a tourist island; they have an incentive to make her

look a certain way. That is not the Ali we know and love." . . .

From "Our Town Says Goodbye" by Kate Cafferty, January 23, 1996, *The Patent Trader:*

. . . Becca Frankel, eighteen and a high school classmate, remembers Alison Brianne Thomas as being a girl who had it all. "She was totally that girl. Smart. Pretty. Great athlete. Awesome dancer. I could probably name ten guys who had huge crushes on her. She got a lot of attention, and you could tell she loved it, you know?" When it was asked whether Thomas was promiscuous, Becca replied, "She was all about Drew." Alison dated classmate Drew McNamara, who is a freshman at Rensselaer Polytechnic Institute, for three years. According to Becca, "They were *the* couple." We could not reach McNamara for comment. . . .

It had been two weeks since I stepped into Clive Richardson's taxi, and at work my productivity had dwindled to almost nothing. Every morning on the subway, I scribbled a to-do list: mail off cover-art proofs, draft the back-cover copy for a movie tie-in edition, write rejection e-mails for half a dozen recent novel submissions. Arriving at the office, I hung my coat in the locker at my cubicle and settled in at my desk with every intention of getting things done. But soon, almost without realizing it, the work at hand was abandoned and I was lost in the digital sea of stories about Alison. None of the mysteries in the books I worked on could compare to my own sister's.

It seemed everyone who had known her, however distantly, had given testimony on the question of who Alison Thomas had been. The articles were filled with tidbits about my sister's last months that were new to me. She had been to an R.E.M. concert at the Meadowlands the fall before she died. She loved the mocha frozen yogurt in the dining hall. She had been a ballerina for Halloween. Each piece of information was like a wound, a reminder of how little I knew about my own sister.

From "An Enigma Abroad" by Sean Winokur, *Esquire,* June 1996:

. . . I meet Richard Conti, Thomas's high school English teacher, at the Station, a diner in the mock-Tudor downtown of the affluent suburb where she grew up. In a town whose quaint main street is crowded with dry cleaners, nail salons, and gourmet take-away shops, the Station stands unmistakably apart. The interior is beyond unfancy — it's downright dingy. Flickering panels of fluorescents overhead, a skein of mysterious stickiness underfoot, a deli case of mayonaissy potato, macaroni, and chicken salads. A jar of magenta pickled eggs occupies pride of place by the ancient cash register on the counter. My western omelet is emphatically mediocre. From the get-go, I wonder at Conti's choice of meeting place. You can sniff out someone trying to control the narrative, hoping to convince the world that Alison Thomas was not a silly little rich girl.

Conti is thirty-three, tall and handsome, with the broad and limber build of the Division I soccer goalkeeper he once was. Despite having agreed to this interview, he is hesitant, at first, to discuss his former student. As he bites into his egg and cheese sandwich, he confides that he almost canceled on me this morning. "I teach English, so I know the same story can be spun a thousand different ways."

But as we speak, Conti grows increasingly comfortable sharing his impressions and memories of Thomas. "She was a very

> bright girl. Not necessarily the most diligent student, but very bright. There's a type of student, and I think it was hard for me to recognize in Alison at first because it's a type that skews male. These kids do the work that interests them and say screw the rest. They turn in papers late but their work is so good you don't want to penalize them for it, even if you know they don't really give a shit what grade you give them, and also that they're kind of banking on that, kind of playing you." Asked if he'd describe Thomas as arrogant, Conti grows flustered. "No, no, no. She was a good kid. She was just a really intelligent, nice, good kid. That's what I'm trying to say. She was a star." . . .

Alison was a drama queen. She was a gentle soul. She was *that* girl. The one everybody envied. The one all the boys wanted. A star. She was what all the dead are: whatever the living make them.

As I pored over the articles, I encountered the same two photographs of Alison over and over. The first was taken after her performance in the school dance recital her senior year. Her cheeks and eyelids are brushed with glittery makeup, so that she seems to shimmer — celestial, angelic. Her smile is soft and dreamy, an unusual facial expression for my sister. Put simply, she does not look like herself. Maybe you've experienced this: you see a photo of someone you know well, and they look like an altogether different person. What makes this phenomenon possible? Is it some trick of the light, distorting the planes and angles of the face? Something about the transference of a three-dimensional form to two dimensions? Is it that we're accustomed to seeing people in motion and the total stillness of an image throws us off? A final possibility seems most convincing to me: We don't know what people look like. We know only what they look like to us. We have an idea of them, shaped by our affections, our memories, and this is the real distortion. In this photograph my sister looks like some romantic ideal of a girl too lovely for this world. A girl fated for death.

The second picture is different. It was taken at a dorm party a month before Alison was killed. The room is dark, lit only by the harsh flash of the camera. The party must have been pajama-themed. Some boys wear boxers. Others are dressed ironically in fuzzy onesies. There is a keg visible in the corner, plastic cups in every hand and cluttering every surface. My sister wears a tiny blue slip — *negligee* would be the proper term, I think. Her nipples press visibly against the silk. She is dancing with her arms raised over her head, a cup in her hand. Her hair is sweaty, her eyes rimmed with smudged eyeliner. She smiles seductively at whoever is behind the camera.

Don't you understand? My sister was an innocent, blameless in her horrific fate. And it was all her fault.

My observation of Clive continued. What I saw was always the same, his habits repetitive and fastidious: that crimson stew and a beer, then a second when he'd drained the first. Silent nods hello to the other regulars. A napkin crumpled in a fist. I watched until he rose to scrape his plate into the trash. Then I hurried down the sidewalk, not slowing until I reached my apartment.

Of course, sometimes I had evening plans, or something came up. For instance, one afternoon Jackie texted that she needed to see me for "emergency girl talk," and that night we met for drinks at her favorite bar near our old apartment. Jackie ran late as a rule. I arrived on time, then sat there twiddling my thumbs and excoriating myself. Why did I always set myself up to wait for her? What was it that rendered me incapable of deviating from this pattern? (I think I know the answer to these questions now. I think I liked this pattern, this banal and benign predicament in which to seethe.) This time, my annoyance was compounded by the fact that Jackie was keeping me from Clive — what if tonight was the night something happened, and I missed it? I worked myself up into quite a state before she arrived, and as usual I shelved this feeling when Jackie whirled through the door, half an hour late and full of apologies.

The reason for the emergency girl talk was that Jackie was "just so overwhelmed." I listened for a long time as she described the sources of her trouble with mounting distress. She wasn't a priority to her boyfriend. She hated her job. She never had time to practice her "craft." (Though she seemed to have plenty of time, I thought, to attend her boyfriend's dodgeball league games and to transform bushels of produce into six ounces of juice twice a day. I didn't say this.)

"Of *course* you're overwhelmed," I said instead. "It's too much."

Jackie nodded. "Right? It would be too much for *anyone*."

There were tears in her eyes. I hugged her. I stroked her hair. I offered what seemed to me rather boilerplate advice: She should deal with one thing at a time. Step by step. Et cetera.

Jackie blew her nose into a cocktail napkin. "How are you so fucking wise?"

We stayed at the bar for another hour.

"So, what's new with you?" she asked as she tossed her credit card down on the check.

I thought of Clive Richardson, of the Little Sweet, of Alison's obituary and the golden-haired, rose-lipped child from *Dying for Fun* who was and was not me.

"Nothing much."

At work one day I went on Facebook to track down Nika Ivanova, Alison's roommate at Princeton. I found her easily. She was Nika (Ivanova) Cunningham now; she lived in Philadelphia and worked for a pharmaceutical company. Her profile picture was a selfie in which she sat sandwiched between two freckle-faced boys on a chairlift. I sent her a message:

> You probably don't remember me, but I'm Alison Thomas's younger sister. I'm working on a project to compile remembrances about Alison. It would mean so much to have a contribution from you. I know you

didn't know Alison long, but she loved being your roommate. Maybe we could arrange a phone call and I can tell you more about what I have in mind?

I felt weird for lying, but pinning my request to a formal project seemed to normalize it. Amazing, the power of a premise.

Nika replied that evening. She would be very happy to help me in whatever way she could. We scheduled a phone call for a night later that week, but a few minutes after we were supposed to talk, Nika texted to cancel. She had forgotten it was her turn to pick up her son's tae kwon do carpool. Twenty minutes later, I was standing outside of the Little Sweet. Stew, beer, nod hello. For over an hour, I wandered the neighborhood, circling back to watch Clive as often as I dared. The streets were busy with people. A mom herding three kids in school uniforms. An elderly man leaning against a storefront and sipping a pineapple soda. The periodic upward rush of bodies from the subway at Nostrand. A stray white kid hefting a mesh laundry basket down the sidewalk. When I circled back once more and found that Clive had departed while I was walking, I was left with the unsettling feeling of a necessary process cut short.

Nika canceled again the next time we were supposed to speak — her other son's basketball game had gone into overtime. Again I left my apartment at once and headed to Church Avenue. Stew, beer, nod hello. Clive maintained this ritual with such consistency that I half wondered if he knew he was being watched and was determined to reveal nothing of himself. At times it seemed to me as if we were engaged in a battle of wills. I had not yet found my way past the mesmeric repetition of his routines. But I was not concerned. I would wait as long as it took. I was patient.

Nika and I finally spoke that Sunday.

"Sorry I was so hard to get on the phone. This week was completely insane," she said, in a rote tone that suggested that for Nika, every week was completely insane. In the background I could hear the crinkle of what sounded like grocery bags being unpacked.

I had a single memory of Nika. When my family arrived at Alison's dorm room to move her in, Nika and her parents were already there, arguing with each other in urgent, whispered Bulgarian as they looked down at her bed. They hadn't known to buy extra-long sheets and now they couldn't make her bed. When they realized we were standing in the doorway, they looked stricken. Nika was dressed in a pleated skirt, a blouse, and loafers with a low, square heel. My sister wore mesh shorts and flip-flops. I understood implicitly that Alison was wearing the right thing and Nika was wearing the wrong thing. In my head she was still the painfully overdressed girl pressed close to her parents.

I told Nika I wanted to create a book of memories about my sister. "I was so young when she was killed. I've been finding it really therapeutic lately to hear stories from people who knew her."

I heard the refrigerator door opening and closing, the garbage disposal churning. Nika's inattention wasn't hurtful, exactly. It was callous in a bland, quotidian way I didn't really hold against her. My tragedy wasn't hers, and that wasn't her fault.

"Your sister was a big deal for me," Nika began. "I could not have been more clueless when I showed up at Princeton. We immigrated when I was ten, but my parents still barely spoke English. I had this horrible bushy hair. I used to go to the dining hall, fill a mug with soup, and go back and eat it in our room because I was so intimidated by the other kids at the tables. I got a sixty-three on my first calculus test. I went to this awful high school in Chicago. I had no preparation whatsoever. I just cried and cried about it. There were tutors you could go to, but I was afraid. I literally thought if I went to them, they'd realize Princeton had made a mistake accepting me and kick me out. I had no idea what to — excuse me a minute." I could hear her hand press against the receiver. *Not now, Logan, Mommy's on the phone.* "Sorry about that. Anyway, right, I had no idea what to do."

"That must have been hard." I straightened a paper clip and used the tip to clean under my fingernails. Her tragedy was not my tragedy, either.

"Your sister made such a difference for me. I'm not just saying that. She included me. The first month of school I made zero friends. I was basically a recluse. Your sister obviously knew everyone on campus within five minutes, and everyone wanted to be her friend. She just had that personal power, you know?"

"She was special," I said vaguely. Charisma, you might call it, though this word doesn't explain the mystery, because charismatic people are all different. It's the feeling they evoke in others, that tipsy glow, that tidal pull, that they share. It's Edwin

Hastie with a passel of children scrabbling over him in the sand. It's a dozen men falling in love with Aunt Caroline as she peels a tangerine in the Luxembourg Gardens. Who was Nika to tell *me* about Alison's power? I thought with irritation. But I composed myself.

"Every time she was going to a party or an event or anything, she invited me," Nika continued. "I must have said no to her a hundred times. I was just scared. Finally one night she grabbed my arm and said, 'You're coming, Nika Nika' — she used to call me that, like the Singing Nun song? — and she dragged me out of our room. We went to this dorm party. I was so freaked out. I'd never had a sip of alcohol. Your sister didn't leave my side the whole night. She introduced me to everyone like I was this extremely cool person who had finally deigned to grace them with my — sorry." Her hand pressed against the receiver again. *Jackson, why do I hear video games? . . . Don't "I don't know" me . . . Five minutes . . . Fine, eight.* She sighed. "Sorry. Where were we?"

"My sister took you out with her."

"Right. Anyway, after that she basically adopted me into her friend group." Nika was speaking more hurriedly now. The video game business had pulled her out of the sea of memory and back onto the shore of her busy life. I could sense she was eager to be off the phone, to check this task off of what was surely a long list.

"And when she died?"

"We were shocked. Devastated. The way it happened. I still feel bad I couldn't go to the funeral. It was the middle of exams and I just couldn't leave. Our group stayed together, though. We're all still friends. We go to Steamboat every winter with our kids. My husband, Alex. Alison was always teasing me that he had a thing for me and I never believed her."

"That's so great."

Nika's hand went over the receiver again. *We don't interrupt people on the phone, sweetheart.* "Sorry. What was that?"

"I said it's nice to know all of this."

"Listen, I'm really sorry, but I have to go. But I have a few pictures and notes and things. I can send you color copies for your memory book." I told her I would like that very much and gave her my address. "I really am sorry to dash off. I need to help my son with this project. We're working on a Prezi about the chaparral," she said sardonically.

"I miss the days of the shoe-box diorama,"

I replied, as if I, too, were a harried mother befuddled by my child's Information Age assignments.

Only after I hung up did I realize that my entire body was clenched. This wasn't a nice story about the good my sister had done in her short life. It was a story about Nika's life. Alison was merely the device by which the universe had conspired to ensure Nika's destiny as Nika (Ivanova) Cunningham, mommy to Jackson and Logan. The dead's stories are lifted away from them; they are sentenced to an eternity as deus ex machina in the stories of others.

"Alison Thomas Autopsy Report, Abridged Text," Special to the *New York Post,* March 25, 1996:

Decedent: THOMAS, Alison Brianne

Authorized by: Cardigan Ralston, Coroner

Assisted by: Diandra Young, M.D.

Identified by: Thomas, Ellen, and Thomas, Richard, parents of decedent.

Date of Birth: September 8, 1977

Race: Caucasian

Sex: Female

Length: 165 cm

Weight: 52.6 kg

Eyes: Brown

Hair: Reddish brown

EXTERNAL EXAMINATION

The body is presented in a black body bag. The victim wears no clothing. Jewelry includes three pierced earrings in the left ear: one gold hoop, one gold stud, and one small blue gemstone, and two pierced earrings in the right ear: one gold hoop and one gold stud. Fingernails and toenails are painted sky blue. The body is that of a normally developed, normally nourished Caucasian female. The appearance of age is approximately as stated. The eyes are closed. The irises are light brown. The teeth are native and in good condition. The tongue is smooth, bloated, and white-gray. The hair is reddish brown, straight, and fixed in a ponytail on the top of the head, secured with a yellow elastic band. It measures 35.5 centimetres at its longest length. The genitalia are that of a normally developed adult female. There is a scar measuring 12 centimetres in length on the lower left abdomen, which the parents of the decedent confirm is the result of an accidental injury sustained in 1981. There is significant bloating and draining of the skin, consistent with the body being submerged in non-saline water.

Injuries
The neck is fractured. There is a laceration to the skull measuring 3 centimetres in length, located on the left parietal. There are abrasions to the vulva which suggest recent sexual activity, but the superficial nature of these abrasions is inconclusive as to whether such activity was forcible. No semen is found within the vaginal cavity, though it is not possible to determine whether this is due to the body's submersion.

INTERNAL EXAMINATION
Lungs: Non-saline water is found in both lungs. Sand granules, beige in color, are found in both lungs.

Gastrointestinal, Cardiovascular, and

Urinary systems are normal.

X-Rays
Total body X-rays reveal fracture of the neck located at the C4 vertebrae.

Toxicology
Blood and vitreous fluids positive for ethanols.
Blood and vitreous fluids positive for cannabinoids.

EVIDENCE

Items submitted to the Royal Police Force of Saint X as evidence include: vaginal swabs; oral swabs; samples of hair, eyelashes, and eyebrows; earrings; hair elastic; fingernail clippings; 3 tubes of blood.

OPINION

Time of Death
Body rigor, livor mortis, and stomach contents approximate the time of death between 72 and 96 hours prior to autopsy.

Immediate Cause of Death
Undetermined

Manner of Death
Undetermined

Remarks
Due to the condition of the body at time of autopsy, it is not possible to determine the immediate cause of death. Possible causes include blunt trauma and asphyxiation as a result of submersion. It is not possible to determine whether manner of death was accidental, intentional, or forcible.

Statement to the Press, Prentice Carter, Chief of Police, April 10, 1996:
The Royal Police Force is aware of the intense global interest in our investigation of the January 3rd death of American teenager Alison Thomas on our island. Our investigation into this matter has been conducted with the utmost seriousness and meticulousness, with the full resources of our department and in close cooperation with the Federal Bureau of Investigation. Our department has conducted interviews with over one hundred witnesses. I can share with you at this time that on the night of her death, multiple witnesses confirm that Alison Thomas was present at Paulette's Place, located at 24 Underhill Road,

where, again, multiple witnesses attest that she appeared heavily intoxicated, a fact toxicology reports confirm. Witnesses describe her as wearing a revealing shirt and dancing provocatively with several patrons. A bartender has confirmed serving Thomas at least four drinks, including a shot of vodka infused with cannabis. Over a dozen witnesses provided testimony that Ms. Thomas was engaged in wild partying during the several nights preceding her death. Every effort has been made by our department to follow every possible lead in this case. Edwin Hastie and Clive Richardson are no longer considered to be suspects in this case; at present, Mr. Richardson is serving a ninety-day sentence for an unrelated charge of drug possession. At this time, there are no other suspects in this case, and we do not find sufficient evidence that Alison Thomas died as the result of a violent crime to continue our investigation.

Statement to the Press, Rick and Ellen Thomas, April 11, 1996:

We, the parents of Alison Thomas, reject absolutely the conclusions of Chief of Police Carter and the Royal Police Force of Saint X. At this time, we plead with anyone who may have knowledge of the circumstances surrounding our daughter's death to please come forward so that this case can be reopened as it should be. We will not rest until those responsible for our daughter's death are found and punished to the full extent of the law.

We want to end with a message to other parents. Please, hug your children a little tighter tonight. We pray that what happened to our beautiful daughter will never happen to another girl.

The beautiful daughter had died. What daughter, meanwhile, had lived?

A cold drizzle was falling the next evening when I made my way to the Little Sweet. I stood beneath the awning of the grocery as usual and watched Clive Richardson sit at the table he always sat at, doing the things he always did.

A few minutes later, I watched him push back his chair, carry his tray to the trash, and scrape the remains of his dinner from his plate. But this time I didn't hurry away. Instead, when he approached the door, I lowered my umbrella, concealing myself behind it. I stayed still until Clive exited the

Little Sweet, walked to the end of the block, and turned the corner. Then I followed after him.

I kept my distance, clinging to the shadows cast by shop awnings, clutching the umbrella, white-knuckled, ready to hide my face should he turn around. He walked north on Nostrand, passing storefronts that would, in the months to come, become intimately familiar to me: Health-wise Pharmacy. US Fried Chicken & Pizza. Immaculee Bakery. Red Apple Nails. Winthrop Hardware. I slowed my pace, letting the distance between us lengthen. KBB Shipping. Beulah United Church of God. I followed Clive for over an hour as he turned right, left, right again, heading in no particular direction, at least as far as I could discern, down the rain-sweetened streets. Finally, he made his way to a residential area not far from where we'd begun, block after block of midrise buildings, their exteriors sand-colored brick zigzagged with fire escapes. In the middle of a block, Clive turned and walked up the steps of a building that looked like all the others. He reached into the pocket of his windbreaker and took out his keys. He fumbled a bit with the lock.

I hadn't planned what I did next. I didn't

even realize I was doing it until it was done, until the shout — "Gogo!" — had left my lips and was coming back to me as an echo off the wet bricks and the soft night air.

I tucked into the shadow of a plane tree as Clive Richardson whipped around.

"Who's there?" he called out. The street was empty, silent. "Who said that?" He stood frozen halfway through the door. "Leave me alone! Do you hear me? Leave me alone!"

He let the door slam shut behind him and was gone.

Gogo

It was the wind. It was someone on the next block yelling, "No, no, no!" It was a dog barking. There are any number of explanations for what he heard: a voice, which surely wasn't a voice at all, calling that name. In the days that follow, he is vigilant with himself. If he catches his mind spinning during his shift, he turns the radio to a Christian station and brings his focus to the words of the sermon. On his nightly walks, when he notices his pace growing frantic, he forces himself to slow down. In the apartment, he busies himself: he wipes down the stove, gives his teeth a long brushing rather than his usual cursory going-over. He even strikes up a conversation with Cecil, listening attentively as his roommate recounts the surprising turn of events from the variety show he watched the night before — a magician was beaten out by a unicyclist for a spot in the grand finale. He nods as Cecil delivers a speech that he has clearly been working out in his head for some time about what makes the show so entertaining; it has to do with the apples-and-oranges comparisons the show requires. How ought one to measure the talent of a contortionist against that of a stand-up comedian? Who is more impressive, a one-in-a-million ventriloquist or an excellent opera singer? Anything to crowd out the voice. *Gogo.* It is not the first time he has heard his name on the wind, there and then gone. He knows where it can lead, and he does not want to go back there.

The voice is mostly dormant in the daylight, so that each day he thinks he has conquered it. But at night it resurfaces, the darkness so thick with it he could choke. *Gogo.* Again and again he tells himself he did not hear what he thinks he heard. After all, how could it be? He hasn't been Gogo to anyone in a long, long time.

It was the first day of second grade and Clive Richardson's grandmother had buttoned his pink uniform polo all the way to the top. They sat together at the kitchen table, where his grandmother had prepared a breakfast of fried jackfish and bakes and bush tea in blue enamel cups. As he ate,

Clive tugged at the collar. His grandmother, who ate her fish in big quick bites, grabbed his hand and held it.

"None of this fidgeting."

He nodded. Things were like this with her, prickly and wonderfully firm. She removed her hand and they continued eating.

"You will make some nice friends today. Good boys."

It was a habit of hers, this way of speaking, as if the future were not in doubt; as if she were merely waiting for it to come along and cooperate. It had been less than a month since he had come to live with her, and as he sat in her kitchen, with its lacy white curtain fluttering against the open window and its smell of allspice and everything in its place — the yellow jug of oil beside the stove, pink beans soaking on the counter, margarine in the dish with the rosebud border on the table — it was still a new, miraculous comfort to be in the care of an adult who was so firmly in command and in possession of such a clear-eyed vision of what ought to happen. He would go to school and make nice friends. He wanted this very much. But he was unsettled, too, because he worried that even his grandmother's oracular proclamation would not be powerful enough to bring about something so unlikely, for he was seven years old and had never had a friend. Not really. Only if you counted Vaughn, who called him "Big Man," but Vaughn was his mother's special friend, so he knew he didn't really count. There was also Jeremiah, who lived down the street from his mother's house, but Jeremiah was simpleminded and it humiliated Clive that one of the only people he might count as a friend was simpleminded, so he did not want to count him.

"Y-y-yes, Gran," he said.

She cupped his cheek with her palm. "You a good boy, Clive." With these words, too, he sensed her trying to speak something into being, to wrangle the loose threads of the past into a neat and orderly present.

Clive had come to live with his father's mother when his mother departed for Saint Thomas to find work. His father was dead, a fact that did not make him sad because he did not remember him. This troubled him, because he was four when his father died, and he did have memories of being four. He remembered getting nipped by a black and white goat, and how his mother spanked the goat on its backside like a naughty child. He remembered Claude Félix, the old fisherman with clouds in his eyes who walked the streets of the village at sundown, stopping at his customers' houses to deliver parcels of fish wrapped in brown paper; he remembered the evening his mother told him that Claude Félix had gone to his eternal rest. But he had no memories of his own father or his death, and so these other memories filled him with shame.

On the day of his mother's departure, she packed his things into half a dozen Goody Mart bags and one of her friends drove them across the island from Bendy Harbour to his grandmother's house in the Basin. She opened the front door when they were still coming up the road. She crossed her arms and stood in the doorway.

"This how you bring my grandchild to me? With he possession all in disarray?" she said when they were standing on the porch in front of her.

"I need the suitcase, Nella."

"How silly I be! *You* need the suitcase."

"How I'm supposed to get on the plane without one?" his mum snapped.

For what felt like forever, his grandmother stood there, her arms crossed, and looked at his mum with eyes as blunt as wood.

"Convenient you not taking he with you, then, or what would you use for he luggage?"

For weeks his mother had spoken heavily

of her impending departure, as if their separation were a thing over which she had no control. Now he understood this wasn't the case. She could take him. She wasn't. What a fool he was, no better than Jeremiah.

His mother knelt beside him and squeezed him tightly. "Mama will miss you so, my love."

His body went rigid. He couldn't let go. Finally, his grandmother pulled him away, uncurling his clenched fingers from around his mother's neck. She held him fast against her as his mother got into her friend's car and drove away. When the car disappeared from view, he began to sob. His grandmother patted his back. "Come, now," she whispered, and led him inside. When he had exhausted himself from crying, she changed him into an old nightshirt that had belonged to his grandfather and tucked him into bed. When he awoke in the middle of the night, aching and confused, she brought him into the kitchen and fixed him a warm bowl of the most delicious pepper pot he'd ever tasted.

It was hard to explain what he felt for his grandmother and his new life in her home. He knew that things were better here. Her house was spotless. For breakfast there was fish and corn porridge or flour pap instead of Frosties with Nido. They went to St. George's Anglican Church on Sundays. She filled a bath for him every evening, and with a rough cloth and a bar of Ivory soap she scrubbed him, a task she completed with an unceremonious physicality bereft of gentleness and harshness alike. He was required to make his bed each morning and read a psalm each evening, and even though he did not enjoy doing these things, he could feel the goodness of them.

At his mother's house he did not have a proper bedtime. Often, she went out at night, and he stayed up, snacking on crisps and pitching marbles on the floor until the house grew dark and he dropped off to sleep. Sometimes he woke in the night to voices and unfamiliar laughter. He would stumble into the kitchen to find his mother and a few others sitting around the kitchen table with the kerosene lamp with the blue base at its center, smoking hand-rolled cigarettes whose smoke tickled his nostrils with its strange funk. "Come here, Big Man," Vaughn would say if he was there. Clive would climb into his lap. "Thirsty?" Vaughn asked him once. Clive nodded. Vaughn handed him his glass. "Just a little sip, Big Man," he said. Clive sputtered as the brown liquid burned down his throat.

Vaughn clapped and laughed and patted him on the head. "Look at you, life of the party."

Yet sometimes he ached for his mother's house. He missed the way she kissed his fingers, one by one. Even when she'd been gone weeks, months, years, his fingertips still prickled with her love and her leaving. He missed the flowers from their yard that she picked and tucked into her hair; sometimes at night when she wasn't around he went out into the yard in the moonlight and touched the flowers and imagined he was touching her. He missed going to the harbor with her at Christmastime, when the boat from Saint Croix brought ice to the island; on the pier, she would hold him up high above the crowd and he would watch as a man threw salt crystals into a machine, turned a crank, and churned out ice cream.

On Sunday evenings, nearly everyone in Bendy Harbour gathered at the home of the only family in the village with a generator and a television. They turned the television so that it faced the yard, and everyone sat outside together to watch. Usually he and his mother did not join their neighbors, so on Sunday nights Clive sat at home knowing everyone else was together without him. But once in a while they went, and he sat on his mother's lap among all the people he had ever known and had never not known as the sun went down. They watched *Rawhide* and *The Wild Wild West,* cheered as Andre the Giant took on Killer Khan or Kamala. When the generator wound down for the night, someone would light a lamp, and the stories would begin. This was what Clive missed most: drifting to sleep in his mother's arms as voices that were as familiar to him as his own skin conjured faraway, long-ago worlds.

There were stories about the men who had left the island at the beginning of the century and sailed to the Dominican Republic aboard the schooner *Lady Ann* to cut cane, or to Trinidad to work in the oil refineries, about fishermen and sailors and their trips to Aruba and Cuba and Curaçao and the things they had seen — the port of Santo Domingo, the club Sans Souci and the Malecón in Havana. There was the story of a cane cutter who came upon a beautiful woman one night along a desolate stretch of road. The next thing he knew, he was waking up beneath a silk-cotton tree in the forest in broad daylight. His shoes were gone — his feet were caked in dirt and blood. When he finally found his way to a road, he discovered he had traveled some twenty kilometers from where he had been walking the night before — he had crossed mountains and rivers but remembered nothing.

There were stories about the *Lady Ann* — how when Jonathan Bell's great-grandfather sailed the schooner back from Santo Domingo to see his dying father, it made the journey a day faster than ever before and he arrived just in time to kiss his father goodbye; of the salt she transported to Trinidad, and how, after the barrels had been unloaded, the deck glittered with fine white crystals like stars. There were stories about salt, how during the reaping months it was not uncommon to pull a cake heavier than a small child from the Thomasvale Pond. There was the story of Harlan Ghaut, who was walking the Old Vale Road past the salt pond when he saw a finned woman sunning herself on the rocks, or so he claimed. Harlan returned to the spot every day, but he never saw her again, until he returned late one night and found her perched on the rock, opening her fin and unfurling two human feet. Twenty years later, Harlan was sitting in his apartment in London watching television when this very same mermaid flashed across the screen.

There were stories about Janet and Alice and Carla and Camille, the great storms that had leveled the island before Clive was born — how roofs lifted off houses and people looked up from their beds into the skies of heaven, how cars spun like bottles in the streets, how the wind stripped houses clean of their paint, and how the paint, carried on gale winds, could cut you up like glass. The sinking of the *Lady Ann* in Britannia Bay.

Then there was the story Clive loved best, the one he begged his mother to tell as she tucked him in, about a long-haired woman with hooves for feet who lived on Faraway Cay.

"Is she real?" Clive would ask.

"For true. Your Great-Aunt Ruth got lured away by she. Poof. Vanish like so."

("Ha!" his grandmother snorted when he asked if she believed Ruth had been taken by the woman on Faraway Cay. "I believe your auntie had she reasons to get lost; that's what I believe.") His grandmother did not tell stories. With her, the world was just itself.

His mother had been gone less than a year when the island's first ice plant opened. You could buy a twenty-kilo block of it; men churned ice cream and shaved ice on the pier year-round. You no longer had to wait for the boat from Saint Croix at Christmastime, and you quickly forgot what a wonder it had once been to sit on the pier, your feet dangling over the flickering sea, and taste the coldness of ice cream while the sun beat hot on your shoulders. Not long after that, electricity came to the island's villages. Soon, lots of people had televisions and the gatherings and the stories ceased. Next the telephone wires went up. In no time, Mayfair Road was paved, and then Investiture Boulevard, and soon all the streets in the Basin. Then the resorts came, and with them the tourists, and everything changed.

And so, for Clive, the sleepy, magical feeling of childhood was inextricably bound up with the island as it was before — with the smell of kerosene and the sounds of stories in the dark — which were, in turn, bound up with his mother. And as the years passed without her she became, like his father, a disquieting emptiness right at the center of him where he thought there should have been sadness.

Horatio Byrd Primary was three times the size of Bendy Harbour Primary, where Clive had attended first grade. It was a low, horseshoe-shaped concrete building painted white with blue trim. On the inside of the horseshoe, children ran and shrieked across the packed-dirt schoolyard. Clive tugged at the collar of his polo.

"Stop that," his grandmother said.

He didn't know how she saw — she wasn't even looking at him. He stopped.

"Go on," she said.

He took a few shuffling steps forward. When he turned to look back at her, she was already halfway across the yard. He watched as she strode in her black shoes through the gate and out of sight.

The classroom was not so different from the first-grade room at Bendy Harbour. The long wooden tables were the same. The girls wore the same jumpers and blouses, only here they were maroon and pink instead of green and white. The boys all wore pink polos and maroon trousers like him, though the other boys did not have their shirts buttoned to the top. He wanted to loosen his but didn't dare. Somehow, his grandmother would know. On the wall above the blackboard there was even the same illustrated alphabet: a balloon for *B,* a goat for *G,* an igloo for *I,* and, his favorite, a mermaid for *M.* He looked at the familiar picture, the pink and green scales of the mermaid's tail, her hair swirling around her head in curlicues, and felt calm.

The teacher, a tall, kind-faced woman

named Miss Forsyth, took attendance.

"Annmarie Bell."

"Present."

"Don Claxton."

"Present."

"Damien Fleming."

"Present."

As she made her way steadily and inexorably through the alphabet, his mouth grew dry until it stuck together, teeth to tongue to roof.

"Edwin Hastie."

Silence.

"Edwin Hastie?"

A boy in the last row shot up as if he'd just jolted awake. "Yes!"

Everybody tittered.

"Yes what, Mr. Hastie?"

"Yes, I be present."

"I *am* present."

"I hope so, Miss Forsyth. You is our teacher."

The class broke into laughter. Clive laughed, too, though his was a nervous laughter; his turn was still coming.

"Sara Lycott," Miss Forsyth said, cutting off the ruckus like thwacking a weed with a scythe.

"Present, Miss Forsyth."

"Daphne Nelsen."

"Present."
"Desmond Phillips."
"Present."
"Ron Rawlins."
"Present."
"Clive Richardson."
He opened his mouth, but his throat wrung itself up. His ears went hot, as if pricked by bees.
"P-p-p-"
Thirty pairs of eyes converged on him.
"P-p-p-"
He searched the ceiling desperately.
"P-p-p-*present.*" The word came out much too loud, like an angry shout. They were all laughing again, harder than they had when Edwin Hastie pulled his stunt.
"Enough," Miss Forsyth said. "Thank you, Clive." She smiled very sweetly at him, which made it worse.
They spent the morning on maths. Miss Forsyth wrote equations on the board. She had beautiful handwriting. Each numeral was like a flower. She called students up one at a time to work the problems out. *If Michael has seven nails and John has twelve, how many more nails does John have than Michael? Marie has seventeen yards of fabric. If she needs four yards to make a skirt, how many skirts can she make?*

Each time Miss Forsyth read a question, Clive's mind flailed. The words tumbled together, twisting into strange shapes in his head. He tried to sort it out while praying he would not be called upon, because in addition to not understanding the questions, he also had to urinate very badly. He had drunk all of his tea at breakfast. But he could not bring himself to ask to use the toilet because he knew he would not be able to get the words out.

"Johnny has a dozen eggs. If he eats four for breakfast, what does he have left? Edwin?"

The skinny boy swaggered up to the blackboard. His trousers were too big for him — they were cinched to his waist with a belt, bunched and sagging. He took the chalk from Miss Forsyth and wrote: *g-a-s.*

The class doubled over with laughter. Miss Forsyth allowed herself a very brief smile.

"The corner," she said. Edwin swaggered there, too. "You see, class, Edwin might be the smartest boy here but he treats everything as a joke so we will never know."

In the corner, Edwin Hastie played with the collar of his polo, flipping it up and down as if he hadn't heard Miss Forsyth. His eyes flashed as if lit by a brewing storm.

After maths, Miss Forsyth distributed copies of the *Higham Brothers Reader* and they went down the rows from the front of the room to the back, each student reading aloud in turn from a story about an American man who planted apple seeds wherever he went. Clive barely heard the words. He was now focused entirely on squeezing his legs together against the unbearable pressure of his bladder. He turned the page of his reader. The American, barefoot and with a tin pot on his head, lay next to a river — blue and white and foamy, full of rushing water. He could hold it no longer. As Daphne Nelsen read in the pinched, nasal voice he would hate forever after, he tentatively pressed his fingers into the air.

"Yes, Clive?" Miss Forsyth said, cutting off Daphne midsentence. The eyes were on him again.

"May I g-g-g-"

It would happen. He would wet himself right here, in front of the entire class, on his first day at his new school.

"May I go — go — go —"

Miss Forsyth saw his anguish and understood. "Yes! Hurry!"

Bent at the waist, fumbling over his feet, he dashed from the classroom. In the hall, he put both hands on his crotch and ran, and when he reached the latrine and released a torrent of urine he felt simultaneously so grateful and so humiliated that his eyes filled with tears.

When playtime came, he made for a deserted corner of the yard. As the girls played marbles and the boys engaged in a rough game of tag, he sat, pulling clumps of dry grass from the dirt. He was himself all over again. In his mortification, he found a certain peace. He had his spot in the yard, and every day at playtime he would come to it and keep his own company. He thought of his mother. Where was she now? Did she know it was his first day of school? He pictured her tapping at a typewriter in a white room.

Boys were coming toward him. The troublemaker, Edwin, was leading a pack of them; he cupped his hands around his mouth and shouted: "Hey, Go-Go!"

The other boys clapped.

Don hooted. "Yes! That's right! G-g-g-go-go!"

Clive kept his eyes on his lap.

"Gogo, man, me speaking with you," Edwin said.

Clive forced himself to look up. To his surprise, Edwin was grinning down at him, his expression teasing but — could it be? — warmly so.

"We having a cricket match, we against they." He gestured across the yard, where a few other boys milled about. Clive sat, uncomprehending, until Edwin exclaimed, "What you waiting for? Get up, man! We need you!"

Clive stood, wiped the dust from the seat of his trousers, and followed.

They won the game, though no thanks to Clive, who, for the most part, stood in one place and hoped not to make a mistake. From then on, he and Edwin were always together. You never saw one without the other, and if you did, it likely meant some mischief was afoot of which you would turn out to be the unfortunate recipient. They did many things, Edwin and Clive and the rest of Edwin's band of brothers, Don and Des and Damien. They caught bait and went to Little Beach, where they fished from the pier, diving and backflipping into the sea when they were hot. They played wind-ball cricket in the sand and had swimming races — first one to the end of the pier, or to the *Atalanta* moored in the shallows. ("I get you back!" Don shouted when Edwin grabbed his leg to slow him down. "I drown you! I gonna drown you!") They built traps and caught turtledoves. They shook tamarind pods from the tree in Damien's yard and mixed the sticky brown pulp with sugar and water. Begged a dollar off Edwin's mother for sugar cakes. When Clive's grandmother baked buns, they stole them right out of the oven, slathered them quickly with red butter, then ran out of the house and down the street, tossing the hot buns in the air.

In fifth grade, they rode their bikes often to the beach that would, a few years later, become Indigo Bay. It was still wild then. The land was covered by pomme-serette trees, and they would pick the fruit, though only one in ten was sweet. The beach stank from seaweed and the seaweed was full of bad things — needles and condoms, which they would lift with sticks and fling at each other. Sometimes they would find two antimen together on the sand. They would sneak and watch them and then Edwin would shout, *Go!* and they would stampede and chase them off.

They scaled the chain-link fence and climbed the island's radio tower, a rickety structure flaking red paint. Clive was a quarter of the way up, far below his friends, when Edwin shouted down to him, "Look *out,* Goges. Why bother climbing if you don't see anything?" He gripped the metal rung as tightly as he could and raised his head. He never forgot it. He could follow the ribbon of Mayfair Road from Horatio Byrd past the governor-general's pink house and the eggshell-blue prison; he could see how the water fanned out around the island in bands of deepening hues — from a pale, milky green like Claude Félix's cataracts to a bright turquoise and finally a deep, sparkling blue. If he squinted, he could make out Bendy Harbour — hardly more than the idea of it, a loose sketch of houses, one of which had been his. He could see his whole life spread before him — past, present, future — and the solidness of this image made him want to collect it like a coin and keep it in his pocket forever.

The island's first movie hall opened when they were thirteen, and Edwin and Clive made a habit of sneaking out of Everett Lyle Secondary to catch the matinee. They waited until five minutes after the showing time so the theater was dark, then snuck in through the side door, vigilant in case Wilmot, the old man who managed the ticket booth, should come down the aisle with his flashlight. The movie hall showed a mix of old movies — westerns and kung fu, mostly — and new releases. They'd sneak into the same movie many times, timing it to catch their favorite scenes. Clive knew *Pale Rider* and *Way of the Dragon* and *Ghostbusters* by heart. Occasionally he discovered that Edwin had left school without him, and he knew that Edwin was in the warm theater, which smelled of stale popcorn and sweat, watching *E.T.* cycle across the face of the moon for the fourth, fifth, twelfth time.

Often the movies had been out in the States a year or longer by the time they reached the island. To Clive this was unremarkable. Everything took time to reach the island. Newspapers came a week late, by way of Saint Kitts by way of Jamaica. The TV stations showed *Bonanza* and *I Dream of Jeannie* and *The Beverly Hillbillies.*

For Edwin, this was a source of immense frustration.

"When you getting *Rocky IV*?" he asked Wilmot one day on the way out.

"What are you boys doing here with no ticket?"

"I ask you first. *Rocky IV* out a year already. When you getting it?"

"When the poster go up. When you think?"

"Come on, man! Bad enough we live nowhere. Why we also have to live yesterday?"

In the beginning, Clive was wary of Edwin's friendship. Why *him*? There were other boys Edwin could have chosen. There was Arthur, for example, not a cool boy by any means and a definite brown-nose, but still miles cooler than him, and besides, Arthur came with the advantages of his father's convenience store with the satellite television in the back room. Yet Edwin had not chosen Arthur. (Nobody had chosen Arthur, who, for some mysterious reason, had been left entirely outside the world of friendship.) Had Edwin selected him merely because of his size — had he been seeking a protector, an enforcer? Or perhaps Clive had been chosen because he was quiet and went along with Edwin's schemes. But despite his wariness, Clive knew the true reason went deeper than this. In the end, friendship was not a thing that could be explained. It was a kind of magic. Either it existed or it didn't. Edwin said they were mates and so they were, and Clive was grateful for it.

Many years later, he would sit in a small restaurant in an unfamiliar city, as snow — a thing he always assumed he'd die without touching — fell from the sky, and he would trace back through his life and conclude that the moment Edwin approached him in the schoolyard was *the* moment. The one after which everything that happened was always going to happen. The one you could wonder and wonder about but never touch: What if he'd simply stayed in the grass?

Ever after that day, Clive was Gogo. First to his classmates, then to his neighbors, then even, at times, to his grandmother. Because it was Edwin who gave him this name, and because it was also Edwin who brought him from the darkness of solitude into the light of friendship, he quickly forgot that the name had begun with his own mortification.

I wasn't trying to "control the narrative" by taking that douche journalist from *Esquire* to the Station. Sure, the kids in this town love the deli because it's a dive; they show up after lacrosse practice, or late night, six-to-a-Beemer, and chat up the counter guys like they're just regular kids. The thing is, I like these kids. For all their privilege, they're mostly unspoiled. It's a town of Nice Kids, really, just a couple of sniveling "My dad is a lawyer and blah blah blah" pains in the ass here and there. But none of that has anything to do with why I suggested we meet at the Station for the interview. It's just my usual place. I'm a teacher. Where else in this town am I supposed to go for a two-buck egg sandwich?

So, no, I wasn't trying to "control the narrative." But there are things I didn't tell him. Things I didn't trust some sleek journalist with. (Horn-rimmed glasses and a tweed blazer, and I'm the one trying to manipulate the optics? Please.) Things it wouldn't have done anybody any good to see in print.

I didn't tell him about her essays. Alison always developed these wildly contrarian thesis statements. Macbeth *can best be understood as a feminist work in which Lady Macbeth is the true hero.* Catch-22 *glamorizes war.* Or my favorite: *While it might seem to depict human nature as savage and anarchic,* Lord of the Flies *ultimately works against the author's own intentions and conveys the endurance of civilization and order.* She was one hell of a writer, and she did crazy acrobatics in the essays to defend what were, basically, incorrect readings of the texts. Intentionally incorrect. She seemed to be under the impression that the best essay is the one that gets people to believe whatever it wants them to believe, even if that thing can't possibly be true. I always wanted to tell her in my comments that just because you win an argument doesn't make you right.

But I always felt a bit nervous critiquing her, to be honest. She was smarter than me,

I have no qualms about admitting it. She knew it and I knew it. I wanted to tell her that just because you're smarter than some-one doesn't mean they don't have things to teach you, but I didn't tell her that, either. I gave her her A's and figured somewhere down the line of her education she'd figure out how to apply her talents in a way that went beyond hot-dogging.

I didn't tell the journalist about the time I closed the classroom door on that poor chubby kid when he was late on test day, and Alison got in a confrontation with me about it, which was entirely inappropriate. The longer the argument went on, the clearer it became that she had the whole class on her side and I was at real risk of losing their good faith in an all-out mutiny that would screw up the classroom dynamic for the rest of the school year. I've always been a really popular teacher, too. Every-body wants to be in Conti's class. That's the sway she had with her classmates.

I didn't tell him about the way she rolled her eyes at these same classmates when they made a comment in class that she found obvious or dumb.

I didn't tell him about the time I went to

the Station for a late-night grading session and she was there, alone at a table in the back, eating cheese fries. She must have come from dance rehearsal — she wore leggings and a sweatshirt unzipped over a black leotard.

"Care to join me, Mr. Conti?"

Fool that I am, I sat.

"Fry?"

I ate.

I asked her how college applications were going.

"Fine," she sighed, as if she hardly cared, which I knew couldn't be true, not a smart, ambitious kid like her. "Can I ask you something, Mr. Conti?" she said.

I told her she could.

"Doesn't it bother you, spending your existence with a bunch of high schoolers?"

I said if it did, would I have become a high school teacher? I felt pretty smart about that response.

"It would make me crazy." She stared right at me as she said that. Under the table, she brushed her foot against my leg.

I told her I had to get going. She smirked, like she thought I was a wuss or something. I was totally freaked out to see her in my class the next day, but she acted completely normal, as if nothing had happened. After a few days, it started to feel that way.

After she died, the last thing she said to me that night kept coming back to me. *It would make me crazy.* What was her game with that, exactly? She was not admiring my capacity for working with young people, that's for sure. No, she was telling me she could never do what I did because she was different from me. Better.

The thing is, from then on teaching did start to drive me crazy. Before, I'd spend hours writing comments on my students' essays, and then I'd see the kids flip straight to the back, look at the grade, and chuck the papers in the trash, and I'd shrug it off. After, stuff like that enraged me. I started to see very clearly the way my life's work was just "second period" to the kids. I started seeing it the way she saw it, I started seeing *me* the way she saw me, and the foundational satisfaction of my life was chipped away at. Not completely, but some.

This is a town of Nice Kids, but Alison Thomas was not one of them. She had talent to burn. She could be very passionate. She had a personal power that she often used as a force for good. But she was not Nice.

EVIDENCE

How frightened Clive Richardson had been when he heard me call that name! The secrets of his past were there, submerged but still hot to the touch. If I played things out right, I was certain I could bring them to the surface. But what then? Was my end game public punishment? Private vengeance? Did I imagine Clive Richardson in handcuffs? Brought to his own watery end in the Gowanus? These possibilities and many others floated in my mind, but I dared not envision any of them too fully. The truth. First I must have the truth.

Autumn continued: the sidewalks grew cluttered with fallen leaves and the pink fruits of ginkgo trees, which released their bilious stink as they rotted on the pavement. I spent an evening battling with Time Warner over my spotty Wi-Fi. Jefe the dog had an accident on the faded green carpet in the hallway. It was determined that

Astrid's latest novel would be titled *The Girl from Pendeen;* the fact that the titles of two of her previous novels contained the word *Girl* was decided, after much discussion, to be a non-issue, even a boon. I continued to call my parents every Sunday, conversations that increasingly became exercises in dissembling. I told them I'd begun attending yoga classes in the evenings.

"That's wonderful, sweetheart," my mother said.

"Yoga is supposed to be great for your alignment," my father said.

(I'd intended to convince them, but was still irritated by how easily they'd been fooled.)

The reality was that my evenings were now almost wholly devoted to Clive. I would linger around the Little Sweet until he departed, then follow him. Clive Richardson, I learned quickly, was a walker. He might stroll for an hour, even two, before heading home. When he reached his brick apartment building, I waited until a light on the fourth floor turned on and then, some twenty or thirty minutes later, turned off again; only then did I make my own way home. On my walk back, I would realize that I was soaked in sweat. I was terrified as I followed Clive — of being seen, of what I might see — but it was a terror that held itself at bay until I was away from him, when it came over me all at once.

On these walks, I experienced what might be described as a state of hypervigilance. I attended to every detail, every movement, searching for any scrap that might provide insight into the man Clive Richardson was and the secrets he was guarding. What ought I to make of the routes he chose? Or of the way he scuffed his black loafers against the pavement? Back at my apartment late at night, I would try to get myself to read through the mounting backlog of manuscripts in my work in-box, but I quickly found myself lost in imaginative labor: What did he think about before he fell asleep? What was in his refrigerator? What did his bedroom look like? (I pictured a stark, simple room — a rough-hewn wood floor, a simple twin bed, a small wicker chair. This mental picture had arrived fully formed, which I took as a testament to my imaginative powers; a few years later, on a visit to the Orsay, I would realize that the image was not even mine — it was *Bedroom in Arles,* Vincent Van Gogh.)

It wasn't only Clive's actions I attended to. Everything I passed seemed anointed by his presence. Graffiti on a brick wall: *Ro-*

chelle, marry me?? A man in a dastaar selling incense on a street corner. A fruit stand with a handwritten cardboard sign: BANANAS 4 FOR 1$! The sweet and sour rivulets of liquid eroding the sidewalk in front of a halal butcher. Did he notice these things? If he did, what did they make him think, want, remember? Clive's world became my evidence — a rush of details, almost unbearably vivid, the landscape infused by a sense of the significance of all things.

From "Secrets on Faraway Cay," *Dateline,* July 12, 1996:

JANE PAULEY: You worked in security at Indigo Bay.

HAROLD MOSES: [nods] For seven years. During which time I was employee of the month on four occasions.

JANE PAULEY: You saw Alison Thomas on the night of her death?

HAROLD MOSES: I certainly did, Ms. Pauley.

JANE PAULEY: Tell me about that.

HAROLD MOSES: [sips coffee] It was eight p.m. I know so because I just return from my toilet break, which I take nightly at seven-forty p.m. precisely. I was doing my rounds. By the swimming pool I see the girl dipping she toe in the water.

JANE PAULEY: Did you say anything to her?

HAROLD MOSES: [shakes head] I didn't want to disturb she. She appeared quite peaceful, like she was having some special time to she self. I saw clearly she had a sweet soul.

JANE PAULEY: What happened next?

HAROLD MOSES: [shakes head sadly] She walked away, over to the bar. This is the last time I see she. But everybody know later that night she went out with those two good-for-nothings. I have a theory about what happened to she, Ms. Pauley. Would you like to hear it?

JANE PAULEY: Please.

HAROLD MOSES: I believe it is a crime

of passion. That girl was pretty. Oh, she was pretty pretty. I have one more thing I wish to say, Ms. Pauley. I want your viewers to know that I carry it heavy in my heart that for this girl I may be the last kind face of this world.

Statement to the Press, for Immediate Release, January 12, 1996:

While on a recent vacation in the Caribbean, I participated in a day trip to an uninhabited island. On this island, as has been widely reported, myself and a companion discovered the body of a young woman who had been missing for several days. Contrary to several grossly misleading recent reports, I had <u>no involvement</u> in the disappearance of Alison Thomas. I have participated in the local investigation to the full extent of my ability. <u>I am not a suspect in this case.</u> Reports suggesting otherwise are an assault on my character. I would like to extend my deepest sympathies to the Thomas family. I ask that my privacy be respected during this time.

From *Tragedy in Paradise: The Untold Story of the Alison Thomas Murder* by Craig Sheppard:

. . . The frantic hunt for the beautiful

teenager continued, transforming the sleepy island with an all-out search that left no stone unturned. Unbeknownst to the police, at this same time, a Haitian man by the name of Siméon Payen was flying from Saint X to Miami, where he owned a palatial beachfront property and was well-known to law enforcement as a key player in La Petite Haïti, a small but notorious Miami cartel. By the time you turn the final page of this book, dear reader, I think you will agree that these two events were anything but a coincidence, and that on a small island, corruption can run deep. . . .

From the "Unsolved Mysteries" subreddit, Reddit.com:

I'm totally new to this sub, so bear with me, but this case is one of my first memories of being totally obsessed with an unsolved mystery and it remains one of my favorites to this day. I've read a LOT about it over the years, and I have to say I've always questioned the Haitian cartel angle, which first came out in the Sheppard book (his book on Thomas is in my personal opinion one of his weaker efforts, and I'm usually a big fan of his). I mean, doesn't it seem like a huge stretch that

Payen would involve this girl in a run, with the risks that would entail for *him*? I know a lot of you here subscribe to the Payen theory, but I've always believed that the simplest and most elegant solution is usually the right one.

Stick with me here. Imagine the police know pretty much beyond a doubt it's Richardson and Hastie. Or it doesn't even have to be them — maybe it's some other local, maybe it's a police officer's kid. A PR disaster for the island, in other words. So what do they do? They fabricate evidence that these two dudes were actually locked up in jail by 1 a.m. or whenever, and once that's done, it's, "Sorry, the timeline doesn't work and there are no other suspects. Case closed, island open for business." This theory works on So. Many. Levels. Think about it. I mean, doesn't it seem just the tiniest bit convenient that the thing that gets those guys off is coming from the *police*?

That message board alone had over nine hundred posts. As I continued to search, I found countless other boards on other websites dedicated to Alison. Across the digital underworld, people were still trying their hands at solving her murder. Scrolling through these posts, reading theory after theory, I felt physically sick. There were thousands of them — these dudes (they were almost all men) using Alison's murder to distract them from their basement-and-weed lives, crafting some loser fantasy that they might be the one to solve it.

It's difficult to separate things out. To determine how much of my disgust at these men was genuine, and how much I was drumming it up, seizing upon an easy opportunity to feel disgusted, indignant, violated by anonymous people I would never know or have to confront. These online forums. Craig Sheppard lining his pockets. The memoir that actor's ex-girlfriend published where she described Alison's body. *Dying for Fun*'s absurd version of her death (Apollo! My god . . .). The whole razzle-dazzle enterprise of the Alison Thomas Economy — did these things actually pain me, did they really touch the heart of my own personal trauma? Yes and no, they did and they didn't, and this is what made it so hard to parse my own feelings, to separate what I did feel from all the things I *could* feel. At times, it could be very difficult to distinguish where my authentic pain over my sister's death ended and where a performative emotionality, a giving over to the drama opened up by *Alison,* began.

As my surveillance spread so, too, did Clive Richardson's power over my life. Before I began to follow him on his walks, he had been contained by the Little Sweet. It had been possible for me to leave him behind not just physically, but also mentally and emotionally — to go to the gym, for instance, and spend forty minutes on the elliptical feeling inferior to the cellulite-free woman on the machine beside me, and wonder what it must be like to have thighs like that, and remind myself that everybody has problems and surely this woman was no exception, and ponder what they might be, and imagine her cowering on a staircase as a girl, listening to her parents yell and throw things, and then, when she wiped down her machine and our eyes met briefly, to smile at her with great sympathy, and only afterward, as I engaged in some perfunctory stretching on a mat strewn with unnerving hairs, realize that I had not thought of Clive in over an hour. But once I began to follow him, he broke free. His routines became my routines, his patterns my patterns.

One night, he stopped at a church and went inside. I sat on a bench at a nearby bus stop to wait. He was not inside long, maybe ten minutes, and when he emerged, his face was composed. Whatever he had been praying over, I could discern no trace of it. Another evening, he walked by a bodega with buckets of rot-edged roses and blue daisies out front. As he passed them, he reached out his hand and skimmed his fingertips ever so lightly against the flowers.

Alison had kept a diary. It wasn't the usual thing, no lock-and-key notebook with *KEEP OUT!!!* on the cover. It was an audio diary, recorded on one of those cassette players for children with a pink plastic microphone. The player had been mine originally, a birthday gift loaded with parental intentions for the shy child — *Look how much fun you'll have singing, Clairey!* I never used it and at some point Alison appropriated it for her own purposes. Many nights she retreated to her bedroom and recorded. I think she enjoyed hearing herself talk. I don't mean she was vain, nothing like that. I used to sit on the floor outside her room, letting her muffled voice wash over me with the distinct sense that on the other side of the closed door something sacred was transpiring — my sister's soul, bared to the night.

I knew my parents had the cassettes

because when I was eighteen I had asked my mother what happened to them. She told me they were in the box on the top shelf of the hall closet, along with Alison's dance trophies and yearbooks and jazz shoes. When I asked if my parents had listened to them, my mother's face tightened. She was going to cry, and I felt at once guilty and angry. Guilty because I had known my question would upset her and had asked it anyway, angry because I was the child and she was the mother and shouldn't she be making things easier for me, not the other way around? "I started to once," she said. "But I only listened for a minute or two. It wasn't right."

On an evening in late October, I called my mother; it was just after six P.M. in New York, dark and cold.

"It's so good to hear from you, sweetie." This was what she always said, as if I were doing some extraordinary kindness by calling her. I winced. I pictured her in their sunny kitchen, living a falsely warm, bright existence — didn't she know it was really night? Didn't she know it was almost winter?

"You caught me in the middle of making white gazpacho. I rediscovered the recipe in this ancient cookbook I bought after college. Very *woo-woo.*" She laughed self-deprecatingly. "You marinate cucumbers, green grapes, bread, and almonds in salt and let it sit a few hours. Then you puree it and whisk in some yogurt. Isn't that a neat technique?"

My mother could always be counted on to prattle about something we both knew neither of us cared about — the plot of a movie she'd seen with my father, a charity auction she had attended and the offerings donated by various local businesses, a nifty trick she'd learned for chopping onions without crying. (She would send me the YouTube.) My mother was not a superficial woman. She was, in fact, in possession of a piercing intelligence, but for some maddening reason she seemed determined to keep this a secret. She'd been a literature major in college. According to family lore, she was solely responsible for getting our father through his own college coursework. ("Your mother's so smart she tricked me into being the breadwinner," he was fond of saying.) On our bookshelves at home, dispersed among our father's legal procedurals and thick biographies of great American leaders, were my mother's volumes of poetry and the slender, peculiar novels of a female Brazilian writer with whom she was enamored. On Saturday mornings when I was a child, as our family life went on noisily around her, my mother would sit on the couch in the living room with her feet curled beneath her and read as if she were alone in a quiet room, which, in her mind, I think she was. But she never spoke to us about the things she read, and when she set down the book she became our mother again, concerned with locating shin guards and checking worksheets, a woman so ordinary and unglamorous that I remember Alison once theorizing to me that she and Aunt Caroline couldn't possibly be blood sisters — one of them must have been switched at birth, or the product of an illicit affair. I think Alison and I both grew up feeling that our mother kept the best of herself *to* herself, that she was guarding something, protecting something, from *us*. So, no, my mother was not a naturally superficial woman; superficiality was a thing she had chosen, and after Alison's death she chose it more and more. I think she was terribly lonely in Pasadena, despite the busy social life she maintained there; it was an existential loneliness that had everything to do with Alison and that therefore could not be cured. With her bland chatter, I think she was trying to talk her way out of the loneliness, to paper over all the unspoken things, but it never worked, it was all still there, and so she went on talking, and hoping, and talking.

"Very neat," I said.

"I made it once years ago but I forgot all about it. I was cleaning out — I've been trying to clean out the bookcases, and —"

"Mom."

"Hmm?"

"I was wondering. You know Alison's diaries?"

"Yes."

"Would you mind sending them to me?"

She was quiet a moment. "Sure, sweetheart," she said finally. "I'll make copies and pop them in the mail as soon as I can."

I knew she would not ask my reasons for making this request, what had happened or what I was thinking and feeling that made me want them. I didn't even bother proffering a made-up explanation. It was a little unkind of me, and I knew that; my request surely made her worry, and I could easily have told her something to assuage her concern, but I didn't. But you have to understand how much it hurt. No, *Honey, are you sure?* No, *Do you think that's really the best thing?* My mother hid away in her fragile sweetness, and I hated her for the ironic way her fragility protected her.

■ ■ ■ ■

A cold, clear night. Clive left the Little Sweet and headed east for some time before coming to a stop; beneath the glare of a single post light, teenage boys, T-shirts billowing from their bodies, were playing basketball on a chain-link court. Off to the side, a few young boys of about five or six played their own small game. Clive stood with his hands resting against the fence and watched. What was it about this scene that so held his attention? I stood some distance away and watched him watching the boys. They seemed to strobe with toughness and sensitivity, the two forces held in an uneasy tension. A boy dribbled the ball gracefully between his legs one moment, barreled into a defender the next. One of the young boys imitated his movements, then forgot the game and stooped to examine the clover growing up through cracks in the blacktop. A man in a tracksuit swaggered down the street in front of me, a tuckered-out girl in a tutu asleep in his arms. On the sidelines of the basketball game, a boy, still in his school uniform, punched a square of gum out of a foil packet and placed it boldly, tentatively, on a girl's waiting tongue.

There were girls and women, too, of course. Heading home from work in suits and pumps, in scrubs. Mothers with children. Clusters of adolescent girls with rhinestones on the back pockets of their jeans. But it was the men and boys I watched. I admit I had not done very much thinking about the inner lives of men. I was a girl with a sister. With my boyfriends, I saw now, I had never dug beneath the surface to find them where they hid. Perhaps I didn't want their pain to compete with my own. Perhaps my story, my tragedy, had a forbidding power over men, and I enjoyed that. Or perhaps, knowing that a man, or men, had killed my sister, I was afraid of what I might find if I looked too closely — gentleness that turned over to shame that turned over to rage; ugly, unshakable desires — qualities that might suggest a universal masculine poison I did not want to know about because it would doom me to be alone forever.

Clive continued down the sidewalk. He stopped at a newsstand and purchased a cup of coffee, which he drank as he headed north. A few minutes later, without breaking his stride, he tossed the dregs of the coffee into the street with a quick, dispassionate flick of his wrist.

■ ■ ■ ■

The material on Alison was endless, so much it seemed I would never get through it. Information on Clive Richardson and Edwin Hastie, by comparison, was thin at best. One day, I told my boss I needed to consult the archives at the New York Public Library to research some details about the Cornish coast in *The Girl from Pendeen* which she had asked me to confirm, and I spent the afternoon at the main branch, searching the catalog for anything I could find that mentioned Clive and Edwin. My first discovery was an academic text, *Dark Travels: Thanatourism, Theory and Practice.*

CONTENTS

PART 1: ASPECTS OF THANATOURISM

Mediations: The Living and the Dead in Public Space
Milking the Macabre: Ethical Considerations
Kitschification and Mass-Consumption
Hospitality in Hostile Spaces: Towards a New Model

PART 2: FORMS AND FUNCTIONS

Genocide Tourism
Homicide Tourism
Disaster Tourism

PART 3: FUTURE RESEARCH DIRECTIONS

To my disappointment, the book contained only the briefest relevant passage, from the chapter on "Homicide Tourism":

. . . While Genocide Tourism is generally structured by government and nonprofit institutions, Homicide Tourism is often ad hoc, and thus represents an economic opportunity for independent local operators. Examples include Kristján Jóhannsson, who leads tours of Keflavik in southwest Iceland, a site of interest in the Guðmundur and Geirfinnur case; and Desmond Phillips, whose guided tours of the island of Saint X include visits to the houses of Edwin Hastie and Clive Richardson, suspects in the Alison Thomas murder, and a boat ride to the nearby cay where her body was recovered for a fish fry lunch. This essay will focus on the case of the Tyrolean village of Zinn am Alberg, which has rebuilt its local economy, previously dominated by dairy farming and the production of Tyrolean speck, around tourism related to the gruesome 1975 murders of the members of the Krenn family. . . .

The next few books were no more informative. An encyclopedia of unsolved mysteries. A media studies dissertation on the differing portrayals of black and white female victims of violent crime from 1970 to 2000. I had high hopes for *A Handbook History of Saint X,* the only book I'd been able to find that focused exclusively on the island. It turned out to be a self-published monograph by a retired customs worker named David Webster, a hundred spiral-bound pages, peripatetic and ambitious in its scope, with five-page chapters on such topics as the history of the salt trade and the entirety of Amerindian civilization on the island.

From Chapter 8, "1950 to the Present Time":

. . . The death of Alison Thomas on Faraway Cay (see Chapter 11: Folklore), had effects upon our island as deleterious as any hurricane. It has been speculated that the closing of the Grand Caribbee and three restaurants on Mayfair Road in a single season may be entirely attributable to the aforementioned scandal. This scandal had the additional effect of dividing the island over the question of whether its primary suspects, Misters Hastie and Richardson, were the innocent victims of a scapegoating mission by the American press, or, alternately and, this author believes, accurately, the parties responsible for single-handedly causing an economic downturn that endured for years and bringing international notoriety to our island and its people. . . .

From Chapter 11, "Folklore":
. . . Tales about the woman on Faraway Cay are prevalent. In the most widespread account of her origin, she washed up on Faraway many centuries ago in a hurricane. Nobody knows from where she came, but she can never return because as is well known, dark spirits cannot cross salt water, as a result of which she is trapped on the cay for eternity. She has white skin and long black hair and hooves for feet. Mention must be made of her odd gait, which appears in many versions of the tale, and is widely believed to be what draws people to her, as humans cannot

resist that dash of salt in their sweet.

As the stories go, she lures people to cure her loneliness. She leads them across the cay and they give chase, desperate to touch some of her wildness. At last, she escorts them to the waterfall at the island's center. She allows them to draw near, but when they reach out to grasp her, she slips away into the mist. They try to follow after her and are drowned. A popular version has it that a new goat appears on Faraway Cay for every person who vanishes there. It is said that you can see the humanness in their eyes. . . .

I shut the book in disgust. A woman with hooves for feet. Humans turned to goats. Had my sister's body been dumped in that waterfall as some kind of sick joke? *Look, the woman on Faraway Cay did it! Hahaha.*

It wasn't until that moment that I realized that, from the time I was a small child, I'd found some solace in the fact that Alison had been found somewhere so beautiful. How many small, unconscious coping mechanisms, how many pretty notions, would be taken from me before I uncovered the truth?

I opened Google Maps on my laptop, a

self-punishing impulse — to lay eyes on it, to force myself to picture her there, her body beneath all that water for days. But Faraway Cay did not even appear on Google Maps. Where I knew the cay must be, there was only blue.

I followed Clive for many nights and many miles. In all that time, excepting the evening when I called his name and he responded with such terror, I never heard his voice. His nights were composed of enormous stretches of silence, and this silence was now mine, too. I would return home near midnight and realize I hadn't uttered a word since leaving work at five-thirty. Sometimes I would speak — "Hello, hello, hello," "My name is Emily," "Today is Tuesday" — just to prove to myself that I was still real. I did not hear him speak, nor did I observe any other evidence to suggest that his life connected meaningfully with anyone else's. Clive Richardson was a man hiding in plain sight, drawing no attention and leaving no trace upon the minds of others. He was an island, isolated and impenetrable.

It went on like this. And something began to happen. At the beginning of each walk, I would be filled with the fear I described earlier, with a sense of the danger posed by Clive and the risk that I was taking in following him. But after thirty minutes, an hour, the experience shifted. It happened without my noticing, like slipping from waking to dreaming. It no longer felt like I was following him, but like we were on this walk together, linked. Eventually, even this *we* faded away; it was no longer the two of us traveling these dark streets, but a single mind, a memory, endeavoring through the *step, step, step* of these constitutionals to travel beyond some perimeter it could never seem to reach. If we kept walking long enough, I would be seized by the certainty that we were not alone; we were being watched, trailed by figures who flickered on the periphery, shrouded in darkness. A hand reaching out, beckoning. The pounding of hooves. A flare of laughter, rising from the streets like steam, then gone. *Shh. Don't tell.*

On Halloween, the old woman in my building sat on the front stoop in her white sneakers distributing Good & Plenty to crestfallen fairies and firefighters. I had been invited to a party at the apartment of a college friend on Pineapple Street and decided that I would go. I'd fallen into arrears with my friends, ignoring messages and invitations; attending seemed an efficient means of digging myself out. The party was an annual thing, and in prior years I'd spent quite a bit of time and effort thinking up and executing my costume — the year before, if memory serves, I'd gone as Frida Kahlo. But this year I had neither the time nor the inclination, and so I put on brown pants and a brown sweater, picked up a few twigs from the tree outside my apartment, and declared myself a tree. My non-costume turned out to be a hit, and at first I was having a pretty good time, sliding into the social rhythm I hadn't realized I'd missed. Gin and tonic in a Solo cup. Jackie squealing, "Where have you *been,* girl?" as she petted my shoulder. Laden chitchat with a guy I'd hooked up with a few months earlier. A group of us climbing the ladder to the peach-soft roof to pass around a joint — smoke and cold air and the stark sounds of our laughter against the glitter of Manhattan across the water.

But when I climbed back down into the hot, raucous party everything was wrong. I looked around — there was a girl dressed as a Warhol painting, her face covered in red dots; Jackie was a "sexy farmer," a canny critique of the Sexy Halloween Costume that nevertheless allowed her to show off her midriff. My gaze pinged from face to face in the semidarkness. What was I doing here? Clive was out there, and I was not with him. I tried to get myself to stay, to enjoy myself, but I was startled to find that I could no longer tolerate a night away from him. I slipped out early without saying goodbye.

Looking back, I can see that my pursuit of Clive Richardson was beginning to be about something more than gathering clues, that I was falling under the grip of something I could not control. But I did not allow myself to see this then. Maybe if I had, it all could have ended differently.

I got a lot of flak for publishing my memoir. People said it was a shameless cash grab. I got called a hanger-on, a fame whore, a star-fucker. I don't think any of those people actually bothered to read my book, because if they had they would have seen that I wrote every word of it straight from my heart.

After I found the girl, I went to therapy. I worked with a life coach. I embraced a vegan diet. I tried Xanax and Zoloft. I got into reiki and did a four-day silent meditation retreat. I even followed this guru for a while. Her hugs were supposed to cure you, it didn't matter what was wrong with you. During her North American tour, I went to see her at the Sheraton near LAX. I waited in line for three hours. When it was my turn, I approached the dais and the guru wrapped me in an embrace so powerful it felt like it originated at the center of my soul. I swear I could feel it wiping everything away. A new beginning. Or so I thought. But on my drive back to Santa Monica, I was stopped in traffic on the 405 and it happened again — the girl appeared in my mind. That bloated white arm, reaching out to me.

My therapist said that intrusive thoughts and images are an extremely common neurological phenomenon. To stop them, I simply needed to retrain my mind; he told me that it is not only possible to rewire the brain's neural pathways, it is easy. Plasticity is exactly what our brains are designed for. Whenever the image of the girl intruded, I was supposed to imagine that I was in the checkout at the grocery store. On the belt were different grocery items and each item was a thought, and the girl was just one of these thoughts, and I knew which items were healthy and which were not, and I could choose which ones I picked up and which ones I put down, and I could watch the unhealthy thoughts travel away down the checkout belt of my mind. I just had to put her down and pick up something else. I spent hours putting down the girl and picking up yogurt, avocados, blueberries. But the longer I spent there, the more I tried not to see her, the more I saw her. The light blue polish on her nails. Her hair swirling upward in the water.

Eventually, I decided my only choice was to accept her into my life. I still see her, but when I do, I just . . . say hi to her. I call her by her name. *Hey there, Ali.* I tell her I like her nail polish. It is not okay, and I don't think it ever will be. But I have found that this way, I can turn her from a body into a girl. And I feel damned proud that I was able to find my own solution when all these supposed experts couldn't help me.

I've been thinking about going back to school to become a licensed mental health counselor. Wouldn't that be a second act nobody expected from me? But actually, I've always wanted to help people. You want to know the real thing the men I dated had in common? It wasn't that they were celebrities. It was that they were broken, broken dudes. He was the most broken of them all. Ironic, isn't it? I made him go to that waterfall because I thought it would heal him, but instead I think it's the thing that broke him for good.

Ghosts

It has happened before. Clive has experienced several periods like this since he arrived in New York nearly two decades ago, seasons of paranoia when the girl is in the wind, when even the hiss of the radiator is full of her fury. It lasts a few days, sometimes as long as several weeks, but eventually things go back to normal. Each time it passes he thinks it will be the last time. It is over, dealt with. But it never is, is it? The old fears, the old voices — *we have found you, we know, everybody knows* — stay dormant for months, years, and then, sure as the tides, they come back.

The littlest thing can set it off. A girl rolling her eyes at her mother in the backseat of his taxi. A whiff of artificial strawberry. During that terrible episode with Sachin, all those years ago, the trigger was nothing more than the hostility with which Sachin looked at him, which made Clive certain that, somehow, Sachin *knew.* This time, it is even smaller than that, a silly mistake. He thought he heard the name that is no longer his, and now she is everywhere. She haunts him, a ghost skulking at the edges of his vision. She shape-shifts, appearing in the forms of other people. She is a girl in an NYU sweatshirt on a delayed subway train, beautifully bored. She is on his block in a pleated charter-school skirt, bathing in the adoration of the boys around her, thrusting out her chin just so. She flashes out from their eyes and catches him in her gaze.

During these intervals, nothing can quell her presence, not his walks, not prayer, for she is inside of him, too, a second self; she feels the freezing floors of his apartment beneath his socked feet, hears a customer berate him over the traffic on the FDR, sees him urinating into a Dasani bottle mid-shift. She reaps pleasure from each small indignity. It seems to him that this life is her doing. She has strung it together, just so. And he feels an anger at her that will never, ever be spent. Then he wonders what it says about him that he has made her into such a vindictive, punishing ghost.

At night she peers into his dreams. He is with Edwin, surrounded by everyone they know; the people shout and leer and hiss.

We have found you, we know, everybody knows. Alison looks on from the edge of the crowd, strokes her scar, and smiles.

Old memories come unburied: Dancing with her, kissing her. The twisted string of blue fabric with which her shirt was tied around her neck. The first day he saw her walking down the beach, her stride so nonchalant he knew straightaway she'd be trouble.

Like any ghost, she radiates. She is not content to remain within her own moment. She inhabits them all — not only her aftermath, but also the time before he even knew she existed, until every memory, no matter how sweet, turns bitter on his tongue.

It was no secret that Clive only had eyes for Sara Lycott. She was not one of the girls most of the boys were stuck on — Daphne Nelsen with her long sprinter's legs, or Saffy Lester with her silky hair and cashew skin, or Joy Vernon who had breasts by the time they were eleven. Sara Lycott's eyes were small and black, and they seemed to cast off bright flares of hostility. She had remained adamantly flat-chested, as if purposefully to deny any boy who looked. She and her mother had come to the island from Saint Kitts when she was a baby. Sara's mother, Miss Agatha, claimed to be the widow of a government minister who was killed in an automobile accident just before Sara was born. Clive's grandmother had declared this a "likely story." Sara didn't talk like the rest of them. She spoke properly, like a teacher, even when she was with her friends, and though she was teased for this, she didn't stop.

His devotion to her had been sealed at the Horatio Byrd Primary Christmas Pageant when they were ten. The pageant was the culmination of a week of festivities that included calypso shows and street jams and the lighting of the mahogany trees along Investiture Boulevard. Clive was an ox. His grandmother had dyed cotton batting with tea and sewn it to an old nightshirt of his grandfather's. (Though his grandfather had been dead for years, she still kept his clothes in a wooden bureau in the corner of her bedroom. It was the one soft thing about her, and it would be many years before he understood that this one thing was really an uncountable number of things, that it was merely the material evidence of an entire unseen world that resided within the grandmother he thought he knew completely.) Sara Lycott was Mary. She wore a flowing blue silk gown and a crown of white flowers. Her performance left him spellbound. Not because it was beautiful or heartfelt or pure, for it was none of these things. Rather, she commanded his attention with her magnificent vacancy. She spoke as if she cared not a whit that she was onstage in front of the entire town, playing the role of the Virgin Mary. How could she dare to give so little, to be so utterly elsewhere? When a fourth-grade boy dropped the porcelain dish that was supposed to be myrrh and the pageant fell for a moment into disarray as the wise men stooped to gather the shards, Sara Lycott reached into her dressing gown and pulled forth a square of coconut candy. There, in the middle of the stage, she bit. He could hear the candy crack against her teeth. Then she released the faintest of smiles, a secret smile at a secret pleasure. Was he the only one who had seen it? The other boys barely gave Sara a thought; if they did, it was only to joke and tease — where did such a funny-looking girl get off being so haughty? But in that moment, her prickly exterior had parted to reveal the truth of her. From then on, all he wanted was to be let back in.

He could not speak to her. By the time he moved from Horatio Byrd to Everett Lyle Secondary, his stutter had mostly faded, but in Sara's presence it came rushing back and took hold of him utterly, so that not only his tongue but his limbs, his organs, the very air inside him, were twisted and bound. His friends reaped endless amusement from this.

"Gogo, ask Sara if she wants to come to Rocky Shoal with we."

"Gogo, ask Sara if we can copy she maths."

"Gogo, Sara left she notebook. Here. Give it back to she," Don said one day in the schoolyard, shoving a yellow notebook against Clive's chest.

Sara was across the yard, giggling with her friends in a bunch tight and lovely as a flower bud. When they saw him approaching they glared at him, a wall of feminine scrutiny that withered his dick to nothing.

"Why, thank you," Sara said when he wordlessly handed her the notebook. The girls were varnishing one another's nails. In the heat, the fumes made him woozy. "How are you doing today, Clive?"

She was the only one apart from his teachers and his grandmother who ever called him Clive. He was at once proud and terrified to be called his proper name by her, to have her attention on him in this way, though he also suspected that it had nothing to do with him; probably, she called him Clive simply because she would not deign to let so foolish a name as Gogo cross her lips.

She smiled. She was tiny as a spider. The way she looked up at him, craning her neck, emphasized his bigness until he felt as if the edges of himself may as well have been miles away, for all he could do to control them.

"I'm well, and y-y-y-you?"

"Quite well, thank you."

She had the power to bind his tongue and she enjoyed it. She turned away from him and thrust out her hand so Saffy Lester could continue varnishing her nails.

He stumbled back across the yard to where his friends were doubled over with laughter.

"Check you out, ladies' man," Des said.

"Wise up, bred. Why you try to love a thing that will never love you back?" Don said.

" 'Sides, I hear she mama crazy crazy," Damien said.

Edwin patted him on the back. "Don't listen to these fools, Goges. Someday that girl will be yours for true. And when she is, you remember it was me who knew it would be so all along."

■ ■ ■ ■

Gogo and Edwin got drunk for the first time when they were fourteen. They were walking home from school one day when Edwin stopped on Underhill Road and struck up a conversation with Jan, a Dutchman who had been on the island as long as they could remember. He wore linen tunics and leather sandals, and he could almost always be found sipping from a paper bag in the shade of one building or another in the Basin. When Jan asked if they cared for a drink, Edwin said, "Sure," as if this were something they did all the time. Jan led them to a bar called Paulette's Place, where he bought a bottle of Olde English. The three of them drank it together at the bar. When the liquid burned down Clive's throat he was back in his mother's kitchen, sitting on Vaughn's lap, the glinting faces of strangers laughing around him. He tilted his glass back again.

"An old pro, are we?" Jan said, and patted his back.

Edwin raised his glass in the air, then took a quick sip. "Sweet like a woman," he said.

"Truth," Clive replied, though neither of them had yet known a woman's taste.

■ ■ ■ ■

That same year, for a few weeks, Edwin and Clive and their friends were seized by boxing fever. As soon as the last bell rang, they traveled in a pack down the center of Gould Road — cars honking at them to move to the side, which they didn't — to Don's house, because his father was in Tortola and his mother didn't get off work until seven. Don's family was worse off than most of theirs. The galvanized roof of his house was badly rusted. Scrawny chickens stalked the yard, pecking at the dirt. There was a rubbish heap nearly hidden in scrub. Against the house, a few desiccated pepper plants grew out of old Nido canisters. The boys liked the roughness of this. In Don's yard their jaws clenched. Their gaits simmered with an itchy energy.

They would stand in a circle and send two from among their ranks into the center. They placed bets. They jeered and clapped and egged each other on. When the sun began to set they squared up with one another, trading coins that were sour and warm from their pockets. Then they dispersed, each sore, bruised boy making his own way down the familiar roads to the lights of home.

When Clive thinks of his youth, it's this brief span of afternoons that pulses most insistently in his memory. They were after something. They ought to have been men, or so they feared, and they were trying to teach themselves the things men should know. None of them expected him to be any good, and he wasn't. Big, clumsy Gogo. He punched the air, dodged too slow, got his lip split over and over.

There was a girl from their form who liked to come around. Her name was Berline, Bery for short, and she was a solid, heavy-shouldered girl who wore her uniform loose, the maroon plaid skirt coming down to her shins. Bery had her heart set on boxing. She showed up every afternoon, lingering and begging to be included. "I been practicing with my brother," she told them one afternoon. "He says I'm better than he."

"We don't want you to get hurt, Bery," Don told her in a voice syrupy with false concern.

"What's it to any of you if I get hurt? You all does hate me."

"Go away, Bery," Des said in a bored voice. "Can't you see where you're not wanted?"

Bery marched right up to Des. "I'm just

asking for one go."

"Sure, Bery," Edwin chimed in. "We'll let you have a go."

"You will?"

"Why not? You is waiting a long time now. Gogo!"

"Me?" he whispered.

"No, my other mate Gogo. Yes, you! Get in there and give Bery she turn."

"I don't want to go with no Gogo! He the worst of all you."

Don got up in her face. "You want your turn or not, Bery?"

She grabbed the gloves angrily from him and stepped into the center. Gogo followed. The worst one, good enough only for the girl. He could hear his friends sniggering as they placed their bets:

"My money's on Bery; her face all wreck like a boxer already."

"Put me on Gogo. Even he can beat a girl. If she even *be* a girl."

They met in the center, glove to glove. He could feel the humiliation in his eyes connecting with the rage in hers, sending off heat.

Don counted down from three and stepped aside.

Gogo swung.

He felt the impact of his punch like biting

into a mango and letting the flesh fill your mouth. Then he heard her scream, saw her hands fly to her face. The circle fell apart as the boys rushed in.

"Bery, you okay?"

"Let we see your face."

When she took her hands away, Clive swooned. Blood spilled from her nose over her lips.

"Shit, Gogo. She all cut!"

Bery scrambled to her feet and ran off, hands over her face. When she was gone, the boys began to laugh.

"What's wrong with you, man? Breaking she nose!"

"Figure he finally throw a good punch *now.*"

Gogo looked from face to face to face. When he saw Edwin, laughing with the rest of them, he was seized by an urge to run at his friend and tackle him to the ground. It was Edwin's fault. He had made this happen, matching him up with her. The blood had been thick and gummy, like the strawberry syrup at Milk Queen.

But when the sun went down and the boys dispersed for the evening, Edwin walked over to Clive.

"What you want?" Clive muttered, and kept walking.

"Come on, Goges, don't be like that!"

"Get dead, Edwin," Clive shouted behind him.

"Slow up, man!" Edwin sprinted after him. "I'm sorry, okay? For true." He put his skinny arm around Clive's shoulders, and though Clive wanted to shove his friend off, he didn't. "You know, I think you finally rid we of she for good," Edwin said. He grinned mischievously, like this had been their secret plan all along, the two of them. And Clive felt better. He smiled back at his friend. Together, they walked the darkening roads home.

When they were fifteen, the island's first big resort, the Oasis, opened on the south coast. A year later came the Grand Caribbee, and then, in quick succession, Salvation Point, the Villas at Sugar Cove, the Oleander, and Indigo Bay. The arrival of the resorts brought other changes. Sir Randall Corwin Airport underwent a massive expansion and began offering direct flights from New York and Miami. It became unremarkable to see a white family gnawing on jerk chicken legs at Spicy's. The sleepy streets near the island's only deepwater port were renamed Hibiscus Harbour as part of an initiative by the island's Tourist Board; Victorian façades were put up on the fronts of the buildings and stores opened selling duty-free perfume and timepieces, T-shirts and batik sarongs, Cuban cigars and souvenir bric-a-brac: palm frond hats and seashell picture frames and bottles of local sand. The port was rebuilt with berthing facilities for fifty yachts and a jetty that could accommodate up to three cruise ships. Within a few years, the island became a popular stop on cruise itineraries; during the high season, Carnival and Celebrity and Royal Caribbean ships moored at the port daily and disgorged thousands of tourists, and as many as half a dozen competing steel bands waited on the jetty to greet them. Paradise Karaoke opened, then Papa Mango's, which became notorious for its thirty-two-ounce frozen cocktails.

The first of their friends to get a job at one of the resorts was Des's older brother Keithley, who became head of water sports at Salvation Point when they were sixteen and Keithley was twenty-two. The resort offered windsurfing and sailing. There were two speedboats for snorkeling excursions. If for whatever mysterious reason the guests wished to, they could cling to a bright yellow banana boat and get dragged back and forth across the bay. At night as the boys drank and smoked wherever they were drinking and smoking that night — at Paulette's Place, or behind Arthur's father's shop (for by then Arthur had given up his honor student ways and was drinking more than any of them) — Keithley regaled them with stories from work. He had watched parents chase young children across the sand for hours like fools, and a child turn inconsolable when his Shirley Temple arrived with only one cherry. His feet had been vomited upon by a middle-aged woman who drank four rum punches before she rode the banana boat. He had been told to "Take it easy, *mon,*" when he insisted that a man wear a life preserver to go sailing, as the resort required. He had gazed upon the supine bodies of teenage daughters and honeymooning young wives as they worked on their tans in the tropical sun.

Keithley had been at the job a few months when he showed up at Paulette's one night with a small key in his hand. They waited until after midnight, then six of them piled into Keithley's car and drove across the island to Salvation Point. He killed the lights and the engine at the entrance to the service road and coasted down the hill to the parking lot. They hurried across the resort grounds.

"Shit, man, check this place!" Don said as they snuck past the main deck with its three swimming pools. When they reached the sand, they broke into a sprint. They pulled off their T-shirts and dashed through the soft waves of low tide with their shirts held in their hands above their heads, to where the speedboat was moored some twenty meters out. Des reeled up the anchor and whispered, "Now! Now!" Keithley turned the key and they sped away from the lights of the resort and out into the night.

For a few weeks, until they got caught and Keithley was fired, they spent their nights joyriding. (After Keithley was dismissed, he would work for a spell at the gas station on George Street before trying his luck in Liverpool, returning three years later with a wife and a son, Jamie, who would die at nine, the freak consequence of a collision on the football pitch behind Horatio Byrd Primary, one of those moments you could puzzle over for the rest of your life — the millimeters and milliseconds by which you had been given this fate in place of all others.) They cut through the placid waters off the coast and limed on one beach or another; they drank and smoked, tussled in the shallows, blasted Public Enemy and Run-DMC, and shouted up at the stars, which wheeled overhead so fine and bright it hurt to try to understand what they were. Just to be a little bad. During the day, the beaches belonged to the snorkelers and picnickers. At night, they became theirs.

From the boat, they discovered coves you couldn't see from land because they were hidden behind thick scrub. One night, they found a small crescent of sand surrounded on three sides by steep rock faces. They returned the next night with a rope. Keithley scrambled up the rocks and tied the rope to a tree at the top of the cliff. They returned to this spot often. They would climb the rope from the beach to the top of the cliff and stand, toes curled over the edge, the moon like a massive searchlight on the water.

"Do it! Do it!"

"Don't pussy out, bro!"

"Three-two-one, man!"

The fleeting infinity between when his feet left the edge and when the water sucked him under was the closest to weightless Clive had ever felt. Don, Des, Edwin, Damien, Keithley — each of them in turn left the world ever so briefly behind. You could hear cars from the top of the cliff; they were less than a five-minute walk through the scrub from Mayfair Road, and from there it was less than half a mile to Indigo Bay, yet nobody saw them, or knew this spot. It was a nameless place on an island where they knew the name of every last dog and dinky fishing boat — a promise that this world, these lives, could break open.

"Someday when I'm making mad cheddar in New York I'm gonna build a mansion right up there, so close to the edge when you look out the window you just see sea," Edwin declared one night. It was three A.M., and they were lying on the sand at the base of the cliffs with the radio turned down low.

"Cheddar," Don snorted. "Man, quit your Yankin'. You're not going to no New York."

"Up yours, Don. Anyway, is what you know about it? When I'm in Brooklyn and you all still live with your mummies, you better not be expecting any barrel from *me*!"

"We'll be sure to keep that in mind," Damien said.

"What you want with New York anyway?" Don asked. "Why freeze your rod off doing shit work there when you can do it here where the weather fine?"

"And hang with we at Little Beach on your day off?" Des added.

"And with we youths," Clive whispered.

He was so stoned his own words flew at his skin like wind.

"With we youths!" Don gasped, slapping his knee. "What the ass you talking about, man?"

"Nah, nah, he right!" Des shouted. "The Goges see it clear! All we liming in the shade with some Cruzan, and we wifeys making chat, and we sons playing windball in the sand."

For a moment they were quiet as the vision Des had painted seemed to take life above them in the dark sky.

"We wifeys nagging and we babies whining, you mean," Edwin said. "Anyway, I'm not gonna be doing no shit work in New York. I got plans, what you think?"

"Hear that, breds?" Don said. "Edwin gonna be a big man! What I think? I think you're full of shit. I think ten years from now you still living with your fat sisters. I think you gonna dead here, same as all we. Except the Doc here."

Damien smiled modestly. He was smart, so smart that he was able to lime with them every night while rising, quietly, to the top of their class at school. Though they teased him for his diligence, they were proud that he was theirs.

"The frig you know about it?" Edwin

continued. "I'll swim off this island, come to that. Gogo will come with me."

"I'm shit at swimming," Clive said.

Edwin pinched the fat on his shoulder. "You buoyant." Edwin shrugged. "You'll float."

"Shit, it's late," Keithley said. "We gotta get back."

They gathered their things, waded through the shallows to the boat, and rode the calm waters back to Salvation Point. On the boat, Clive, too stoned to sit up, lay on the floor and let the wind blow over his open eyes as he stared up at the sky. New York was Edwin's dream, and though he spoke of it as a place they would go to together, Clive sensed the unlikeliness of this; instead, Edwin's desire for New York seemed to prefigure a future in which he would be left behind — on the island, and in the past.

For hours after that, until his grandmother woke him the next morning, he could feel Edwin's fingers on his shoulder as if they were still there, like the ghost of someone who was already gone.

"We liming on Faraway tonight," Keithley declared as the boat sped away from shore one evening.

"We can't," Clive blurted out before he

could stop himself.

"Why not?" Keithley asked.

Clive looked down at his hands. "You know why," he mumbled. In his mind he saw her — the long black hair hiding her face. Hooves for feet.

Keithley clapped his hands in delight. "Goges, man, don't tell me you still believe that old-folk fuckery."

"But my great-auntie disappear there!"

"Who don't have a great-auntie who disappear there?" Des said.

"Don't stress, Gogo. If she turn you into a goat, we'll set you up fine in my yard," Don said.

"Beside, if that sket would choose any of we to lure away with she, it would be me," Edwin said.

"Is that so?" Damien said.

"A lady all alone like that needs a man who can sort she out proper. Can I help it if all the ladies know I'm the only man for the job?"

As Keithley slowed the boat and guided it to shore, Clive was filled with an unease he felt helpless to counteract. The other boys climbed down the ladder and hopped into the shallows one by one. When it was his turn, Clive couldn't move.

Then he heard Edwin's voice in his ear.

"It's okay, man."

"But my mum —"

He knew he should be past believing, but he couldn't rid himself of the story. It was what he had of her; it was the pocket watch, Bible, lock of hair she'd left behind for him.

"To hell with she. You don't need no mum. You have a brother."

Clive climbed down into the water, with Edwin right behind him. The moon that night was so bright they didn't even need the flashlights they'd brought. Beneath its light, the sand seemed to glow white — in his memory of it, it almost looked like snow. He hesitated again before he stepped ashore, shaken by the feeling that he was about to break something that could never be put back together. He glanced back at Edwin, who nudged him forward.

"Hurry up, you fools! We going to check out the goat lady's watering hole or what?" Don called.

"Wait up!" Clive shouted. Together, he and Edwin sprinted up the sand.

It was one of those nights whose every pleasure is multiplied by all the future moments when, you imagine, you and your friends will gather and reminisce about it. They tramped through the jungle in the moonlight, casting behind them a trail of crisps bags and still-smoking roaches. When they came upon a goat, they shouted and chased it into the bush, whooping with delight. At the waterfall, they peeled off their shorts and cannonballed in. They swam and roughhoused and pulled off stunts — leaping from the highest rocks, pratfalling into the water, swimming under the falls' churn and shouting "Fuck Daphne!" and "Fuck Joy!" and fuck all the other girls who wouldn't fuck them into the obliterating roar. As the night rose, growing wilder and wilder still, Clive felt himself sending it all away — the stories and the ghosts. His mum.

Later, they returned to the beach. Too drunk to make their way back to the mainland, they lay down on the shore, using their balled-up shirts for pillows and letting the soft sand love their stoned, tingling skin as the sound of small waves rocked them to sleep. That was the night they had everything. The night they brought friendship to the divine edge.

And the girl was already there. As they leapt and roughhoused and plunged into that cool, clean water she was beneath them, at the bottom of the pool, waiting to undo them.

Tuition for Jayson and Stasia at Porter's International School. A Manchester United jersey for Jayson. Stasia's pink dress for prom. A satellite dish with eight hundred channels. Life insurance. Jemma's salon visits. Her annual shopping trip to Saint Kitts. Bikes for Christmas. Our house in Crofton Hills. A loan to Don when he was hard up. A surprise trip to Kingston with Jayson to see Man-U play the Jamaican national team. Miss Verna to clean the house weekly. Jemma's smooth hands. Stasia's acne treatment. Jayson's club football fees. The headstone for little Jamie's grave, pure granite. The diamond on Jemma's finger.

I used to feel mad guilty over all of it. We never could have lived this way if I didn't start giving these tours. Pawning off my friendship with Edwin and Clive as secret insider information. Alison Thomas: Behind the Headlines, I call it. Ninety dollars a person, kids under twelve half price. On the tours, I'm careful to call it an unexplained death, not a murder. As if that makes what I'm doing any better.

I tried to stop once. I told Jemma it was dirty money and I had to put an end to it.

She took my face in her hands and made me look her right in the eyes. "Don't you ever apologize for providing for this family. You're a good man. You hear me, Desmond Phillips? You're a good man leading a good life."

I want to believe that.

If it weren't me, I guess it would just be somebody else getting rich driving Yankees past the houses where Edwin and Gogo came up, and the building where Paulette's used to be, and boating folks out to Faraway. But it's not somebody else, it's me. They were my brothers.

VOICES

My name is Alison Brianne Thomas. I am fifteen years old and this afternoon I ceased to be a virgin. I've been thinking that I should keep a record of my life so that someday when I'm completely bored with my suburban-lady existence, which I really hope I never have, I can listen to myself and remember what I used to be like and maybe I'll shake some sense into myself or something. Anyway, I figure today is the perfect day to start.

The first thing you should know is that this afternoon you cut dance rehearsal. You put on a fantastic performance for Mrs. Conyers about your horrible period cramps, which you obviously didn't have, and you went to Drew's house. The crazy thing is, after all this time, we didn't plan it. Today when I woke up I just felt different. I knew today was the day. Honestly? I didn't really enjoy it. The actual act was sort of uncomfortable. But that's fine. I'm not one of those idiots who thinks her first time has to be some perfect whatever. It's knowing I've done it that matters.

Anyway, when it was over Drew kissed my neck all over. I love when he does that. It just . . . gets to me in the best way. He kept whispering over and over, "You're so beautiful. You're so beautiful." Middle-aged Alison, wherever you are and whatever you're doing, I hope you have that. I mean, I'm not a dingbat, I know it probably won't be with Drew. But I hope you have someone who feels that way about you. The neck kissing. I *love* that.

It had taken my mother several weeks to make duplicates of the tapes and send them to me. I imagined her hovering over them, fretting about whether to grant my request. When I returned home from work one evening in early November and saw the box addressed to me in my mother's handwriting in the building's foyer, it took me a minute to realize what it was. Opening it up on my bed, I saw that there were dozens of tapes, many more than I had expected. My mother had even taken the time to photocopy their labels, each one in my sister's bubbly teenage penmanship: "Frosh,"

"Sweet 16," "Seniorz," "Summah!" They were arranged in chronological order, beginning with "Fifteen" (the *i* dotted with a heart). At once, I put this tape into the dusty brown cassette player I'd purchased weeks earlier at a pawnshop on Flatbush Avenue and pressed play.

As soon as the first entry ended and Alison's voice faded to silence, I stopped the tape. With trembling hands I took the cassette out of the player and put it back in its case. For weeks, I had been waiting to listen to these tapes, to be held and soothed by my older sister's voice. But the voice on the tape was not what I had imagined at all. Alison sounded so much younger than I had expected, so shockingly girlish, and I was filled with shame. I was an adult listening to the private confessions of a child. Why on earth had I expected anything different? Then and there, I vowed I wouldn't listen to any more.

For a while, I managed it. I kept myself busy. I'd fallen terribly behind at work, and I endeavored to catch up — reading manuscripts, combing through the mixed reviews of the new Mann for phrases that, with a few strategically placed ellipses, might suggest positive endorsement. At night, I walked with Clive. Flowers outside of a bodega. Boys on playing fields. *Special! Persimmons!*

One night I had a work function to attend — one of our books was a number one *New York Times* best seller, and the whole office was going to happy hour at a bar in midtown to celebrate. I calculated that I could easily put in an appearance and make it to the Little Sweet in time to join Clive on his nightly sojourn. But the Q stalled on the Manhattan Bridge for over twenty minutes. It was announced that a rider on another train was in medical distress, and as I sat there, waiting with increasing impatience for us to move again, I decided this rider was a man who'd gotten stumbling drunk at his own happy hour, and I hated him as the minutes slipped away. When at last I arrived at Church Avenue, I dashed up the stairs and down the block. I arrived at the Little Sweet breathless, but I was too late. He was already gone. I would have to wait an entire day to see him again, an amount of time that felt no different than an eternity.

When I arrived back at my apartment, the man in the NASCAR hat was just coming in from walking Jefe, and he held the door open for me. Jefe, who had never paid me any attention, began to growl, a deeper and more menacing sound than I'd thought the poor animal capable of producing. *"Cállate,"* the man said. The dog lunged at me. His little claws scraped at my tights. He bared his tiny yellow teeth. The man jerked the leash and scolded him, plainly shocked at his dog's behavior, but Jefe would not stop. He glared up at me with his milk-white eyes.

"I'm sorry," I said, though what I was apologizing for I couldn't explain — it seemed to me that I had been seen by this pitiful creature, naked right down to my soul. I fled down the stairs to my apartment. Quickly, before reason or willpower could creep back in, I plunged my hands under my bed, yanked out the package from my mother, and threw the cassette back in the player.

I just had this memory I haven't thought about in forever. When I was really young we had this tape of Irish folk songs I was totally obsessed with. I used to jig around the living room in my nightie. I remember singing along, trying to do this Irish accent which I thought was so romantic, and in my head I was one hundred percent prancing across the highlands in a tartan dress, which I guess is actually Scottish, but you get the idea. I was, what? Five years old? And I already sensed that there was this thing missing from my world. Like, *depth.* Or maybe, *rootedness.* I already got that I was from a totally superficial place. People do not exactly write books or make movies about their poignant childhoods in Westchester, you know? My family doesn't really have a heritage, or a religion, or any of that. Alison. What even is that name? I'm not named after anyone. It doesn't have some meaning. My parents just thought it *sounded* nice, as, apparently, did a million other parents, dooming me to a life as Alison T. At least they had the decency to spell it the good way. But it's like my entire identity from that first moment when they named me — it's not *about* anything. It's like our only culture is this very nice life we have.

Tonight for homework I have to fill out this career quiz for health class for whatever freaking reason, and the last question is, "What are you afraid of?" I'm honestly stumped. I mean, I can tell you the stupid things. I'm afraid of being home alone at night because every time I hear a sound I think there's a murderer. I'm afraid of mayonnaise because it's disgusting and I hate how it gets on people's fingers. Loose teeth totally skeeve me out.

But real stuff? I guess the thing I'm most afraid of is that my life won't be what it can be. I have everything, everything going for me. I have no excuses. And what if I still blow it?

When I broke my promise not to listen to Alison's diaries, I broke it fully. There were so many hours of tape it seemed I would never get through it. Much of it was rambling and not particularly illuminating. For twenty minutes she leafed through her high school yearbook and developed a ranked list of the ten cutest senior boys. She sang along to the entirety of a Counting Crows album. I didn't fast-forward. I listened to every word. She talked about Drew a lot, about the romantic things he did for her, like taking her out on real dates to restaurants and the movies while other boys just took girls to the pond and parked. She talked about her friends. Lisa was her "soul sister," Amanda was driving her "just bananas"; a week later, Lisa had been demoted to "o*kay,* I guess." She complained about her teachers. Mr. Conti kept sticking her with the "chalk eaters" for group projects, which she had decided was a deliberate attempt to teach her some lesson, and let him try. The more I listened, the less I considered whether it was right to listen. What did it matter? I couldn't stop. I gorged on Alison until I could hear her voice even when I was away from it — her breath hidden in the hum of a ceiling fan, her laughter tinkling within the piano track of a song I was listening to on the subway home. She was with me as she hadn't been in years.

Hey there. Me again. Hahaha. You're so diverting, Alison. Jocular. Convivial. Uproarious. Titillating. Winsome. It's March and as you may have guessed, you took the SATs this morning, and let me just say, the SATs are to actually being smart as having a pretty voice is to being a talented musician. Analogies are to meaning as a puddle is to the ocean. I'm pretty sure I did awesome, though. But that's not what I want to talk about. This afternoon, Claire went to this birthday party for some girl in her class. Stacy? Anyway, the party was at that Chuck E. Cheese–type place, and my parents asked me to pick her up when it was over. When I get there, all these kids are racing around together playing tag and some girls are pretending to be horses or whatever. I'm looking everywhere and I don't see Clairey. Finally I find her. She's in the ball pit by herself. She's holding a green ball and just turning it in her hands and looking at it like she's figuring something out about it. Then she started doing her writing thing, where she moves her finger around in the air like that? I wanted to run up and shake her and say, *Just stop doing it, kiddo. Just stop, easy peasy.* But she can't. She can't change or she would change, right? Nobody *wants* to be the weird kid.

But also? I feel terrible saying this because she's my sister and I love her, but sometimes I don't actually like being with her, because it's like her life — she's only six years old and I can already see every single way it's going to be hard. Meanwhile, for whatever nonreason, the same stuff that's impossible for her comes easily to me. I'm not trying to brag. It is what it is. When I'm with her, sometimes I feel so freaking relieved I'm *not* her, and then I feel horrible for feeling relieved. I don't deserve anything I have, really. Then I took her out for ice cream even though she already had birthday cake, and the end.

I remembered that day. Alison was close with "Stacy" — the party was Tracy Donofrio's. Our whole class must have been invited, otherwise I never would have been included. I remembered picking pepperoni off of greasy arcade pizza. I remembered that there was a My Little Pony cake with a buttercream flower border, and I wanted to get a flower on my slice, but other girls begged for them while I just silently hoped for one with all my might, so I didn't get one. What I remembered most vividly, though, was how excited I was as I sat in that ball pit, because soon, any minute now, my big sister would arrive and all of my classmates would see that she had come to pick me up, that she was mine. Could anything be better? But she had already been there, she had been watching me, and she had pitied me.

There was more. As I made my way through Alison's tapes, I discovered that there were many entries about me, more than there were about our parents, or Drew, or her friends. My sister had watched me. Analyzed me. Puzzled over me much as I was puzzling over her now, like I was a riddle to be solved and like maybe in solving me she would crack open some truth about herself.

There was this moment at the swim club today that totally killed me. Claire's going into second grade in the fall, which means she's officially old enough to go in the deep end of the pool. So the big thing for the kids her age is to jump off the diving board. Not the high dive or anything, and not dive, just jump off the low one, a few feet. Today was ridiculously hot, and we all went to the club together. All of Clairey's little peers are jumping off the diving board, and she's just watching them while she licks a Popsicle next to my mom. Then when my dad left to do his laps, my mom asks her, very calmly and low-pressure, if she wants to give it a try. Clairey nods uncertainly, and they go over together. My mom goes in the water so she's ready to catch her. When it's Clairey's turn, she steps up onto the board and walks really slowly to the end. I'm watching from my lounge chair. We wait and we wait and we wait. My heart was pounding out of my chest. My mom says, "Come on, sweetheart. You can do it!" Then some ten-year-old asshole waiting on line starts chanting that *Jeopardy* song and the rest of the kids join in. Fuckers. Finally, Claire looks at my mom and shakes her head, and my mom tells her if she doesn't want to go she should get down. My mom got out of the water and Claire sort of fell into her arms.

But right before that, I saw it happen. It was a tiny flash, so quick I've never, ever caught it before: My mom, just, swallowing everything of herself, just pushing whatever she was feeling down, and smiling really brightly at Clairey and telling her it was fine! Who cares? She'd do it later this summer! Which she can't possibly believe. Why is life so hard for her? What are you so afraid of, Clairey?

It went on and on: Clairey came home early from the first slumber party she'd actually been invited to. Clairey refused to go up onstage when a magician chose her from the audience to be his special assistant. Clairey was too shy to order her own dinner at a restaurant. Clairey hid out in her room when Mom's college roommates came to visit with their kids.

What is there to say about listening to these entries? It was devastating, humiliating, awful. How I wished I could slip into the past and tell my sister I would not be that weird little girl forever. I would grow up to have friends, boyfriends, a cool job, a life. But what would she think if she could see me now, skulking in the shadows, collecting details about Clive Richardson like some eccentric hobbyist? What clearer evidence could there be that I was exactly who Alison feared I would be? The friends, the boyfriends, the job — these might have been things I'd managed, but were they really me? Who was I? Didn't you hear what Alison said? The weird kid. A coward. What if our situations had been reversed? *She* would have known just what to do. She wouldn't have been afraid, either. She would have done whatever it took. *What are you so afraid of, Clairey?* I sat on my bed, hugging my knees to my chest and hearing her words over and over as my eyes filled with tears. I rubbed my fingertips together, and for the first time in years I felt that old prickling feeling. I raised my index finger in the air. *A-L-I-S-O-N.*

I knew what I had to do.

It was an evening of brewing winds, the Brooklyn night an inimitable hazel. I arrived at my post across from the Little Sweet earlier than usual and pretended to examine the shelves in the grocery as I waited for Clive. At the usual time, I saw him coming up the sidewalk. A few moments after he entered the Little Sweet, I crossed the street. When I reached the entrance, I hesitated. Then I opened the door and stepped inside.

My nights following Clive had not prepared me for this proximity. I took my place behind him in line, inches away from him. I could smell his aftershave. I could see where the cuffs of his windbreaker were worn thin. His hands — fingertips drumming lightly against his pant leg as he waited his turn. I couldn't do this. I was about to turn and run out the door when I heard a voice, clear as anything, in my mind. *Get a grip, Clairey. It's like this: He is just some dude who found your phone a few weeks ago and you are just some girl who digs authentic ethnic food and you're just going to get to know each other.* I stayed where I was. I forced myself to stare at his hands until I was able to convince myself that they were not *his* hands, not *the* hands, and as I did this, I felt my terror subside. In the coming months, I would play this game over and over. I split Clive Richardson in two: there was the man with whom Alison had spent the last night of her life on Saint X and there was this man in this restaurant in Brooklyn, and they were not the same.

When he looked up, I smiled at him politely and vaguely, then pretended to do a double-take, as if I'd just recognized him.

"Clive, right?"

"Yes . . ."

"Emily," I said. "You found my phone last month?"

He exhaled. "That's right. Nice to see you again." He squinted at me, and I could feel the question in his gaze: What was I doing here?

Come on, Clairey. You know the words.

"After I met you here I looked this place up on Yelp and saw the rave reviews. I figured I'd better come back and try it."

I was surprised by how convincingly this explanation came out. Who was to say I wasn't the sort of girl always on the lookout for the city's best arepas, curry, dim sum? Maybe I should have been alarmed by my facility for lies, by the ease with which I spun myself into someone else, but I wasn't. Alison beamed. *Well done, Clairey.*

"Pepper pot and Carib, my dear?" the woman behind the counter asked Clive when he reached the front of the line. She was short and heavyset, and her natural hair was close-cut.

"Yes, Miss Vincia," Clive said.

"Pepper pot and Carib, pepper pot and Carib," the woman clucked as she ladled crimson stew onto a plastic plate. "And who do you have with you tonight?" she asked, her gaze hardening as it shifted to me.

"Oh, we're not —" Clive began.

"I'm Emily."

She raised her eyebrows. "And what would you like, Emily?"

I looked up at the illuminated menu. I wanted to pick something quickly and confidently, but with the exception of jerk chicken, the items were mysterious to me, and I was determined not to order jerk chicken, which I was certain would mark me as a rube. Buss-up-shut. Roast bake. Souse. Aloo pie. Accra. As I scanned the menu, I could feel my face heating up and Vincia's eyes on me, and sensed (or perhaps imagined) her annoyance. Oxtails dinner. Doubles. Festivals. Sea moss. Peanut punch. "I guess I'd better trust the expert," I said finally, smiling at Clive. "I'll have a pepper pot and Carib, too, please."

Vincia filled another plate, and Clive and I slid our trays down the counter side by side to the register.

"My treat," I said when Clive pulled out his wallet.

He looked at me uncertainly.

"Please? You'd be doing me a favor. I've been feeling totally guilty you wouldn't accept any reward." I smiled my best silly-me smile.

"Okay," he relented. "That's very kind of you. Thank you."

After I paid for our meals, Clive lifted his tray from the counter and looked at me. He hesitated. "Won't you join me?"

By paying for his meal I had hoped to create in him a sense of obligation, and it had happened just as I expected.

"Oh, I don't want to disturb you," I said, looking down shyly at the floor.

"Please. I insist." He said this without conviction. He didn't want me to sit with him. That much was clear.

I smiled. "Okay, then. Thank you."

I recognized this turn as absolutely crucial. Because now, if Clive ever began to wonder about Emily, and why she was so interested in him, he would remember that he was the one who had insisted that she join him that first night. She hadn't even wanted to — had tried, at first, to refuse.

He gestured to the table beside the potted palm tree, and I took my seat across from him. He wiped the table clean of straw wrappers and grains of rice. The table was covered in a yellow oilcloth and adorned with a vase of artificial carnations. A mural on the wall depicted a party on a tropical beach. On the television mounted on the wall, a game show was on — people in costumes competed to win bedroom sets and Jacuzzis.

"You must come here often," I said.

He looked alarmed. "Why would you say that?"

"I mean, because she knew your order by heart."

He shook his head and chuckled at himself. "Of course. Well, it's a good place to pass the time." He picked up his fork and began to eat, and I did the same.

I swooned when I took my first bite. "Mmm. This is amazing." In truth I was too full of adrenaline to notice the taste. My reaction was a performance, and I could feel the falseness of it — the theatrical *Mmmm,* the big eyes.

"Vincia's food is the best in the borough." His manner, too, was performative. He was saying what he thought he ought to say to me.

What now? *Keep it simple, stupid.*

"So are you from the Caribbean?" I asked.

He nodded.

"Cool. Which island?"

He said the name and I squinted as if it were unfamiliar to me.

"It's small," he said hurriedly. "Most people here don't know it."

"How long have you been in the U.S.?"

"Seventeen years."

He'd left less than a year after Alison's death.

"So what made you decide to leave home?"

He rubbed his hand back and forth against his cheek. Guiltily, or merely uncomfortably?

"It became difficult to find work." He bent his head toward his plate, scooped a forkful of crimson stew neatly into his mouth, and chewed silently, mouth closed. Was there something off about these tidy habits? An attempt to distract, or to mask, or to convince oneself of one's own tidiness of character? I wanted to ask him why it had become difficult to find work and see what he would say, but I was wary of pressing him.

"You miss it?" I asked instead.

For a moment, a distant look came into his eyes. I imagined that in his mind he was back — the crystalline water, the sandy roads, a small white house that had once been his.

"You get used to things."

"Do you visit often?"

"Never." He said this quietly and definitively. He yawned.

"Long day?"

"I got a flat. I went to a garage downtown

to get it fixed, but the nut was stuck and they couldn't repair it. I had to go all the way back to the fleet garage. It used to be any garage could fix this."

"Nothing works the way it used to, does it?" It was a false stab at commiseration, and I cringed inwardly. But he seemed to appreciate the comment. Or maybe he'd merely grown very good at appearing to appreciate comments like this from people like me.

I sipped at my Carib, and for a while we ate in silence. I wanted to move the conversation forward, but I understood that above all I must not do anything to make him suspicious. But why would he be? Wouldn't he just assume I was exactly what, in a way, I was — another white interloper in the new Brooklyn, my interest in his life motivated by a desire for self-assuagement, to prove to myself that I was a good community member, I cared about lives unlike my own, et cetera?

He cleared his throat. "What about you? Where are you from?"

"Nowhere. Well, pretty close to it. Indiana," I said with droll self-deprecation. "Starlight, Indiana, to be precise."

My response was not premeditated. The location rose to my lips by instinct. In the fourth grade we did a unit on the fifty states and, much to my disappointment, I had been assigned Indiana. (I'd had my heart set on Louisiana. Wild alligator swamps. Mystical voodoo.) I made a diorama on foam board with Crayola cornfields, brown sand for the plains, plastic cattle. I remembered Starlight because this name had seemed to me to be the state's single redeeming characteristic.

"Starlight. That's beautiful."

"Yeah, well," I said, rolling my eyes. I leaned toward him. "I don't visit, either." I conjured an expression of guarded sadness, designed to intimate some deep ocean of painful personal history: my childhood difficult, my reasons for leaving Starlight, Indiana, equally so, as if to say to Clive Richardson, *See? I have secrets, too. I, too, live in exile.* "It's funny. I've been in New York three years now, and it still feels sometimes like this is someone else's life I'm living."

It was only after I said this that I realized I really did feel this way. Though I didn't know it then, this was to become my method during these evenings at the Little Sweet. With Clive, I confessed to feelings I had not previously articulated even to myself. Yet these emotional truths were presented within a fictional architecture. My feelings of alienation from my own life, for example, were not caused by some banishment from Indiana. It was Alison's death that had cast me into the simulacrum.

"Just so." He tucked back into his food.

"I can't believe your partner left you with a flat. People," I said with a scoff.

"People." With his spoon, he gathered the last of the crimson sauce.

We stood in unison and threw away our trash, slid our trays onto the stack on top of the garbage bin. On the television, a woman dressed as a squirrel had just won an all-expense-paid trip to Bermuda. From behind the counter, Vincia watched us as we walked out of the restaurant and onto the street.

I'm not sure I will ever be able to explain what it was like to sit across from Clive Richardson at the Little Sweet. I had never felt anything like it before and I haven't since. I suppose it might best be called clarity — a sense, bestowed as if from some source outside of myself, that I was exactly where I was supposed to be, doing exactly what I was supposed to be doing. On my walk home that first night I was breathless, the danger of what I'd just done swirling with euphoria at how skillfully I'd managed it. I didn't delude myself that he'd especially enjoyed our interaction, but it was a beginning. I would figure out who he needed and I would become that person. I would gain his trust, insinuate myself into his life. And I wouldn't be alone. Alison had been with me that night, giving me words I would never have found on my own. The closer I drew to Clive, the more powerful her presence became, as if they were a unified system, the two poles of a closed circuit, amplifying themselves within me.

All of this sounds crazy, I know, and when I look back on it, on how far things went, it's difficult to understand how I allowed myself to be pulled under so deeply. But I had stepped into Clive Richardson's taxi. One can understand how such an unlikely occurrence could make a person believe she had a purpose, a fate, that transcended the ordinary realities of her world. Even all these years later, knowing what I do now, I cannot disabuse myself fully of the notion that forces were at work that season that defy easy explanation. At times I wondered, and wonder still, if Alison hadn't strung all of this together from some perch beyond this world.

As the city released itself from the showy burdens of fall and grew quieter and colder, my life steadily reduced until it revolved entirely around two intertwined rituals: I could not stop listening to Alison's diaries and I could not stop seeking out Clive. Her voice and his, that was all.

So last night at dinner, my parents were having this totally riveting conversation about the dead patches on the lawn and my mom gets that Very Nice expression on her face that means exactly one thing, which is, *I'm about to say something positive about a black person,* and she goes, "It's never looked the same since John died," and my dad says, "That man was a miracle worker." Then my mom turns to me and says, "You remember John, don't you, sweetie? You loved him. You were so sad when he died. You cried and cried." She smiled her sweet little smile. Whatever, it's not worth getting into with her because it's beyond her limitations to understand, so I just smiled a sweet little smile back, but in my head I was thinking, *Wrong. Incorrect. That is not even remotely what happened.*

Maybe you don't even remember John anymore, Old Person Me. I don't know what you still remember and what's been crowded out by the fascinating life I really,

really hope you're living. John was our gardener when I was really little. He died when I was maybe four. Cancer, I think. I remember he had this pure white, lamb's-wool hair and extremely dark skin. He came once a week to mow the lawn and every week my mom took me outside to say hello to him. He always tried to talk to me, but I always hid behind my mom's legs. My mom would say, "She's so shy," which wasn't true, I was a really gregarious kid, and obviously my mom knew that. I remember being completely terrified of John but not knowing why. My fear of him was totally inexplicable to me. I just *felt* it.

I remember when my mom told me he died, and I wasn't crying because I loved him. I was crying because here was this really nice old man who had just wanted to be friendly to me, and on some level I got that my fear of him was bad, and maybe it hurt him, maybe *I* hurt him.

My mom just drives me crazy. Like, you do not get to choose to raise your family in a place with only white people plus a few Indian and Chinese doctors and then convince yourself that your kid desperately loved the black gardener who you took her outside for some beneficial interaction with, and that this love is proof that even though you made the choices you made, it doesn't matter, because your kids are good and you are good and you are all just so very, very good.

I returned to the Little Sweet again a few nights later. Clive looked up when I walked through the door. He did not acknowledge me, and I pretended not to notice him. I got in line. I could feel him watching me. Vincia was curt with me, all business. I paid for my food. Then I turned and let my eyes fall on him as if I'd just spotted him. I walked over to his table.

"Back again," he said.

"You caught me. I think I'm officially hooked. May I?" I gestured shyly at the empty chair across from him.

My request flustered him. But I figured he wouldn't be so rude as to say no, and I was right.

"Please."

In the weeks that followed, I went to the Little Sweet many times. Each time I feigned sheepishness when I asked to join Clive, and each time he said yes. I grew quite adept at playing the role I had created for myself, that of a lonely exile in New York, a girl from far away, all alone. While Clive did not exactly seem to welcome my presence, it seemed to me that, gradually, he was warming to me, or perhaps I should say to Emily.

What did we talk about? We traded stories from work — a boorish passenger, a temperamental author. We commiserated over the various urban creatures making incursions into our apartments — silverfish in my shower, mice in his ceiling. I told him about my short-lived kickball career, and he told me he'd played in a cricket league until a shoulder injury a few years earlier sidelined him. But mostly, as New Yorkers are wont to, we talked about the city itself, which provided for us a language of common approval and disdain: De Blasio's carriage horse crusade — a lost cause. The MTA — abysmal. Pedicabs — a nuisance.

I told stories composed of inventions and half-truths about a childhood in flyover country, hoping that these confessions would elicit some from Clive in return. I would try — carefully, so carefully — to ask questions that might lead to a revelation of some kind. Did he plan to go home someday? Did he miss his family? What was he like as a child? Nothing. Often, I caught him telling small lies. For instance, take this exchange, from our third night together:

"Have you been driving a taxi since you

moved to New York?"

"Yes. Though I only switched to the day shift a few years ago."

"I hope you won't think this is weird, but I looked up the island you're from online. It looks, like, ridiculously beautiful."

"Yes, it was quite beautiful."

"What's it like, like, living in a tourist destination?"

"New York is also a tourist destination."

"I guess that's true. Did you drive a taxi down there, too?"

"No."

"What did you do?"

"Odd jobs, mostly."

Another example, from a few weeks later:

"How was your day?"

"The traffic was terrible."

"This time of year must be the worst, huh? With the holidays coming?"

"There's always something. In spring, it's the parades. In fall, it's the UN summit. The tourists are quite bad now. Today I picked up a family at St. Patrick's that barely spoke English. They asked me to take them to Rockefeller Center. I tried to tell them it's just around the corner, but the mother kept saying, 'Skating! Skating!' Finally I just drove them there."

"I haven't been skating since I moved here."

"I've never been."

"Really?"

"We didn't have a lot of ice growing up, miss."

"Right, I'm sorry. That was stupid. We used to skate all winter long, as soon as the Wabash froze over. I remember my feet would turn so numb that when I took off my skates I'd cry." (Truths nested in lies nested in truths. The pain of numb toes warming after skating — a memory as visceral as any from my childhood. But the Wabash River? A strip of blue cellophane in my fourth-grade diorama.) "All the kids from my neighborhood would be playing some game together on the ice, and I was always just skating by myself off to the side. It was like I couldn't figure it out somehow. You know, I don't think I've ever really had a best friend?"

"Me, neither."

Tonight was my senior dance recital. I've been practicing for months. I choreographed the dance myself. I probably spent a hundred hours practicing. But as soon as I stepped onto the stage and went up for my first pirouette, I knew I would fall short. It was like it had already happened and there was nothing I could do about it.

I danced and it was fine. I didn't mess up or anything, but I wasn't inside the music the way I wanted to be. When the recital was over I put on my sweats and went out to the lobby and there's twenty people giving me flowers and accosting me with praise. "Oh my god, Alison, you're so amazing." "You're so talented." "That was so great." Blah blah blah fanfucking-tastic.

Are most people so insensitive to what's going on that it all looks the same to them? I mean, how did everybody totally miss what actually happened tonight? I didn't make a single mistake, not one, and I still completely failed.

Flowers and white teeth. This was my image of my sister, taken from this very recital. She had seemed to float with happiness that night. What a shock to learn that she had in fact been seething with self-criticism and hostility. How well she had hidden it! I had not thought my sister capable of such deep dissatisfaction.

I flew to Pasadena for Thanksgiving. I resented this disruption to the progress I was making with Clive, but could see no way around it. It was the same small gathering as always: me, my parents, Aunt Caroline, and a man my mother referred to, in a tone that managed to sound simultaneously empty of and loaded with judgment, as "the flavor of the month." This time he was an acupuncturist of Argentine extraction. Aunt Caroline was in her sixties and skinnier than ever, her lips plumped to the edge of tastefulness with Restylane. The acupuncturist looked to be about forty-five. Aunt Caroline had been dating forty-five-year-old men since she was twenty and it seemed she had no plans of stopping now.

Before the meal we assumed our usual positions, my mother and me in the kitchen, Aunt Caroline, the boyfriend, and my father chatting in the living room. ("I promise I'll stay out from underfoot," Aunt Caroline said to my mother, as if she were doing her a favor by sitting on the couch getting tipsy on Cab Franc.) At the dinner table, things proceeded the same as always.

"The garden is looking magnificent. What's your secret?" Aunt Caroline asked my father, who launched into an animated discourse on his approaches to fertilizing, pruning, watering, pest control.

"And what's new with you, darling?" Aunt

Caroline asked, leaning toward me.

Before I even had time to concoct a convincing reply, my father chimed in. "Em's getting into yoga."

"How fabulous!" Aunt Caroline said. "I have a friend who swears she grew two inches when she started practicing yoga."

"It's fantastic for your alignment," my father said. "And it transforms the way your body processes carbon dioxide."

"Is that right?" my mother asked.

"NPR." My father shrugged.

The conversation moved on to other subjects — the consulting project my father had picked up in his retirement, the dash of fish sauce my mother had added to the roasted Brussels sprouts this year, the half marathon in Huntington Beach my father had registered for and the nagging knee injury that would likely prevent him from running it.

As the meal progressed, its mundanity began to feel increasingly phantasmagoric. How was it possible they didn't realize something was happening to me? The conversation continued — my mother couldn't take this new contingent that had joined her book club, they never read the books, she was honestly considering defecting. I clenched my fists under the table, digging my fingernails into my palms. This, I now saw, was exactly how our family had maintained itself since Alison's death, by not squinting too closely at one another, not knowing one another too well.

As soon as we'd finished the pie, I announced that I was feeling terribly jet-lagged and headed to bed early, though I lay awake much of the night, staring out the window at my father's violets, which held perfectly still in the dry, windless dark.

On Saturday morning I woke up early. Aunt Caroline and her boyfriend had flown home the night before. My flight to JFK wasn't until the evening. I found my mother in the kitchen.

"Coffee?" she asked, already opening the cabinet and reaching for a mug.

"No."

"Oh. Tea? Orange juice?"

I shook my head.

"How about some breakfast? I can make eggs?"

"Stop, Mom. I don't want anything."

I went to the dishwasher and began unloading the bowls.

She put a hand on my shoulder. "You spoil me."

I shrugged her off. She winced and shrank

back from me with a wounded expression. Suddenly I felt nothing but revulsion for this fragile bird of a woman, my mother. I wanted to hurt her, and not like I just had, not with some minor daughterly rudeness, but to really hurt her, in a way she could not evade or dismiss.

"Do you remember Alison's last dance recital?" I asked.

She looked down at the floor. As a family, we were not in the habit of bringing up Alison without warning. I kept going. "The one where she danced to —"

My mother hummed a few bars of the song, then laughed quietly at herself. "Your sister was so beautiful that night." My mother never said her name.

"She hated it."

"Hated what, darling?"

"That whole night. Everything about it."

"What are you talking about, sweetie? She was on cloud nine."

"You're wrong. She was furious."

My mother hugged herself as if the room had grown cold. "You listened."

"How would you know? You said you stopped after a few minutes."

My mother held my gaze.

"You listened, too."

"Years ago. You were in college and your

father was away on business for the week. I just —"

"Couldn't help it."

She nodded.

"Then you know what I'm talking about. You know how upset she was that night."

My mother sighed. "I know that's what she said, sweetheart. But I was there. I saw her. She was so happy."

"Apparently not."

"All I can say is I know what I saw."

I gritted my teeth. It was so like her, this aloof denial of an unpleasant truth.

"Honey, what was that?"

I stuffed my hand in my pocket. "What was what?"

"Your hand. I thought I saw . . ."

"An itch."

Strange, how something can lie dormant in you for years, so long you forget about it, and then it's back like it never left. It had been happening for a few weeks now, the need growing more difficult to suppress — words prickling in my fingertips, desperate to get out. *S-o h-a-p-p-y.*

"Sweetheart, are you getting enough fresh air?"

Fresh air? *Fanfuckingtastic.*

It's tempting to paint my nighttime meetings with Clive retroactively with a shiny gloss, to suggest that after a while we achieved an easy rapport, and I want to be careful not to mislead in that way. Even after we'd spent hours together, our conversations remained stilted. Clive often gave only the most perfunctory answers to my questions before falling silent for long stretches. There was one topic, though, that he seemed truly to relish, and that was his job as a hack and the things he had seen, the stories he had to tell. He told me about the crazy conversations he'd overheard. The time someone left a two-hundred-dollar tip on a ten-buck ride. Getting held up in the nineties.

"I had a man once who started talking to himself," he began one evening. "He was talking about a heist he was going to execute with a partner. He said, 'Here's the plan. I'll go up to the teller, I'll show her the gun and tell her she has twenty seconds. When I put my hand in my pocket, you get the customers down on the ground.' He kept going like this, how they will get into the vault and what they will retrieve from it and where the getaway car will be parked. I began to worry that perhaps *I* was the getaway car. I was thinking about how I might drive to a police station without him realizing where we were going when he said, 'So? How did I do?' He was an actor. It was opening night of his first off-Broadway play."

"No."

"It's true." He grinned. "I've also driven three women in labor to the hospital, one of them in a blizzard. She told me she would name her child after me. I remember when I told my son that he said, 'But what if she had a girl?' If you ever meet a Clivette, I guess she has me to thank."

"You have a son?"

He appeared flustered, as if he hadn't meant to reveal this. He nodded. "He'll be turning twenty-one soon."

"He lives here?"

"Oh, no, no. He's back home, back — with his mother."

"Your wife?"

He shook his head. "She was a difficult woman. Troubled."

"Are you and your son close?"

He broke off small tatters from the napkin in his fist and collected them in a pile on the table. "I tried at first. She didn't permit me to be involved." He cleared his throat. "Here's another story for you: Would you believe I once picked up Mike Piazza two hours before a home game? His driver was stuck on the Bruckner. It was just after 9/11 and traffic was very bad. I got him to Shea just in time."

Clive had spoken the words "my son" like a kiss to a warm forehead. I hadn't known he had a child. If the boy was twenty now, then he had been two or three years old when Alison was killed. Bile rose in my throat. Clive had been a father when it happened. He should have looked at Alison and seen someone's child, not whatever she was to him instead: A way of injecting excitement into a life saddled with a kid and responsibilities he wasn't ready for? The unlucky victim of a man's anger toward another woman, a "difficult" woman? Had Alison known Clive had a son? As Edwin Hastie slid a cigarette between her lips in the sandy staff parking lot, had Clive told some precious story about his toddler, and had this story made her think these men sweet and safe?

"Wow," I said. "That's amazing."

"Only in New York. Before he got out I told him, 'Mike, I have a confession. Usually I'm a Yankee fan. But tonight I'm rooting for the Mets.' "

Happy birthday to me. Woo-hoo. Today, old lady Alison, you are sixteen years old.

So I can drive now. Very exciting, blah blah blah. For my birthday my parents got me . . . drumroll, please . . . a new car!

That's right, my dad bought me a brand-spanking-new Audi. So inevitably we had a big fight about it. I wanted a used car. Something low-key. Because, come on. I'm sixteen. Why on earth should I own a brand-new Swedish or German or whatever . . . why should I have this luxury car that I'm inevitably going to fuck up because I just started driving and, news flash, I don't know how yet? When I told him that, he was all, "That's exactly why we want you to have a good, safe car."

I mean, he's *right.* On the one hand, I completely understand why if you could afford it you would buy the best car you can for your kid. On the other hand, I'm mortified. Not just for me. For my friends, too. On be*half* of my friends, especially the ones who are, like, super-excited about their new luxury vehicles and see no issue here whatsoever. We're teenagers and people are just giving us these ridiculously nice cars. We should be embarrassed, right?

But being embarrassed only makes it worse, because if you're lucky enough to be given a nice, safe, fancy-schmancy car, isn't it brattier to yell at your dad about it than to just be glad you have it? But then — I feel like there's this really slippery slope between being glad you have something and thinking you deserve it.

When my mother had told me that, despite what Alison said in her diary, she was certain my sister had been on cloud nine at her last dance recital, I'd thought she was sticking her head in the sand. But the more I listened to Alison's diary, the more I began to wonder whether it could be trusted. I began to detect a self-conscious, performative aspect in the things she said. Take Alison's insistence that she did not want the new car my parents gave her. Are we really to believe that she did not, on some level, want it? Are we really going to accept that she didn't enjoy having it? Isn't it more likely that she loved the car — its new-car aroma, its elasticity around a sharp bend, its blue gleam in the school parking lot — but that her own materiality embarrassed her, or she thought it ought to — that she knew a purer person *would* be embarrassed by it, and she wished to believe she was such a person? Isn't it more likely that the extended diatribe on the subject that she recorded in the diary was an attempt to reassure herself of her own virtue?

Or let's return to the recital. What if my mother was right and Alison was simply giddy eating up compliments after her performance? That's how I remember it, too. You can see how a diary might become a useful tool, how it might be used to rewrite history, to recast the pivotal moments of one's life to suggest a humbler, more critical self.

At the same time, the urgency and raw emotion in Alison's words were unmistakable, her turmoil palpable. She was grappling with herself. I believe that. Alison at least *meant* to be honest with herself. Here we run up against yet another problem — the obstacle of her youth. How much does a girl of fifteen or sixteen really understand about herself? How accurate can she possibly be?

The diary was a slippery thing, weaving together confession with self-delusion, truth with distortion. No — the weaving metaphor isn't right. That suggests truth and distortion are strands and, therefore, separable. I think it would be more accurate to say that truth and untruth were present in Alison's diary as hydrogen and oxygen are present in water. The challenge is not one of separation — for what use are either hydrogen or oxygen in understanding the nature of water? — but of understanding these moments *without* attempting to separate them. I had to find a way to understand how truth and untruth make each other.

One day at work, a Facebook invitation appeared in my inbox. Jackie was throwing herself a birthday party: dinner at an all-you-can-eat-and-drink sushi and sake joint, followed by karaoke in Koreatown. I could no longer imagine attending such an event. How frivolous to be twenty-five and doing sake bombs, what a joke, what a cliché. What a cliché, even, to possess some ironic relationship to your own clichéd birthday party, as Jackie did, to affect a pose of self-mockery toward oneself and the basic things one loved. (*Yes, we're doing this. Bon Jovi non-negotiable,* the invite said.)

Before I set out for the Little Sweet on the night of Jackie's party, I texted her: *Sorry, I have a thing tonight, but have so much fun!*

Jackie texted back immediately: *You're bailing on my bday?!? Is everything okay??? I'm worried.*

Her worry opened something in me. For a moment I wanted to go to Jackie's party and have stupid fun there the way I would have just a few short months ago, but I knew I couldn't; it was simply no longer possible for me to get wasted and eat bargain-basement spicy tuna rolls and belt out "Sweet Caroline" like these things were somehow relevant to me, and there was loss in this, too. Briefly I considered telling Jackie everything. I typed and deleted half a dozen messages, but in the end, I gave up. I never replied.

I began sleeping less and less, and erratically. Night after night, through the dark hours, I listened to Alison. I had not experienced insomnia like this since I was a child, churning out fatal scenarios in the darkness, and the feeling now was familiar: I wanted to stop listening, to give myself over to sleep, but I couldn't. To press stop, to extinguish Alison's voice, seemed dangerous in a way I cannot explain rationally, but which felt absolutely inviolable to me. I was almost grateful when the man above me began his nightly guitar practice at two A.M., the music sifting down through my ceiling providing an alternate and utterly ordinary explanation for my wakefulness. For the first time in my life, I was sleeping through my alarm and arriving late to work.

I just got back from a trip to Becca's ski house. First of all, the trip was a freaking blast. I seriously think I have a six-pack from cracking up so much. I feel like I've been really, I don't know, *blah* lately, and this trip made me remember that I really, really love my friends. A few highlights: Matt and Andy losing a bet and streaking across the yard in the freezing cold. Staying in the hot tub for hours drinking beer and talking. Getting ridiculously stoned one night and taking all the blankets onto the deck and lying there looking up at the stars while it snowed. After a while I couldn't even tell if the snow was falling or the stars, it was just this beautiful mess. High stargazing is seriously the best.

Did I mention I broke my wrist? True story. It happened on the last day, otherwise the trip would have been a total bust. I fell coming off a big jump. Everybody else was in the lodge for a hot-cocoa break, and I went off on my own to get in one more run. I had a three-seater to myself on the chairlift. You know how sometimes the world just rips open and you find yourself in a moment that is totally sacred? This was that. The trees high up on the slope were coated in snow and glittering. The snow had that bluish glow, and it was like it was all here for me. I actually started to cry because I just felt so *moved.* I was still in that energy when I decided to take this jump on the way down. There was that moment when I was hanging in the air, that weightless, almost-flying moment when you start to realize your body is no longer under your control, then splat.

Ski patrol came and brought me down the mountain in one of those gurney thingies. Once my friends figured out where I was, they were all crowding around me in the med hut, and then at the hospital with me later for the X-rays and everything. I didn't cry. It hurt like hell but I was a total champ. I'm really proud of how tough I was. But then again, the only reason I didn't let myself cry is because I wanted the medics and my friends to tell me how brave and amazing I was, which is exactly what happened. So does that even count as toughness, or is it actually appalling?

I'm leaving for college next week and my parents said I have to sort through my so-called "junk" before I go. Today I was going through these boxes of old essays with my teachers' comments and school photos of my friends, and every stupid trophy and medal from swimming and dance. All of a sudden I was like, "Why have I held on to this crap? Why is it so damned precious to me?" I got these heavy-duty black garbage bags from the garage and I started filling them. I got into this rhythm . . . trance is too dramatic, but I got to this headspace where I couldn't see any reason to keep anything. The only memento I didn't throw away was my prom corsage from Drew, and I only kept that because I kept imagining he was in the room with me, and how hurt he'd be just killed me.

As I was throwing everything away I had this vision where I had pared down everything I need in life to a black attaché case, like people use to hand off dirty money in espionage movies. Then, like, what if you got rid of not just things but parts of yourself? Memories you'd been holding on to and random skills and knowledge and all the books you'd ever read that didn't matter? What if you pared yourself down to one essential part? What would that one grain be? It occurred to me that I have no freaking idea.

I broke up with Drew today. It was awful. He was crying in my bed and begging me to take it back. I know this makes me seem terrible but the begging actually made it easier for me. I kind of lost some respect for him, you know?

Now my mom is all concerned. "It was just so *sudden,* sweetheart!" Like sudden is this problem. But I did something that had to be done. We're going to college, for one. But it's more than that. I am totally settled into Drew, and I can see how it could just go on and on, and something in me is saying, *No, no, no.* Like, is that really where it's supposed to lead? But seeing Drew cry and knowing I did that really sucked.

I had made my way through all but the final tape. I was terrified to reach the end, but I couldn't slow myself down. I called in sick at work. I stayed in my apartment and listened.

Do you ever wish something terrible would happen to you so the world could see how strong you are? People probably think I'm this delicate flower because nothing bad has ever touched me, but I'm not. This is fucked up to say, but I think I would be amazing in the face of a tragedy.

"Humiliation is purification, because it

causes the most corrosive, the most painful awareness." We're reading *Notes from Underground* in my World Lit Survey and Dostoyevsky is officially my new favorite writer. Dude gets it.

I really shouldn't be recording right now, because I'm going home tomorrow for winter break and I need to pack everything I need for home and for the annual Thomas family vacation to a culturally devoid tropical resort, and I haven't even gotten my suitcase out yet. But this thing from last night has been bugging me and I have to get it down. So I was at this dorm party and this extremely hot junior from the lacrosse team was there. We went back to his room and we're sitting on the futon in that pre-make-out phase and he's touching my hair and everything's great. Then he launches into, "Have you ever wondered what if your green is my purple?" I told him I was really tired and left. Honestly, if I meet one more pseudo-intellectual, actually *so* stupid boy here, I'm going to lose it. Let me go on record and say that the number of dumbnuts at one of the best schools in the country is mind-blowing.

That was it. *The number of dumbnuts* and then the barely audible spooling of blank tape. Right away I took out the tape, swapped in the first one, and started back at the beginning.

Today when I woke up I just felt different. I knew today was the day.

*S*he's only six years old and I can already see every single way it's going to be hard.

Fanfuckingtastic.

The more I listened, the more I felt that I was far out in the ocean, swimming down, down, down. I knew I should rush up to the surface for air, but I couldn't help myself. There was something at the bottom I was after, and I couldn't stop.

Maybe it hurt him, maybe *I* hurt him.

I didn't make a single mistake, not one, and I still completely failed.

Blah blah blah.

True story.

This beautiful mess.

It had grown dark in my apartment, but I didn't turn on the light. I listened to my sister's voice in the darkness until I could scarcely remember a time when I'd heard anyone but Alison. I had the feeling then that I was entering my sister. I stretched and filled her, head to toe. I opened my eyes and looked out through hers. Together, in our body that was Alison's body, we descended through lilac clouds.

■ ■ ■ ■

The Real Wherever

■ ■ ■ ■

They arrive at sunset, slipping beneath pastel clouds as the sun slips into the sea. For a moment it seems to Alison that the plane, too, will slip into the sea, but the tarmac rushes beneath them just in time. As the plane brakes down the runway, a ghostly whoosh fills the cabin. The minute it subsides, her parents and the majority of the white passengers unbuckle their seat belts and stand to retrieve their things from the overhead compartments: carry-ons, rackets, straw hats. Her dad edges out another dad in the aisle. A third dad edges out her dad. The pilot comes on the intercom and requests that everyone remain seated, but he is ignored. Heaven forbid their vacations start thirty seconds later. Once the plane door opens and people begin to move, her dad looks back at the black woman he had been seated beside on the flight; "Welcome home," he says to her, before hurrying along. When they get to baggage claim, the carousel is empty and motionless. Everyone prowls around it, staking out the most strategic position. Ten minutes pass. A guy with a winter coat unzipped to reveal a Hawaiian shirt walks past her muttering, "Unbelievable." She smiles. Let these dopes wait.

"You know that woman next to me on the plane was a lawyer?" her dad says to her mom on the walk to the arrival gate, once their luggage finally arrives. "She's from here. She was just in New York on vacation."

"Huh," her mom says.

"Imagine that, Dad. They have lawyers here," Alison says.

The shuttle to the resort is late, too. Alison's family stands on the curb with two other families, next to a white sign with gold letters that say INDIGO BAY, for quite some time. Everybody grouses and makes small talk. The other families are from the Upper East Side and Bedford Hills. The irony of traveling over a thousand miles to spend the week talking to other people from the New York metropolitan area does not seem to be dawning on anyone. The moms talk to the moms. The dads talk to the dads.

"How old are you?" Alison's mom asks a girl who must have changed out of her winter clothes in the airport bathroom — she is wearing bike shorts and a cropped T-shirt with a rhinestone heart.

"Twelve," the girl says wearily.

"She's on a birthday trip!" her mother says.

"Mom, why are we waiting?" the girl asks.

"I don't know, sweetie. Daddy booked this vacation."

When at last the shuttle arrives, the driver begins to load their suitcases.

"Is all of this going to fit in there?" a dad says, looking skeptically into the back of the van.

"Not a chance," Alison's dad contributes.

They are wrong, everything fits, and soon they are pulling away from the airport. On the drive to the resort, the small talk continues, but Alison doesn't hear it. Her face is pressed to the window. She sees scruffy dogs and houses with rebar sticking up out of the roofs. Three goats bite at the dirt outside of a small white building with a shingle out front: CENTRE FOR DENTAL AESTHETICS. Everywhere she sees piles of . . . *stuff.* Rubble? Junk? Supplies of some kind? There are houses with porches but no railings. A white concrete staircase ascends out of the scrub, the top step touching only air. As she watches the world pass by, she is filled with disquiet at her inability to parse the things she sees. Are the diminutive chickens pecking at the side of the road malnourished, or are they some breed of chicken she has never seen before, or is this what a chicken is *supposed* to look like? Do they belong to someone or no one? Is this place in the process of being built or unbuilt or rebuilt or none of these — maybe something is happening here that she lacks the experience to comprehend.

The van trundles past a girl standing in a yard along the road; she wears a purple T-shirt and yellow cotton shorts. When they drive by, she runs into the road and chases after them. Then she plants herself in the middle of the road, puts her hands on her hips, and thrusts out her tongue. The shuttle judders on over the uneven road and the girl disappears into the haze of dust and twilight.

Alison is mortified to be in an air-conditioned van with her family and her fellow resort guests driving past it all. In her Global Justice class, she learned that two billion people, more than a third of the humans on earth, live on less than two dollars a day. (Are the people on this island *those* people? Are the things out the van window poverty, or just people living their lives? She doesn't know how she would even begin to know.) Anyway, it's not like she didn't know people were poor before — she isn't a complete idiot. In high school she volunteered at a soup kitchen. But her lasting memory of that experience is not of bearing witness to poverty, or of any good she did; it's of the men . . . looking at her, calling her pretty with their ruined mouths. "You're coming home with me, little girl," a man in a giant tan parka told her one night. He pointed his index finger at her, then curled it toward himself and laughed madly. She felt afraid, though she was pretty sure he was messing with her, making himself into a caricature to mock her — like, *Boo!* The acrid smell of male bodies and the simultaneous unease and pleasure she felt in their gaze — this is what she has kept.

So the things she sees out the window do not *raise her awareness,* or whatever. They just mortify her. An old woman limping down the road. The accusation of that little girl's sharp pink tongue. That girl is really millions of girls. You cannot permit yourself to forget that. How is she supposed to square millions of these girls with her own life? And how, in turn, to square millions of girls with a trillion trillion stars? She has been born on the one temperate, unhostile planet in the universe, in the richest country on that planet, into a family whose wealth places them at the tippy top of that country. It is a disgusting amount of luck. You could never be forgiven for such good fortune. Sometimes, when she thinks of her teeny-weeny life and how *obsessed* she is with it, she feels physically sick.

She is also mortified that she will spend the next week darkening her skin on a chaise lounge alongside other oil-slathered tourists, while people whose skin is darker than hers will ever be (and darker than she wants hers to be) bring her beverages and fresh towels. And she is mortified that her parents see nothing wrong with the whole arrangement. No, that isn't exactly right. They do see something wrong with it, but they think something along the lines of, *We're fortunate, they're unfortunate, and it's neither our fault nor theirs because we are all part of something that is beyond any of us, and we just as easily could have been born them and they just as easily could have been born us, but we weren't, so here we are.* Welcome to paradise. Honestly? She doesn't even want to be here.

Her first night at Indigo Bay, after her sister is asleep, she walks out onto the balcony to look at the stars. The warm breeze ripples against her skin. Venus burns a cold, clear blue. She unzips her dress. Just because she can. You can stand on a balcony and have an utterly ordinary moment, or you can let your dress fall to the cool terra-cotta tiles, unhook your bra, and offer yourself up to the night. Possibilities are everywhere, hidden in the fist of each moment, yet most people don't see them, or they see them but leave them untouched.

She wishes she could see the picture she makes with the white curtains billowing behind her, hair fluttering in the wind, breasts lit by a fingernail of moon. She surveys the resort grounds below her. No one. This pleases her, not because she would be embarrassed to be seen, but because it means this is a secret moment. Hers alone, then, *poof!* Gone. When she thinks of all the secret moments locked within this instant — of all the people on earth doing things no one will ever know — her heart feels so full it could crack.

She looks at the starry sky, the dark shimmering sea, and tries to savor the beauty of it all, but she can't get herself to really feel it. The view from the balcony bleeds together with too many other views on other vacations in other paradises. Which island had the pink sand beach? Which one had those zippy orange birds? Where was it you could wade out a quarter mile from shore before the water deepened? Somewhere she saw a sunset like a bloody sacrifice and a woman tossing white petals into the surf. She is eighteen and beauty already seems such a cheap thing. She can behold it and behold it without feeling a thing.

She sleeps late, then spends an embarrassing amount of time appraising herself in the mirror in the marble bathroom before making her entrance on the beach. When she finally emerges, her family is already set up, with a row of four chairs with white cushions in the shade of two white umbrellas. These resorts often have an obsession with white. White buildings, white floors, white linens, white uniforms. Like they're trying to convince you you've died and gone to heaven, or like you've arrived at some hedonistic sanatorium because you're afflicted by something and you didn't even know it but now you will heal.

Her parents start talking at her. Cruise ship, slide, something, something. She pulls one of the lounge chairs into the sun and lies down. She takes out her Walkman and lets "Big Poppa" drown her dad out. A minute later her father hails one of the beach waiter guys like he's a cab. Awful. But the guy doesn't seem to notice, or care, or something. She turns up the volume on her Walkman and pulls the headphones down around her neck, hoping he'll hear what song she's listening to. He introduces himself. He's Edwin. He is skinny and super-friendly with her parents, like all his life he's dreamed of meeting the Thomases of Westchester, who are totally eating it up. Her dad orders her a fruit punch, which . . . she guesses he can inhabit whatever alternate reality he wants.

When Edwin comes back, he's hunched under the weight of a tray of excessively garnished cocktails and she wants to disappear, because lying on this chaise lounge while he labors is so uncomfortable. The thing she can't figure out is, if she is honest with herself, she does not find this arrangement uncomfortable because a person is doing something for her, but because a black person is doing something for a white person. Which doesn't mean she doesn't want him to have his job. So what does it mean, exactly?

When he asks if she'll come play in the volleyball game in the afternoon, she shrugs, tells him maybe.

"More of a sunbather, are we?" he says.

Her entire body flushes. *Not me!* she wants to tell him. *I'm not just some ditzy sun worshipper.* But there is no way to convey this without protesting too much and coming off even worse.

He winks at her and continues down the beach.

Her fruit punch, actually, is delicious. The sun on her skin is delicious. Maybe she is wrong to have such a stick up her ass about the whole situation. Maybe she should, as a general thing, just shut up and be grateful. But lately she is beginning to suspect that gratitude (as an emotion, as an action) is a colossal scam. Rich, poor, it doesn't matter — everyone is expected to be grateful for what they have, whatever that is. Once, in high school, she snuck into the city with her girlfriends to smoke clove cigarettes in Washington Square Park and try to get invited to an NYU party, and on the way downtown from Grand Central they had a taxi driver who'd been a chemical engineer in Pakistan. When she asked if it frustrated him to do what he did now, he said no, just the opposite, he was grateful. It was a familiar story. In my country I was a lawyer, I was a doctor, I was a professor, but I'm grateful to drive this taxi in America, I'm grateful to bus these dishes in America, I'm grateful to clean up the vomit of fraternity brothers in this dormitory at an Ivy League university in America. Meanwhile, Alison is expected to be grateful for her Audi, and for she doesn't even know how much her parents pay for her college tuition, and for their beautiful vacations and the beautiful teeth she possesses after years of orthodontia. So what is gratitude, really, but reverence for a system that gives and deprives at random? No, not at random. The non-randomness is exactly the point, right?

That afternoon when she hears Edwin yelling about the volleyball game, she pushes herself up from her chaise lounge. She will show him who she is.

"Want to come watch me play, Clairey?"

Her sister's face lights up at the invitation. Sometimes her power to make her sister happy terrifies her.

She's nervous when she pulls her tunic up over her head. Though she knows she's pretty, cute, arguably even sexy in a girl-next-door way, she is always nervous when she reveals her scar to people for the first time. She isn't insecure about it, exactly; it's more like the nervousness she feels at a dance recital just before she leaps onto the empty stage.

When her torso is exposed, it happens like it always does. Her teammates stare with the obviousness of cattle. When she catches them at it, they avert their eyes oh-so-politely. She loves catching people looking at her scar, shaming them with a glance.

As the players manage the ball back and forth over the net in sequences of sloppy bumps and sets, she imagines them imagining what happened to her. A wash of dark scenarios projects like a movie montage against the limpid blue sky. She sees herself thrown from a car onto one of those boggy meadows beside the highway, gnashed by a neighbor's Akita, cut open on a surgeon's table.

The real story is her favorite, but she guards it closely, not wanting to dull it by too frequent visitation. She was four. It was summer, and her family, which did not yet include Claire, was at a campground on a lake. They went every summer, and she never liked it. The bottom of the lake was soft, like stepping in dead things. It was night. She was sitting around a fire with her parents roasting marshmallows. Her parents turned away for a moment and when they looked back, she was in the fire. Her father dove in and scooped her out — she was in the flames for only a few seconds, just long enough to be marked by them forever. At the hospital, when her parents and the nurses asked her what happened, she just shook her head, unable to explain. As her parents tell the story, it is a mystery: whether she tripped and fell or whether, dazzled by the flames or propelled by some wild impulse, she jumped.

"I could have died," she told Drew the first time she let him see it. When he touched the smooth, pink surface of the scar gently with his fingertips, as if it might still hurt, she loved him. It's true — she *could* have died. In a way, her whole life grows out of that moment. Edwin will begin to see it now: she is a person to whom things have happened.

A woman on her team is talking through the earth-shattering conundrum of whether she and her husband should go on the excursion to the old sugar estate and rum distillery. "I wanted to go, but I've heard it's a drag. Apparently it's mostly about the history of sugar cultivation on the island, the plantation system and that stuff?"

That stuff, i.e., slavery? Alison purses her lips to indicate to Edwin that she does not approve of the woman's comment. She hears everything her teammates say twice

— once as herself, and once as she imagines he hears it. The woman's husband, a man with dolphins on his pink swim trunks, serves the ball into the net.

"Almost, honey," the woman says. "I would just like to have a week here where I don't have to think about how awful the world is. I'm a defense attorney. I know it's awful."

Fair enough? Alison isn't sure. You don't get to decide, do you, when to care and when not to care, when to see the big picture and when to zoom in so super-close on your own life that your desire for a massage fills your entire field of vision?

There are a few other college kids playing, and they set about the unavoidable business of identifying the hall mates, teammates, bunkmates that connect them. "Small world," remarks a boy who initially says he goes to school in Connecticut, and only when prodded lets "Yale" cross his lips, a confession he makes with an irreproachable mix of sheepishness and élan. *Small world. Small world.* Like it is some crazy cosmic coincidence, rich people overlapping with other rich people. If he weren't so cute — yellow-haired and tall, with a certain anemic quality she finds appealing — she would be done with him already. Instead, she flirts.

The other girl her age squeals when the ball comes near her. She adjusts her bikini top to maintain just the right revelation of boob. She says, "Did I do good?" in a baby voice when she sets up a spike for one of the guys. Alison doesn't get it. Okay, fine, she *gets* it. In a way you can hardly blame the girl, because it works. The boy with the hemp necklace is eating it up. But can someone please explain to her the appeal of a guy who can be reeled in by that kind of thing? What you want is a guy who is a little afraid of you. And you want to be a little afraid of him, too.

While the other girl swats the scary ball away, Alison leaps and spikes and pushes off powerfully from the sand. She can feel eyes on her — Connecticut boy's, Edwin's. A vacation is its own world, compressed and powerful, like a planet with stronger gravity. If you play it right, it can teach you things about yourself you can't learn the other 358 days of the year. It is her first day here and already it is happening. The vacation is finding its promise.

When the game is over, Connecticut boy approaches her. She can smell his sweat. It makes her think of Drew, salty and nice. He tells her about the bar in the white marble lobby where the liquor is watered down but where he'll be, anyway, tonight, around ten P.M. He touches his hand to her shoulder, then trots off down the sand.

I might have it all wrong. Maybe Alison did not stand naked on the balcony on our first night on Saint X. Perhaps she did not play volleyball with such vim and vigor in order to impress a boy from Yale, on the one hand, and a local employee, on the other. Perhaps the scar on her stomach was not her most sacred vanity. I'm trying to triangulate the truth, to inhabit my sister's mind. Impossible tasks, to be sure.

What I can say is this: While the details of this story may be products of my imagination, I trust its broad strokes and core themes. I believe that for my sister, our family vacation coincided with one of those brief, intense intervals of identity formation we all experience from time to time in our lives. She arrived at Indigo Bay at that critical moment when the girl cuts herself on the shards of her own reflection and watches, baffled and thrilled, as the blood begins to flow.

Alison wears her pale pink slip dress. Her "fuck-me, I'm-a-baby" dress, as summarized by her friend Dan, who was in love with her but not *something* enough for her to consider a viable romantic option.

Connecticut is already there.

"Hey," she says, exquisitely low-key.

"Hey."

He is drinking a rum and Coke. He is even cuter than she remembered from earlier. He has one of those old-fashioned faces, the kind you can picture in black-and-white. For a moment she sees him in an army uniform and one of those little caps. The image excites her — a young man in the trenches, the secret personal sufferings of war, but also the part where she takes him and implants him in this scene while he sits here next to her in his button-down and has no idea that in her mind his face is smudged with dirt and he is living on rations of tinned meat.

She orders a tequila shot. She opens her throat and drinks it in one go, and though it burns she does not permit herself to react. She is a girl in a tiny pink dress, downing tequila like a champ.

They talk. In addition to playing cello in the Yale Symphony Orchestra, Connecticut is a German major.

"Why German?" she asks.

"I wanted to be able to read Rilke in the original." He rolls his eyes at himself, which she recognizes as the correct move. Nobody likes a snob, but everybody likes the discernment that allows for snobbery.

"How do you say, 'You must change your life,' in German?" she asks, raising her eyebrows like, *Of course I read Rilke.* Actually, she doesn't — she remembers this quote from a paper she wrote freshman year of high school comparing and contrasting Rilke and, for some reason, Keats. She got an A. Mr. Conti put the paper up on the projector as a positive example.

"Du musst dein Leben verwandeln," Connecticut says. "Or something like that. So what about you? Do you know what you're going to major in?"

"Probably something that will drive my parents crazy."

They talk awhile longer, letting the thing build. He asks if she wants to go for a walk and she says yes. He charges her drinks to his room, which would be romantic if his parents weren't obviously paying for it. They leave the bar for the beach. They kick off their shoes. The sand is soft and cool as cream. For a few minutes they walk along the water's edge, their fingertips brushing against each other's, letting their banter slow and the force of the night and this thing they are creating together fill them.

When they reach a cabana he gestures at it, she nods, and he takes her hand and leads her in. Easiest thing in the world.

She has kissed quite a few boys since Drew, and Connecticut is particularly enjoyable. He does not use his tongue a lot, which she likes, because sometimes in the midst of making out with a boy she will think about what a tongue actually is and feel paralyzed. He kisses her neck a lot and she likes that, too. It is all very, very nice. But there is something about this niceness that doesn't sit right. She feels it like a cold gel applied to the moment. She is moving through this scenario the way she would work through a math problem she knows she will get right.

She knows why it is so easy for her, this and so much else. She knows the substance of the reserves inside herself that make the world a comfortable place to navigate. It is her mother and father loving her like crazy. It is the dappled lawn of her childhood home with its soft mown stripes of green and darker green. It is "fantastic insight!" written in a teacher's delicious cursive in the margin of an essay. It is the gothic magnificence of the Princeton campus, through which she strolled all autumn in mesh shorts and flip-flops and a messy ponytail. It is every witticism she's ever tossed off in a circle at a party and the impressed faces of the people who heard it. It is the people she knows and *their* reserves — their happy childhoods, their bright memories, their educations, all the beauty they have seen, out and out like ripples on the glassy surface of a pool in a secret glade they carry collectively within them. They are spinning it together, she and Connecticut, good fortune igniting on itself under the tropical stars. Is there anything more obvious in the entire world?

When he touches her thigh under her dress, she freezes. Not *actually* freezes. She keeps doing what they're doing. But inside. She is not very experienced, truth be told. She was with Drew forever, but she's learned in the past few months that all that experience is actually just one experience. They were babies when they started dating and they figured everything out together, and what if they figured it out weird? She hasn't had an orgasm with anyone else and she knows it's because she's afraid that if she does, the guy will look at her funny because her orgasms are weird and she didn't know it. She doesn't want to be here anymore. She wants to take the nice kissing with her and leave.

She presses a finger delicately to his lips. "I should go," she whispers.

"Are you sure?" He strokes her thigh higher up this time. It is the first thing he does that she doesn't like. He looks down at his lap, where his boner pushes against his khaki shorts. Her stomach flips. Back in her room with her sleeping sister — that's where she wants to be.

"I'm sure." She scrunches her nose, cute as a button.

He wraps his arms around her waist. "But I want to kidnap you," he says, and buries his face in her hair.

"Not tonight," she says.

"Tomorrow?"

"We'll see."

She stands, smooths her dress. He reaches for her hand, and she holds his for a moment, then lets it slip through her fingers as she turns and walks back toward the lights of the resort.

"Tell me something," her father says the next day, as Clive gathers up the french fries he spilled in the sand. "Where do you recommend for some local food? You know, something authentic."

Alison winces. Her father asks this every year, at every resort, on his bullshit search for some local color, the Real Wherever. She can't stand how pleased he is with his question, like he expects Clive to be superimpressed by his desire to get off the beaten path. (Does he think Clive wants his favorite local spot to be invaded by hordes of tourists?) Her father wants to be able to say, *Now,* this *is delicious,* of the conch creole at some hole-in-the-wall, whether or not it is better than the conch creole served at Indigo Bay. Her mother wants to tell the cook on the way out, *You have a beautiful restaurant,* with her sweet little smile, when the truth is if she thought folding chairs and ceiling fans instead of AC were so great, she'd eat at places like this back home, too, which of course she doesn't. Then her father wants to take his mediocre photos of the place and blow them up and hang them on the living room wall so their friends will inquire about them at dinner parties and he can tell them about *this amazing little spot* he discovered.

That isn't fair. As parents go, hers aren't so bad. Isn't it better at least to have the inclination to leave the bubble? Well, maybe better for *them,* but shouldn't the people who live here get to keep some places to themselves? But maybe the people who live here *want* people like her parents to come to their restaurants; maybe her notion that they'd rather the tourists and their money stay away is just that, a naïve little notion. She could go around like this forever, trying to decide.

"People like Spicy's. Their roast crayfish is quite popular," Clive says.

"Roast crayfish," her father says. "Fantastic."

Later that afternoon, Alison finds Edwin standing behind the open-air restaurant. "Hey, Mr. Carnival Sandcastle Champion."

"Watch out. The girl's feeling frisky today."

She snorts.

A cook calls out from the kitchen, "Order up!"

"Duty calls?"

"Nonstop till three."

"What's at three?"

"Break. I usually take it down there, past those rocks at the end of the beach."

When the hour comes, her parents are snoozing away. She tells her sister she's going to the bathroom. At the jagged black rocks that mark the end of Indigo Bay, she scrambles up and over, stumbling, then regaining her footing. She crests the rocks and sees Edwin sitting in the sand. He looks up.

"What are you doing here?" he says sternly. For a moment she worries she misunderstood. Then he tosses back his head and laughs.

"Ha ha," she says. "You're hysterical."

The beach here isn't groomed like it is around the resort. You can barely see the sand, it's so covered in stuff: green beer bottles, nests of odorous seaweed studded with cigarette butts. Three tires tied together with yellow rope. An old cardboard campaign poster with a picture of a woman in a blazer, the blazer still bright red, the woman's face so faded she looks like a ghost. She has to step carefully as she makes her way to him. He's eating fried fish out of a grease-spotted paper bag and smoking a cigarette.

"You know those will kill you," she says as she sits down beside him.

"Only if something else doesn't kill me first."

She nods at the cigarette with her chin. "May I?"

"I insist, miss."

She rolls her eyes at this word. *Miss.* She likes the way he calls her this with a subversive smile, like they're in on something together. He passes her the cigarette and she takes a slow, assured drag. As she exhales, she looks out at the water and tries to work her face into an expression that suggests she finds something very personally meaningful there. She passes the cigarette back to him.

"If you're looking for something more, me and Gogo usually lime in the car park for a bit after work. Smoke some herb, you dig?"

"Oh, I dig."

"Maybe we'll see you there sometime."

She shrugs. "Maybe. Anyway, I should get back before they send out a search party." She stands and brushes the sand from her legs.

"You're bleeding," he says.

She looks at her calf. She must have cut herself when she stumbled; a few long scratches bubble with red blood. She shrugs again.

"Tough girl."

"Oh, yeah. So tough."

"How did you get that?" He is pointing at her scar. She feels filled by a gust of bright wind. It is happening so right, his eyes riveted to the pink glaze on her stomach.

"I don't like to talk about it." It's like the words find her. She turns and walks back the way she came. She doesn't glance behind her once.

At the end of the day she makes her way to the parking lot. She finds Edwin and Clive leaning against a shabby, eggplant-colored car.

"Miss! What a fine surprise to see you here!" Edwin says.

She rolls her eyes. "Right. What a coincidence. What are you two upstanding gentlemen up to, I wonder?"

Clive stiffens.

Edwin slips a joint from his pocket. "Nothing much." He twirls it in his fingers.

"Mind if I do *nothing much* with you?"

Alison's father summons Edwin to their chairs.

"What can I be getting for you this afternoon?" Edwin asks.

"How's the penne?" her father asks, which makes Alison want to crawl into a hole and die.

"Excellent, sir."

They place their lunch orders.

"And to drink, a Red Stripe for me and a rum punch for my wife. Girls?" her father says.

"Sprite," Claire says, then adds in a

whisper, "with a cherry."

"Your wish is my command, little miss. And you?" he says to Alison. He doesn't use her name, as if he doesn't know it.

"I'd love a daiquiri."

"Virgin," her father says.

"Of course," Edwin says, at the same time as Alison says, "I thought that was implied, Dad."

When Edwin returns with their order, Alison takes a delicate sip of her daiquiri. It's full of rum. She looks at him. He has his eyes on her, steady. He puts her father's tip in his back pocket and continues down the beach.

"I needed that," she says later, when she finds him beyond the black rocks.

"You're most welcome, miss," he says.

"Stop calling me that," she says, and leans her body playfully against his.

It's a clear day. Faraway Cay appears unsettlingly close.

"So how are you enjoying your holiday?"

"It's fun I guess," she says. "My parents are driving me nuts."

"Family's always that way. You need a break."

"Seriously."

"Come out tonight. With me and Gogo."

"Out where?"

"We lime at a place in the Basin. We can pick you up in the car park. Eleven P.M. Just make sure it's all right with your parents, okay, miss?" His eyes twinkle.

"Right. I'll be sure to secure their permission."

"You'll come, then?"

A hermit crab scuttles across the sand. She picks it up and holds the shell close to her lips, then blows gently across the opening, drawing its legs out into the air.

"We'll see," she says, with a sly smile she thinks irresistible on her lips. She stands and begins to walk away. When she reaches the rocks, she glances back. He has his eyes on her, watching her go.

Once her sister is asleep, she changes out of her pajamas and into the outfit she decided on that afternoon, her yellow dress with the plunging neckline. She glances one last time at her sleeping sister before closing the door quietly behind her and stepping out into the warm night. The resort late at night is a vacant place — lounge chairs stacked six feet high on the sand, the fertile scent of washed clay rising from the tennis courts, everything dark save the dim illumination of lanterns along the gravel footpaths. The water has changed, too; the ocean is glossy and black as oil, the pool glows ghostly green. Every surface echoes her nervy energy back at her.

She can hear the distant sounds of chatter and merriment at the hotel bar. So *satisfied* with their margaritas and Marley. She imagines Connecticut sitting at the bar, looking over his shoulder frequently to see if she's coming. She feels his lips on her neck, dry and nice like warm stones. She sees his blue eyes under the thick fringe of his lashes. She shakes the image away. It is to be expected, this residue of desire, this lazy craving.

What does she want from tonight? She's not totally sure. She knows only that she wants these men to take her somewhere new, out past the familiar borders of her life. She is only waiting in the parking lot a few minutes when the eggplant-colored car pulls in.

"Look who decided to grace us with she presence," Edwin says.

"It was a tough decision. There are so many fun things to do at the hotel at night."

She climbs in the backseat. The car smells strongly of body odor and air freshener. The seats are upholstered, and the fabric is held together with tape where it has ripped open to reveal beige foam. In her head, she's sitting on her bed in her dorm room, telling Nika, *Then I snuck out with them and we went to this great local dive.* She loves the feeling that she is doing something she probably shouldn't with men who scare her a little. Life is about escalation: men instead of boys; a wilder wild night; more and more and more. In her mind, she sends the image of her in the car with these men to Drew. He sees her and is worried, and his worry makes her swoon and long for him. But the feeling passes quickly, and then she pities him. She has left him so far behind that he is nothing but a nice little memory. Besides, what could possibly happen to her on a tiny island where everyone knows everyone?

"What's this place we're going to?" she asks.

"Paulette's," Edwin says. "Best dance spot on the island."

"Do you dance, Clive?" she asks playfully.

Edwin palms Clive's head with his hand and rubs it. "Gogo's a fantastic dancer. Just you wait to see his moves. Isn't that so, mate?"

Clive turns to look back at her and makes an expression that is a smile but not really.

Paulette's is more of a shack, honestly, the exterior strung with orange Christmas lights. Inside, there is a plank floor covered in sawdust, speakers spitting tinny music, the smells of sweat and liquor, an old mutt sniffing the ground for scraps. There are maybe twenty people, some dancing but most just talking. Alison sees a woman she thinks she recognizes as a waitress at the resort restaurant, but she isn't positive — black people *do* look similar to her; it's embarrassing but it isn't her fault, is it, that she's been raised in a white place and made white friends and had sex with exclusively white men? Well, three of them, anyway.

Nobody seems surprised to see her here with Edwin and Clive. It occurs to her she is probably not the first girl from the resort they've brought here, but did she think she was? She did not. She isn't an idiot.

"I'll get drinks," Edwin says. "You keep the Goges company."

She stands with Clive at the edge of the dance floor, which isn't an actual dance floor but an area marked off with yellow electrical tape. She smiles warmly at him and he smiles uncomfortably back.

"Do you guys come here a lot?" she asks over the din.

"Quite often, miss."

"You don't have to call me 'miss,' you know."

"I'm sorry, m—" He looks down, shakes his head at himself.

"It's fine. Seriously."

He looks out at the dance floor, like it is an absorbing show he doesn't want to tear himself away from. She knows he's just trying to fill the time until Edwin gets back. He doesn't know how to talk to her.

"I brought you something special," Edwin says when he returns. He hands Alison a shot glass filled with something murky — it looks like the water in Claire's fish tank when she hasn't cleaned it in too long. "See if you can guess the secret ingredient."

Alison holds the glass up to the light. "What is it?"

"Do you trust me?"

Does she?

"Yeah," she says coolly. She snaps her head back and takes the shot in one gulp. "It just tastes like grass."

He claps his hands. "That's a fact. Vodka infused with fine Jamaican ganja."

"It's not bad," she says. She laughs. "It's actually pretty good."

"You going to drink any fool thing he hand you?"

She turns. A woman is standing a few

inches away from her, looking at her critically. She wonders if the women here all watched her gulping down the mystery drink and thought, *Dumb, dumb, dumb.*

The woman breaks into a laugh. "I'm just playing," she says. "He's all right. He's real sweet."

"This is Paulette she self," Edwin says.

"Nice to meet you," Alison says reflexively.

Paulette smirks at her, amused. God, she feels clueless.

"She's bent all the time to messing up my game," Edwin says.

"Is this your game?" Alison says, eyebrows raised.

Paulette laughs. "She's a live one."

She is doing it. She is really doing it. *A live one.*

"Do you want to dance?" Edwin asks.

"With *you*?"

"Sassy."

She takes his hand and pulls him onto the dance floor.

I searched for Paulette's Place online but found no trace of it. It must have closed sometime in the intervening years. I do not know what the bar where Alison was seen with Edwin and Clive really looked like. I know only that it was in the Basin and that, according to several witnesses, Alison was there four nights in a row, including on the last night of her life. But I have a mental picture of the place to which, in this version of things, Alison reacts. When she sees my Paulette's, she is pleased by its shabby authenticity, which affirms that she's found the real fun to be had on the island, something better than the lame hotel bar where empty-nesters stay up past their bedtimes slinging tequila and laughing at their milquetoast naughtiness.

Is the bar I've created a terrible cliché? If so, how much does it matter? What happens if you replace the wood floor coated in sawdust with a proper dance floor? What if you nix the mutt and add a cocktail waitress, sub a sound system for the tinny speakers on the bar? Now what does Alison think, say, do? What quantity of truth resides within a story's details?

Alison sits on the putting green at Indigo Bay in her purple bikini and watches Connecticut drive golf balls into the lagoon. They are alone, at the far edge of the property. On the putting green there is a golf bag stuffed with clubs and a tin bucket of balls, special ones that float. At some later time, Alison assumes, a staff member will go out onto the water in a boat to collect them. So much effort so that they may have this moment.

The lagoon is a wide stretch of shallow water separated from the ocean by dunes and a thicket of sea grape. This spot feels private, secret. She understands this is why he has brought her here. She recognizes the strategy of this, but she can still feel the place working on her. It's quiet. The only sounds are the swoop of the club, the crack as it makes contact with the ball and, after the passage of an impossible number of moments, the distant plunk of the ball slipping into the water.

"You're good," she says. She sits with her legs straight out in front of her, leaning back and propped up on her elbows.

"I'm just okay," he says with a shrug that makes her heart skip.

She feels him taking in the inches of her. It's so easy it makes her want to wring the sky — his wanting and her not giving and his wanting more.

It begins to rain. The first drops cool her sunburned shoulders.

"Should we go back?" she asks.

"A little rain never killed anyone," he says. She can tell he likes how it sounds. He swings and sends a ball whooshing out over the water.

When it begins to pour, he slots the club back into the bag and sits down beside her. He tucks a wet strand of hair behind her ear. He leans in to kiss her, and she kisses him back. Then she pulls away.

What's wrong with her? Why can't she give this to herself? Ivy boy and Ivy girl, la-di-da, easy peasy, ashes ashes we all fall down. It makes her . . . what? Embarrassed? Ashamed? She could kiss him, and then they could have sex in a secluded corner of a resort on a tropical island as the rain falls around them. For a moment she wishes with everything she has that she were a different girl, one who would see this possibility as the pinnacle of something.

"I'm sorry," she whispers.

"It's fine," he says. "Whatever."

She seeks out Edwin and Clive more frequently. In the afternoons, she sneaks away to meet Edwin past the black rocks. She wakes at dawn and swims in the ocean while they set up the lounge chairs on the beach for the day. Before they depart in the evening, she finds them in the parking lot and they pass around a joint. She learns that they have a sideline keeping the guests of Indigo Bay supplied with marijuana and, occasionally, harder stuff — cocaine and Ecstasy, mostly.

"Sometimes we forget to pass on a small amount to our customer," Edwin says one afternoon.

"So technically this joint is the property of a stockbroker from Millburn?" she says.

"Maybe so."

"So are you, like, stoned all the time at work?"

"Not *all* the time, miss," Clive says with a grin — the first time she's seen him actually smile.

Her whole body feels charged with the delicious secret they've divulged. She has been chosen, brought to the other side of the wall that separates tourist from local. They tell her about the soca band that will be playing at Paulette's later that week; about the cup of spittle Nestor the bartender keeps under the bar, next to the maraschino cherries. When Clive asks, Alison declares college "pretty boring." When Edwin prods him, Clive recounts the story of a guest who crashed a Sunfish into a fishing boat in the bay.

"Tourists," Alison scoffs, then blushes.

Edwin asks her about New York. He tells her he has a cousin there, in Queensbridge.

"Cool," she says with an air of native

authority, as if she has any clue where Queensbridge is; as if, when she was a kid and the school bus took them through Harlem en route to midtown for field trips — museums, Broadway — she didn't press her face to the bus windows with the other kids and stare at the spectacle of a world of black people. "I was born in the city," she adds after a pause. "My parents lived in this tiny apartment on the Lower East Side. It's this immigrant neighborhood."

Clive and Edwin nod blankly in response. Her face burns. She wanted them to know her family hasn't always been filthy rich, but it didn't land how she wanted. What's wrong with her, bragging about how her parents were poor for, like, five minutes, before she was even born? She's been doing this kind of thing at college, too. Just the other day she told Nika a story from last summer at her family's "cottage" at the shore, and now she's stuck, because she wants to invite Nika out there to visit this summer, but then not only will Nika see just how rich Alison's family is, she will also know that Alison is the kind of person who refers to a huge freaking beach house as a cottage, which is even worse than the huge freaking house itself. It's not just her, though. Every rich kid at college does this.

They all have a "cottage," or forebears they seem very keen to talk about who came to America from some shtetl or Irish potato farm, or they're "from Chicago" when really they live in Winnetka. (In the past three months she has learned the fancy suburbs surrounding all of the major cities in the country.) They are pathological minimizers, telling their half-truths and hoping for some kind of credit.

"It drives me nuts that my parents moved out of the city to raise us," she says, changing tack. "I mean, you're in the greatest city on earth, and you leave for some lame suburb?"

"But isn't New York quite dangerous?" Clive asks.

She shrugs. "You just have to pay attention."

One evening when she is standing with them in the parking lot after work, Clive proposes they go down to the water for a swim.

"I'm game," Alison says.

"Nah, nah. My boy's stalling," Edwin says with a mirthful shake of his head.

"Am not. The water's just looking nice today."

"Gogo has to go see he baby boy and take

the shit from he lady," Edwin says with a gleam in his eye.

"You have a kid?" she says. She's been hanging out with them for days and this is the first she's heard of any baby. The information tickles her. In her head, she tells Nika, *Then Clive had to go take care of his son,* as if it doesn't ruffle her at all.

Clive's face has gone blank. Maybe he doesn't care about the kid. Or maybe he does care about him and he's ashamed to be standing here getting stoned with Edwin and some girl while his child waits for him and he doesn't want to think about it.

"He'll make three soon," he says softly.

"Wait. Are you *married*?"

Clive shakes his head.

"Relax, Goges." Edwin claps a hand on his friend's big shoulder. "If Sara never consents to marry you, more time to lime with me."

Clive nods, his face empty. She can hardly bear it, and at the same time cannot look away from it, his gentle, pained way of being in the world; he reminds her, in a way, of Claire.

She touches his arm. "She don't know what she's missing."

"She *don't* know what she's missing.

You're turning into a proper island girl, now," Edwin says.

Every night, after her sister is asleep, she crosses the dark resort grounds and meets them in the parking lot and they drive to Paulette's Place, where they drink and smoke and she and Edwin dance while Clive stands near them on the dance floor, bouncing his large body not quite to the beat. At times it seems clear to her what Edwin wants — he flirts, manufactures opportunities to touch her. One night, his crotch grazes her hip as they dance and she feels that he is hard. Her skin turns to gooseflesh. His erection scares her. Well, Drew's scared her, too, at first, didn't it? Connecticut's hand on her thigh scared her. But she knows it is not the same.

Suddenly she sees John the gardener's face — his soft lamb's-wool hair, his dark skin. Is that all this is, what she's doing with Edwin? An attempt to absolve her frightened child self? And she still can't do it. She feels him against her and she tenses.

But nothing comes of it. When the song ends, he buys her another round at the bar, complimenting Paulette on her dress while they wait. He is loose and jovial again, as if their pressed-together dancing didn't happen. She is starting to see something new about him, a controlled aspect simmering just beneath his charming surface. The moves he makes — letting her feel his hardness, then striking up a conversation with Paulette when she fully expected him to lead her off to some dark corner — seem, beneath the offhandedness with which he executes them, studied, like there is nothing he says or does that he hasn't thought through. Maybe this will go where she thinks it's going. Or maybe nothing will happen. When she considers this possibility she is humiliated but also, in some way, relieved.

On a rainy day, after picking up a puka shell necklace for Claire at the gift shop, Alison finds Edwin taking his break behind the restaurant. "No beach today?" she asks.

"Can't." He points out at the black rocks. Waves crash against them, sending spray high into the air and blocking the path to his usual spot.

"We could swim there," Alison says.

"You crazy? Look at that water."

"Bet you two joints I can do it. Around the rocks, to the beach, and back."

"I'm not betting your death sentence, miss," he says with a laugh.

"Suit yourself." She walks down to the water. She peels off her tank top and shimmies out of her shorts, revealing the new bikini she got for this trip, blue with white flowers.

"What are you doing?"

She dives in. The waves are swollen, but it isn't as bad as it looks from shore; besides, she's a strong swimmer. She strokes through the waves, keeping her head when she sees them rise up above her. When she is out past the rocks she begins to arc around. She swims until her limbs are stiff with exhaustion and every part of her tastes salt. She loves this feeling, the rush of hanging off the edge of your comfort zone but still knowing you have a solid grip on it. When she returns to shore she hands Edwin a shard of green sea glass.

"Proof," she gasps, breathing hard but trying not to show it.

That afternoon in the parking lot, he gives her the two joints she has won. "I think I've been underestimating you," he says.

"Is that right?"

He nods. "You're a dangerous girl."

On the last night of vacation, she can't help herself. She goes looking for Connecticut. She finds him by the bar in the lobby. He wears khaki slacks and a blue-and-white-checked shirt. He is freshly showered. His blond hair still holds narrow ridges from the tines of a comb.

"Hey."

"Hey."

She reaches into the pocket of her jean skirt. "Want to?" she says, revealing the joint in her palm. Easiest thing in the world. Connecticut grabs one of the Indigo Bay matchbooks from the glass bowl on the bar. She leads him to the parking lot. She puts the joint to her lips. He strikes the match. When she exhales, she coughs.

"You okay?" he asks, a hand to her back, a show of rather than actual concern — he is a good guy and wants her to know it. It's nice, though, his hand there.

She nods and passes the joint to him.

"How'd you manage to get this?"

"Let's just say I have my ways."

He leans closer, whispers in her ear, "I like your ways." He kisses her neck. Her body shivers, but she shakes the pleasure away. When they have finished the joint, she drops the roach on the ground.

"You're really not going to tell me where you got it?"

"Well . . . ," she says.

"So secretive, Alison." He twists a strand

of her hair around his finger.

"It's no big deal, really. Edwin gave it to me." She says it like it is the least interesting fact in the world.

"Oh," he says, stiffening. "Well, lucky us. We'll have to thank him." He pulls her hair away from the back of her neck and kisses her again.

"I have to go," she says. She pecks him, quick and delicate, on the lips.

"Come on, why don't you —"

"Shhh," she says. She is the star in a script she knows by heart. "Later. I'll find you."

She begins to walk away, but he holds on to her hand.

"Where?" he asks.

She smiles coyly. "I promise."

Does Alison seem awful to you? I admit that, as I channel my sister, I sometimes have an urge to shake her. I find her incessant judginess toward our parents and her fellow resort guests self-righteous and bratty, especially the judgments she renders on the blond boy, who is practically her double: bright, privileged, attractive, and tasteful enough to know to be self-deprecating about such things. Equally frustrating is the way she exempts Edwin and Clive from her judgment. How desperate she is for their approval, their special attentions, how badly she needs them to know that she is more than, better than, all the basically decent people from her world.

What I can't figure out: Was Alison insufferable in a perfectly ordinary teenage way, or was something darker at play? Was her behavior typical or troubling? What destiny lay ahead of her as she toyed with the blond boy and danced at Paulette's Place and swam out beyond the black rocks in the rain-swelled surf? Who *was* she?

As the eggplant-colored Vauxhall Astra (how she loves that name!) rumbles down Mayfair Road, she sees her last night on Saint X spread above her like a sky dense with stars. She feels the night's promise in the itch of the upholstery against the backs of her thighs and in "Boombastic" blasting from the radio. She wears a turquoise halter top and a short jean skirt; she is an island girl, flying away from Connecticut at the speed of light. *I think I'll stay in tonight. Honestly, Nika? These campus parties just feel very tame to me lately.*

It is hot inside Paulette's Place. Sweat gleams on skin. "Buy me a drink," she tells them. She takes a shot of rum, then another, and struts onto the dance floor. She sways her hips and presses up against Edwin, then spins away to uncertain Clive, back and forth. Irresistible. She sees herself from outside herself, from somewhere up in the mantle of stars, like the story of her life is already burned in light and she has only to navigate by it to make herself into herself.

Once Clive is a few drinks in he is not so hesitant. When she dances with him, he holds her hips.

"Check you out, Goges!" Edwin hoots.

Clive grins.

She winks at Edwin and moves in closer to Clive.

His hands, so clumsy and searching, stir something in her. As they dance, his eyes wander from her breasts to the floor to Edwin to the ceiling, never settling anywhere, as if looking at any one thing too long is just asking for punishment. An image comes to her, a baby boy with damp black curls and eyelashes to the horizon.

It's then she understands. It isn't only Edwin she wants. It is the two of them together, the power of two men so different from each other, and all eyes on her. They will dance a few minutes longer, and then she will say, "Let's get out of here." They will go to some deserted beach, or they will sneak into an unoccupied hotel room at

Indigo Bay, or maybe they will only make it out behind Paulette's, to the scruffy patch of sand and grass at the edge of the parking lot, hidden from view by an old junked van. Things with Edwin will reach their natural conclusion. Even as she does it, she will be telling Nika, *It was pretty good. Not, like, earth-shattering or anything.*

Then she will turn her attention to Clive. She will push onto her tiptoes and kiss him on the mouth. He will surprise her. She will expect him to be timid and awkward, but he won't be. He will hold the back of her head and kiss her hard, so that the whole weight of him is contained in his kiss. He will take her ponytail and squeeze it in his fist like a rag. He will take her hand and thrust it down his pants. The more afraid she feels, the more she will want it.

He will lay her down on the ground. The stars will wheel overhead, fine and white, and in them she will see herself, years from now, looking back at her as she is in this moment, beautiful and reckless as a young woman ought to be. She will have this night forever. She will carry it like her scar, a thing she can always feel, even when she isn't touching it. He will move over her like she isn't precious at all, like he is barely aware of her beneath him. She will feel so small in his arms, and she will like this so much it will suck the air out of her — the way she disappears, the way she becomes nothing at all. She will finally feel like she is in this place without herself, and maybe that is all she ever wanted, for her little life to vanish right out from under her.

She will stare into the sky. The stars will rush at her across time and space like spears. They will slash her up with their cold white light.

I didn't have sex for almost a year after she died. At first I didn't want to. Next to Alison, the girls at college were so mind-numbing. I'd go to parties and they'd be wearing all this makeup and this perfume or fruity shampoo or whatever makes them smell like that, and while they were talking to me they would pose and giggle like it was an audition, and it made me feel dead.

Later I wanted to, but I couldn't. I'd go back to a girl's dorm room and she'd light a vanilla candle or something, and all of a sudden I just had to get out of there. The girl would be embarrassed and hurt and insulted. She'd say, "Did I do something wrong, Drew?" I'd pull on my pants real quick and bolt. I'd go back to my apartment, which was a real shithole I shared with these guys I'd ended up living with, and drink beer and play *Mario Kart* until four A.M. I haven't kept up with any of those guys. I can't. I thought Alison was the love of my life and she was dead and that was it for me.

But things changed. Alison changed. With time, she stopped being this guilty conscience or this barrier or whatever she was. She became a way of . . . opening up, I guess. I told Shannon about her after two months, in the Sheep Meadow in Central Park. I told Anjali after only two weeks, when we snuck away from a friend's housewarming party. I'd tell the girls about Alison and they'd tell me about their mother's drinking, or their brother's depression, or being bullied.

I told Hayley after three months, on a road trip to her cousin's wedding in Cleveland. After I told her, she stroked my arm and said, "You poor thing." I drank too much at her cousin's dumb wedding. I got loud and obnoxious with her blowhard father. I spent the rest of the night puking into the toilet at the Best Western. Hayley stayed awake all night taking care of me and the next morning she sucked apologies from me and I gave them to her, tail between my legs. I did behave badly. It would take a few more months for me to admit to myself that I hated her; I'd hated her from the moment she stroked my arm in the car like that.

With Rachel, I waited almost a year. I didn't want her to feel like she had to compete with my murdered high school sweetheart. When we got married, Alison changed again. She became a past I was ready to leave behind. A ghost I no longer invited inside. We're divorced now, but that was about other things. She wanted kids, I thought I did but changed my mind. "But don't you want to see who we'd make?" she'd say, like she thought it could only end well.

Sometimes I can't help it. Alison forces her way back in and I start litigating the whole thing all over again. She had a temper, no doubt about it. I think about how riled up she could get about things that were, I don't know, just the world being the world. Like when Nick cheated on Becca and Alison slapped him. Or that teacher, I forget his name, but he had this policy where if you were late he shut the door, and if there was a test, tough luck, you failed, and once this kid Paul, this poor fucking fat kid everybody gave a hard time, I think he was probably gay, too, and this was before you could be, he showed up late on test day and this teacher wouldn't let him in, and she went off on him. The star student challenging the teacher in front of the whole class. The rest of us sat there slack-jawed. She thought everything was her business, I guess is what I'm saying. I'll think about that and wonder if maybe it got her into trouble. Maybe she stuck her nose where it didn't belong.

But I don't spend nearly as much time thinking about this stuff as I used to. Alison's death is a mystery like God or Stonehenge or intelligent life in the universe — if you aren't careful, that shit will consume you, and in the end you'll still be no closer to solving it. I'm thirty-seven years old, and if I've learned anything it's that you can live a pretty decent life without unpacking life's mysteries.

Sara

In his years driving a taxi, Clive has observed that there are two kinds of passengers. First, there are those who ignore him. They spend the ride as if they are alone. They may make telephone calls about sensitive matters. A few times he has heard about the merger between two large corporations, or the resignation of the CEO of a Fortune 500 company, before the news appears in the papers; *I could have been a wealthy man ten times over with all the insider knowledge I've overheard, if I had any money to invest to begin with, hahaha* — he's heard this joke a few times around the garage. In his presence customers have called divorce attorneys ("I want him fucked, do you understand me? I want him fucked so hard his head spins.") and parents with dementia ("Mommy, I need you to listen to Nurse Jen, okay? Can you do that for me, Mommy?"). They may belch or pick their noses in the backseat, and they will not be surreptitious about it, for to these customers, the taxi is that rarest thing: a private enclave in the midst of the city. In his backseat he has seen grown men sob. A teenage girl hold up a small mirror to pop her zits and scowl hatefully at her reflection. A father slap a son across the face.

Then there are those who talk to him, seeking, he supposes, the wisdom that films and television shows have taught them to expect from taxi drivers. These passengers unburden themselves to him of their darkest shames. Affairs, addictions, a stepdaughter's birthday forgotten. To these passengers, the taxi driver is priest, the rider penitent.

Ultimately, though, these types are not as different as they seem. Both those who ignore him and those who entrust him with their most precious secrets do so because, in the end, he is no one to them.

It used to be that when he came home after his shift he could leave these people behind, but the neighborhood is changing. Last year, a white family moved into his building, a couple with a green-eyed, black-haired little girl, Maeve. It won't be long before somebody opens a wine bar nearby. Before too long, one of those food halls might open in Flatbush, and maybe the Little Sweet will have a stall there. The white family in the building are polite and very friendly and at first it seemed there were some advantages to their arrival. When the boiler broke last winter, it was fixed within forty-eight hours. The white family, it turned out, had called 311 about it. He'd overheard them chatting with a neighbor in the vestibule, the neighbor explaining that in the past they'd gone as long as two weeks without heat, the white couple expressing outrage at the landlord's tenant treatment. But now his roommate Cecil calls the family the 311s, because they have also called on more than one occasion to lodge noise complaints, leading to police visits. "Why can't they just knock on a door?" Cecil grumbles, though he must know the answer to this question, as Clive does. They are afraid. Not afraid that their black, foreign neighbors pose a threat to their safety, but afraid that a confrontation will mean losing the approval they feel they've earned with their "Good morning"s and their "Let me get that for you"s. He remembers something Edwin used to say: *Nice* is some real fuckery.

So he knows what this girl, Emily, is doing at the Little Sweet. After all, she's not the only white kid who's become a regular recently. There is also the man with the sketch pad. (*What is he drawing?* Clive wonders. *Scenes of locals in their natural habitat?*) It's not enough for them to live here, to overrun every last space — they need everyone else to be happy about it, too. Every time he catches himself enjoying her company, he reminds himself that's what he is to her. Her local friend. Her badge of approval.

But the more time he spends with her, the more he forgets to remind himself. She is such an odd girl, so young to be so alone in the world. Some evenings, looking across the table at her pale hair, skin, lips, a disquieting notion washes over him: She is not real. She materializes each night so that they may speak, then melts back into the city, dissolving into the salt-whitened streets.

She may be trouble. Funny — from the time he was a child, he has always thought of himself as a person who avoids trouble and complication at all costs. Yet the facts of his life tell a different story. Sometimes he wonders if it is his fate to be controlled by people with the tug of stars, to let himself be pulled into their trouble again and again and learn nothing from it.

■ ■ ■ ■

When they were seventeen, Edwin and Clive and the rest of their class graduated from Everett Lyle Secondary School, all of them except Arthur, who had dropped out a year prior and who, as everybody save his sweet father knew, was into some serious shit by then. He could be found many nights loitering outside the bars and discos around Hibiscus Harbour, sometimes dealing to the tourists, sometimes looking to score. Damien continued his schooling; he would do well on his O-levels, receive a local scholarship, and go on to study biology at the University of the Virgin Islands. His picture would appear in the island newspaper, along with those of the other students from their form who would be attending college off-island, bound for Saint Thomas, Barbados, Miami, Washington, D.C.

"You better not come back all assified," Don would tell Damien when they gathered to see him off.

"I'm right behind you outta here, Doc," Edwin would say.

The rest of them found work. Don got a job in his uncle's auto repair shop. Des, good with boats like his brother Keithley, scored a gig aboard a party boat that took tourists — mostly American college students on spring break — for all-you-can-drink tours up and down the island's south coast. The boat had a dance floor, and the nightly tour included a dance competition in which a dozen or so girls vied for the prize of coupons for five free drinks at Papa Mango's. Often as they danced, the girls shed their clothes — flinging their tank tops into the crowd, sliding their panties down their legs. Des had been at the job a month when he confessed to his friends that there might be such a thing as too much pum pum. After four months, a naked woman was nothing to him. He would look at the girls flaunting their hips and breasts and feel an emptiness like water.

Despite his grandmother's disapproval, Clive joined Edwin in pursuing what Edwin referred to as his "business ventures." It was not uncommon for them to have four or five such ventures going at any one time. They started an agency doing paperwork for charter boats on the cheap. They went to Philipsburg, on the Dutch side of Saint Martin, stocked up on Guess jeans, and resold them in the Basin. They went out into the shallows of Britannia Bay at midnight and hunted sea crayfish, which they sold by the pound to the restaurant at the Oasis. “Nobody ever got rich working for somebody else,” Edwin was fond of saying, as they hefted enormous trash bags filled with jeans through the streets of Philipsburg, or when Clive got his hand snipped by a crayfish at two A.M. They were earning a pittance, less than any of their friends, but Edwin was certain it was just a matter of time before they stumbled on the right idea, at which point they would finally have the cash to “make a big move,” which Clive understood meant leaving — for the States, for New York, someplace with a stage grand enough for his friend’s ambitions.

His life took on a familiar shape. He worked with Edwin. At night, they drove to wherever they were liming that night. (Officer Roy pulling them over with some regularity and tossing them in jail for the night to sober up.) When he arrived home, he stumbled into bed and slept until his grandmother swatted him awake, and then the whole thing began again.

He was nineteen the day Edwin did something that would change his life forever. It was Carnival. They had spent the afternoon with their friends at the Grand Parade along Investiture Boulevard, watching the revelers and passing a bottle of rum among themselves, cheering when their favorite local band went by on a truck with speakers blaring, catcalling Miss Island Queen with her silly crown. As the festivities wound down, they spotted Sara and her friend across the parade route.

"Your girl's looking fine today!" Des said.

"Check she out, dressed like a sket," added Don.

Sara Lycott was wearing a yellow dress that ended just below her ass, a thing that was altogether unlike the proper, innocent girl Clive had known all his life.

"You going to ask to walk she home or what?" Edwin said.

"Stop fooling," Clive mumbled.

"Who's fooling? This is your moment! She dressed like a sket because she's hungry for it."

Clive took a swig from the bottle of rum.

"Look at he, too puss to even try!" Don said.

Then Edwin grabbed him by the shoulders and looked at him with such conviction it shook Clive to his core. "You want to live your life or what, man?" He didn't wait for Clive to reply. "Go!" With that, he shoved Clive, who stumbled out into the parade. He hurried across the street and found himself standing before the tight female circle of Sara and her friends.

It was over a mile from Investiture Boulevard to Sara's house. They walked along the side of the road. Sara wore peach pumps, her ankles wobbling on the uneven ground; she stopped periodically to brush the dust from her shoes. For some time, they walked in a silence that seemed to concern Sara not in the least, while Clive was desperate to break it but could come up with nothing to say, his mind at turns swirling and blank. He didn't understand how it had happened. She'd stood there surrounded by her friends, arms crossed, as he stuttered his invitation. "M-m-mmmay I walk you home?" Once he'd gotten the words out, he looked up at her, awaiting her rejection. But something had changed in her. It wasn't just the dress. Her eyes, usually so sharp and flashing, held a dull detachment, as if she were watching herself in this moment from some great distance. She opened her mouth and said, "You may."

"How did you enjoy the parade?" he tried finally.

"The parade is the parade."

They walked on.

"You look nice today," he said.

"No, I don't."

"Yes, you do. You always do. You're beautiful, Sara." He had wanted to say this to her for years, but had never believed he really would.

"You're the only one who thinks so." She paused to dislodge a pebble from her shoe. "Shall we go to Milk Queen?" She pointed down Tillery Street in the direction of the ice-cream parlor.

She ordered a banana split with peppermint ice cream. He got nothing for himself. He would have felt foolish eating in front of her. Sara ate her ice cream with the same weariness with which she'd responded to his compliments. She picked at it, licking tiny spoonfuls with a tongue like a cat's, setting the spoon down, then sighing and picking it up again, as if this were merely one more in an endless line of tasks she must complete before she could be dead. Why had she said yes to his invitation? He wanted to touch the secret world inside her. Instead, he watched dumbly as she ate. When at last she'd scraped the glass dish clean, she murmured, "You'd best take me home now."

They didn't speak on the walk from Milk Queen to her house. His throat felt clutched by a hand. He had not the faintest idea what had happened in the past hour, and he supposed that was what everybody meant when they talked about the mystery of women. There was some consolation, at least, in joining the ranks of mystified men.

Sara's house was a single-story cinder-block-and-plaster home like everybody else's, but the paint was fresh — white, with sunshine-yellow trim. The short front walkway was lined with purple flowers and there were no enervated donkeys or dogs cluttering the yard. All of this contributed to an air of gentility that Clive felt befitted a minister's widow and daughter brought down by circumstance. The only discordant feature was an old, tumbledown cookhouse out back, with a rusted galvanized roof.

As they turned off the road and walked up to the house, Sara's mother appeared in the doorway. Miss Agatha, like her daughter, was a meager woman, no taller than a child. Growing up, he had seen her at church every Sunday. But as she stood in the doorway, her stance slack and desultory, her eyes darting like a hen's, it occurred to him that he had not seen her there in years.

"G-g-good evening, Miss Agatha," he managed. The mother had the same effect on him as the daughter.

She did not respond, just continued to

stand in the doorway with her arms at her sides. Past where she stood, he could see the parlor. There were piles everywhere, and dirty dishes stacked on a table. A framed painting hung askew on the wall; beneath it a planter held the brown husk of a dead plant. As he took it in, mouth agape, he thought of Sara's pristine speech and dress, everything that made the other boys call her *snob* and *prude.* He thought of his grandmother's house, its smell of bleach and not a thing out of place. He thought of his mother's house, and of his mother. When he felt Sara looking at him, he tried to avert his eyes from the scene, but he was too late — she had seen him seeing it. She bent her head. He wanted to tell her that her secret was safe with him. He wanted to tell her he understood how the shame came not just from being from a home like this, a mother like this, but from loving a home like this, a mother like this. But before he could do anything but fidget, Sara shook her head, and when she raised her eyes to meet his they were rinsed clean, bright and flashing as always. Miss Agatha turned and walked back into the dark house.

"Your mum vex?" he asked.

"My mum is nothing."

"I hope you did have a good time," he said

pitifully.

Sara kept her eyes fixed on the ground.

Clive turned and walked down the porch steps, past the purple flowers that lined the front walk. He was about to turn back onto the road when he heard footsteps behind him. Then he felt Sara grab his hand. He turned, and she met his gaze. Her eyes were shining, he couldn't tell if there were tears or if it was the moonlight. She pulled him off the walkway.

"Where are we going?" he asked.

"Hush," she said. She led and he followed, around the house to the yard and into the old cookhouse.

Two months later, when Sara told him that she was pregnant, Clive had the feeling that this eventuality had been waiting for him all along. He was scared as shit, but it had a rightness to it. Clive and Sara. He looked at her belly and tried to get his mind around the truth that a person who was half him and half her was inside, blooming into being day by day. It seemed like a thing that could not possibly have happened to anyone else ever before.

"I want you to know I'm going to take care of you," he told her. "Both of you."

"You don't even have a job," she whispered. Her voice was not angry or accusatory. There was nothing in it at all. She blinked.

"I'll get one. We can rent a place of our own. Buy a car. It will be okay. I promise."

"Didn't anybody ever tell you not to make promises you can't keep?"

"I will keep it, Sara. We can be married. We can be a family."

He did not stumble on the words. He had at last found something worthy of his conviction.

Sara looked right past him. "What kind of family would we be? You out all the time carrying on with your friends, and me . . . you've seen how I did grow up."

"It won't have to be like that. I'll stop all of it. We can give this child everything."

"I might be crazy like her. I know I might." Her voice was a whisper.

"Sara." He took her hands in his, but she yanked them away.

"You think because you did rut with me like a goat in a shed I must marry you?" she snapped.

He wanted to tell her he would weather any storm with her. He wanted to remind her that what happened in the cookhouse had been her idea; that as he emptied himself into her in the pitch-dark, breathing in the smell of must and rusted metal, he felt such sadness, because he didn't want to do it like this, that he would be angry with himself forever for letting it happen the way it did.

"I know you come from a good family," he said instead. "I'm prepared to set you up how you deserve."

She stared at the dirt. "If you believe I'm a minister's daughter, you're a fool for true."

"Sweet boy like honey. Always stick to the most venomous girl." His grandmother said this as if it could not be helped. Clive had waited nearly a month to inform her that he was going to be a father, telling himself he was withholding the news simply because it was none of her business.

"Sara is not venomous."

"Don't give me that backchat."

"You don't know anything about her."

She snorted, then released a laugh like vinegar. "I know she crazy mother. I know goat don't make sheep."

He slammed his fist on the table. "She's the mother of my child and I won't let you speak low of she!" he shouted.

For the first time in his life his grandmother averted her eyes from him. Looking back, he would realize this was the moment when she relinquished him to himself; never again would she pester him about his late-night liming or encourage him to enter a training program so that he might learn a vocation.

"Oh, you're a real man now," she whispered.

He wanted to press himself to her and weep.

He began looking for a job the day Sara told him she was carrying his child, but found nothing. He was beginning to despair, and to think that Sara was right when she'd told him not to make promises he couldn't keep, when Edwin announced he'd secured interviews at a new resort for both of them. "I thought nobody ever got rich working for somebody else," Clive said when Edwin told him.

"What you think, I'm going to abandon my bred in he hour of need? Beside, we gonna make mad service charge."

What would he do without Edwin? They were hired. The job came with a uniform, crisp and white, with *Indigo Bay* embroidered on the breast pocket in gold thread. When he went to Sara's house in the uniform after his first day of work and gave her the tips he'd earned, she smiled the secret smile he'd seen all those years ago at the Christmas pageant, the one he'd been chasing ever since.

Clive made plans. He spent a Saturday at the small island library, paging through a mildewed book about pregnancy. He brought Sara ginger candies to quell her nausea. He purchased bottles and diapers and a soft brown bear he imagined would become his child's favorite. He made sure Sara had the phone number for the back office at Indigo Bay so he could be reached when it was time.

But in the end, Sara went into labor at night, three weeks early. He was at Paulette's with his friends. He stumbled home that night the same as usual, woke from his hungover sleep the next morning like always. It was only when he went into the kitchen and saw his grandmother sitting stiffly at the table that he knew something had happened.

"You have a son," she said.

He could not square in his mind how, as he'd been drinking with his friends, elsewhere, he was becoming a father. He would never know exactly when it had happened. The moment he went from being one thing to another was lost to him forever.

When he went to Sara in the hospital that

morning, she would not look at him.

"How could you?" she whispered. She held the baby, his son, asleep in her arms, swaddled in a pale blue blanket.

But how could he have known she would go into labor so early? Didn't she see all he'd done to prepare? Didn't she know he was not the deadbeat she seemed to want to make him into? He was about to say all of this to her, but the look in her eyes stopped him. It was not sadness, or hurt, but a brittle, impassive stare. The world had disappointed her once again, as she always expected it to, only this time he was the one who had done it.

The baby began to cry, a desperate wail that sucked the air out of Clive.

Sara turned away from him as she rocked the child. "Hush, Bryan. Hush, my sweet love."

When Clive told me I was beautiful, my heart cracked. All my life I had waited for a boy to say that to me, and now one had, and it didn't matter, because I could not let myself believe it. I had finally gotten what I wanted and it was no good because I was who I was and I always would be. Everything was like that, ruined just because it was me it all happened to.

Sara Lycott. So proper and well spoken, so devout at church, so obedient at school. How my friends would have recoiled if they saw who I became at home with my mum, how we yelled and yanked and scratched.

Behind its freshly painted exterior, our house was a wild place. We were not so much mother and daughter as two women suffocating together, breathing into one another until all the air in the house had been warmed by the insides of both of us.

There was nothing in life we were not tired of.

Though we fought all the time, we only had a single argument, which we repeated over and over until I was insentient to it as stone. Our fight was like the walk home from school, marked by familiar signposts: the Scotts's orange front door, the pothole shaped like a heart on Underhill Road. I think there was comfort in knowing we would only hurt each other in familiar ways. I think I hoped each time that the argument would finally take us somewhere new, out beyond the hating and loving and hating that was all I had ever known.

It went like this: I would sass, or leave a mess, or be a disappointment to my mum in some other way, and she would scold that I should be better, for I was the daughter of a government minister and I could not afford to forget it. I would shout back, call her hypocrite. "When was the last time you did clean we house?" I would say, and off we would go, shouting about all the ways the other had failed to live up to the kind of family we both pretended we were.

On the morning of the Grand Parade, we had found ourselves deep in the mud of this same fight once again. She had come into the parlor to find me scratching at my scalp. She grabbed my elbow.

"Stop that. Where are your manners?"

" 'You're a minister's daughter,' " I mimicked. I wrenched my arm free and went right back to sliding my fingernails beneath the irresistible dried skin on my scalp.

"Don't you mock me."

"And you're a minister's wife. Must be some other lady I saw in we house yesterday itching she pum pum."

"It's a good thing your father's dead. How ashamed he would be to hear you speak this way to your mum!"

How many times had she said this to me? A dozen? A thousand? But this time the anger I felt was different, feral and hopeless, sharp as teeth.

"You never tell me again whose daughter I be!" I shouted. "The only person I see I'm the daughter of is you. A sket like everybody say!"

I screamed so loudly my throat would be raw later that day, when I told Clive Richardson he could walk me home. I held my mother's gaze and sucked air through my teeth. I swear the whites of her eyes turned black.

Her hands fell to her sides. "You think I'm nothing but your mum," she whispered. "But someday you'll see." Then she turned and walked slowly to her bedroom at the back of the house and pulled the stained curtain across the doorway.

Oh, what a fine actress, my mum, playing the victim of my cruelty. Where did I learn how to lash with words if not from her?

I changed into the shortest dress I owned. I snatched my purse and slammed the front door behind me. At the end of the parade, when Clive Richardson stumbled up to me and mumbled his invitation, it was like God or fate or whatever thing I lacked the time or proclivity to wonder about then was handing it to me, just giving it to me for free: a chance to take my life into my own hands and spoil it before it could disappoint me; to break my mum's heart and free myself from our suffocating life together; to prove I was every bit my mother's daughter.

Though in the end, the cost would be more than I could have imagined.

The Secret City

In mid-December, a food deliveryman on a bicycle turned the corner by my apartment too sharply and mowed down pitiful Jefe mid-elimination. I was at the other end of the block when it happened, returning home from work. I did not see bike and pup collide, but I heard Jefe's high-pitched yelp and witnessed the aftermath: The man in the NASCAR hat gathering Jefe in his arms like a baby. The deliveryman putting his hands up defensively and repeating, "Sorry," in heavily accented English as the old man berated him in Spanish and passersby craned their heads to watch, sometimes pausing as if they might intervene before averting their gaze and hurrying along. The deliveryman backed slowly away and got on his bike (plastic bags of takeout still hanging from the handlebars). He rode quickly around the corner and out of sight.

The old man carried Jefe to the front

stairs, sat on the lowest step, and rocked him. I'm not sure whether the dog was still alive or whether he'd already departed this mortal coil. As I approached them, I thought I ought to say something, but when I reached the steps it seemed that to intrude in their final moments together would be obscene, so instead I walked quietly past them up the stairs.

As I disappeared into the vestibule, I heard the man whisper, *"Nos vemos pronto, viejito."*

When I was underground in my apartment, it occurred to me that now there was not a single soul in the building whose name I knew. So began winter.

An entire season had passed since I found Clive Richardson. I had been conversing with him for several weeks, and an ironic reversal had transpired. In the beginning, our proximity had terrified me. Now it was just the opposite. When I was away from him I became unnerved, agitated, itchy, feelings that festered until I was sitting across from him again, our trays of stew and beer before us. I'd catch myself prolonging our evenings despite being aware that he was ready to leave, because once he was out of sight the dread would set in all over again, and I would face the long night hours alone with it.

When I was not with him, I was thinking of him. On the surface, I could be conversing with my mother on the phone about which produce it was most important to purchase organic (blueberries: essential; bananas: not), or racing past the travertine-and-glass grid of the Grace Building in the sleet on my way to work, or eating a lunch of anesthetized midtown falafel with my fellow bright young coworkers, and I might pull all of this off convincingly, but really I was with Clive, imagining hypothetical interactions we might have that would lead to his confession. I imagined, for instance, that there might be a fire at the Little Sweet, and that after making our escape I would dash back into the building to rescue Vincia; afterward, as I breathed through an oxygen mask in the back of an ambulance, Clive would be so stricken by my self-sacrifice and my goodness, and by his own shame, that he would prostrate himself at my feet and tell me everything. Another scenario found us at the Heidelberg on the Upper East Side, washing down käsespätzle and sauerbraten with steins of Dunkel. I would remark that the saying about the impossibility of stepping into the same river twice could be applied just as aptly to New York, a place as transient as it was eternal, the Germans of old Yorkville disappearing into the sediment and making way for new inlets and curvatures — Little Brazil, the Nepalese of Jackson Heights. This comment would strike Clive as so utterly insightful that he would decide that he had finally found a person worthy of being entrusted with his secret.

During this same interval, winter took firm hold of the city. It was the coldest winter anyone could remember, global warming be damned. Ice-breakers turned the Hudson to shards. At crosswalks, pedestrians maneuvered around moats of frigid, gravy-colored slurry. The subway trains smelled of the particular sweat of overheated young financiers in puffer coats. That winter in New York was a period of collectively borne brutality, the sort during which it is possible for a passing glance between strangers on the sidewalk to contain an entire conversation about the awfulness of the season. Yet I had never felt more distant from my fellow urban denizens. As December wore on, I came to feel as if a pane of glass had slid between me and the rest of the world, a division so impregnable that when I collided with a man coming out of my office building one evening, I was so bewildered that I made my way to the subway at a near-gallop.

I said earlier that in general Clive did not speak about his life before New York and, in general, that was true. But there were a few exceptions to this rule, and I'd like to set those out here, because I can see now that they told me everything I needed to know, though I didn't understand this then. There were small things, mentioned in passing: I learned that Clive had worn a pink and maroon school uniform. I learned that he was raised by his grandmother, though he did not say what had become of his mother and father. I learned that when *Ghostbusters* came to the island's only movie hall, he snuck in at three forty-five every afternoon, just in time to watch the Stay Puft Marshmallow Man stomp through Columbus Circle (though he didn't know it was Columbus Circle then — New York, he said, had seemed to him a blur of traffic, graffiti, and crazy characters, an impression that remained unchallenged until he touched down in the city himself over a decade later).

Clive shared these stories with me in his reserved way. He chose his words carefully, set each scene with a minimum of detail.

Sometimes he would begin to tell me something, then shake his head and stop. "Never mind," he'd say. "It's boring." I suspect he didn't think I would understand, and maybe I wouldn't have. Often, he paused for long stretches, during which I supposed he was reliving unspoken aspects of the stories privately, and I understood that these gaps were where it all resided, that my challenge was to parse these omissions, to decipher the negative spaces carved out by his stories.

One evening, after I told him a story about the late-night joyriding of my youth (a story lifted from the freeways of Southern California and transposed onto the streets of Starlight, Indiana, which were surrounded, in my telling, by endless fields of corn), Clive chewed his lip and said, "My friends and I used to take a boat out and party on beaches all around the island. Drink a bit, smoke a bit. I remember one night, we went to this cay called Faraway . . ." He paused. Smiled. "I used to know how to have a pretty good time."

He uttered the name of that place as if it were nothing at all.

In one of Ian Mann's novels, the private investigator explains to the parents of a victim that most murderers return to the scene of their crime, and this is how a surprising number are caught. They can't help it, the investigator explains. The place tugs at them and they can't resist. Was this what Clive was doing? Was saying the name of that place to me a way of returning to the scene? Did he reap some perverse pleasure from conjuring it indifferently, as if it were nothing more than the site of some fun party from his youth? For the first time in a long time, I felt afraid.

"That must have been super-fun," I said, forcing a smile.

"Super-fun," he repeated, laughing. "You've no idea."

The galleys of *The Girl from Pendeen* arrived. On the cover, a woman in a flowing white dress strode barefoot along a cliffside path, her hair in a long, windswept braid down her back. It was my job to compile a list of twenty or so authors at least as well known as Astrid, track down their addresses, and mail them copies for endorsement. My boss had also acquired a debut novel — a thriller set on a commune in the New Mexico desert — which we had agreed a few months earlier I would edit. When the manuscript came in, just before the Christmas holiday, she called me into her office. The manuscript sat on her desk, a stack of paper six inches high. She drummed the stack with her fingertips. "I wanted to be sure you feel up to this?"

"Absolutely!" I said too loudly.

"It's just — you're behind on things, Emily. The backlog is piling up. You seem . . . Is everything okay?"

"Everything's great! I'm super-sorry I've gotten behind, things have been a little crazy, but I promise I'm going to catch up."

"Okay, then," she said with a strained smile. She nudged the pile toward me and I carried it back to my cubicle. I opened my locker and placed the manuscript on the bottom, next to an umbrella and a growing accumulation of Tupperware that needed to be washed and taken home. I piled the early copies of *The Girl from Pendeen* on top of the manuscript and closed the locker door.

I always went to Pasadena for Christmas, but this year I could not tear myself away from New York. I told my parents the only lie I could think of that was big enough to justify missing the holiday, but which would not cause them to book the first flight out to New York. I said I'd met someone, and we had decided to spend the holiday together in the city. Oh, my parents were so happy! *Yes,* I absolutely *must* stay in New

York! We should enjoy Christmas just the two of us! How giddy they became, how altogether unable to conceal the things they hoped for: That I would marry, and give them grandchildren, so that they might enjoy the sweet pastures of old age. After all, I was their only hope. Their enthusiasm made it utterly transparent that they feared they would be let down by me, that they worried I would remain alone. I was furious with them, and yet my heart broke for them, for the ordinary happiness they still hoped would be theirs.

"Tell us about this guy," my father said.

"What do you want to know?"

"Throw us a bone, Em, what's he like?"

"I guess he's a lot like me."

I ate a hefty cancellation fee on my flight and bought a knee-high artificial tree, which only made my apartment even more dismal. Two days before Christmas, a package arrived — panettone and peppermint bark from Williams-Sonoma.

For you and your "special friend."
With love, mom.

Christmas in New York: tinsel snowflakes on lampposts, holiday markets popping up like toadstools, infinite off-key renditions of

"Silver Bells" on subway platforms — saxophone, mariachi, marimba. On Christmas Eve, I went to the newly opened Whole Foods in Gowanus and purchased the fixings for a Christmas dinner for one: a single filet mignon, a potato, sprigs of rosemary, a handful of haricots verts. A ruse, a performance for my own audience — I had no intention of staying home. I halfheartedly snapped the ends off a few beans, then grabbed my coat and headed out.

The Little Sweet was open, though nearly empty. Vincia stood behind the steam table as usual and a few men hunched over their regular tables. In the corner by the potted palm, Clive sat reading the *Daily News.*

I'd thought that seeing I had nowhere to be on Christmas might soften Vincia to me, but I was mistaken. (*You do have somewhere to be, you just chose not to go,* I scolded myself, but I believed completely in my own sorry aloneness.) She took my money with the same cordial displeasure as always. Though I had been hoping for a reprieve from her surliness, I found myself grateful not to receive it. I took my tray, nodded my thanks, and made my way across the restaurant to Clive's table.

"You, too?" I asked.

"Afraid so."

We ate in quiet fellowship. When Clive finished his Carib, he bought two more, one for each of us. We smiled and bounced our heads when "Feliz Navidad" came on the radio, belched softly as we drank our beer. It grew late. Across the street, eerily quiet on this night, a man pulled the grate down over the storefront of the grocery. One by one, the other patrons departed the Little Sweet, until Clive and I were the only ones who remained. When Vincia began wiping down the steam table, Clive looked at me hesitantly. "Would you care to walk?"

We stopped at a bodega to buy tallboys of Bud Light.

"A toast!" I declared, raising my can with a wry smile.

"Happy bloody Christmas," Clive said.

We tapped our cans together and drank.

We walked without speaking, choosing our route by silent accord. Light seeped onto the street from every window: families and trees and carols sung in warm rooms. It was on that Christmas Eve walk I finally understood that I had begun to care for Clive Richardson. I don't mean that I had become any less suspicious. When I forced myself to imagine what he might have done, my blood ran cold. Yet when I did not force myself to imagine it, I was able to believe the lie that

Clive was just a taxi driver with whom I'd struck up one of those unlikely urban friendships you hear stories about. (A hair colorist officiating at the wedding of a client who has become a dear friend. A manicurist and an Upper East Side mom brought together by a passion for mah-jongg.) A few months earlier, I had to exert tremendous mental energy to convince myself that the man before me was not the same man Alison had known, simply to bear being near him. Now that same process was effortless — the separation of one man into two was total, complete.

As we walked, it began to snow. The light from the streetlamps caught the falling snow in big, soft halos.

"Beautiful," I said.

He shrugged.

"But not home, right?"

He didn't respond.

"Why don't you go back? I can tell you miss it."

Clive's face tightened. "It's for the best."

"But not even once? Not even to see your son?"

He shook his head.

"You have secrets."

He stopped walking. "Pardon?"

I took his hands in mine. "It's okay. I just

mean, you have your secrets and I have mine. That's why I know I can trust you. Because you understand what it's like." He started to protest, but I continued. "You don't have to tell me I'm wrong. We don't have to say anything about it. Not unless we want to."

One night I dreamed I was riding with Clive in his taxi. We were in New York, but it didn't look like New York. It looked like Saint X. We drove down sandy streets lined with palm trees, past fish-fry stands and pink motels; I understood that this was the secret city, a submerged place that existed beneath the city where harried workers and dithering tourists cluttered the sidewalks — if I listened, I could hear the shuffle of their footfalls filtering down from some distant, forgettable world high above. On a long straight stretch of road, we came upon a girl crossing the street. It was Alison, though in the dream this meant something different — my heart did not leap to see her, she had not been dead and was not now alive; she was simply a girl taking her sweet time in the middle of the road. Clive honked. She idled. He explained to me that this was always happening, that it was one of the primary aggravations of his job, these girls in the road. He honked again, but Alison was not the least bit concerned, and I started getting annoyed. I shouted, "Move! Move!" Clive honked and honked, and as I surfaced from sleep I realized that the honking was my apartment buzzer. It was eleven o'clock on a Sunday morning.

"Who is it?" I asked groggily.

"Emily, thank *god.* It's *me.* Please, please let me in."

Jackie. I looked around my apartment — it was a disaster, an easy visual symbol Jackie would be eager to latch on to, physical disorder as a sign of emotional disorder, and so on. "Wait there. I'll come up."

I threw on some clothes and met her at the vestibule, where she at once threw her arms around me.

My body went rigid. "What are you doing here?"

"Don't you know I would never, ever forget? I'm not just going to leave you alone today of all days, even if you have been a totally awful friend lately. You and I are going to a barre class that starts in twenty minutes."

I didn't move.

"Come on, Em, get your butt downstairs and get changed."

"No."

"No what?"

"I'm not going with you."

"Of course you are. I have a whole day planned. After barre class there's brunch at this amazing vegetarian place on Bedford. They do a homemade chai that is life-changing."

I tried to walk around her, but she reached out and put her hands on my shoulders.

"Excuse me," I said.

"What the hell? Are you seriously going to walk away from me?"

She held me firmly and our eyes locked. In that moment I saw many things clearly that had previously been opaque to me. Jackie was a basically good person, but I did not like her and I never had. It wasn't just Jackie. It was all of my friends. They were dramatic, self-absorbed, ridiculous people, and I had always thought so. I had cultivated friendships with them not for intimacy and connection but to be able to judge them, and to extract from our every interaction a sense of my own superiority. Look what I had been through! And still I was better than the lot of them. What was wrong with me? Why was I the way I was? Alison, Alison, the answer was always Alison.

"Excuse me," I said again.

Jackie's eyes filled with tears. She released me.

As I hurried down the street I heard her call after me. "I'm trying to help you! Can't you see I'm trying to help you?"

When a person you love dies, the calendar becomes a minefield. Anyone who has lost someone knows this. There is the loved one's birthday. One's own birthday. Various national and religious holidays, if one is religious. All of these days are difficult in their own ways. The loved one used to call you and sing happy birthday over the phone, awful and tone-deaf. Cranberry relish was the loved one's favorite Thanksgiving food, they used to eat and eat. But the anniversary is different. On the anniversary of the loved one's death, you slip backward through time to this same day one, five, ten years ago. (Eighteen years . . . How could it be? She had been gone as many years as she was alive.) You live it all over again, minute by minute.

I made my way to Clive's apartment building just before noon. I was sitting under the faded blue umbrella then. We were sorting through the woman's basket of beads together, picking out purple and white beads, colors I had chosen not because they were my favorite but because they were hers. As I walked east on Cortelyou, I felt the brisk, delicate movements of the woman's hands braiding my hair.

The light was on in Clive's window. I walked to the end of the block and sat on a front stoop diagonal from his building to wait. I'd left my apartment in such a hurry, what with Jackie's unexpected appearance, that I hadn't even grabbed my coat. I wore jeans and a sweatshirt, and within minutes my ears burned with cold. Alison pecked me on the forehead. She walked down the beach and was gone.

More than two hours passed before the light in Clive's window finally went off. A few minutes later, the front door opened and he stepped out onto the sidewalk. He walked first to the bodega a few blocks away. He was inside for just a minute and emerged empty-handed. We headed south on New York Avenue, passing block after block of red-brick midrise apartment buildings, interrupted occasionally by a blip of row houses. Clive turned onto Nostrand at Avenue H. I expected him to loop back up after a few blocks as he often did, perhaps to stroll the lawns and brickery of Brooklyn College and then take Flatbush back to Farragut back to New York. But he continued south. We passed Avenues I, J, and K. At Avenue L we briefly left the city behind and entered a mirage-like stretch of Japanese car service centers — Acura, Honda, Toyota, Hyundai — which we exited to find ourselves deep in Jewish Midwood. Men draped in prayer shawls sporting enormous fur hats, girls in long dark dresses and black loafers crossing streets blanched white with salt. It was midafternoon. She was lying on the beach, sipping a Diet Coke in the sun. I wanted her to play with me, but I didn't want to annoy her, so I didn't ask, I waited. *My, you a patient child.*

We walked through Sheepshead Bay on Avenue U, then took Coney Island Avenue down into Brighton Beach. While the neighborhoods we traveled through each had their differentiating features — Hebrew giving way to Cyrillic on shop signs, Kosher then Georgian then Russian bakeries — it was the landscape's repetitions that began to take hold of me, the endless cycling of deli, slice joint, Key Foods, MetroPCS, and the thousands of thousands of brick apartment buildings. The farther we walked, the more disoriented I became by the *on* and *on* and *on* of the borough, by its vast peripheries and the impossible number of people living their lives out past anyplace I had ever wondered about. We passed Avenues X, Y, Z. Neptune. We had been walking for nearly two hours. It seemed the brick apartment buildings would go on forever, and when we turned onto Oriental Boulevard and, after a few more minutes, found ourselves standing on the sand of what I now know to be Manhattan Beach, the sight of the ocean stretching before me was like stepping into a dream. I clung to the perimeter of the beach while Clive walked forward. The sand was a gray crescent, the sea a sheet of shale. A man in a parka sat on a bench, tossing shards of bread to the gulls. The sun was already beginning to go down. We were in the water, one last swim before the flight home the next day. The salt water stung then soothed the bites on my legs. Alison dove into the waves, surfacing and disappearing again and again. Clive stood at the water's edge for a long time, staring out at the ocean.

Before he turned to go, he pulled something from the pocket of his jacket. From where I stood, it took some squinting to discern that it was a chocolate bar, which must have been what he'd purchased at the bodega. He removed his gloves and unwrapped it. The sun set without fanfare, its weak light spilling briefly and colorlessly across the clouds. Clive ate the chocolate bar slowly, never turning from the water. Then he crumpled the wrapper, stuffed it in his pocket, and headed home.

How did I pick Saint X? Easy. I knew not a soul there and not a soul knew me. I had two suitcases and Sara. She was four months old, a scrawny babe with a head of dewy curls and an aroma like boiling milk turning to caramel. I wore the prettiest thing I owned, my floral dress and ivory pumps. The pumps had cut up my feet before Saint Kitts was even out of view, but so what? They would heal somewhere else, and that was all that mattered. I was seventeen.

When we debarked at Bendy Harbour, a gentleman in a linen suit offered to help me with my luggage. When he asked my name, I told him I was Agatha Lycott, which wasn't true. All my life I had been Agatha Hodge, but over my dead body would I be her here, too. Lycott was the surname of a girl in the form above me at school. I always thought it elegant, the sort of name that, of course, belongs to somebody else. From that day forward it was mine and, above all, Sara's. To anyone who asked, I told the story I had dreamed up awake and alone and growing bigger in the dark in my father's house, about how my husband, a government minister, had died in a tragic automobile accident just weeks before our daughter's birth. To make the story more convincing I told everyone I was twenty-four, though I was such a small thing I could more easily have passed for twelve.

But this one's cousin on Saint Kitts knew that one's friend on Saint X, and so on. I had been on the island less than a month the first time I told my story and was met with suspicion rather than compassion. The rumors trailed me even here, to this sand-and-rock speck where they make their curry with vulgar quantities of allspice and where not even the teachers speak properly.

You can never start over. They will not permit it, neither the ones who shun you nor the ones who are kind to you so they may lord their kindness over you. In the end they are all after the same thing, all so very curious to know the truth about the origins of the daughter of that skinny little Kittitian sket. I will not give them the satisfaction, though the truth would make them beg for my forgiveness. I will carry the secret of Sara's paternity to my grave.

Before Sara was born, I imagined that my love for my child would be a sweet blooming inside of me. I was desperate to have someone to love this way, desperate for love to swoop in and soften my sharp edges. But there are other kinds of love. What I got instead was a love that filled and terrified me, a love I knew as intimately as my own body; it was my mother's love for me, a thing I never, ever wanted.

When Sara told me she was pregnant, I knew I had been naïve to think a new name would be enough to put an end to the passing down of this broken mother's love. I never should have let her leave the house so angry that day, the day she brought Clive Richardson home. *Wait! Don't go! Sara, I love you. Sara, forgive me. Sara, my child.*

At night, I plead into the darkness, hoping with the force of my love to undo the past so she may begin again.

But answer me this: If I'm such a sket, then why have I been lonely every day of my life?

though the truth would make them beg for my forgiveness, I will carry the secret of Sara's paternity to my grave.

Before Sara was born, I imagined that my love for my child would be a sweet blooming inside of me. I was desperate to have someone to love this way, desperate for love to swoop in and soften my sharp edges. But there are other kinds of love. What I got instead was a love that filled and terrified me, a love I knew as intimately as my own body; it was my mother's love for me, a thing I never, ever wanted.

When Sara told me she was pregnant, I knew I had been naïve to think a new name would be enough to put an end to the passing down of this broken mother's love. I never should have let her leave the house so angry that day, the day she brought Clive Richardson home. *Wait! Don't go! Sara, I love you. Sara, forgive me. Sara, my child.*

At night, I plead into the darkness, hoping with the force of my love to undo the past so she may begin again.

But answer me this: if I'm such a skeт, then why have I been lonely every day of my life?

Snow

After they found the girl, Clive became untouchable. When he was released from prison he tried to return to his life, but Don and Des closed ranks. Even Arthur wouldn't touch him. He couldn't find work, not cutting grass, not even scrubbing toilets at Papa Mango's. He and Edwin kept their distance from one another. As far as he knew, Edwin had also been shut out of polite society, but it was different for him. He hadn't been to prison, for one thing. He didn't have a family to support, for another.

For weeks after his release, Clive went to Sara's house and begged to see his son. But Agatha wouldn't let him past the front door. Finally, one day, he waited down the road until he saw Agatha go out. Then he went up the front walkway. "Please, Sara! Let me talk to you!" he shouted as he pounded on the door. He didn't care who saw.

The door swung open. "Hush," Sara

scolded. "You'll wake him."

He told her everything he had planned during his time in Her Majesty's Prison. He was sorry. He would do whatever it took to make it up to her. He would quit drinking and smoking. He had messed up and he knew it, but he would fix it.

"And what kind of mum would I be if I let you into my boy's life after this mess?"

"But I'm innocent! I swear it! Don't you believe me, Sara?"

"It doesn't matter what you are," she snapped. "Innocent, guilty, can't you see? It's all spoiled."

"I know it must seem that way right now. But with time, maybe —"

She shook her head. She had her hand on the door, ready to close it.

"Please," he begged.

She paused. She smiled a small, sad smile. "You know, I think you're the only person who was ever really sweet to me," she said. Then she closed the door.

Growing up, Clive had known more than a few people who had returned to the island from abroad, and it was from them, long before he ever thought their stories would be relevant to his own life, that he learned what it meant to leave home. Almost all of these people had gone either to New York or London, though he knew a few who'd gone elsewhere — to Glasgow, Birmingham, Toronto, Miami. A few years before he left, a boy who'd been three forms above him at Everett Lyle Secondary flew off to Houston, but last Clive heard he, too, had washed up in New York.

For most of his childhood, New York and London were roughly interchangeable to Clive, big, gleaming cities, more Dominicans and Haitians in New York, more Jamaicans in London. But when Keithley returned from London with his wife and the baby boy who was destined to die on the soccer pitch behind Horatio Byrd, he began to understand that the people who returned from New York and those who returned from London had changed in distinct ways. Though Keithley had left home determined never to return, he appeared relieved to be back, and this seemed the case for many people returned from London. It was true they had failed to do what they had set out to do, to build a big life *away.* But in London it had become plain that this plan was naïve and misguided. The city had taught them that the big life was nothing but the delusion of a person from nowhere who didn't know any better. They rarely spoke of their time away.

The New Yorkers, too, appeared relieved to be home. New York, like London, had been drab and crowded and unforgiving, and the winters were colder and the summers hotter and more humid than in London. But their relief was thin, a skin covering the flesh of longing. They spoke of New York constantly, as one turns over a riddle one has not managed to solve. They seemed convinced they had missed the big life by inches. It had been there, set plainly before them, but some narrowness of vision had prevented them from grasping it. Now New York was over. They had not grasped it and they could not figure out why.

Clive knew he was not like these men. He did not want to leave home. New York had been Edwin's dream, never his. He arrived with no grand plans, no conviction that in New York the world would finally recognize his special deservingness. He hoped only that his time away might make it possible, someday, to go home and reclaim the only life he'd ever wanted, a quiet existence with Sara and his son. Mates and a drink after work. Picnics and cricket in the sand at Little Beach on the weekends. Perhaps another child eventually, a daughter, chubby like him. People did not forget, but they might decide, eventually, that they no longer cared.

Most of the people he knew who had gone to New York had settled in the Bronx, but he did not want to run into people from home. He chose Flatbush because it was the largest Caribbean neighborhood in the city; a place, he hoped, he could get lost in. He found a room in an apartment on Farragut Road, in a building whose dim hallways smelled of mice. The apartment had four small bedrooms, each shared by two men, and a common space with a kitchenette against one wall. When he moved in, a bunch of rotting bananas atop the fridge cast off a sickly sweet smell. In the bathroom, toothbrushes balanced precariously on the rim of the sink, which was lacquered with a pale blue chalk of hardened toothpaste; the floor around the toilet was littered with cardboard tubes. He could hardly believe this filthy apartment was New York, and he was thankful that it was he, not Edwin, who was here to see it.

The unwritten rule of the apartment was that the men pretended not to see one another. In such close quarters, it was the only way to keep the peace. They took wordless turns in the bathroom, slept and woke and pretended not to overhear one another's phone calls home.

Only two of them disrupted this dreary concord. The first was Ousseini, Ouss for short, the youngest among them at twenty-two and the only one not from the Caribbean. He was short and sprightly, with the simultaneously curious and sleepy countenance of a child. On Clive's first night in the apartment, as he unpacked his suitcase in his bedroom, Ouss stood in the doorway in his mesh shorts and undershirt, elbow against the doorjamb, and confessed he'd been socially and sexually deprived ever since he arrived in Brooklyn from Burkina Faso three years before.

"I desire a wife with such ardor I can think of nothing else."

Clive was hot and tired and wanted only to lie down on his thin mattress and sleep. On the opposite side of the room his roommate Charles was flipping through a sports magazine, diligently ignoring Ouss and eyeing Clive every so often with a glint of warning.

"You're young," Clive said succinctly.

Ouss shook his head sadly. "This is what I thought, but it was an error. I have five brothers in Ouaga, and all have children. When they were marrying I thought they were foolish to start families. I thought I was so smart to remain free to pursue my dreams. Now I fear I am too late. I want a woman who will be my partner. I want to start a business. But what woman in New York will love me? We need women. All of us here. You, too, Charles!" Charles kept his eyes on his magazine. "You see! You see! We are becoming dysfunctional. To live in this world of solitary men is not natural."

Ouss talked on and on and Clive, not wanting to be rude, nodded politely and offered small words of comfort. Later, he understood that this had been his critical mistake. The other men ignored Ouss absolutely. This was how Clive became the recipient of Ouss's laments, a position he found somewhat irritating, though ultimately not as disagreeable as he supposed he should, because, as Ouss had said, theirs was a solitary existence, and it was nice to have company.

Then there was Sachin, as surly as Ouss was talkative and romantic. Sachin left his briefs on the bathroom floor, his old food in the fridge, was often drunk and prone to picking arguments. (Those were his bananas rotting atop the fridge when Clive moved in.) He took an immediate dislike to Clive, who found himself on the receiving end of much of the man's vitriol. "It's not personal," Ouss assured him. "He possesses a lot of anger. He had a wife and daughter back in Trinidad who died in an accident after he left. I think he should go home and begin again, but he's afraid. Jean-François says he speaks to them in his sleep."

In New York, with these men, he became Clive again, as he hadn't been since Edwin christened him in the schoolyard at Horatio Byrd Primary. Gogo. That name, that world, that life. At times it seemed to him like one of the stories his mother used to tell him, vivid and vaporous as a dream.

New York surprised him. He expected a rough, gritty place, and while this vision was not exactly inaccurate, there were things it failed to capture. The pleasure of a nine P.M. summer sunset. In spring, in the parks, the quiet grace of what seemed like all the people in the world spread across the lawns. He had expected a place where there were a million things to see, but also where what you saw was what you got. Instead, New York seemed to tremble with the unseen. Subway tunnels whooshed people through the earth, the warm steam rising from street grates the only sign of this subterranean world. He had heard that the layers of the city went down ten meters, that below the city of today were buried houses, streets, and cemeteries, and he could sense this past beneath his feet. Walking at night, he sometimes feared someone would grab his elbow, and he would whip around to find himself staring into the eyes of his dead father.

It took him three months to get his hack license. He submitted the dozens of pages of paperwork for the application. He got a medical exam from a Dr. Khutsishvili in Midwood. He took defensive driving at Safe Taxi Academy and sat for the six-hour exam: *What landmark is located at the intersection of 33rd Street and 5th Avenue? Which of the following streets runs parallel to Adam Clayton Powell Jr. Boulevard? How many roads cross Central Park, and where are the transverses located?* When he found out he had passed, the first thing he did was call Sara.

"I'll be making decent money," he told her happily. "I'll be wiring some home to you and my gran as soon as I can."

"My mum needs new tires for her car," she said bluntly.

"Your mum?"

"Yes, she needs new tires for the car I use to take your son to the doctor and to do the shopping. Although you cannot see us,

Clive, we are living every day down here, and every day has its expenses."

He took a deep breath in. "Can I speak to him?"

She sighed. "It would only confuse him."

For a moment neither of them spoke.

"Clive?"

"Yes?"

"Be careful on those roads."

He leased a night shift because he heard it was more profitable.

"Last chance to change your mind," said the manager at the fleet garage, a middle-aged man named Larry in an old, beat-up Mets cap calcified by sweat and grime, before he took the money for Clive's first night's lease.

"You'll never see him without that filthy thing," the driver behind Clive in line said, gesturing at the hat.

"Don't even take it off to screw my wife," Larry said proudly.

Clive handed him the money.

"Don't say I didn't warn you," Larry said with a smile. "I've got hacks getting mugged on the regular. Half these guys have diabetes, and you can say sayonara to your kidneys unless you want to piss in a bottle all night."

In the months that followed, Clive found that the things Larry said were true. It was the most punishing work he'd ever done. Customers ran off without paying. He was regularly accused of taking a slow route on purpose. (How was it that these people, these *New Yorkers,* didn't know he made less, not more, the longer each fare took?) Some nights, his first fare found him stuck in gridlock on the FDR bound for JFK, where he waited another hour in the holding area for his next fare, and when this happened he knew the best he would be able to do on his shift was to break even, and he would spend the next ten hours laboring simply not to lose money, after which, bone-tired on the bus home, he might see a white woman seated next to him clutch her handbag and smile kindly at him; at first he was perplexed by this sequence of behaviors, but he came to understand that these women did not trust him, but they also did not want to appear distrustful.

In spite of all this, the work also had its pleasures. The drivers inhabited a secret shared world. He liked to linger after his shift in the garage, where men played checkers and polished off takeaway containers of curry and jollof rice in the break room, retreated into the prayer room with its three threadbare rugs, groused about the new weekly lease rates in Punjabi and Urdu and Haitian Creole. He found comfort in the ritual details of the garage — its smell of motor oil, the rainbow slicks on the concrete floor, the clouds of yellow dust cast off as the mechanics touched up paint. He learned a hidden archipelago within the archipelago of New York: the Pakistani curry-and-chai cafeterias on Lexington, the Haitian spots in Harlem, the dwindling gas stations, the bodegas that carried meter paper. He learned to feed himself in New York from the examples of his fellow drivers. Deals: two plain slices and a can of soda; egg roll and sesame chicken combo. Egg and cheese on a roll from a bodega, scarfed down on the sidewalk, gone before he tasted it. Foods from home, too, peas and rice and pumpkin soup and fish stew with dumplings, though none of it satisfied him; the scent of island food carried on cold air delivered a sense not of nostalgia, but of error. So much of New York was like that, not-quite-memories and almost-evocations that slapped him with his distance from home . . . the sonorous coos of the turtledoves of his youth emanating from the filthy iridescent throats of pigeons in the streets.

There was something about the night

shift. He discovered that his favorite New York was the one you could only know at four A.M.: The darkness, which was never true black but a trembling blue, as if the city exhaled the residual light of day all night long, and against which the vivid green of traffic lights on the avenues — block after block of them to the edge of sight — was that rarest thing, beauty as pedestrian as it was exquisite. New York was the city that never sleeps, but it did, and as he drove its empty, witching-hour streets and sailed across its starry bridges, he sometimes felt that the city had been abandoned to him, that every other living soul had vanished into the air.

He left the garage around six in the morning. On his walk to the bus he watched the sun come up behind the buildings. The oystershell light of dawn. How it tugged at him, reminding him of his old bike ride to work at Indigo Bay. Even this daily sadness he did not mind, exactly. The ache of it was its own pleasure.

Be careful on those roads. He heard Sara's voice all the time. *Be careful,* when a car cut him off on the BQE at sixty miles an hour. *Be careful,* in the pouring rain and when his eyes yearned for sleep. Her words were the most meager of gifts, a small seed of hope that he had not been completely forsaken, and he held fast to them.

On a night in December of his first year in New York, he picked up a man in a suit outside of an office building in midtown. Once the man had hefted his briefcase onto the seat beside him and closed the taxi door, he declared, "We're going to Westchester." The man told Clive the name of a town at the northernmost edge of where he was required to take passengers, and proceeded to spend the ride alternately reading documents and directing Clive. Up the Henry Hudson, the river a black abyss, the cliffs of Jersey twinkling across the water. On to the winding ribbon of the Saw Mill. After nearly an hour, the man directed him off the highway. A few minutes later, Clive found himself on a narrow road driving through what could only be described as the country. It was his first time this far out of the city. He drove up steep hills from the crests of which the villages below glittered like something from an old movie. In a moment of wonder and terror, a silvery deer leapt out from the woods into the road; Clive slammed on the brakes and narrowly missed hitting it. "Jesus," the man in the backseat muttered without lifting his head from his papers.

Clive wondered if this man had ever vacationed on the island that had once been his home, or if he would be going soon, this Christmas, even, or to celebrate a promotion or anniversary.

"Sorry for dragging you up here," the man said when they arrived at his house, which was huge and had a turret on one side. In the illuminated square of a window Clive saw a pretty wife in jeans and a sweater. The man handed him a generous tip. "Right, right, left will get you back to the highway," he said. As Clive watched the man walk up his front steps, and his pretty wife open the door and push onto her tiptoes to kiss him, he felt himself fill with anger he didn't like and didn't want.

Right, right, left did not get him back to the highway, and soon he was hopelessly lost. He passed a silo beside a barn, a hillside where pine trees hugged the curve of the earth. Then the sky filled with white. His first snow. In the beginning, the flakes melted as soon as they hit the windshield, so he hardly saw them. He pulled off the road at a park to piss and pull out a map. The parking lot was beside a pond surrounded by trees and hills. He urinated into the gravel of the parking lot, studied a map for a few minutes before giving up. (Half an hour later he would stumble, mercifully, upon an elderly woman walking a dog, and she would direct him back to the highway.) The snow picked up. He was shocked by the lightness of it; it fell faster than it seemed a weightless thing should be able to fall. He stood and watched the snow melt into the pond. As he looked at the snow on the water, the blue hills beyond, he saw his own sadness stretching out in tandem with the landscape, as if the land knew his affliction, as if it were weary with the burden of human secrets. Suddenly the colors of home struck him as flat and cheap, a prettiness like white sugar. (And it was really only the water that was pretty at all. The land was dry and covered in gray scrub. The towns were overcrowded with concrete houses.)

The girl was from here, or a place like it. Any one of these big houses might have been hers. Standing in the snow in the middle of who knows where, he tasted the berry of her lips. He saw her dancing; she raised her arms in the air and her shirt lifted to reveal that touchable, touchable scar. He heard her say again all the disparaging things she'd said about the place she was from. She had lied to him. They all had. All the vacationers who went on and on about how beautiful his island was, how lucky he was to live there, how jealous they were. What bullshit. They had *this.*

Every season in New York had its indignities. The stink of urine on pavement in summer. Trash cans stuffed with the corpses of umbrellas during the rainy, blustery days of early spring. By his second winter in New York, Clive saw the season as yet another thing to be gotten through, the clang of the radiator at night, the black snowbanks that uglied the city (or rather, that revealed the ugliness that was always there). Their landlord kept the building like an icebox. This was illegal, but so was everything about their situation, so what could they do? The shower did not get truly hot; the water came so close to warming him without actually doing so that he came to dread bathing, the *almost*ness of it, comfort held just out of reach.

Roommates had come and gone by then, Ouss and Sachin and Charles the only ones who remained. Sachin was as volatile and Ouss as earnest as ever; he'd recently been promoted to assistant manager at the hardware store where he worked, and was convinced this would turn out to be his "big break." The others had been replaced once, twice, three times over, the men different in their particulars, though these differences hardly mattered to Clive. Jean-François kept a laminated picture of his father back in Dessalines in his jeans pocket. His father was ill, and Jean-François would be stuck in New York until he died, paying his medical bills. After four months he was replaced by Dennis, a bachelor who had sent home enough money over a decade in New York for his sisters' weddings and houses and schooling for his nieces and nephews. He went home once a year, for a week.

Clive had begun to wonder by then if Ouss hadn't been correct on that first night — maybe this temporary existence was changing them in ways more permanent than they could fully comprehend. He thought of Hamid, another night-shift driver, who loved to brag about the accomplishments of his four children back in Pakistan, but whose plans to bring them over to join him always seemed to get pushed back to the next year, and the next. He thought of Neer, a baby-faced driver who had returned to Gujarat for the month of December for years. When December arrived that year and Neer was still at work, Clive asked if he would be going home at another time, and Neer told him he would not be going at all. Had something happened, Clive asked, was something wrong? Neer shrugged evasively, and Clive was frightened to find that Neer didn't need to explain. He understood. The family Neer had longed for, eked out this lonely existence for . . . it had been too long. The noise and chaos of children early in the morning, a wife's hopes and desires and disappointments — these things were too much now. He had grown too accustomed to a life he'd never wanted in the first place to give it up. That December, the sight of Neer — gazing impassively at the television in the break room, smoking a cigarette on the curb in front of the garage after his shift as the sun tried uselessly to break through the clouds — was enough to bring tears to Clive's eyes. He missed Sara and his grandmother, missed being in the company of and under the care and brusque direction of women. He was determined not to let what had happened to Neer happen to him. He would not become one of those men for whom family became too difficult, a thing better surrendered than reclaimed. Yet he could feel it happening to him, bit by bit, as seawater erodes rock. He wired money to Sara monthly, but he called less frequently now. Sometimes he asked if he could speak to Bryan, but sometimes he didn't try, even when he could hear cartoons in the background, punctuated by his son's airy giggles.

Sometimes, he could never predict when it would happen, he would be plunged into Bryan's life. He was stuck in traffic on the Major Deegan. He was trudging through the snow on an unshoveled stretch of Forty-seventh Street. Then he was in the yard at Horatio Byrd, invisible and watching, as a pack of boys (all much bigger than Bryan — in his imaginings his son was a small and delicate child) shoved him and called him bastard. He watched his son curl into himself and cry. Then Bryan turned and looked at him. He was not invisible anymore. His boy ran to him, and he gathered him in his arms, taking Bryan's small, heaving body into his large one, absorbing the tears and the runny nose and the brave trembling lip into himself, and in that moment he understood, finally, what his too-big body was for. There had been a reason for it all along: to take into himself the suffering of his child.

Then he was back — the taxi inching along the asphalt, the snow soaking into his shoes. And he felt emptier than it had been possible to feel before he'd had a child to be absent from his life. He should never have left. He should have found a way to stay. If he had not been able to regain Sara's trust he should simply have demanded it, so that he could remain on the island and in his son's life. No, he had done the right thing. Sara needed space and time. Eventually she would soften. It might all work out in the end. He felt better, except sometimes he didn't. Could you ever undo it when a father and son became nothing to one another but voices? He could never decide — he would wonder for the rest of his life — whether his departure was his single most courageous act or just one more example of his cowardice.

In bed at night, he closed his eyes and sent himself home. His grandmother's house, white curtains in the kitchen and the oleander tree in the yard. The potholed streets, Mayfair and Gould and Princess Margaret and Underhill. The three-legged goat in Daphne Nelsen's yard. The secret, nameless cliffs from their nights joyriding with Keithley. Conch fritters and limeade at Perry's Snackette. The gas station on George Street and the salt ponds with their pleasant stink and clotheslines on which school uniforms crisped in the sun. The spots where the buildings, the hillocks, the scrub parted to reveal flickering glimpses of the sea. The sea itself. He sat on the sand at Little Beach and looked out at the water. He was not alone. On the beach were all the people he had ever known, the old and the young, the living and the dead. They, like he, sat still and solemn with their eyes on the sea, waiting.

For what?

Then it began to snow.

It was January of his third year in New York when Clive stopped for gas at the Shell on Hudson Street and the man at the next pump said, "Clive Richardson? Is that really you?"

He looked up and saw a man standing beside a Range Rover, and after a moment he realized it was Ron Rawlins, who had been in his form at school and who had gone on to attend university in the States. In school Ron had been a square, mercilessly teased for his eczema and acne. He looked good now. His skin had cleared and he wore a gray suit with a lavender tie.

"I heard you left for here, and here you are!" Ron said.

He could feel the weight of what Ron hadn't said. Surely Ron had heard about everything that had happened to him in the years since they had last seen each other.

"What are you up to these days?" he asked Ron, who happily accepted this shift of focus to himself.

"Real estate. The market's hot right now, my man."

How he and Edwin and their friends would have laughed and mocked Ron if he had dared to call any of them "my man" back home.

"You know Berline's up here, too," Ron said.

"Bery?"

"I set her up working in the same optometry office as my girl. She's saving for art school."

Clive forced a smile.

"Hey, man, good on you for making an honest living here," Ron said, gesturing at the taxi. "Keep it up, you hear?" He pulled out his wallet and flicked a business card at Clive. "You need anything, call me."

Early the next morning, when Clive got back to the apartment and flipped on the light, Sachin leapt off the couch.

"The fuck, man? I'm sleeping here," Sachin shouted, his eyes crazed. Drunk.

"Sorry. I didn't know you were out here."

Sachin spread his arms before him. "Well,

here I am. Trev's driving me mad. I can't stand to sleep where I can hear that joker breathing."

"Sorry," Clive muttered again, and fled to his bedroom. He had to piss, but he didn't want to go out and face Sachin again, so he relieved himself into a Big Gulp cup from the day before, his urine swirling with the inch of flat cola at the bottom. He lay down, but though he was tired he couldn't sleep. He imagined Ron Rawlins and his girl and Bery sitting together in a diner. Ron had his arm around his girlfriend, who was small and pretty and American. "You'll never believe who I ran into," he would say to Bery, swiping a fry through ketchup and tossing it in his mouth. After he said Clive's name, Ron and Bery would tell Ron's girlfriend about him: an illegitimate child, drugs, jail, the girl. Then Bery would snort at a thought in her head. "You know, he punched me in the face once," she'd say, without bothering to explain the circumstances.

In February, his roommate Charles returned to Saint Thomas. Three days later their landlord came to the apartment with his replacement. Fazil was a diminutive man with mantis-like limbs and a tidy beard dyed with henna. He was much older than the rest of them, in his fifties at least, and he kept nearly silent. He prayed five times a day, and Clive liked this about his new roommate, though he had no interest in religion himself. It seemed to him that Fazil had released himself to the universe in a way that made him, not happy exactly, but reconciled to his life. He had a habit of picking his nose and flicking his excavations into the corners of their small bedroom, but other than this he was unobtrusive (in his sleep he was completely soundless, so that Clive sometimes worried he was dead) and fastidiously neat, and Clive accepted his one vice as the cost of a roommate who was much better than he might have been.

Not long after Fazil arrived, Clive was working on a Monday night when, barely an hour into his shift, he pulled over on Amsterdam and vomited a salmon-colored froth onto a hardened gray snowbank. He was so suddenly and intensely ill it was all he could do to drive the taxi back to the garage, stopping periodically to be sick again, and then struggle home. He thought he'd eaten something bad and figured he'd be back on his feet the next night; instead, he awoke drenched in sweat and delirious with fever. The illness lasted for days. Fazil moved his mattress against the wall to create as much distance between them as possible. Ouss cared for him to the extent possible when he wasn't at work, bringing him soup and medicine and washing Clive's sheets at the Laundromat.

Just an hour before he fell ill, Clive had paid his weekly lease, six hundred dollars he now had no chance of recouping. When he was finally well enough to return to work, he showed up at the garage only to have Larry tell him he'd found another driver for his shift. He would have to wait until a spot opened up. Two weeks passed.

Sara called. "I expected you to wire us something last week."

"Things are hard up here at present."

"Well, down here at present your son is growing like a weed and needs new polos and trousers and shoes."

"You think I don't know your extensive list of demands, what with how you do remind me?" he snapped.

For a moment Sara didn't speak. He could hear her breathing into the phone slowly and deliberately.

"This is not about me and you. It is about your son."

He hated when she called Bryan *your son* — as if Clive didn't know, as if he needed reminding.

Rent was due but he couldn't pay it. Their landlord came to the apartment and told him in front of Fazil and Trev and Sachin that he had a week to pay. That night he took Ron Rawlins's business card from his wallet and turned it over in his hands. He walked to a pay phone. He dialed the first digits. Then he heard Ron's voice, *Good on you,* in his head. He hung up. He tore the card in pieces and tossed them in the rubbish bin on the street corner. He did not trust himself with it.

Two days later, he returned to the apartment after a day spent fruitlessly walking the city looking for HELP WANTED signs, his feet aching, and found Sachin sitting on the couch. Sachin looked up at Clive, his green eyes sparking. "Where is it?"

"Where is what?"

"You know very well."

"Please, Sachin. I'm too tired for this today. If you're vex with me, say so and be done with it."

"You bet your dick I'm vex. This morning I had four hundred dollars in an envelope under my mattress. Tonight, I don't."

"You think *I* took it?"

"I know you owe rent."

"But I've been gone. I've been out since

this morning."

"Says you," Sachin spat.

Clive heard the sound of a key in the lock. Fazil stepped inside. When the small old man saw the two of them, frozen and glaring at each other, he hunched his shoulders and disappeared quickly into the bedroom.

"I'm giving you a chance to make it right, Clive. You give me what you did take and we'll be cool."

"I didn't take your money, Sachin. How would I even know where you hide it?"

Sachin clapped his hands and released a dark, amused laugh. "How would you know?" He was wired; he spoke with a red-hot smoothness. "Clive, even you could find a stack of cash in a room that's nearly empty."

"I don't know what else to say," Clive whispered. "We've lived together a long time. You know me. You know I would never —" He heard the floorboards creak in his bedroom beneath the light weight of Fazil's body settling onto his mattress and he knew. Small, silent Fazil who never bothered anyone. He also knew there was no point in accusing him to Sachin, who would never believe him, blinded as he was by his anger. "I wouldn't," Clive said finally, uselessly.

"You have until tomorrow night." Sachin

stalked off to his bedroom and closed the door behind him.

He should not have thrown away Ron Rawlins's card. It had been exactly the wrong thing to do. What else was new? The next evening, he went to the Little Sweet. He planned to stay there until closing, then remain out until two or three A.M., by which point, he hoped, Sachin would have blown through his anger and turned in for the night. He ordered his pepper pot and Carib, then another beer and another. Vincia pursed her lips but did not comment. The radio was on; the local Caribbean station was broadcasting a cricket match, Barbados Pride versus Leeward Island Hurricanes. By his sixth beer, he could feel the grass on the pitch like velvet beneath his fingertips. He closed his eyes and said a silent prayer that when he opened them he would be sitting in his grandmother's kitchen. She would be rinsing dishes in the sink. She would swat a mosquito and scowl, and how happy he would be.

When he opened his eyes, he was in the Little Sweet, his empty plate before him. He looked through the storefront at the street. Sachin was standing on the sidewalk, staring at him through the glass.

■ ■ ■ ■

One afternoon when he was fourteen, during the boys of Everett Lyle Secondary's brief love affair with boxing, Clive took a punch to the gut so powerful it knocked the wind out of him. His mouth opened and closed like a fish's on land as he waited what felt like an eternity until the air rushed back in. It was Thomas Hinton who had walloped him that time, a shy, handsome boy, well liked by the girls, who would go on to become the landscaping foreman at one of the resorts on the south coast. Clive remembered the intensity of the punch, but he did not recall feeling any pain at the moment of impact. This must have been partly because of the adrenaline of the fight, his body thrumming with it as he tried to get off his best shot to a chorus of cheers and jeers. But mostly it didn't hurt because Thomas was his friend. So were Damien and Des and Don, and because they were his friends, his body seemed not to believe the physical seriousness of their blows. Those matches in Don's yard never hurt. It was the great irony of their contests. They administered injury to one another in order to teach themselves something of the violence of manhood, yet each blow was carried on the wings of fraternal love; you could feel it as plainly as you tasted the tang of blood seeping from your split lip. Because of this, those afternoon sessions were no preparation at all for what finally did come, on a frigid February night in New York. As he understood very quickly after he left the Little Sweet and followed Sachin around a chain-link fence to a vacant lot (broken glass glistening like jelly in the moonlight), it was not the physical power of a blow but the contempt which fuels it that makes it so terrible.

Why did he go with Sachin? That's what he would ask himself after, leaning against the fence and spitting blood onto the sidewalk, his face mangled and swollen. He could not explain it. Sachin had stood on the sidewalk outside the Little Sweet, staring at Clive through the glass with such coldness. He curled his index finger, gesturing for Clive to come out as if offering an invitation. Clive felt his body rise from his chair. He had the feeling that he was walking toward something he'd been trying to avoid for a long time, that Sachin had something to show him about himself, and that it would be the truth.

When they entered the vacant lot, Sachin

stumbled on the uneven ground, then swung his arms wildly to steady himself. He was very drunk. "This is your final chance," he slurred. His voice was brittle and ironic, as if this were a poorly acted performance they were both in on, as if his own anger were hilarious to him.

"I didn't take your bloody money," Clive grunted through clenched teeth. He was suddenly furious, because he understood now that Sachin didn't even really believe he'd taken it, but it didn't matter. He was hated.

The first sloppy blow glanced off Clive's jaw. Sachin spun on his own momentum, regaining his footing just in time for his chin to meet Clive's fist. Clive heard the gnash of Sachin's bottom teeth smashing into his top teeth, saw his head snap back.

Well, Clive thought, he'd given Sachin his chance. It wasn't his fault if Sachin had shown up too drunk to put it to use. He turned and walked over the uneven ground toward the sidewalk. He was almost at the fence when he heard the pounding of feet behind him. Then Sachin was on him. An arm hooked around Clive's neck, the crook of an elbow crammed against his windpipe. He fell to the ground and Sachin sprang on him. Clive felt every blow — on the rim of his eye socket, his throat, his chin. Finally, he was able to grab hold of Sachin's shirt and shove him off. Sachin flew backward. Clive heard a crack. Skull hitting concrete.

The night filled with a terrible stillness. Sachin lay on the ground, motionless. "No," Clive whispered. "No, no, no."

Then Sachin raised his arm. Clive had never felt such relief in his life. Sachin brushed his hand against the back of his head, held it up to the moonlight to confirm a gummy swipe of blood. He pushed himself off of the ground and rushed at Clive. Clive let Sachin pummel him, too terrified of what he'd almost done to retaliate.

Sachin began to laugh. "Is the big man scared?"

He punched Clive in the gut. Clive did not respond.

"Does that make you angry? Does that get you going, big man?"

Sachin's pale eyes never wavered from Clive. He was a father whose child had been taken from him; his loss was black magic, allowing him to see through Clive and know the things that he had taken. When Sachin delivered a swift, fierce kick to his groin, Clive fell to his knees, spat into the dirt. The world began to swirl. Sachin kicked at his ribs like he was trying to dislodge a stubborn flat tire. He kicked and kicked — he was moaning, Clive realized. The sound had been going on for some time. It filtered down from far above his body like the voice of God.

Then footsteps, stumbling away. He caught a fleeting whiff of berries. Tinkling laughter. A final howl: Sachin's? His? Hers? Clive sailed away on it.

He could not stay in the apartment. It wasn't just Sachin. After that night, he could find within himself only pity for Sachin, whose family was gone and always would be, no matter how he tried to batter the truth of his life out of existence. But he hated Fazil. (Where would the money he'd stolen end up? Clive wondered. He imagined grandkids in Guyana opening a package of Nikes and CDs. Or maybe Fazil had no one back home and would spend the money in small morsels on himself; he saw him hunched over a large slice of red velvet cake in a café, scraping every last bit of frosting from the plate.)

Ouss loaned him the money for his back rent and the deposit on a new place. He found an open bed in an apartment shared by five roommates just a few blocks away. Not long after that, a shift opened up at the garage, and Clive returned to work. His first night back, in early March, was the first warm night of the year, a promise of spring. When he got off in the morning, he decided to walk. He crossed Manhattan on Forty-second Street, Times Square so early in the morning empty, his. When he reached First Avenue he turned south. He walked past the United Nations, its sweep of flags snapping in the wind, past the brick projects of the Lower East Side, quiet and softly lit at this hour. At Delancey, he turned onto the pedestrian ramp for the Williamsburg Bridge. He crossed the bridge, pushed forward by westward winds and fanned, at intervals, by ephemeral breezes from bikes whizzing past. When he reached the bridge's apex, he stopped. At the edges of the panorama, the silver tip of Manhattan and the brown façades of Brooklyn aproned the river; the water was a rich, indeterminate color, as if the essence of the city had been condensed into a dark, sparkling broth, and here he was above it, catching its cool upward breezes.

Things would get better now. He would be able to wire money to Sara and his grandmother soon. His cuts from the fight with Sachin had scabbed over. His whole body felt tight and new as a bud. At the foot of the bridge, he got on the B44 and rode Nostrand all the way down to Snyder. When he got home, the phone was ringing. He picked it up just in time. It was Sara.

"I was just thinking about you," he said.

"Oh?"

"I'm back at work. It's all sorted out. I'll be wiring money in a few days."

She said nothing.

"Sara?"

"That's wonderful." She paused. "I want you to know I'm proud of you, Clive. I know it hasn't been easy there." Years later, the memory of it was enough to pull tears to his eyes. "I'm calling because I have something to tell you." Her voice sounded neither happy nor sad.

"What is it, Sara?"

"I'm married."

For a moment he couldn't speak. "You're — Sara, did you say y-y-y—"

"Yes," she snapped. "I said I'm married. I got married. Last week."

"No."

"I'm sorry, Clive."

"You should have told me. You should have given me a chance to —"

"To what? To try to stop me? I'm sorry, Clive, but I couldn't do it anymore. I've been here, all this time, raising our son alone."

"While I'm up here slaving away for that boy."

"And how do you think it's been for me? You don't have to take the stares when all you want is to buy groceries."

"Please, Sara. Listen to me. I love you. I —"

"It's Edwin," she said. "Do you hear me? It's Edwin." Her voice seemed to study the words, as if she only half believed them. "I married Edwin."

Bery Wilson, Sculptress. That's what it says on my business card. These days every actress wants to be called an actor, every waitress wants to be a waiter. But I'm a woman and I want every last person who sees my work to know it. My artist friends scoff when I show them my card. They think it's vulgar, like I'm an electrician or an accountant hocking my services. But I'm making a living doing what I love, and I want the world to know that, too.

In my twenties, when I was new to New York, my love affair with the city just beginning, I salvaged my materials from its streets: twisted bike rims, concrete, pigeon feathers, lots of metal. My latest pieces are different. In this place of my adulthood, I resurrect the spaces of my youth.

Rubbish Day went up last year in a pocket park in the West Village. If you're not from where I'm from, you'd see it and think it was just a sculpture made of castaway items, but anyone from home would see the bottle of Maggi and the box of Sazón Goya, the Ivory soap and Crix crackers wrappers, the bottles of D&G pineapple soda and Vita Malt and the canister of Nestlé Klim and know it was a love letter.

School Girls was installed in front of the Adam Clayton Powell Building in Harlem a few years ago. A circle of straw-and-plaster girls with painted-on skirts and blouses, maroon and pink. On the opposite edge of the plaza there was another girl, alone, looking back at the others and flaying them with her eyes. The piece was up November through March. The decay of the materials over the course of the winter was part of the project from its inception. I used to ride up there to see how people interacted with my work. Hardly anybody noticed the lone girl. I would watch her as if held there by something. Watch the snow settle on her shoulders, pigeons peck at her straw, sleet lash her wide-open eyes. I wanted to take her home and make her cinnamon tea and tell her, *Just you wait.*

Faraway Woman will be my next project, on Governors Island. I've only done sketches so far, but I know she will be larger than life. A woman twelve feet high with locks of black hair six feet long and bright white haunches thick as tree trunks. Hooves for feet. I want people to fall in love with her. I want her to give them nightmares.

When that girl died on Faraway, I knew it was the woman who took her. You might expect me to believe it was Gogo Richardson, on account of the afternoon he punched me so hard my legs flew out from under me. But that afternoon wasn't what I thought about when I heard that he and Edwin had been taken into custody. Instead, I thought of a morning many years earlier, the first day of second grade, when Gogo's terrible stutter almost caused him to wet himself in front of the entire class. I felt such rage at him then. Rage for allowing something so humiliating to happen to himself. Rage that he couldn't just *fit in.* I know, I know. Irony is a live wire. It seems to me now that for years of my life, rage is all I was. It lived in my skin and crackled in my teeth. I would have followed it anywhere.

Starlight

You get far enough into winter and you no longer believe it was ever warm or ever will be again. The trees seem as unalive as the other fixtures of the city's sidewalks: newspaper boxes, abandoned bicycles, hydrants (their tops covered now in little ushankas of snow). During the day, the light seems filtered through a dishrag, and by late afternoon, day is gone; the surrendering blue of a four o'clock twilight becomes your whole world.

When I try to get myself back into that winter, to reenter my psychic state during those frozen months, I find that I can no longer do it. I can remember that period in an external way, using the things I did and said to reconstruct what I must have felt. But I can no longer inhabit those memories as I can inhabit even more distant ones: Sipping espresso with Aunt Caroline in the Place des Vosges. My skin peeling in the days after Alison's death. *Me say day me say day me say day.* The best I can do is to describe how the world around me seemed altered. Before that time, the city was for me what I believe it is for most people: a commons, all of us grazing together in its glass-and-steel meadows, a place the most salient feature of which is not, in the end, its skyscrapers or its cacophony, but the excruciating and ecstatic demands it places upon our empathy. To push through the crowds in the Times Square subway station, zigging by tourists with suitcases, zagging around bankers in suits, brushing past people hawking churros, EPs, God, veering around a troupe of young men performing backflips above the hard tile floor, and squeezing onto a train so packed your chest compresses in the crush of bodies, and to know that every one of these people is in the thick of a life every bit as complex as your own, that you are all extras in one another's dramas — isn't this the quintessence of urban life? But during those months, it was different. The city seemed not public but private, a place created for me and the things that were playing out in my life. New York was mere backdrop, a screen painted with buildings and delivery trucks and dog-walkers and children on scooters, in front of which I enacted my life. I did not care what people around me thought of me because I did not entirely believe they were real. On the subway I bit my nails with impunity; I traced words in the air without bothering to disguise my behavior.

The significance of Clive's pilgrimage to Manhattan Beach was clear to me. He had been marking Alison's death. It had been months since I had entered his life, and I knew it was time to move things forward. Either I'd gained his trust or I hadn't, and it was time to find out. Every night before I stepped into the Little Sweet, I promised myself this was the night I would press him, the night I would bring the conversation around to the secrets of his past. But these were false promises; even as I made them I don't think I believed them. Instead, I spent our evenings lamenting the hideous condo tower rising on Fifty-seventh Street. We groused about the disastrous snow removal after the most recent storm. Clive explained to me the workings of cricket and the Windies' tumultuous history of shame and glory. On the walk home afterward, I would excoriate myself for my cowardice, though I knew it wasn't really cowardice preventing me, but something else, something I wouldn't be able to fully understand for a long time. In truth, I had altogether lost sight of the purpose of my time with Clive Richardson. The winter, these nights, this man — it stretched on and on. I could see no end in sight.

I guess what happened next was inevitable. On a Tuesday in early February, I called in sick at work. Clive was off on Tuesdays, and I spent the day trailing him as he ran various errands. The next morning when I arrived at work, my boss called me into her office. As I sat across from her, she proceeded to describe to me the events of the day prior. Astrid Teague had come in for a marketing meeting. When she was ready to leave, it was sleeting, but she didn't have an umbrella. My boss took her over to my cubicle, hoping to lend her one, and in my locker, amid an accumulation of dirty Tupperware, they discovered the stack of copies of *The Girl from Pendeen* which I had never mailed, along with the untouched manuscript by the debut novelist, which my boss would now have to edit herself in a hurry.

I was told to pack my things. I did so quickly. I removed the pushpins that had for the past three years affixed my photographs and decorations to the wall. I gathered my belongings from my locker. Everyone around me was very quiet. My coworkers avoided walking by my cubicle, except for the few who made a point of it, stealing pitying glances at me as they passed. I think this was when I understood that I would lose things in pursuit of the truth that I could not get back, that my life might be derailed in ways I could not recover from.

I couldn't tell my parents I had been fired. How on earth would I explain it to them? I couldn't tell Jackie. She had given up on me — there had been no texts, no attempted interventions, since the morning I brushed her off at my apartment. The only person I could talk to was Clive. That night, when I told him I had lost my job, he said the usual comforting things. It happens to everyone at some point. I would find another. That old chestnut: "Everything works out for the best."

"You can't actually believe that," I said.

He cocked his head back. "I guess not." He furrowed his brow, chuckled.

I began to cry, tears that were at once utterly genuine and a command performance. "What should I *do*?" I reached for his hand, and he took mine in his. He stroked the inside of my wrist with his fingertips. When our gazes met, it seemed they were both filled with the same question. I leaned toward him. I closed my eyes.

It is impossible to say how much of this action was strategy and how much of it was desire. These two tracks had collapsed in on each other. I had reached a level of cognitive dissonance that seems almost impossible to me now, but of which I had only the most submersed, peripheral awareness then: I simultaneously trusted and distrusted Clive Richardson absolutely. I loved him and loathed him. I wanted to destroy him and was terrified of losing him.

Clive dropped my hand. He leaned away from me.

"I'm sorry," I blurted.

His eyes darted from the floor to the television to the table, looking at anything but me.

"God, I'm a shit show tonight," I said, wiping the tears from my eyes. "Can we just pretend that never happened?" I attempted a lighthearted smile.

"I'm sorry if I —" His gaze had fallen on my hand.

I shoved it under the table. "A cramp." I'd been doing it without even realizing, tracing a finger through the air: *N-e-v-e-r. N-e-v-e-r.*

N-e-v-e-r. He looked warily at me, and a rush of embarrassment flooded me.

"I think we could both use a drink," I said. I got up and went to the counter and bought two cans of Carib.

When I turned to walk back to our table, Clive was gone.

He wasn't there the next night, or the next. I sat at the Little Sweet alone, lingering until closing in case he should appear. By the fourth night, I was in a panic. I had pushed things too far, driven him away with the very expressions of intimacy with which I'd hoped to pull him closer.

"Clive hasn't been around lately," I said casually to Vincia on the fifth night of his absence, as if I were merely making conversation. She pursed her lips and continued scooping rice onto a plate. "Do you know if he's, like, away or something?"

"I know if he didn't tell you, it's none of your business."

After that, I didn't go inside the Little Sweet. I spent hours every night walking the streets, looping past his building to see if he would emerge, which he never did. Back in my apartment, I occupied the liminal space between sleeping and waking all night long, and in the mornings I couldn't say for sure whether I'd slept at all. I had nowhere to be during the day. I returned to Alison's diaries, searching her voice for some hint of where to go from here. I roamed the streets of Manhattan, looking in every taxi for his face.

As the days without Clive wore on, a vision of who I was and would be from then on began to sharpen in my mind. I was not one of the city's bright young things after all, but one of its invisibles. You know the kind of person I mean. You see me hauling myself up the subway stairs in the summer heat, or down them in winter with bags of groceries banging against my knees. You see my brown parka, which is not even utilitarian but actively — intentionally, it seems to you — ugly, and if you are a person with a full and busy life, you cannot even understand the logic behind such a sartorial choice, and the life behind such logic, except to feel sorry but also, well, irritated — all the lonely people clogging the world, making you see them when all you want to do is take the subway home and deal with your own problems and engage in your own small pleasures. Don't you deserve that? Well, sure, you do.

A week later, when I looked in the storefront

at the Little Sweet through a light snowfall and saw Clive sitting at his usual table, I thought I was imagining it. He looked up and spotted me through the glass. He smiled and waved.

"You were gone," I said as I took my seat across from him.

"I had some things to take care of. Did you miss me?" He smiled jokily.

"With all my heart."

"Did you hear about that flasher on the J?"

"It's always something with the J, isn't it?"

Just like that, we slipped back into our normal conversation. There had been a coyote sighting in Hamilton Heights — apparently it had scavenged a carton of General Tso's chicken from a trash can. An abandoned Mickey Mouse suitcase had led to the evacuation of Times Square and snarled traffic all afternoon.

When we finished our food, he proposed a walk. The halal butcher. Immaculee Bakery. The fruit stand (KUMQUATS FRESH!). Winthrop Hardware. The bookstore. (*The mother puts the children to bed. He waits for the bus. They say goodbye.*) What a relief it was, passing these familiar places with Clive again. When we came to a bench, Clive gestured at it, and we sat. It was a frigid night. Our breath left white contrails in the air. Clive said he'd heard on 1010 WINS that the Gowanus Canal had frozen over.

"I guess now we know the freezing point of whatever the hell is in the Gowanus Canal," I said.

He laughed. Then his face became serious. "There's something I've been wanting to tell you, Emily, and I don't want to put it off anymore. If I put it off I'm afraid I'll never say it."

My chest tightened. "Yes?"

"It's about what you said on Christmas Eve. About how we both have secrets. I think I'm ready. I want to tell you. I want us to tell each other."

"I want that, too," I whispered, half afraid that if I spoke too loudly I might shatter the moment. My eyes filled with tears. *Bravo, Clairey.* "I want that very much."

"I trust you. I know you would never do anything to hurt me."

"Never."

"But I'm afraid," he continued. "It's not easy for me, what I have to tell you. Maybe you could begin? With what happened to you in — what was it called, again, the town you're from?"

"Starlight."

"Where you skated all the time on the Wabash River."

I nodded.

"That's a lie, Emily."

"What are you talking about?"

"I looked it up. The Wabash River is all the way across the state from Starlight."

I looked down at my lap. Snow had gathered there, and I brushed it off automatically. "I'm sorry," I whispered. "I've wanted to be honest with you for weeks now. For months, really. The truth is I'm from California. Pasadena. That's where I grew up. You have to understand — when I talked with you that first night I had no idea you'd become part of my life the way you have."

He didn't reply.

"I said I'm sorry, and I am. But I told you I have secrets. So I tell people I'm from one place when I'm from another. Does it matter so much? Are you going to sit here and tell me everything you've shared with me is the whole truth?"

He shook his head.

"Please don't be angry with me. We can still tell one another our secrets, just like you said. Forgive me?"

He held me in his gaze. "Who would I be forgiving? Emily, or Claire?"

Sometimes you close your eyes and you are back at the beginning. You are walking down the beach. The sand is warm beneath your feet. The water is aquamarine, a wonder, yet when you cup it in your hands it is clear, and this is the biggest mystery you know. Your hand is in her hand. You see the apricot freckles crowding her milky skin, her hair in its messy bun with the yellow elastic band, the billowy white tunic that hides her secret. She looks down at you and smiles. She is yours, a beautiful sister made only to receive and return your love.

Somehow you understand that if only you can hold this moment firmly enough in your mind, if only you can plunge deeply enough into it, the two of you can break off from the world. You can erase the future through an act of will and live together with your sister in this moment forever, see the blue sea stretching before you forever, walk forever down the warm sand, the black rocks up ahead receding at the pace of your approach so that you never reach them. You can remain here until the world forgets you.

But you can never quite manage it, can you? In the end, you always let the world back in. You could have everything you ever wanted, but you spoil it. You spoil it every time.

"How did you know?"

Snow continued to fall. Steam rose from a grate in the street. I kept my eyes fixed on the interface where the steam and snow melted into one another to keep me from slipping off the edge of the moment.

"The thing you did." He traced a finger through the air. "You used to do it then, too."

"I could never help it," I said softly. I pressed a fingertip to a snowflake on my coat and felt it melt away to nothing.

"There was a night a few months ago. I was walking home and I thought I heard — did you follow me? Did you call my name?" He bit his lip and squinted down at the sidewalk as if he could scarcely believe what he was asking me. Then he looked up at me, his eyes so full of foreclosed hope that for a moment all I wanted was to be able to tell him I hadn't and have it be the truth.

I looked back down at the sidewalk. "Yes."

He shook his head. "I thought I was losing my mind." He was facing away from me, speaking to the sky, the snow, the brittle February night, and I understood that these words were not meant for me, but for someone else.

"I don't know what to say."

"I'm sure you'll think of something. You're so good at thinking up things to say. All these nights. I hope you did have a fun time."

"No."

"Bullshit," he whispered.

"You think I *wanted* to do this? I've given up everything. All I ever wanted was the truth. For Alison."

"For Alison," he echoed back. It seemed to me that his mind was far away, only the most gossamer of threads tethering him to this bench on this sidewalk here with me. He looked around — at the shop fronts across the street, the snow on the sidewalk, the black sky overhead. "Fuck," he shouted, punching his fist into his open palm. His shout echoed down the deserted street.

"I'll go," I said. I stood. "I'm going."

He grabbed my arm. "Sit."

"I'm sorry. I shouldn't have —"

"Sit."

"Please let me go. Please don't —"

"Don't *what*?"

"I'm sorry. I just wanted —"

"The truth, *Clairey*?"

I nodded.

"The truth is you're a fucked-up girl."

"I know," I whispered.

"Just like your sister."

"Please don't do this."

"The truth is Alison destroyed my life, and from what I see, she destroyed yours, too."

"Please just let me go."

"No. You want the truth, Claire, and I'm going to give it to you. You're going to sit here and listen to every word of it. And then I never want to see you again."

The Girl

Every week there's a girl. Every week she's pretty. Some weeks she's tall, some weeks she's short, some weeks her hair is blond and silky, other weeks it's red curls. She has big tits or flea bites, it makes no difference to he. He does like them with freckles.

He picks this one straightaway. I see it happen. She gallivants down the sand to the volleyball game and when she arrives she takes off she shirt. I was some distance away, but I saw it. He went still. I followed his eyes to she belly, where she has a big pink scar. Edwin and me have been breds since second grade. I know his mind and how it turns. He likes them with some twist to their pretty. He picks her then. I know even before he.

On the sideline, the girl's pale little sister spectates. She does something funny with she finger, waving it through the air. She's burning, but it's not my place to say so.

After work, me and Edwin smoke in the car park. We count up we tips on the hood of Edwin's car. Me, twenty dollars. Edwin, thirty-four.

"Figure," I say.

"What I tell you? You're too serious. *Yes, sir. Yes, ma'am.* Yankees want to be your friend."

He's right, but so? When I try to make chat, the guests' faces go crooked. When Edwin tells a wife she looks lovely, her husband smiles because he loves to hear how his wife is pretty. When I say the same thing, the husband thinks it's none of my business how pretty his wife be. I can't do the job the way he does it. But I'm polite. I'm prompt. Some days, anyway.

After, I bike to Sara's house to see my boy. When I arrive, Sara's standing in the doorway with Bryan in she arms and displeasure on she face. Agatha is on the sofa in the parlor, scratching at she scalp.

"You're late," Sara says. I feel annoyed, though she's right — I am late.

She tries to hand Bryan to me, but my boy clings to his mum. When I take him he cries. I stroke he ringlets. My boy is handsome, and I'm not just saying so because he's mine. His ringlets have light in them. "There, there, my Bry," I say.

The next morning I wake up to pounding on my bedroom door as usual. Gran.

"What's wrong with you? You late!"

Shit, woman.

I don't say this. I get up and stumble to the toilet. How sad is it for a man to look forward so much to his morning piss? When that relief may be as good as his day will get? But it's such a good feeling. It could have gone another way. God could have made a world where good things feel bad. Pissing, eating, banging. Maybe he would have been doing us a service.

I bike Mayfair to work. I'm hungover as usual from liming at Paulette's last night. My bike is old and rusted and squeaks with every pedal. When cars pass, they stir up the dust and leave me in it, and I hold my breath until it settles. But this hour, the streets are mostly quiet. The only sounds are roosters and women sweeping and cartoons inside houses. I feel myself on the bike, a big thing on a little thing. I'm of two minds on this ride, always. It's a mortification, but so peaceful. When I set out, as long as I'm not running too late, the sky is still smoky blue, like something far away. As I ride, it turns the color of an oyster shell. The breeze still possesses some coolness. Dogs wake. The skinny black hound with the white belly trots alongside me sometimes. Early morning feels like church, when I did go.

When I pass Arthur's father's store I'm close. I ride past the gas station on George Street where Keithley used to work, past the three-legged goat tied to a post in Daphne Nelsen's yard, past the clinic where the antimen go when they're deading. Past Prosser's School Uniforms — pink for Horatio Byrd, yellow for All Saints, blue for Sir Northcote. Past the scrub that leads to the nameless cliffs. Past the house where my father was born. It's abandoned now. The roof is more sky than galvanized. Chickens roost there. I crest a hill and the ocean appears, a color nobody can describe. Damien once told me science says mankind came up in the sea — we started as lizards with fur or some shit. It's only recent we left the sea for land. Maybe that's why the sea feels so, like a house in a dream you wish so badly to enter, but where's the door?

Indigo Bay is the last resort on Mayfair Road. When I look at it, I see it twice at once: the white buildings and the clean sand, but also as it was when we were boys, with wild pomme-serette trees and needles and condoms in the seaweed and the anti-men who loved this spot. With its stink and sand flies, nobody bothered they. Well, nobody but we.

Morning is morning. Edwin and me carry the lounge chairs out from the storage house and arrange them in a crescent, just so. Next, the chair cushions. I carry them four to a stack on my shoulder. Finally, the umbrellas. A bit later, the early birds arrive. By nine, the beach is crowded. Then it's towel, bottled water, adjust umbrella, drag chair, fresh towel, fresh water, all morning long. Today, a man with dolphins on his swim trunks and a pretty Asian wifey orders a Red Stripe.

"Peace, *mahn,*" Edwin says when he sees the bottle on my tray. Edwin thinks it's fucking daft how Yankees love to order Red Stripe here. But Jamaica's not so far from here. I see their point. Later, Edwin will chat this daft fucking Yankee up to see what else he likes. Guests who order a drink in the morning often turn out to be good customers.

When I bring his drink, the man reaches in the pocket of his swim trunks, pulls out five dollars, and says, "Get yourself one, too." He smiles.

"Thank you, sir," I say. His smile goes flat. He wants me to make some chat, but chat is Edwin's thing.

Midday, the girl's daddy asks me where the locals eat. I'm glad he asks me and not Edwin. It pisses Edwin off when guests ask for recommendations for authentic island food. A few weeks ago we had a guest order only curry goat and conch creole for lunch all week.

"Fucking dolt," Edwin said to me one day after he took the man's order.

"Last week you say the same about the lady who only ate burgers and pizza. What would you like they to eat? How can they do right by you?" I thought I had him then.

He shrugged. "Maybe they can't. What I care about it?"

"That sounds fair." I rolled my eyes.

He snorted. "Gogo, man, you so soft it get you someday."

When he takes break past the rocks at the edge of the beach I see she, gallivanting down the sand toward he.

This job's not so bad. The Yankees who go to Papa Mango's and stay at hotels near the Basin and shop in Hibiscus Harbour where the cruise ships dock act like they're royalty because they bought some budget Caribbean cruise package. The guests here are so rich they can relax about it. They're polite, mostly. The food trays are heavy, the chairs are heavy, the umbrellas are heavy, but that's just usual job shit.

One thing I do mind. While I walk the beach, I feel the guests' eyes on me. It's like I'm onstage, but at the same time, the audience is not even interested in me. I feel so big under their gaze, like if I open my mouth I may swallow the world by accident and leave myself alone.

Everybody knows Yankees are fat, but at Indigo Bay, most of them are thin. All day they eat and drink and sleep like babies. I walk back and forth carrying trays heavy with they cheeseburgers, coconut shrimp, and conch fritters. Food so oily it shimmers. So how are they thin? It seems like someone somewhere just decided it.

Not all the guests are beautiful, but they all have a certain something. A wellness, maybe. Terrible things may happen to any person, rich or poor, white or brown, and I'm sure terrible things have happened to some of they, but they don't appear so. They appear like they believe the universe loves them, and maybe it does.

A few guests are not so well maintained.

At present, we have a fat woman with skin like cottage cheese and a Frenchie man with a hard round belly. They don't cover up; they lie out like everybody else. When we're waiting at the bar for our orders to be ready, Edwin says, "You check the belly on the old fucking Frenchie?" and puts a finger in he mouth like he's gagging. I laugh. But when I'm not with him, laughing at they, it's different. These fat people, almost naked under the sun — I'm amazed by they.

Fleet. I learned this word from Jan, the old Dutchie we used to lime with when we ditched school. One day when Edwin and me were walking to Paulette's, it started to pour. Edwin took off he shoes and sprinted through the rain and I followed behind, panting all the way. When we arrived inside, all soaked through, our school polos stuck to we, Jan said, "Edwin, how fleet you are!"

English was not Jan's first language or he second; first came Dutch, then German, then French, then English, but he still knew this word I didn't.

I never looked it up, but I have the idea of it. *Fleet.* A thing I'll never be.

We have a customer. The man with the dolphin swim trunks. Edwin chats he up after volleyball one afternoon. Turns out his lawyer wifey needs to relax. This morning, after my daily highlight morning piss, I reach under my bed and pull out the lockbox. The combination is Bryan's birthday. First, so I don't forget it. Second, to remind me I do this under under business for he. When I open the box, the ganja scent rushes out. Gran must smell it, but she's given up being up in my business. This is why the lockbox stays at my place. Edwin's sisters are nosy as shit.

The lockbox is how I do my part. Edwin chats up potential customers. Edwin makes the sale. I keep the lockbox under my bed. We split the profits even. I weigh out ten grams. Most I put in one baggie. Enough for two spliffs, I put in another. This bag's for we.

I wait in the car park, and when Edwin arrives I hand he the big baggie. In the afternoon, the man with the dolphin swim trunks has a rendezvous with Edwin by the tennis court. The wifey's there, practicing she serve; she pauses in she little white skirt and watches. The man gives Edwin sixty dollars. Edwin gives me thirty.

Sundown is sundown. Insect coils with their sweet fake smell, last call, a posse of children chasing Edwin around the sand.

Girls and boys tug at he legs and tickle he, and finally he lets them take him down. The girl's pale little sister doesn't join. She watches. Her finger turns and turns.

When the guests leave the beach we collect the towels, hundreds of they — damp and sandy and smelling of salt. We take down the umbrellas. We drag the chairs across the sand and stack them up. After a day trudging in the sand beneath the hot sun, we uniforms have the same strong, mothy smell as the boys' P.E. changing room at Everett Lyle Secondary, full of sweaty plimsolls and pinnies. We change out of them and throw them in the bin for the wash lady. In the car park, we roll a spliff with the extra herb we skimmed from we sale.

Evening, I give Sara my tips plus the money from the sale. If she suspects where the extra money comes from some days, she never says so.

Today, when we're smoking in the car park after work, I see the girl coming up the path, swaying she hips before she even spots us. "What the ass?" I whisper to Edwin. He shrugs, as if her arrival is unexpected for he, though we both know it's not so. When she asks what we're doing here, Edwin takes a spliff out of he pocket, twirls it in he finger, and says, "Nothing much."

She raises she eyebrows. "Mind if I do *nothing much* with you?"

This girl appears cunning.

Word gets out from the man in the dolphin swim trunks. A few newlyweds purchase from we. Some retirees also. We sell some pills to the girlfriend of the actor on holiday. She has a body like a porn star. "That man have it made," Edwin says. "So old he balls must sag to his knees and still the women line up to be fucked." The actor appears shy to me. He touches his girlfriend's body, but he doesn't appear to enjoy it. That's some Yankee shit right there — rich, famous, porn-star girlfriend, and still he's so low.

One day I arrive at Sara's with fifty dollars, and do you know what she says?

"Look at you, high as a kite! How can I leave him with you now?"

"I'm not high as a kite, Sara."

She places she hand on she hip. "You smoked before you showed up here. Do you deny it?"

"Don't be like that. I'm out there breaking my back ten hours a day for you."

"You think I'm not breaking my back all day, caring for this child?"

"Me and Edwin just smoked a bit. A man needs his breds."

"What about me? When do I get to see my friends? As if I have any left, anyhow."

Here's some words of wisdom for you: Don't ever try to out-talk a woman. They store the right language up so it's ready to throw down when the time comes. Her face goes bitter, but then she changes it — she crinkles she eyes and gives me this injured look, like she's a gentle woman without a nasty bone in she body and in the face of all the poor treatment I dole out she feels only this soft, pretty sadness. Such fuckery.

"All I ask is one hour's reprieve from taking care of him, Clive," she says. "One hour. So that I might bathe and, heaven forbid, lie down and put on a little perfume and listen to the radio." She's crying now. I can't tell if it's more pretty acting or if she's crying for true.

I look past she. Through the window I see the dead yard, the clothesline, and the old cookhouse. We were together there, in the dark. She led and I followed. What was I thinking? Only one thing: Sara. It was Sara pulling me through the dark yard. It was Sara opening the door, and Sara unbuttoning me, fast and urgent like she would combust if she didn't manage it soon, and it was Sara's small, narrow hips I was pulling the yellow dress away from with my shaking hands. It was Sara pulling me against she, Sara I entered, Sara who I had loved for so long. I look at the woman before me, her eyes so tired it's like she's been watching this life since the beginning of time, and I wonder how we got here.

"I'm sorry," I whisper.

"I'll see you tomorrow, Clive," she says. Then she closes the door.

Night, Edwin picks me up. When we get to Paulette's, Don and Des are already there. Edwin buys two rums, one for each of we, though we know I'm going to drink both. Edwin hardly drinks, though I'm the only one who notices. He holds he glass, then when I finish mine, we switch. It's been this way so long I don't recall how it became so.

"Tonight's spliff brought to you by the Yankee in the pink dolphin swim trunks," Edwin says.

"You shitting we," Don says.

"Antiman?" Des asks.

"Nah. Hot Chinese wifey."

"Women in America must be desperate," Des says.

"Man must be filthy rich," Don says.

"Man be nice," I say. I don't know why.

Maybe because it's true. He tipped nice, too.

Edwin grabs the spliff from me and takes a puff. "Nice," he snorts, "is some real fuckery."

The next day I arrive at Sara's sober and on time. Bryan's toddling on the floor. I sit beside he, make some silly faces. My boy gurgles when he laughs. His eyes are big and round like his daddy's.

While I entertain he, Sara takes a bath. She comes out looking refreshed. She wears a scarf around her hair the color of grass on a cricket pitch. Sara has parts of she so small sometimes I wonder how God did manage it. She tiny toes, all lined up. She leans down and tousles Bryan's ringlets. He gurgles. Her small small feet carry her to the kitchen. She takes the lids off the pots on the stove and ladles food onto a plate.

"Dinner, Mum," she says.

Agatha stops she scratching in the parlor and trudges to the kitchen. She sits down at the table in such a way. I can't explain how she does it, what it is she does with she eyes or she back or she jaw or she hips, but she manages to sit down at a table in a way that says that she — she! scratching lady in the parlor! — is too good for this, and that it takes all she has to abide she daughter, who falls so far below she expectations. Here's the thing about women: If the world was only women, there wouldn't be language at all. They don't need it.

Sara pretends she doesn't notice the way her mum sits. Her pretending pains me.

Agatha takes a single bite, then sets down she fork and says, "There's grit in the callaloo."

I lose it a bit then. I walk to the table and stand over she. I pick up the fork and hold it out to she.

"Eat," I say.

Agatha looks at me with she black beady eyes of a hen.

"Sara does everything for you! She cooks and cleans and tends to Bryan while you sit around with your feet up like some grand woman you never was, scratching at your nasty head. Now, *eat.*" For a moment our eyes lock. Then Agatha takes the fork. She eats.

When I leave, Sara walks me to the door. "See you tomorrow, Clive," she says. She smiles.

Tonight, when Edwin turns left onto Mayfair instead of staying straight on to Paulette's, I feel the evening congeal like old porridge.

"Edwin," I say.

"One stop." Like the stopping's the problem.

"You promised."

"Relax."

When we pull into the car park the girl is there, waiting pretty against a palm tree. So many weeks the girl waits against this same tree. Women always know their best angles.

"How would you like to stick your cock in that?" Edwin whispers to me as she walks toward the car.

"Girl decked out for you." I never know how to stay vex with he.

"Ten dollars say she decked out below-deck, too."

We laugh at this, at she, as she approaches. He loves to laugh at they.

"Look who decided to grace us with she presence," he says.

This one is perfection when she rolls she eyes, and she knows it. She climbs in. This is happening, no stopping it. Though Edwin promised how many times this shit be finished, we're driving to Paulette's with somebody's daughter in the backseat.

This week's girl keeps appearing. When we arrive at the beach in the morning she's in the water, stroking. I've never seen a pretty little thing swim with such power. She stays in the sea a long time and never pauses to look at we.

"Oh, hey," she says, back on land, like she's surprised to see we. Who does she think she's fooling? We know she's performing for we. For he. The girls always do so. Sometimes they do it by sunning themselves in their tiny bikinis. Sometimes they do it by getting drunk and crazy at Paulette's. There was a girl a few months ago, Callie, who climbed onto the bar and danced, and when she was up there you could see straight to her pum pum because she wasn't wearing any panties. Edwin and me lost it. I think he still fucked she in the end, but he fucked she like it was the funniest thing in the world. Sometimes, if they're shy, they even do it by pretending to ignore him, but the way their gaze keeps flicking back at him gives them away — their walk, their pretty dresses, even the way they read their book on the beach like it's so interesting they can't spare a moment to look up at he as he passes — it's all for he.

Volleyball, she's there, flashing she scar. Everybody watches she. Edwin, the Yankee boys. On the sideline, her sister spectates and does she tracing with she finger in the air. Poor little girl — such an odd child, and she sister so pretty.

Sundown she's there, too. She comes around the car park and shares we spliff like this is she usual routine. People see she with we, and I don't like it. Waitresses arriving for the dinner shift. Gardeners departing. Sometimes women shake their heads as they walk past us. Sometimes they do nothing, but still I know they disapprove. Let me take this even further for you: Women don't even need bodies to tell us exactly what they think. They could be ghosts, all air, and still men would walk through this air and know just how vex they be with we.

Night, she's waiting in the car park for we, in she little dresses with she little sweaters over she little shoulders for the chill. This girl can hold she liquor, and when Edwin compliments her on this, she says, "The value of a college education," and rolls she eyes. When the dancing begins, I stand to the side and watch she motion. How does a body know and choose everything it does like that?

Sometimes in the afternoon I see she gallivanting down the beach after he. She flashes over the black rocks and gone. What they do there, just the two of they, I don't know. He's not fucking she yet. At least, I'm pretty sure, though this is the one thing my chatterbox friend doesn't speak about much. Don't get me wrong, he makes plenty of big talk about banging these rich-daddy girls. But when Don or Des bang a girl, they go into the particulars . . . this girl smells like fish down there, that one knows how to work she teeth, another one has nipples wrinkled up like walnuts. Edwin stays on the surface, no matter how we pump he for details. Still, I gather he waits for the last night to fuck they. He likes pursuing them even more than he likes fucking them. Fucking is easy for he. Waiting's what he loves, and making them wonder: Did their pretty little performance work?

Another thing: I think he waits because this way, if the girl regrets it, by the time the feeling sinks in, she's on the plane to Chicago or in she pretty purple bedroom in Boston, and what's she going to do then?

A few months ago, a girl almost made everything go bad. Julie. A California blondie, pretty pretty. Julie was quieter than the ones Edwin usually picks. A good girl. She barely touched her drinks at Paulette's, and when we offered her the spliff in the car park, she said, "No, thank you," like she was declining a fresh towel on the beach. I thought she was a lost cause, but then she spirited Edwin away one sundown to she room. With Julie, he didn't wait; he went right along with she. When she bled, he knew it was a mistake. Virgin girls are not a thing to mess with. They think they know what they want, but how can they? And a virgin Yankee girl who decides this is how she wants to lose it? Holy shit.

After that, Julie started acting funny. Her daddy wasn't stupid. He knew something was going on. One sunup when we arrived at work, he was waiting for we in the car park. He marched up to Edwin and grabbed his shirt and told us to stay the hell away from his daughter and threatened to get both our asses fired and to beat the shit out of we if he found out Edwin had laid so much as a hand on his little girl. First time I ever heard a guest threaten to beat the shit out of someone. We were lucky. Julie was so embarrassed she kept she trap shut about what happened. Ever since, Edwin waits. You never know when a girl will get vex. You never know what a vex girl will do, or say.

These girls have a danger to they. He likes that, too.

When we meet the girl in the car park after work today, she appears troubled. Restless.

Maybe it's the rain. It fell all day, constant. Her fingers keep moving like they're not ruled by she. She drums she fingers on the hood of Edwin's car. Then her fingertips circle she scar, around and around. Maybe something happened between she and Edwin. Maybe with this one, so pretty, he failed to wait. Shit.

Then she furrows she brow and says a thing I never expected.

"When I was swimming today I saw a woman on Faraway Cay."

For a moment nobody says a word. I look at Edwin. I expect him to grin and brush her off, but his face is dead serious, even a bit afraid. I shiver.

"Jesus, Mary, and Joseph," he whispers.

"What?" she says. "Do you know her or something?"

"Woman you say you saw — she have long hair, black black?" Edwin asks.

The girl nods.

"White white skin?"

She nods again. "She was, like, staring at me."

I'm thinking, it can't be. But this girl freaks me out a bit. She fingertips never stop tracing she scar. A silly notion comes over me that this scar is the source of she power.

Edwin looks across she to me. "Tell her, Gogo."

I tell her about the Faraway woman's hooves for feet and her wildness. I tell her how she lures people to Faraway and leads them across the cay, how if you follow the woman to the waterfall and see the stars reflected in the water you will lose all sense of up and down, earth and sky, you and she, and they say that's how she takes you.

"I saw her," she says when I finish.

I shiver again.

Edwin snorts. He claps his hands, tosses back his head, and laughs.

"Check you two," he says. "Girl, only thing you did see was a goat. Faraway's overrun with they."

I should have known he wasn't being serious with his Jesus, Mary, and Joseph.

"It wasn't a goat," the girl says. "She had black hair and white skin, just like you said."

"Old nanny goat, probably." He shrugs.

"Why you think Faraway is overrun with they in the first place?" I say. I turn to she. "Every time someone vanish on Faraway, a new goat appears. She turns they."

Edwin cracks up. "Goges here's the only one under sixty who believes that nonsense. Tell me something: What you ever see a goat do beside eating, shitting, and rutting? How do *you* think that cay became overrun with they?"

"How you explain the planes, then?" I say. I can't tell anymore if I'm defending she from Edwin's ridicule or fucking with she, too. Maybe it's some of both.

"Oh, yes!" Edwin says, grinning. "Let it be known that there are not one, not two, but three downed planes on Faraway Cay."

"And they form a triangle," I say.

"Three things *always* form a triangle," Edwin says.

He's right. Shit.

The girl appears nervous.

"But the triangle's not the point," I say. "Guess what's at their center? The waterfall. She lures they. How else you explain it?"

"Drug runners. In shit prop planes."

The girl chews she lip and looks down at the ground. "Maybe I didn't see it as clearly as I thought." I'm pretty sure she only says this to please Edwin, though, because she gazes past the parking lot in the direction of the cay with this dreamy look, like something legit is happening to she. Like she thinks she's special now because we local folkloric creature has taken an interest in she. I feel so annoyed then I wish I didn't argue with Edwin on she behalf. Anyway, he's probably right. Must be a goat she saw.

We change the subject. We smoke we spliff. We pass around a bottle from Edwin's car — hot, unpleasant liquor. We're ready to leave when the girl asks, "Why is it called Faraway Cay anyway, if it's so close? Is that supposed to be, like, a joke or something?"

"No, miss," Edwin says. "This is a deadly serious matter. This name protects us from the cay's proximity." He snorts. "Typical superstitious island shit, thinking if we call it so, it will be so, when that goat-infested cay is staring we right in the face. Better take care, now, girl. The Faraway woman has she eye on you."

Today when I arrive, Sara opens the door with a basket in she arms. "I thought I'd take him to Little Beach," she says.

"Oh," I say. "I guess I'll see you tomorrow, then?"

She looks at me with softness in her face. "Come with us."

We stop off at the food mart on Hopper Lane and I buy three Cadbury bars, one for each of we. We arrive at Little Beach at that magic hour just after sunset when everything is veiled in blue — the sky, the sea, the sand. The guests at Indigo Bay miss this hour. They take their photographs of the sunset and then they go inside and they miss it. Little Beach is quiet, but not empty. We choose a spot a bit away from the others. Sara takes a cloth from the basket and spreads it on the sand. I set out the Cadbury bars. Bryan pets the sand beside the cloth like it's a living thing. Sara lies down, closes she eyes, and lets the remains of the day warm her.

In the distance, one fishing boat is still out, a small dinghy with a fishing pole planted at the bow. The boat is a black silhouette. The fishing pole appears to lance the clouds. At the water's edge, a shirtless man in track pants sprints down the sand. A few strays follow after him, yapping and so happy. Boys scamper onto the pier, then dive into the sea. Not long ago this was me, and someday it will be Bryan. The lampposts on the pier are rickety and their white paint is nearly all flaked away. The lampposts have no lights and they never have and I've never known why, and I like this.

"Should we draw shapes, my Bry?" I say.

He doesn't reply. A shy day. I hoist myself from the cloth and squat in the sand. I trace a balloon with a squiggly string. A bird. A sailboat. Bryan looks at the shapes with interest and also some wariness. "Do you know what that says?" I ask, pointing. He shakes his head. "*B-R-Y-A-N.* That's you, Bryan."

He murmurs something.

"What's that?"

"A nana."

"You want me to draw a banana?"

His lips part and release the faintest, "Yes."

I do my best, a thin shape that looks more like a crescent moon. "Like so?"

He nods. "Thank you, Dada."

It's not me who taught him *thank you.* It's Sara. Already she's showing him good manners. I didn't even notice it happening.

Bryan is still shy with me when I tear the corner off a Cadbury wrapper and show him how to press out the melted chocolate. My boy accepts the chocolate I squeeze onto his finger like it's something holy. He licks it off with his small pink tongue. Sara's tongue.

Sara sits up. "Should we go in?"

I undress Bryan and take off his nappy. My son's skin is dark and even and supple. His belly button is a small sweet nut. Sara removes her shirt and her skirt to reveal her swimming suit. I take off my polo, so I'm down to my shorts and singlet. I'm a bit embarrassed for Sara to see me, but she doesn't stare.

With Sara beside me, I take Bryan in my arms and carry him into the sea. At Indigo Bay, the guests pause on the sand before they walk into the water, as if some sort of preparation is required. It's different here. We walk into the sea as easily as taking our next step. We are not alone in the water. I see a father with a daughter. A woman in a pink bathing cap. An old man holds an old woman by the arm and guides her through the soft waves.

We wade out until the water comes to Sara's waist, Bryan nestled in the crook of my arm. The water is warm, almost the same as the air. Then I feel something warmer on my arm. At first I think it's the last of the day's heat, but the warmth is moving, flowing. I look at Bryan. My boy is laughing — big laughter, full and free. Sara and I look down at my arm at the same time. Urine, trickling in a small channel. We laugh, too. Then Sara closes her eyes, leans back, and floats.

I see us then, a family together in the sea. And something happens to me that maybe I can't ever explain. On this evening, I am a father. Later, Sara and I will tuck Bryan's sleeping ragdoll body into bed. Later still I'll lime with Edwin. For the first time ever, my life feels like my life.

■ ■ ■ ■

Isn't it the fuck of it all that tonight of all nights, when all I want is to lime with my mate, to feel my life being my life, we're saddled with the girl? We're in the car on the way to Paulette's. Engine sputtering, chicken in the road, and she. Tonight's she last night. Edwin knows what this means and from the way she's dressed in a short skirt and a top that ties with a string around she neck, she knows it, too.

"You ready for a wild night, girl?" Edwin says.

She scoffs. "Paulette's is not exactly the pinnacle of wild."

"Maybe we'll take you out to Faraway," he says with a grin. "See if the goat lady take an interest in you."

"I'm down for whatever," the girl says, like it makes no difference to she. But I see she hidden smile, so pleased to think we're going to do something big for she last night. What is it about this one, so convinced she's special? I want to tell she there was Julie and Callie and Lisa and Lauren and Molly before her, and there will be plenty of pretty pretty girls after her. She may be a bit sharper than most, she may be quicker with her tongue, but in the end she wants what they all want: to take home the story of how she fucked the man who brought she towels on the beach. But so what? She's using him, but he's using she, too. They get their story and he gets them.

At Paulette's, Edwin buys all of we a round of ganja shots. Next, rum. At some point I must switch glasses with he, because soon both of ours are finished. I buy another, and another. I'm getting good and gone now. Music playing, bottles clinking, mutt begging. Sounds of Edwin and the girl.

I watch them dance. She does have a nice sway. Together they move so right. You can't learn this. You want to know the secret of life? You will never be they. *They* is always someone else.

We're at Paulette's an hour or so when the girl says, "I'm bored. Let's get out of here."

"Where do you have in mind?" Edwin says.

"I thought we were going to Faraway?" she says with a glint in she eyes.

He laughs. "You mad, girl?"

"But I thought you said —"

"I was just messing with you. Anyway, how you think we would get there?"

She looks down at the floor. "Whatever,"

she mumbles. "Forget it."

"Relax. Plenty of wild places to go."

Next thing we're in the car. Edwin drives fast. Windows down, radio blasting. The potholes give a good *bump* — the girl bounces so high she head hits the roof, hard, and she laughs. We're all good and drunk. Ready for the night to take we.

When Edwin pulls off the road at the spot where the scrub leads to the nameless cliffs, I turn a hard gaze on he. I don't want to take some Yankee chick to this place. But Edwin pretends not to notice. He turns off the car and climbs out. He grabs a bottle of rum from the car and says, "Follow me."

We walk single-file, Edwin then she then me. We've limed here pretty regular over the years since we found the spot in the boat with Keithley, and there's a path carved into the scrub, so faint you have to know it's there to find it. But the ground is uneven and the path is narrow and the scrub is so thick sometimes you have to shield your face as you walk. I see the girl turn around and look behind she. The road is gone.

"Where are we going, anyway?" she asks. She tries to make her voice calm, but she's nervous, and I feel a bit pleased to see this cocky one brought a little low. She stumbles as she walks. This is she drunkest night yet.

"This wild enough for you, miss?" Edwin replies.

She wraps her arms tight across she chest like she's cold. She's scared for true now, and just when I'm about to break and tell she everything's fine and where we're going, the scrub parts and we're here. The stretch of smooth, flat rock that leads to the edge. The ocean lit up by the moon. The girl doesn't hesitate. She dashes right up to the edge, so fast for a second I think she's going to go right over.

"Shit, girl, watch yourself!" Edwin says.

She turns to us. "This place is amazing." She kicks off she sandals and we do the same, leaving we shoes in a pile. She walks the edge like a high-wire walker in the circus, up on she tiptoes with she hands out to she sides. Next, she stands with she toes curled over the edge, looking out. In the distance, Faraway is a black shadow against the black sky.

Edwin nudges me. "She ripe to be fucked or what?"

Then he runs at she, his bare feet soundless against the rock. When he reaches she, he puts his arms around her and she shrieks. He scoops her up. He twirls her around.

"You scared the shit out of me!" she says, laughing so hard she's gasping. She hits him, but not hard; she's not angry, she's flirting. She leans back in Edwin's arms and looks up at the stars and kicks her feet like she's swimming through the air. He puts her down and we sit together on the rocks.

Edwin passes the bottle of rum around. He pulls a spliff from his pocket. We're having a real bacchanal now, the three of we. The rocks are smooth and cool. The sky offers we everything: crescent moon, stars so bright it's like they're fucking with we.

She tips the bottle back and lets the liquor flow down she throat. She blows smoke into Edwin's face and he breathes it in. I reach for the spliff. She shakes she head, wags she finger.

"Not yet." She takes another hit, brings she face close to me, and exhales. Then her mouth is on my mouth. I'm so gone I don't wonder what or why. Her tongue twists around my tongue. I take she hips in my hands. She berry lips. She little tits pressing against my chest. I feel myself going hard.

She pulls away. There's a twinkle in she eyes. She turns to Edwin. Then her mouth is on his mouth and I watch she kiss he. Her ponytail tosses in the wind. He unties the string around her neck. He runs his hands up and down she sides and groans.

She pulls away from he, same as she did

from me. I look to see if something's wrong, but she still has the twinkle in she eyes. She twirls her ponytail with her finger, like she's alone here, amusing herself. Then she looks at we. "Your turn."

I laugh.

"What's so funny?" she says.

"You shitting we," Edwin says.

"You scared, boys?" She makes a big show of tying the string around her neck again, though she's so drunk she does it sloppy. "I thought you were up for something wild. Never mind, I guess."

Edwin shakes he head. "Fucking girl." He grabs me and pulls me toward him. Next thing I know, his lips are on my lips. His tongue pushes into my mouth. Quick, he pulls away. He wipes the back of his hand across his mouth and I do the same. We spit onto the rocks. He kissed me hard, like a smack across the mouth. At first I want to laugh. Can you believe what we just did? Can you believe how far my bred will go to fuck a girl? But then I look at he and he looks at me and something in his face stops me. For the first time in we life, Edwin appears afraid.

I hear the girl clap, slow slow. I hear she say, "Bravo." We don't move. "Guys?" she says. "Hey, guysss." Out of the corner of my eye I see she stumble. She falls to her hands and knees like she's going to be sick. Then she lies down on the ground, curled up like a baby.

Edwin snaps back into the moment then. He turns away from me and faces she. "You satisfied, *miss*?" he says.

"Shhh. The stars," she mumbles. Her eyes are closed.

Edwin goes over and sits next to she. He takes the string of her shirt in his fingers and pulls. She lets him. She shirt falls down to she waist. She's not wearing a bra. Her tits are like Sara's, small small, the kind that remind you a woman was a girl. He unbuttons his trousers. He runs his fingers up she leg, she thigh, under she skirt.

"Mmm." She says it so faint I barely hear it.

I go off to give them space. I walk to the edge of the rocks and lie down and listen to the sea crash. I close my eyes and for a moment I'm falling, weightless. Then I hear Edwin.

"What the fuck?" he says.

I look over.

He's wiping his hand on his trousers. "Girl, quit slobbering!" he says.

I laugh. "Edwin, man, she passed out!"

He groans and shoves she away. In the

starlight her scar glistens like a thing that could slither away. He lifts she arm and lets go. It flops.

"Typical," he spits.

Edwin leaves her there and walks over to me. He lies down near me, right at the edge, so close he hangs one arm over it and swings it back and forth through the abyss above the sea. We look up at the stars. A memory comes over me like a breeze, of lying like this back in this same spot in secondary, when Keithley would take us out in the boat and sometimes, amid the bacchanal, the night would find its stillness. I'm drifting off now. Ground cool and smooth. Air cool and smooth. Sound of waves far below.

Then I feel Edwin's hand on my hand.

He turns and looks at me. I don't laugh or pull my hand away. It all happens fast. He unbuttons himself, then me. I make my mind go empty. I make myself all body. Not because I know what I want or don't want, but because this night has taken us to a place we may never find again, and I need to be there with him before it's gone. I don't believe we're doing this until he places my hand around him. He's warm, like my own self. It's he or me or we — I don't bother to understand, just touch and rub, touch and rub, until the world goes tacky with we. We're together beneath the cold stars, and then the stars groan and unleash their white light and the night goes so thick and sweet with our chlorine I swear that perfume will last until the stars are dead.

Then I'm on the ground. Shoved off by he, hard, and at first I don't know why, but then I sit up and rub my eyes open and see she looking at we.

"The fuck you staring at, little girl?" Edwin says.

Her eyes open wide. Her mouth makes an *O* and a sound comes out so small the wind takes it.

She stands, gathers she sandals, and runs.

FARAWAY

"At first, I believed she would turn up."

People disappear and are found. A mother at a department store plunges into panic until she hears a muffled giggle coming from inside a rack of clothes. A husband is late on a rainy night, but eventually the headlights come up the driveway. The girl is sobering up somewhere. She is swimming in the ocean, in the pool. She is a bit late, is all, to the breakfast buffet. For a time, the missing person is everywhere. Then, sometimes, just as quickly, she is nowhere.

Clive and I sat on the bench on the sidewalk. Snow had collected on our coats and on Clive's gray wool hat. The traffic light at the end of the block bathed us in its shifting light — green, yellow, red. It was after midnight. I felt as if I had been walking for days, for years, and now that I had finally arrived at my destination, this faraway place the reaching of which had been my sole object for so long, I didn't want to look around. I didn't want to take in the sights or know anything about what kind of place this was. I was only tired.

I said nothing and he continued. "When she ran off, I started to go after her, but Edwin said to let her go, and I did. We were only half a mile from Indigo Bay. We weren't abandoning her in the middle of nowhere. I figured she'd find her way. On the drive home, we got pulled over and the police officer took us in to sleep it off. You must know about that, I guess. We were in a cell together all night, only the two of us, but we didn't talk. We just sat there together. But it wasn't a bad silence. It felt like we had time, is what I mean. We didn't have to say anything to each other yet about what we'd done. Then the next day we found out she was missing and everything changed."

"What did you do?"

"When he heard the news, Edwin came up to me on the beach and said, 'Listen. We limed with she at Paulette's and then we drove her back here. That's all.' So when the police questioned me that's what I told them. I knew how it must look. The two of us with her all night, and now she happened to be gone? They knew I was hiding something, but what could I do, tell them what had happened?" He shook his head. "The police came and searched my grandmother's house. They were looking for drugs. I don't know how they knew. Edwin — he wouldn't have done that to me. I still believe that. My grandmother watched me get taken away, with all the neighbors out in the street." He ran his hand over his face.

Clive told me the rest of his story, and I did my best to listen, though I confess I found it difficult to focus on the details of a life that I saw now had very little to do with me. He told me about his time in the eggshell-blue prison, where he and the twenty or so other incarcerated island men did nothing much as they waited out their sentences. At night, he was troubled by dreams. In them, he was back at the cliffs with Edwin, together beneath the stars. He looked up and saw everyone he knew standing in a circle around them, watching. *We have found you, we know, everybody knows.* He woke from these dreams soaked in sweat. Then he reminded himself that the girl was the only one who had seen them together, and she was dead. He felt so relieved, and right on the heels of this emotion came the next one — filthy, gut-twisting shame that he was relieved that a girl was dead, and in these moments it seemed to him that they must have willed her death somehow, that their desire to protect their secret had made it happen.

In prison he had time to think. Mostly, he thought about Edwin. They had not spoken since Edwin instructed him on what to say to the police, so Clive was left alone with the mystery of that night and what it meant — a mystery that cast its shadow back to the beginnings of his boyhood. He went over it and over it, sifting through the smallest moments and details of their shared life. He thought of the antimen on the beach before Indigo Bay was Indigo Bay, when Edwin orchestrated the ambushes to chase the men away. He thought of Jan sitting in the stifling afternoon air of Paulette's, his eyes bloodshot with drink, his thumb beating like a heart against the sticky bar. *Fleet.* What was Jan's interest in them, in Edwin, really? He thought of Alison and Julie and all the rest, the whole parade of Edwin's pretty American daughters. Edwin always said he went after them because the local girls were either prudes or skets or gossips, and Clive had always been impressed with himself for knowing better than to believe this. He had thought Edwin pursued these girls because they came from the places he dreamed of going, because he hated them for their stupid good luck even as he tried to draw himself closer to his dreams through their sweet-smelling skin. And maybe that was part of it. But what if there was something else, too? What if he chose these girls because whatever happened, or didn't, they were leaving, gone?

No matter how much he thought about it, without knowing what that night had meant to Edwin, it was impossible to determine what it had meant to himself. What would have happened next? What future was thwarted because that girl went off and got herself killed?

Edwin did not come to see him in prison. His grandmother did, every Sunday. She sat stiffly across a folding table from him in the visitors' room, beneath an overhead fan that ticked as it uselessly stirred the warm air. It was from her that he learned that Edwin was looking in on Sara and Bryan in the evenings. He had been fired from Indigo Bay, of course, but recently he had started a new venture silk-screening island-themed apparel — T-shirts with palm trees, neon sunsets, a pineapple wearing sunglasses, slogans: I'M ON ISLAND TIME. WHAT HAPPENS ON THE CRUISE STAYS ON THE CRUISE. His merchandise was already in a few of the souvenir shops in Hibiscus

Harbour. He was giving Sara money. Clive was grateful. Edwin had always helped him, and he was helping him now, as Clive still believed he always would.

Two months after his release from prison, he flew to New York. He thought Edwin might come to say goodbye, but when the time came to drive to the airport in his grandmother's church friend Verna's car and Edwin had not come, he was not surprised.

He made his way in New York, as he had already told me. He built a life passed in the fellowship of other solitary men. He had been gone three years when Sara told him she had married Edwin. That was over fourteen years ago, so long that it was difficult to believe it wasn't always true, that there was a time before the mother of his child married his best friend. He had been through so much. He had lost his father and been abandoned by his mother, gotten a girl pregnant and become a father too young, been a suspect in a murder, gone to prison, started over in a new country, had the shit kicked out of him in a vacant lot in Brooklyn. Yet it seemed to Clive that the man who lived through all that was still an innocent, for he had not yet lain awake at night imagining his son walking between Sara and

Edwin, one hand in each of theirs. His boy, laughing with delight as they lifted their arms and swung him into the air.

Why had Edwin done it? Did he love Sara, or had he only married her to hurt him, to reject the love that had hung in the stars like an open question on their last night together? Or maybe marrying Sara had been a way of holding on to the only part of Clive that Edwin could have — Bryan; maybe Edwin's most wounding action was also his greatest act of devotion.

Two years after Sara and Edwin married, Clive received a letter from his grandmother. It was autumn. He remembered because just before he found the letter in the metal mailbox he shared with his roommates, he paused on the stairs outside the apartment building to scrape the tacky samara wings from the bottoms of his shoes. He read the letter in the dark hallway. Buried in updates about the renovation of St. George's, about the local election and Verna's nieces from Toronto, was the news that Sara had given birth to a son, Edwin Jr. Eddie for short. Clive saw his son and Edwin's growing up together. More than mates, more than breds. Brothers. The thought of it was so sweet to him his chest ached. He knew that to feel this way after what Edwin had done made him a chump. Edwin had stolen the only life he had ever wanted, a quiet existence with Sara and children and not-so-bad work and Sunday afternoons at Little Beach. Yet he was grateful. It seemed to him that this life was better off without him in it, for surely he would have spoiled it with his clumsy touch.

What if he had known everything that was waiting for him? What if, when Edwin approached him in the schoolyard on the first day of second grade, back when he was only Clive, you had shown him all that was going to happen and said, *Will you take this life?* What is there to say? He would have walked right up to Edwin and joined the game. Because of Edwin he'd lost everything, but without him, he would not even have had these things to lose. He needed Edwin. He could make no sense of his life without him.

Years passed. He was thirty-five. One summer evening he was walking through Prospect Park — the air redolent with charcoal, laughter and music wafting into the huge night above the lawns — when he heard his name.

"Gogo? Clive fucking Richardson, is that you?"

It was Bery Wilson. She marched right up

to him and wrapped him in a tight embrace. "I've thought of you," she said. That was as close as she came to talking about the past. She told him she was an artist now — something about the city as canvas, pain as art. She wore her hair in a Mohawk, shaved on the sides and natural on top. In the purple twilight, he could make out tattoos of birds on her arms. An Asian girl and a white guy ambled over and said hello. Bery introduced them to him as members of her collective.

"Join us," said the guy.

"We have veggie dogs," said the girl.

"Yes, please, come sit," Bery said with a smile. How had she managed it? The anger seemed to have evaporated out of her altogether.

He told her he was running late, though the truth was he had nowhere to be.

"I understand," she said. Then her face turned serious. "You've heard about Edwin?"

Clive spent the months after Bery told him that Edwin was dying waiting for his friend to reach out to him. ("Cancer," she'd said, and when he asked what kind she said she wasn't sure, she only knew that it was everywhere now.) He imagined it so many ways. He would be getting out of the shower, or paying for dinner at the Little Sweet, when his cell phone would ring. "He's asking for you," Sara would say. Clive would fly home, arriving just in time. The house would be dark and quiet, Bryan and Eddie having been sent out to occupy themselves despite their protestations, for they knew their father was dying and did not want to leave his side. Clive would walk through the kitchen and the parlor to the bedroom. When he first saw Edwin in the bed he would gasp. His friend would be unrecognizable — his skin ashen, his cheeks sunken, the sockets of his eyes alarmingly prominent.

Hey, Gogo, Edwin would say, as if it had been only hours since they'd last seen each other.

They would talk. About the boys. About their own boyhoods. Remember the time we climbed the radio tower? Remember sneaking into *E.T.*? Remember, remember, remember. Edwin would close his eyes, as if drifting off to sleep, and for a minute Clive would think he was gone. Then Edwin would open his eyes again, and when he did they would be glazed with tears. He would look up at Clive with that old grin.

Will you miss me? he would say.

Clive would take Edwin's trembling face

in his hands. He would lower his head and kiss his best friend lightly on the forehead, and they would know without having to say it that all was forgiven.

But Clive did not hear from his friend, and one day his grandmother called and told him that Edwin had died. He tried to wrap his mind around the truth that Edwin was not still down on the island, away from him, unseen for years, but still there, still *here,* but he couldn't. It was only then he recognized that all these years he had held on to the buried belief that someday, somehow, they would be brought together again, and that in their new, shared aftermath they would have all the time and words and silence they needed to understand together everything that had happened. Now this would never be. He had moved into another chapter of his life, one in which he would have to live without the possibility that the central mysteries of his life would be demystified.

Ever since, his days passed like walking downhill. He drove his taxi, moved from apartment to apartment. He kept apprised of the news in the lives of his friends and acquaintances. There was a gallery in Fort Greene where from time to time he saw Bery's sculptures on display. He and Ouss still got together once or twice a year for a meal. Ouss and his wife owned a hardware store on Tremont Avenue. They had four girls; the eldest was on a full scholarship at Exeter.

At night, he walked. Every evening when he set out, the details of the neighborhood were overwhelming — a lover's quarrel on the sidewalk, blinking lights in the windows of an electronics store, peaches at a fruit stand so ripe their perfume made him woozy. But the longer he walked, the more the city receded, until the world around him rendered itself invisible and he began to hear water lapping against the edges of the metropolis, which became water lapping at the edges of another island, and then he was not walking through New York anymore, but through the landscape of that other world, that other life. He would stop at a basketball court or a playing field to watch the boys at play, and he would see them all there, shouting and tussling on the pitch, Edwin and Des and Damien and Don. Sometimes a boy left the raucousness of the game behind to sit in the grass, or to hum a song to himself, and Clive knew that he was Bryan; his boy was beautiful and sweet and everything good. And once a year, he walked to Manhattan Beach with its gray sand and its mangy gulls swirling overhead and ate an American chocolate bar that tasted all wrong but was the best he could do, and in this way he marked the day he lost all of them forever.

If only Alison hadn't found it so necessary to stir up the shit between him and Edwin, to intrude in things she didn't understand. If only she hadn't gone off and done whatever she did. It wasn't just her own life she was risking — had she thought about that? Had it occurred to her for even a moment?

And if only . . . if only they hadn't taken her out with them. If only they hadn't been taking pretty white daughters out with them for months like the world was a place it most definitely wasn't. If only he had gone after her when she ran. If only he'd called out to her. "Wait, don't go," and maybe he wouldn't be sitting here now, with his hands numb and the snow falling on his coat.

"But I never would have. He told me to let her go and I did." He put his head in his hands.

"You couldn't have known," I whispered. I placed a hand on his back, but he jerked away from my touch. He stood and brushed the snow from his windbreaker.

"What are you doing?"

"What does it look like?"

"You can't just leave! There's so much more I want to ask you. I know there must be more you want to ask me, too. We can be open with each other now. We don't have to hide."

"You wanted the truth and now you have it. What more could you want from me?"

I understood then what I did want, what I had wanted for months. There was a version of this story in which two lost souls whose lives had been irrevocably altered by the same long-ago night found each other in New York and, in one of those unexpected turns you hear about with surprising frequency, built a new life together. It was the best version of the story, one with the power to salvage everything that had happened. At the same moment it became clear to me that this was what could have happened, I also understood that it would not happen, and that from then on I would be living in a different aftermath — no longer the aftermath of Alison's death, but of this winter in New York with Clive Richardson. For, whether we're aware of it or not, we are always living in the aftermath of something.

"It has to mean something that I got into your cab. Don't you see? All of this was supposed to happen. Please," I said uselessly.

He looked up at the sky and shook his

head. "The crazy thing is I knew. I must have, right? That something with you wasn't . . . You just seemed so lost and lonely."

"I am lost. I am lonely. Clive, please. It's still *me.* I was just a little girl." My eyes filled with tears.

For a moment, as he looked at me, he seemed to be peering into the past, seeing the strange sunburned child I once was. He nodded. "I know." Then he slipped the wool hat from his head and stuffed it in the pocket of his coat. "Goodbye, Claire."

He walked down the street and disappeared into the falling snow.

For weeks after that I circled the Little Sweet hoping to find him. Maybe we could reconcile. Maybe it wasn't too late. But he never came back.

One night when I was walking past, Vincia spotted me. She left her post behind the counter and came outside.

"He's gone," she said.

"Gone?"

She nodded. I expected her to be angry. Instead her expression was sharp with loss. It occurred to me that I might have misapprehended her prickliness toward me; maybe Vincia had harbored her own ideas about two lonely people in this city who might have found happiness together. "I heard he left in the middle of the night."

"Where did he go?"

"As if I would tell you if I knew!" She turned and marched quickly back inside.

I suppose that in the days before he confronted me, Clive must have been settling his affairs in New York and making plans for wherever he was heading to begin again once more. I stopped returning to the Little Sweet after that. It was as Clive had said: I'd wanted the truth and now I had it, as much of it as I would ever have. It was enough, wasn't it? There are many versions of the Alison Thomas story and I suspect there always will be. The police have theirs. So do the interweb conspiracy theorists and *Dying for Fun.* Now I had my own. One I could accept. One I could, perhaps, move on from.

Alison wakes from her stupor on the cliffs to the sounds of lovemaking. She turns and sees them, these men for whom she has performed her spectacular self all week.

The fuck you staring at, little girl?

Suddenly she feels very young and very foolish. How impressed she had been with herself! How pleased their approval had made her and how convinced she was of her appeal to them. How clearly she had seen it: she would get their groans of pleasure, their black skin against her white skin, the night a souvenir to remind her who she has the capacity to be. How humiliated she is to realize this night isn't about her and it never was, to see Edwin and Clive together beneath the stars and to know with corrosive, painful clarity that there is not a thing in her own life as true as this moment between them.

She gathers herself up and she runs, sandals in her hands, through the scrub. When at last she breaks through to Mayfair Road, she continues to run along the ditch on the road's shoulder, not caring how the rocks cut her feet, wanting it, even. Up ahead, she sees the lights of Indigo Bay. The illuminated fountains and the perfect lines of palms. She smells the floral air, feels the road turn smooth and loving beneath her feet. And then?

Some months after my last night with Clive Richardson, a package arrived from Philadelphia, a slender bubble mailer addressed to Claire Thomas.

I'm sorry it's taken me such a ridiculously

long time to send this to you. I hope it's helpful. Sending you all my best.

Inside was a color copy of a poster for the Princeton Modern Dance Ensemble's "Winter Extravaganza." Polaroids from parties. Messages scrawled on scraps of notebook paper: "12:15, just left for dining hall. C u there?" "Free ice cream at student center tonight. Let's do this!" A postcard. On the front, a consummate sunset, lilac infinity over a tropical sea. On the back:

> Nika Nika,
> Greetings from paradise! Haha, not exactly. Hope your parents aren't driving you as crazy as mine are. On the bright side, I met the *cutest* boy. Guess we'll see!
>
> Love ya,
> A

Where does she turn after everything with Clive and Edwin falls apart? Isn't it obvious? She finds him at the bar doing tequila shots as "Redemption Song" is piped in over the speakers, or sipping a Red Stripe on a lounge chair by the pool, or participating in a game of beer pong on the Ping-Pong table off the lobby, his enthusiasm changing to cool boredom the instant he spots her. Better than nothing, she tells herself. Even before it's over she knows it isn't enough, not even close. It is worse than nothing. It is all wrong. This boy whose baby-blue eyes match his baby-blue polo shirt match her baby-blue manicure. It only makes her feel more acutely the exact problem of her life: No matter what she does, no matter how she tries, she cannot get out beyond herself. She can only ever be Alison.

But suppose you told her she could have a different life, swap out hers for one she'd deem more acceptable as an offering to this beautiful, brutal world? Though it would be pretty to think she'd say yes, she knows what she would really do: She would snatch up her cute dresses, her A's, her orthodontia-sleeked teeth, the many dappled lawns of her life . . . the gothic dormitory washed in eventide bells, flip-flops in autumn, fresh powder on the mountain. She would take it all and she would run. There it is, her most shameful secret: She loves her life. Oh, how she loves it.

It is very late now, and she is desperate for something, anything, with which to salvage this night, this vacation that has gone so awry from her carefully cultivated plans. It's then that she looks out into the water and sees Faraway, a black silhouette etched against the sky. She hears the soft wash of waves. She walks across the beach to the water's edge. She unties her halter top, unzips her skirt, shimmies out of her panties, and lets them fall to the sand at her feet. She considers moving her clothes higher up the beach in case the tide should rise and carry them away. Instead, she leaves them. Let the sea do what it will. What a story it would be, what a thing to be able to remember. She steps into the water.

Maybe, as she strokes through the sea to the cay, she believes she is being lured there by a black-haired woman with hooves for feet who has chosen her, and into whose wildness she can finally lose this self she loves and hates in equal measure. Or maybe she does not believe any of that. Maybe her strokes are powered by a desire she can't name, a need going unmet and unmet and unmet. Maybe she simply wants to give herself her wildest wild night; proof, to some older, duller version of herself, that she was young once and didn't squander it.

She follows the starlit path inland, her feet sensing their way over roots and rocks. In the darkness, the spray cast off by the waterfall is a vaporous fog, soft as a caress on her skin. Maybe she slips on the moss-slicked rocks close to the water and falls in. Maybe she dives, the water appearing deeper than it really is in the dark, and hits her head. This version, too, has its blank spaces. Things I'll never be able to know. These are the secret moments. Hers alone.

But first . . .

In the dead of night, a little girl opens her eyes. As she surfaces from dreams, she smells the tang of blood. She has been scratching in her sleep. Then she hears rustling. She calls her sister's name and her sister comes to her.

"Where were you?" she asks.

"Shhh."

Her sister crawls into bed with her and wraps her arms around her. When the little girl is on the edge of sleep, her sister kisses her on the back of the neck and slips out of the bed.

"Where're you going?" the little girl mumbles.

"Far away."

"But —"

"Shh. Don't tell." She pads across the room, opens the door, and is gone.

The little girl doesn't tell. Not when her parents ask. Not when the police question her. At first she doesn't tell because it's a secret, and she is good at keeping secrets. She is patient. Later, when her sister has been missing too long, she doesn't tell because she is scared she did something wrong by not telling and everyone will be angry with her. Later still, when they tell her that her sister is dead, she knows she will keep the secret forever, because it is the last thing she has of her sister and she wants to keep it for herself. She keeps it so long, unspoken, that it becomes difficult to believe it happened at all.

Don't go.

If she had said this, maybe her sister would have listened. Her sister would have rubbed aloe over her itchy skin, and in the morning she would have woken to her sister's warm body beside her in bed.

Feeling better? her sister would ask.

Don't go. That was all she had to say. But what kind of thing is that to know, really? Because to have said those words, she would have had to be a different person altogether. So, in the end, what is the tragedy of her life if not being, again and again, the person she is?

“It will feel good.”

I actually said that to her. Like I knew better than she did. Like she was under some naïve misapprehension that sex might be unpleasant and here, let me clear it up for you. She had found me at the bar and we had gone out to the beach. We were alone, it was late, and we were pretty drunk. We were doing what, for lack of a better term, I’ll call making out. She was taking the lead and I was just happy to be taken along for the ride. At Yale, I was not exactly a Casanova or a Vronsky. I was a German major in the orchestra; I played the cello, for Christ’s sake — these are not cool things now and they were not cool things then. But sometimes when you go someplace where people don’t know you, they get an impression of you that’s different from who you are in your regular life. I remember thinking that this girl was way out of my league, but lucky me, she hadn't figured that out yet. I'm not talking about the night she died. This was before, on her first night at Indigo Bay.

I wouldn't call her aggressive, but she was forward. There was no coyness to what was happening between us, no game being played. When I put my hand on her thigh and she pulled away from me I was genuinely confused. I thought we'd both been pretty clear where this was leading and, like I said, she was the one doing the leading. I was moving my hand up beneath her skirt, and she stopped me. She said she should go. She looked nervous, which threw me because until then she had seemed so confident. That's when I said it. I stroked her hair and said, "Are you sure? It will feel good." Then — Christ, this is embarrassing — but I sort of, not sort of, I *did,* I nudged her hand toward the crotch of my shorts, toward my boner, if you want to call it that. I hate the language we have for this stuff: *boner, horny, making out, feeling up, eating out.* It's so crass and graceless. Hanna teases me; she calls me a prude because I can't say these words out loud. I'm not a prude. But these words make me feel like I'm an animal.

After I said that, I was actually relieved when she didn't give in to me, when she said good night and left. Turns out all I really wanted was to go back to my room and jerk off and pass out. But there's this script, a script all boys know, and I didn't write it and I didn't even really want to say it, but there we were, and it's not like I was some player with a stockpile of great lines, so that's what I said. It scared her. *I* scared her.

For months after she died, I was terrified something would surface and my life would be destroyed. When everyone thought those men raped and killed her and I knew they didn't, I felt terrible. But what could I do? When the police came to question me, it wasn't even a conscious choice — I simply told them she'd been doing drugs and who gave them to her. When I told them I saw her early on the night she disappeared, and only briefly, and they asked if I was sure I didn't see her again, I nodded my head and said, "Yes, I'm positive," so decisively I almost believed it. It was not a choice, but something I knew I must do. To tell the truth, to tell them she had been with me after those men had already been put in the drunk tank, would have been unthinkable, tragic, foolish. It would have yanked me into this horrible mess, and for what? My life wasn't meant to be derailed by one night on vacation.

It was late, and I was making my way back to my room from the bar, scuffing my Top-Siders against the pool deck, when I saw her. Her hair was a mess. Her mascara was smudged around her eyes.

"I promised, didn't I?" she said. She smiled that sly smile that had teased me all week. Something was different, though. She was agitated, I might even say frantic. I was pretty sure she'd been crying. She grabbed my hand and I let her lead me to one of the beach cabanas. She wasted no time. She pulled off her top, her skirt, and her panties with a pragmatism that both chilled and aroused me. She pointed at my khakis with her chin. I unbuttoned them.

It was unlike any sex in my admittedly slender library of experience. She pinned my arms above my head and held my wrists so hard they still ached the next day when the police questioned me. (There were faint bruises there, which they would have found if they'd looked.) Then I moved on top of her. She placed my hands around her neck.

At first I jerked them away, but she grabbed them and wrapped them around again. I squeezed. She closed her eyes and smiled faintly, like I wasn't even there. So I squeezed harder, and her eyes popped open. I'll never forget it. The violence she unearthed so easily in me, like she knew it was right beneath the surface.

It was about something other than pleasure for her. Something was wrong but I didn't know what and I didn't ask. When I remember it, my dick goes limp, but I was twenty years old — capable of enjoying all kinds of misguided sex. When it was over, she dressed and ran off so quickly I was still dribbling cum into the sand when I lost sight of her.

At first I felt horribly guilty. Maybe if I'd asked her what was wrong, or if I'd done something different, then . . . I played that game over and over until it nearly drove me crazy. Back at Yale, I paid penance in all kinds of ways. I tutored a low-income New Haven kid. I called my parents more. For a brief period during my senior year, I seriously entertained joining the Peace Corps. But with time, I grew comfortable in my life again.

I've never thought of myself as a secretive person, but I am practical, and practically you can't tell this story, and I never have. I lead a good life. It is not as grand as the life I assumed would be mine when I was young — I haven't changed the world with my goodness or brilliance or bravery. I haven't made a giant splash with my existence, but I'm well respected in my field. I'm an architect. Hanna and I own a boutique firm together. She's Dutch. We met during a summer studio in Budapest in graduate school. I love her frankness, which can come off as arrogance to those who don't know her because she is beautiful, tall and slender and erect. I love the space between us, the gap our different native tongues and cultures opens, and the privacy this affords.

I read somewhere — okay, not somewhere, I saw it on this fairly lowbrow pop-psychology website — that each of our lives is anchored to a single moment, whether disturbing or traumatic or euphoric or inscrutable, from which we never move on, and that the age at which this moment occurs is our Eternal Age. This strikes me as true. Hanna's Eternal Age, for instance, is twenty-eight, when she gave birth to our son. But mine isn't thirty-two, my own age when he was born. My moment came years before I met my wife, and maybe that explains the distance between us: I shared her moment with her, while she doesn't even know mine exists. My eternal age is twenty. I see him, this lanky kid I was, with a mop of unruly hair, so erudite and charmingly, forgivably assured, and I'm a bit in awe of him, to be honest.

"It will feel good." Sometimes I wonder whether this thing I said, this juvenile horndog pressure I put on her at the beginning of the week, is to blame in some small way, like it set her on a course. Then I scold myself. I tell myself that it's vanity, thinking something I said was powerful enough to do all that. I tell myself that just because I didn't behave perfectly doesn't make me responsible. I remind myself, finally, that I barely knew her. Still, sometimes I wake up in the middle of the night and the darkness is full of her.

Remember This

I once read that evolution has predisposed us to see ghosts and spirits, to find signs and omens in the ordinary: a sudden swell of wind, answers revealed in dreams. This impulse toward the mystical has its basis, so I read, in neurology. Our brains hunger for order. The early man who could make sense of the patterns of deer, the migration of birds, the movement of clouds, lived. From the beginning, our survival has hinged on our ability to look at the miscellany of the world, to sift through its deluge of details, and find the story. Stories, this article claimed, are the essence of human endurance.

But on the radio last week another expert, a neuropsychologist, explained it differently. Stories, this woman said, are our Achilles' heel. Our desperation for them leads us to live in a perpetual state of delusion. Early man, at the mercy of animals, weather, each other, invented Artemis, Ra, Vishnu. Our hunger for stories leads us to mistake a distracted spouse for an unfaithful spouse, an earthquake for divine punishment. A death for a murder.

Aren't they both right? Stories lead us to the truth and they lead us astray, and how are we to know the difference?

Slowly, the city began to thaw. The air turned wet and clean. Trees unfurled vivid newborn leaves. The man in the NASCAR hat sat on the front steps with a fluffy white puppy beside him.

"Isabella," he told me with a grin.

I took Jackie out to brunch to apologize for my recent behavior. She forgave me quickly, and over mimosas and eggs Benedict she updated me on her drama of the week.

My parents flew out for a visit. We did the things we always did when they came to New York — the Met, brunch at Sarabeth's, a show. One afternoon my father had plans with an old college friend, and my mother and I found ourselves in Central Park. Lines of girls in powder-blue pleated jumpers and sneakers followed teachers onto the park's muddy fields. The last gray snowbanks were almost gone, and the melt from them darkened the footpaths. We bought ice-cream bars. ("Naughty us," my mother said with a conspiratorial smile.) We sat on a bench to eat them. We talked about the television show everybody was watching that spring. About the vacation my parents had planned for October, a two-week river tour, Basel to Barcelona. Then we fell into the uncomfortable silence of a mother and daughter who know that mothers and daughters ought to be able to speak to one another endlessly.

"Mom?" I said finally.

"Yes, sweetheart?"

"What happened when I went to Paris with Aunt Caroline? When I came back everything was different, but I never knew why."

My mother pursed her lips, and I feared she was going to give me the kind of evasive nonanswer I was used to from her.

"I told your father it had to stop. Not just him with the police. Me, too. Both of us."

"But why? Why did you just give up?"

"We didn't give up, sweetheart. But we had to leave it behind. Because we had you, and you were everything. You *are* everything. We wanted you to have a life."

I think Alison was wrong about our mother. I was, too. We thought she was a fragile, timid woman. But as I looked at her on the bench, a smile flickering in her eyes as a young boy toddled unsteadily past us holding a small pink ball, I saw her differently. It took strength not to allow oneself to be subsumed by a thing that loomed so large.

(Not long after my parents' visit to New York, a Hollywood agent would drive out to Laurel Canyon, let himself into a midcentury modern house nestled among eucalyptus trees, and find the actor, dead in his bed. Foul play not suspected. Oxycontin, Ativan, and cocaine found on the nightstand, according to an anonymous paramedic. Most of the articles about his death were accompanied by the same photograph, a recent paparazzi shot in which the actor gave the impression of abundant unwellness: long unruly hair, a too-big suit and sandals, gin-glazed eyes and coffee-yellow teeth. I would stare at that photo, looking him in the eyes across time and space, life and death, and he would seem to look back at me.)

It has been several years since I stepped into that taxi. I live in Charlotte now. I work in ad sales. My condo is spacious and bright, the walls painted an institutional peach I don't really mind. I drive a little red Honda that gets great mileage. A few weeks ago, a coworker sent me an old article from *The Onion,* "Horrified Man Suddenly Realizes He's Putting Down Roots in Charlotte," and I laughed because it reminded me of me. I go by Claire here. At first hearing that name on the lips of my coworkers and new friends unsettled me. But I've grown used to it.

Clive Richardson has disappeared from my life as completely as he entered it. I find comfort in not knowing where he is. Sometimes I close my eyes and send messages to him. I tell him I hope he's found a place beyond the grip of his past. I tell him it wasn't all a lie. I ask him not to judge me too harshly. The winter I spent with Clive is a locked room inside myself, one which, I'm reasonably certain, I will never open again. (Though still, now, when I find myself back in the city, I will climb into a taxi and hope that when the driver says hello it will be Clive's voice I hear. And when, inevitably, it isn't, I summon that voice, those nights, the city as it was that winter, and I tell myself, almost sternly, *Remember this.*)

I can see now that during those months, I fooled myself into believing I was after closure, when all I really wanted was never to let go. Because, as Alison's scar was her most sacred vanity, her death was mine. Because I needed a murder mystery. Without one, what choice did I have but to be angry at Alison for making herself so indispensable to me, to all of us, and then being so careless with herself? (Drinking and drugs, a reckless swim, a stupid accident. The police had suggested this basic scenario from the beginning, but my parents had refused to accept it. Why would they have? Why would anyone accept such a sad and pointless story, a tale that was not even cautionary but simply tragic, a shame?) What choice was there, finally, but to admit that I hated Alison every bit as much as I loved her? I hated her while she was alive for the way her dazzling, spectacular self took up the entire spotlight, and I hated her even more for the oppressive shadow she cast with her death. How could I ever be enough? How could I possibly compare to someone who never had to grow up?

Had she lived, perhaps in her twenties Alison would have been like Jackie, a person who might say to her friends, over craft beer or picklebacks or whatever beverage would have been de rigueur then, "I need to find time for my *dancing,*" in a way that suggested that her dancing was something the world needed. If I was visiting her, in Williamsburg or the Mission or Silver Lake, say to celebrate my sixteenth birthday, then I would have rolled my eyes when she said this, and I would have gotten to experience the wrenching, liberating moment when your idol becomes just another person. She might have grown to be a woman like Nika, preoccupied by her children's homework assignments and video game habits. Perhaps she would now be living a life not so dissimilar from our parents'; maybe she would take her own children to Caribbean resorts and reflect, as she read a memoir beneath an umbrella's shade, on the trade-offs she had made for a life that was, it turned out, more than enough.

I still haven't told my parents — not about Clive, or Alison, or what happened to me that winter. Maybe someday I will. The thing is, I haven't decided if telling them would do them any good. For so long it was all I wanted. The truth! The truth! Good, fine, but for what? With the truth we will do what, become what? And in gaining the truth, what do we lose? It seems to me now that some truths will never be enough to seal the mysteries that precede them. I think in her own way my mother understood this all along — that there is nothing the truth can give you that you cannot give yourself. That in the end, you just have to decide. To live. To continue.

Saint X

Look down upon Saint X from above and it will appear as if little has changed. In the Basin, children in pink and maroon uniforms still run and shout through the yard of Horatio Byrd Primary. Her Majesty's Prison, eggshell-blue, still stands beside the bank. Along the winding ribbon of Mayfair Road there are now billboards for Digicel and FLOW broadband, but the white stucco churches remain, as does Perry's Snackette, and the radio tower with its flaking red paint, houses with galvanized roofs and sandy yards. Float up and over Devil Hill and there it is — Little Beach. It is late afternoon, and everyone has gathered here. They have their umbrellas and picnic baskets, their coolers filled with cola and Carib. Constellations of families float in the sea. Children clamor out of the water and run onto the pier, not even pausing before leaping off the edge back into the water, again and again in an unbroken loop.

Search among the faces and you will see a woman seated on a blue and white cloth, a point of stillness amid a lively family gathering. Her eldest grandchild dribbles a football down the sand. The youngest is curled asleep in the shade cast by the woman's own body. Her daughter-in-law hushes and soothes and doles out kisses and tamarind balls. Her sons, Bryan and Eddie, laugh together as they let the workweek's troubles lift from their shoulders. Sometimes she cannot quite believe that all of this is hers. Sara Lycott is neither as young as she once was nor as young as she still feels sometimes, until she catches herself in a shop window, startled by the silver flash of her own hair. It has been years since she first laid lisianthus on her mum's grave. Remarkable, isn't it, that a woman her age, who has not been anyone's daughter in a long, long time, still, hearing a funny story on the news, or picking the first ripe sugar-apple in the yard, opens her mouth to call out, "Mum"? On some nights, she is still laid low by a longing for her mother's house. She longs for bedding that smells human and that has grown soft as oil with unwashing. The plink of a sink that leaked throughout her whole childhood. The odors of old fruit in the refrigerator, of her mother's urine in the bathroom. In her own house, she washes and presses the sheets on Tuesdays. She keeps the bathroom scrubbed and smelling of bleach. When a thing breaks she fixes it. When a thing is empty she disposes of it.

The best thing she ever did was to behave in front of her children. If all she could give them was to contain the dark, squalid rooms within her, then that is enough. If to other people it seems like very little, well, she knows that it is everything. She has freed them from a burden they do not even know exists, that of being tormented by a deep, unsolvable ache for all the wrong things.

She has outlived them all. Her mother. The father whose name she never knew, whom she assumes must be long dead. Edwin, whom she nursed until his last breath but who never, not even then, truly let her in. (Yet did two boys ever have a father who adored them more?) Only Clive is still out there somewhere. Rumors reach the island. Last she heard he'd left New York for the West Coast someplace. According to a friend of hers, he got married out there and has a daughter. But this is secondhand knowledge at best. She does not think of him often. A difficult chapter in her life, from when she was very young. It has been so long since any of them were here with her that her own endurance confounds her. Lately, she has the oddest notion that she might go on living forever.

The baby beside her on the blanket stirs and cries. Before she can reach out for him, Bryan is there, scooping the child into his arms.

"There, there, my boy," he whispers. "You're all right. You're just fine."

Travel to the edge of the island's south coast and you will find yourself on a different beach, where the sand is soft as cream. At the water's edge, children turn cartwheels and bury one another in the sand. A boy lifts a conch to his ear and hears the secret sea. A mother considers grabbing her phone to capture this moment; instead, she just watches him. A cruise ship glides soundlessly across the middle distance. Somewhere, in another world that is also this world, it is snowing.

Farther up the sand, a little girl sits beneath an umbrella as a woman braids her hair. In the sea, brothers on boogie boards ride the gentle waves. A teenage boy picks up a girl and threatens to dunk her, and she squeals with delight.

A woman pauses on her walk down the beach and watches them all. This place is much as she remembers it. The pool in the shape of a lima bean, the open-air restaurant where last night she ate conch carpaccio and drank rum punch on the veranda and felt the cool ocean breeze. As with all places remembered from childhood, it appears smaller now, more ordinary. The domed ceiling of the marble lobby is not quite so high, the sand not quite so white, as they are in her memory. They've changed the name, too. Indigo Bay is the Royal Hibiscus now, and has been for years; a rebranding effort after the things that happened.

One more thing is different: Several years ago, a French conglomerate purchased the development rights to Faraway Cay. Now it is a private island resort and spa with bungalows built on stilts in the shallows. According to the resort's website, the restaurant is helmed by a celebrated Nordic chef who "marries his farm-to-table ethos with the local Caribbean bounty." The spa's offerings include a hot volcanic-stone massage, a local salt scrub, and a two-hour "Arawak Ritual" that promises "complete purification of both body and spirit." The downed planes on the cay have been preserved. There is a picture of one in the website's photo gallery, a yellow wing choked in sea grape. *Stroll past the island's mysterious relics en route to your own private waterfall.*

The goats are gone. Exterminated, one assumes.

When the woman reaches the black rocks that mark the end of the beach, she sits in the sand and looks out at the cay. The white beach. The cliffs tufted with growth, a vivid green unlike any she has seen before or since. She can make out the bungalows that ring the shore and, if she squints, people on the beach — husbands with wives, parents with children. The woman stands, brushes the sand from her legs, and walks back in the direction from which she has come.

On the volleyball court, a game is under way. The players are newlyweds and retirees, thirty-somethings and teenagers. They bump and set and spike. When a girl who is a bit of a weak link serves up a winner, both sides cheer. After a teenager takes a running dive into the sand to save a point, a retiree slaps him five. "Appreciate those," the man says, and points to the boy's knees. "They'll betray you someday."

The woman watches, as she watched years ago. It occurs to her that this game is always under way; that, in a sense, it never ends.

In the shallows, two pairs of legs poke out of the water — a handstand contest. A moment later, two sisters surface.

"I win!"

"No, me!"

"First one to the buoy!"

They are off, swimming away from shore.

AUTHOR'S NOTE AND ACKNOWLEDGMENTS

From New York City's John F. Kennedy International Airport, it is possible to fly direct to nearly twenty Caribbean islands. One can reach Jamaica, Haiti, the Dominican Republic, Cuba, Turks and Caicos, the Cayman Islands, Saint Martin, Saint Thomas, and Puerto Rico in under four hours; Antigua, Saint Lucia, Barbados, Saint Kitts, Grenada, Trinidad, Aruba, and Martinique in under five. Some 15 million American tourists visit the Caribbean each year. The islands are so close, American tourists visit them so frequently, and yet most of these visitors know so little about them. For a long time, I have been fascinated by the place the Caribbean seems to occupy in the mind of the American tourist as an "escape," or, as I put it early in the novel, a "lovely nowhere."

This phenomenon was at the heart of my decision to create a fictional, unnamed island, Saint X, for my setting. Building the world of Saint X was a process I undertook with a great deal of questioning about what it means to invent a fictional island within a place that is not fictional at all. In a region where every island has a rich and distinctive history, culture, dialect, cuisine, flora and fauna, and on and on, how does one approach creating a fictive space that embodies without simplifying, that is none of these places, exactly, but is also never pure invention? I have done my best to create in Saint X a cohesive place that, I can only hope, will inspire readers who don't know much about the Caribbean to learn more.

In this process, I am especially indebted to the wonderful series of Caribbean histories and guides published by Macmillan Caribbean in the nineteen eighties and nineties, in particular: *Nevis: Queen of the Caribees* by Joyce Gordon, *Anguilla: Tranquil Isle of the Caribbean* by Brenda Carty and Colville Petty, *St. Kitts: Cradle of the Caribbean* by Brian Dyde, *St. Lucia: Helen of the West Indies* by Guy Ellis, *Grenada: Isle of Spice* by Norma Sinclair, and *St. Vincent and the Grenadines* by Lesley Sutty. To the *Dictionary of Caribbean English Usage* and the *New Register of Caribbean English Usage,* both edited by Richard Allsopp. To *Island People: The Caribbean and the World* by Joshua Jelly-Schapiro (see also the beautiful map "Archipelago: The Caribbean's Far North" created by cartographer Molly Roy in *Nonstop Metropolis: A New York City Atlas,* edited by Jelly-Schapiro and Rebecca Solnit). To *Caribbean Folklore: A Handbook* by Donald R. Hill. And to Jamaica Kincaid's seminal work, *A Small Place.*

When it came to rendering Clive Richardson's life in New York City, some key sources included *Taxi!: A Social History of the New York City Cabdriver* by Graham Russell Gao Hodges, *Taxi!: Cabs and Capitalism in NYC* by Biju Mathew, and *Islands in the City: West Indian Migration to New York* edited by Nancy Foner.

I am incredibly grateful to those people on Anguilla who gave so generously of their time when I visited the island for research. Thank you to Josveek Huligar for being such a fun and helpful guide. My deepest gratitude to Anhel Brooks, Trevon Liburd, to M., to A., to M., and to J. for sharing your stories with me. Thanks also to Scott Kircher for the introduction to Trudy Nixon, and to Trudy for sharing her experience as an incomer on the island.

Thank you to Melissa Borja for sharing her knowledge on conducting oral histories and interviews.

To Stephanie Stokes Oliver and Crispin Brooks for reading the manuscript with such brilliance and care. To Graham Gao Hodges for so graciously reading the passages about Clive's working life in New York.

To wonderful friends who shared geographic and linguistic expertise with me: Margo Levin, Kate Rubin, Dave Serafino, Geraldine Shen, and Erin Zimmer. To Marisa Reisel for . . . everything.

To the brilliance and generosity of Greg Jackson and Lulu Miller, who read this book when it was a mess and saw so clearly how it could become less of one. To my teachers: Christopher Tilghman, Caroline Preston, Ann Beattie, Deborah Eisenberg, Chang-rae Lee, Joyce Carol Oates, and Wendy Phelps.

I thank my lucky stars daily that Henry Dunow is my agent. He is the wisest reader I know, and he worked with me patiently over many years and many, many drafts to help this book find its footing. Thank you also to the wonderful Arielle Datz and everyone else at Dunow, Carlson & Lerner.

To my fabulous editor, Deb Futter, who sees everything so clearly and who made this process more fun than I could have imagined. To Rachel Chou, Anna Belle Hindenlang, Randi Kramer, Christine Mykityshyn, Jaime Noven, Heather Orlando, Clay Smith, Anne Twomey, and everyone else at Celadon: I feel so fortunate to be in your capable hands. Thank you also to David Cole, Elizabeth Catalano, Cheryl Mamaril, and Jonathan Bennett for their wonderful work on this book, and to the incredible Callum Plews at Macmillan Audio for his work on the audiobook.

Our son was born a year before this book was completed, and I never would have finished it were it not for the people who cared for him so lovingly in his first year. To Meg Sweet, Cate Nowlan, Roberta Sweet, Carly Knight, Allison Haley, Maria Mastrandrea, and Molly Egger: Thank you.

To Shawn, Walter, Charlie, James, and Kelsey: I'm so lucky to be able to call you my family.

To Dona, Keith, and Brian: my rocks, my favorite people, from the very beginning.

To Emerson, our baby, our big boy. We are the very luckiest to have your light and spirit in our family.

And, always, to Mason, whose faith in me is the most profound thing I've ever known. I love you.

ABOUT THE AUTHOR

Alexis Schaitkin's short stories and essays have appeared in *Ecotone, Southwest Review, The Southern Review, The New York Times,* and elsewhere. Her fiction has been anthologized in *The Best American Short Stories* and The Best American Nonrequired Reading. She received her MFA in fiction from the University of Virginia, where she was a Henry Hoyns Fellow. She lives in Williamstown, Massachusetts, with her husband and son. *Saint X* is her debut novel.

The employees of Thorndike Press hope you have enjoyed this Large Print book. All our Thorndike, Wheeler, and Kennebec Large Print titles are designed for easy reading, and all our books are made to last. Other Thorndike Press Large Print books are available at your library, through selected bookstores, or directly from us.

For information about titles, please call:
(800) 223-1244

or visit our website at:
gale.com/thorndike

To share your comments, please write:
Publisher
Thorndike Press
10 Water St., Suite 310
Waterville, ME 04901